BY THE HORNS

BERKLEY TITLES BY RUBY DIXON

ICE PLANET BARBARIANS

Ice Planet Barbarians

Barbarian Alien

Barbarian Lover

Barbarian Mine

Barbarian's Prize

Barbarian's Mate

Barbarian's Touch

Barbarian's Taming

Barbarian's Heart

Barbarian's Hope

ROYAL ARTIFACTUAL GUILD

Bull Moon Rising

By the Horns

RUBY DIXON

✳

BY
THE HORNS

ACE

New York

ACE
Published by Berkley
An imprint of Penguin Random House LLC
1745 Broadway, New York, NY 10019
penguinrandomhouse.com

Copyright © 2025 by Ruby Dixon
Penguin Random House values and supports copyright. Copyright fuels
creativity, encourages diverse voices, promotes free speech, and creates a vibrant
culture. Thank you for buying an authorized edition of this book and for
complying with copyright laws by not reproducing, scanning, or distributing
any part of it in any form without permission. You are supporting writers and
allowing Penguin Random House to continue to publish books for every reader.
Please note that no part of this book may be used or reproduced in any manner
for the purpose of training artificial intelligence technologies or systems.

ACE is a registered trademark and the A colophon is a trademark of
Penguin Random House LLC.

BOOK DESIGN BY KATY RIEGEL

Library of Congress Cataloging-in-Publication Data
Names: Dixon, Ruby, 1976– author.
Title: By the horns / Ruby Dixon.
Description: New York: Ace, 2025. | Series: Royal Artifactual Guild; 2
Identifiers: LCCN 2024058993 (print) | LCCN 2024058994 (ebook) |
ISBN 9780593817056 (hardcover) | ISBN 9780593817063 (ebook)
Subjects: LCGFT: Fantasy fiction. | Romance fiction. | Novels.
Classification: LCC PS3604.I965 B9 2025 (print) | LCC PS3604.I965 (ebook) |
DDC 813/.6—dc23/eng/20241223
LC record available at https://lccn.loc.gov/2024058993
LC ebook record available at https://lccn.loc.gov/2024058994

Printed in China
1 3 5 7 9 10 8 6 4 2

The authorized representative in the EU for product safety and compliance
is Penguin Random House Ireland, Morrison Chambers, 32 Nassau Street,
Dublin D02 YH68, Ireland, https://eu-contact.penguin.ie.

For the OG inspiration

Isabella Bird

The first woman to join the Royal Geographical Society

CONTENT WARNING

ALTHOUGH THIS BOOK takes place in a fantasy setting, it deals with emotionally difficult topics, including cave-ins, claustrophobia, murder, corpses and decay, rats, rampant misogyny, scapegoating, servant abuse, unprotected sex, a pregnancy scare, poverty, and self-harm. Readers who believe that such content may upset them or trigger traumatic memories are encouraged to consider their emotional well-being when deciding whether to read this book.

—Ruby Dixon

BY THE HORNS

ONE

GWENNA

Dere Ma,

Aspeth is helping me to rite to you. She is teeching me my letters so I can better myself. I am still a repeeter at the guild but we will have recruitment day soon and I hope to be picked as a flegling again. If I can work for the guild I can send money home. I have enclosed a few coins. Please pay someone to rite back and let me know you are well. I love you.

Love, Gwenna

THE DEAD MAN in the alley is really bothering me.

Not that I killed him, of course. I just know that he's there, and I can't tell anyone.

Nor can I tell anyone that I've been able to sense the dead lately. I don't know why. I don't know how it started. All I know is that if there's a dead person somewhere nearby, my skin itches and crawls as if a hundred bugs were moving over my body.

It makes it damned impossible to concentrate.

I swipe at the window I'm supposed to be cleaning, hoping no one notices that I'm not truly giving my all. I need to keep my head down and stay out of trouble to remain as a repeater, one of the workers for the

Royal Artifactual Guild. Repeaters have a strange sort of position in the guild. We're considered "failed" students, but because we've been students in the past, we're also allowed to be first in line when it comes time to sign up with a new guild master for the next year's training. If I piss off Mistress Umala, though, she'll drop hints that I'm a bad, lazy employee, and she could ruin my chances to get picked as a fledgling for the next year's tutelage. True, my best friend is married to a guild master, but I can't count on Aspeth to grease the wheels for me. I need to earn my place, and as a woman in a male-dominated guild, I need to make doubly sure that my record is impeccable or people will talk.

Focus, I remind myself. Concentrate. Ignore the dead man in the alley and how hard your skin is buzzing because it must be a fresh murder—

A throat clears behind me.

I lower my arm, turning to greet Mistress Umala. She's an elderly woman with thick coils of white hair atop her head, and she wears a severe, high-necked dress in guild colors, along with a repeater sash at her waist and a second one at her shoulder. She's not a repeater, though. It's just part of the uniform. I'm told that she's a guild member's widow who decided to take up cleaning to keep her husband's pension, and now she just makes all of us who clean miserable. I really wanted to like her, because we maids should stick together, but Mistress Umala made it clear from day one that she didn't think much of me because I'd actually "dared" to try to be in the guild.

"Is there a problem?" she asks, looking down her sharp nose at me. Her skin is so pale that she looks unhealthy, and for a moment, I wonder if she's the corpse I keep sensing.

I put on my sweetest smile. Only one more month until recruitment day. Then I'll be free of drudgery. "Why would there be a problem, ma'am?"

She arches one hairy silver brow at me. "You've been rubbing that window with a dry rag for ten minutes now."

I . . . have? I glance down at the rag in my hand and sure enough, I've forgotten to wet it. "Just getting a few of the worst smears taken care of," I say cheerfully, and rub the window with the rag again as if this is all according to plan. "See?"

"I do not see," Umala hisses. "All I see is a young woman not doing her job properly."

Biting back a retort, I keep the smile on my face and take the shit she shovels at me. It's the servant's lot in life to smile through their true feelings, to never let their employers know what they're really thinking or else they'll get the boot. After years of working as a kitchen girl, and then a maid, I know all about how to look fawning and humble. "I'm very sorry, ma'am. I've no wish to be a bother. I'll finish up this window quickly."

And then I scratch at my neck and the high-collared uniform I'm wearing, because by the gods, that dead man is going to make me crazed.

I keep on scratching as she harrumphs. "See that you do. And then get the windows on the second floor. They look filthy."

I nod and bend over to dip my rag in the soapy bucket at my feet. "Of course, ma'am." One more month. One more mucking month. "Even the rooms with the patients?"

"Absolutely. They deserve clean windows, too." She turns and sweeps away, the conversation ended.

Now that her back is to me, I make a face at her retreating spine. Bitter old puss. She never rides any of the other repeaters as hard as me, nor any of the women who are employed under her. It's the fact that I am an actual repeater *and* a woman that really makes it difficult for her to mask her resentment.

After nearly a year of working as a repeater, I'm used to it.

I turn and clean the window correctly this time, scratching wildly at my skin through my uniform as I do so. The buzz of the dead man's presence feels as if it is burrowing directly under my flesh, and I wonder if I should say something.

Not to Umala. She already hates me.

I can't say anything to the guards, either. I notified them about a dead man in an alley last week because I'd *felt* him. A second one would be less of a coincidence and would point a finger at me. If they find out that I can feel the presence of the dead . . . my fledgling career would be over.

Everything would be over.

I scrub the window frantically, trying to distract myself. A song? No.

Counting? That won't help. Reciting guild rules? I can't remember enough of them. I end up biting the inside of my cheek until it bleeds, but the pain helps me focus. After I get done with these windows, maybe I'll volunteer to go dust in the archives. That should be far enough away from the guild hospital, where I am currently. And maybe Umala will be pleased with my initiative.

By the time I finish the windows downstairs, my crawling skin is driving me mad. I glance around, looking for Umala, but she's talking with someone near the front hall and I won't be able to slip past her and leave. I dig my fingernails into my palm, but my hands are callused from years of housework and it doesn't give me the bitter pinch I need to focus my mind. The inside of my cheek has been bitten so much that it feels like ground meat.

I need something to distract me until I can leave this place. Biting back a whimper of frustration, I grab my bucket and dump the rag in. "Heading upstairs," I call out to Umala.

She's deep in her conversation with a guild master and shoots me an irritated look as I interrupt. Right. Well, if there's one thing Umala likes to do, it's let everyone know how important her work is. I suspect that guild master isn't going to be able to get away from her for a while. Her cornering him might be to my advantage.

I need something to distract me so I can finish my job. The buzz of the dead man is only growing more deafening, and it's starting to scare me. What do I do if it doesn't stop? What do I do if no one finds him and it just keeps going and going and going?

Head down, I bite back a whimper of frustration as I go up the stairs.

"Be sure and get the patients' rooms," Umala calls after me.

"Yes, ma'am," I yell back, probably more forcibly than I should. Maybe one of the patients will have something I can use to get this feeling out of my head. A bottle of wine would be nice. At this point, I'd even be willing to cut myself with a knife if the pain would distract me enough, though I won't be able to work if I carve up my hands. I need a better solution.

I race down the hall as quickly as I can, opting to start with the rooms that overlook the alley, since they're the ones closest to the body. Get it over with already. Maybe I can open a window and pour the soapy water down on someone on the street and force them to veer into the alley.

Then again, maybe it's not a dead body. Maybe I'm panicking. Maybe it's something else. Didn't Ma say once that she grew up in a house where the cook couldn't eat shellfish or his lips puffed up? Maybe this feeling I have—like I'm being gnawed from the inside—is like that. As I approach the room farthest down the hall, though, the sensation grows stronger. I get to the window, but I don't even have to look outside to know that there's a dead man there.

I can feel him. He's about my age. Throat cut. Been there a few hours now, limbs stiffening. Spirit lurking until he can go to Romus, the god of the dead.

And I'm terrified about the fact that somehow I know all of this.

I'm just a maid trying to be a guild artificer. Not a mancer. Mancers are trouble. Mancers are burned at the stake because they're a threat. Because magic is outlawed and forbidden, unless it's in one of the old artifacts.

I just want to blend in. Get a decent job that doesn't involve handling other people's chamber pots or a broom, maybe make a little coin to send back home to my ma so she won't have to work so hard for that skinflint Lord Honori.

I'm not a mancer, though. I can't be. I'm not anything special. This must be a sickness. That must be it. Scrubbing the window viciously, I tell myself the dizziness is due to something I ate last night. Nothing more. Soon enough I'll get the sweats and then go running for the garde-robe. I mean, I *am* sweating. But as time passes, more bits about the dead man leak into my brain. That he was a repeater, just like me. That he was doing a stint on guard duty. That he was supposed to meet someone in the alley last night for an exchange when someone came up behind him and a hot flash moved over his throat. Then he couldn't breathe—

Choking on air, I grab my bucket and haul it toward the next room. The moment I'm inside, I slam the door behind me and lean against it, gasping.

"Who's there?" asks someone with a deep, irritated male voice.

Shit. Mucking shit. I must have awoken the healers' patient. Sure enough, when I look over, there's the big, pale white form of a Taurian sprawled over the bed, which seems far too small for him. He's naked except for a sheet tossed over his loins and what looks like a cloth covering his eyes. His bed has an overly tall footboard, upon which his hooves press. I guess that's more comfortable for him on his back than lying flat like a human would, because his legs bend backward at the knee. He looks mucking grumpy that I'm here, too.

"Sorry, sir," I chirp, sliding into my old friendly-helpful-maid persona. I step forward, clutching my bucket, and notice that his eyes aren't just covered, they're blindfolded. Good. He won't be able to say it was me who interrupted him. "Name's Sarya."

Maybe I shouldn't lie about my name, but I figure he doesn't need to know who I really am. If I annoy him, the last thing I want is someone reporting back about how terrible Gwenna is. I set down the bucket near the window and then glance back toward him. This is the guild medics' main hospital, so I reckon that he's a guild artificer. He's enormous, this Taurian man. There's a glinting golden ring in his bovine pink nose, and his shoulders are so broad that his arms hang over the sides of the narrow bed. His horns jut forward over his bandaged brow and look sharp and deadly. Someone, one of the nurses perhaps, has tied a bright red ribbon in a colorful bow on the end of each one so the staff notices if he swings his head.

I don't think they're necessary. He's impossible to look away from. I've seen him around guild headquarters, but I don't know his name, just that he's one of the guild's hardworking Taurians. His barrel chest is nothing but muscle and the occasional scar, with two flat nipples decorating his delicious pectorals. The hooves on the footboard are equally enormous, and his tail swats the side of the bed with irritation. He's magnificent.

Grumpy as muck, but magnificent.

The Taurian grunts, shifting his big body on the bed. "You're the female they sent up?"

To clean the windows? "Aye, that'd be me. I'll get you taken care of and then I'll be on my way, promise."

"Good" is all he says, and then he drops the sheet covering his loins to the floor and gestures at his fully engorged cock.

RAPTOR

I'm a terrible invalid.

It goes against everything I am to lie abed all day, doing nothing at all. I should be in the tunnels, digging for artifacts. I should be scouting for new paths. Five hells, I should be drinking in a tavern for all I care. Just not in bed with my eyes glued shut by a thick paste under a bandage. Granted, the paste is cool against my burnt skin, and the healer assigned to my care reassures me my vision will come back soon, but each day that I'm here, I can practically hear the coins clinking. The guild loves to charge for everything. Meals. Uniforms. Medic services. *Everything.* I'm going to be in so much mucking debt after this, just to get back to normal.

It's my own fault. I shouldn't have let the new guy in our Five handle the artifacts. I should know to duck and cover when someone says, "I wonder what this button does."

I'm lucky all I got was a pair of flash-burnt eyes and some scorches on my hands. I'm told Romald—sorry, *Bustard*—didn't make it. That means our Five has an opening again, and it means we'll have another new guy. I mucking hate new guys.

Shifting on the narrow bed, I try to ignore how my back aches. Truth be told, more things are aching right now than just my back. My cock throbs like a swollen tooth. My knot hasn't been drained in days now, and it's been a lot longer since I've had a dose of the illegal potion that keeps my ever-present hungers in check. I can't exactly go out and get it myself, not without my vision, and it'll be at least another week before they release me from the clinic.

Nor can I demand someone go to the underground mancer's shop and ask for my weekly dose. Without my regular dose of the potion, my needs have come rushing back. The god's hand—which the potion stays—has returned with a roar. My sexual hungers are making me twist in agony. Most Taurians are only god-touched during the Conquest Moon, but some of us are god-touched permanently, and it makes us insatiable.

"Can I get you anything?" the healer asked me earlier.

"A woman," I managed. "A sex worker."

"Oh." The healer seemed flustered at the request. "Is there a Taurian moon—"

"No." I pull the sheet off and show the permanently swelled knot at the base of my cock. "God-touched."

"Oh. Oh, mercy." The elderly healer made a few other fluttery, anxious noises, but I couldn't see her face to know if she'd agreed or not. It's been hours now, though, and I was about to get up from the bed—wounds and all—and demand that someone send a female to me. Anything to get this wild ache out of my groin. I can't even take care of it myself because my mucking hands are bandaged.

But it seems as if my request has been fulfilled after all. I lift my nose, trying to pick up her scent. Normally human females smell like sweat and musk and all kinds of delicious things. This one just smells like . . . soap. Soap and cleaning supplies, and lemon. They love to soak this hospital in astringent things, though, so my senses might be numb after days of being here. She *sounds* female at least. "You're the female they sent up?"

"Aye, that'd be me. I'll get you taken care of and then I'll be on my way, promise." Her voice is sweet and cheerful, all business. I like that.

"Good." I'm so relieved I could jump out of this bed and do a jig . . . but the burns on my body wouldn't be too happy with that. Instead, I simply pull the sheet off my groin, my already stiff and aching cock leaping free. "As you please."

There's a little pause. "Is that a knot?"

Inwardly I stiffen. It's something I despise hearing. Something I hate having to go over with every new sex worker, because it brings up problems. Some fear my size, as my knot just increases the girth of my already-large Taurian cock. Some are anxious and don't want to be knotted under any circumstances and will scream it loudly to all who will listen and make me feel like a monster. Most behave like I'm an unforeseen issue that can only be solved with a lot more coin. No matter what, I'm treated like I'm a problem, and I hate it. I go through the rote explanation I offer to every sex worker I encounter, my voice tight. "Some Taurians are 'blessed' by Old Garesh to have a knot at all times. It makes our need constant."

"That sounds . . . distracting." Her voice grows breathy. A moment later, I hear the click of the lock in the door. "Lucky for you, I'm all about distraction today."

I groan. Gods, yes. This is exactly what I need—an eager, willing partner. "I'm yours to play with, woman. Be as rough as you like."

TWO

GWENNA

WHAT IN ALL the mucking hells am I doing? The thought bounces in my head even as I lock the door to the Taurian's quarters and approach his bedside. He clearly thinks I'm here for a hand job—or more—and not that I'm here to clean the windows. I should tell him no.

And yet . . . I love this idea.

I've been crawling out of my own skin all afternoon with the dead man nearby. Haven't I been going on and on in my head about how I need some sort of diversion? A release of some sort to distract my body? This is perfect. Anonymous, delicious sex. Zero strings attached, tons of distraction. "I'll do it," I tell him, setting my bucket down quietly. "But I have rules."

"Rules?" He huffs, his snout turning in my direction. "What rules, exactly?"

"I want to come, too. If I get you off, I need at least one orgasm of my own or else I'm not touching you."

His mouth curls into what looks like an amused smile. When he speaks, his voice is a low, sultry purr. "Oh, sweet female. That's an easy task. Just come climb on my knot and I'll make you feel very, very good."

I shiver, and this time not because there's a body in the alley. This time it's because of anticipation.

"Do we need to discuss your payment?"

"Already taken care of by the guild," I lie. No need to point out that I'll be using him as much as he's using me. I shimmy out of my bloomers and skirts, then strip my tunic off after a moment's hesitation and kick off my boots. Umala likes for the nestmaids to wear skirts, repeaters or not, so my clothing is a bastardized version of a guild fledgling's uniform, along with the black repeater sash. But if he realizes that, he won't think that I'm a hired sex worker, so it all goes by the wayside. I leave my frayed and much-patched corset on, since it's trickier to get on and off, and move to the edge of the bed.

He immediately reaches for me, gripping one of my butt cheeks in a bandaged mitt. The Taurian's groan of pleasure is loud in the room. "Nice, thick flanks. My favorite."

And he squeezes even as he hisses with pain.

I bite back a squeak because his handling makes me slippery with arousal. The buzzing from the corpse in the alley below is fading behind nervous excitement. I'm not the type to jump into bed with just anyone, though I've had my share of lovers in the past. Before, I'd always had a relationship of some kind with my sex partner.

Before, they'd always been human. The sheer size of this Taurian and the knot are all new to me.

But new is definitely distracting. It's just what I need.

I reach out and stroke his cock, fascinated at how thick he is. A long strand of pre-cum glazes the head of his cock and I run my fingers through the wetness, using it to slick my hand.

"Spit," he tells me.

I lean over and spit on his cock, clenching my thighs together even as I do. He knows what he wants to the point of being pushy, and for some reason, it really turns me on. He's so big I have to spit a second time, and the lubricant quickly dries up with a few strokes of my hand.

"You're too large," I tell him, amused. "I don't have enough spit. I don't know that *any* woman does."

He chuckles, reaching for me. "Use your mouth on me, then."

"You don't tell me what to do. I'm in charge here." And I reach up and flick his nipple.

The big Taurian stiffens on the bed, and for a moment, I wonder if

I've gone too far. But then he groans, his hips pumping instinctively at the air. "Bossy little wench. Fine. You're in charge. Spit, use your hand, whatever. Just touch me."

"I've a better idea than spit," I say, sliding away before he can grab me. I love the frustrated growl he makes as I slip out of his grasp. Heading over to the small table nearby, I spot a pot of lotion. I noticed the other day when cleaning that most of these rooms have extra lotion on hand. The constant bathing and soaps make skin dry, and so the healer is constantly lotioning her patients after washing them.

But I've got a far naughtier use for that lotion. It's mild and unscented, which makes it perfect for sex. Scooping up a handful, I move back to his side and slather his cock with it. He sucks in a breath, no doubt surprised at the cool sensation, but when my hand wraps around him again, his irritation turns to pleasure.

"Aye, that's it," he growls, reaching for me again. His bandaged hand drifts through the air, searching, and I drop it on my breast. "Just like that. Nice tits on you, too. Are you tall?"

I am short and absolutely stout, but who cares in this moment? Certainly not me. "Tall and blond."

"Mmm." He handles my breast, his wrapped palm big enough to practically cover one. When he feels my corset, he slips the ties over his hand and tugs them loose, my breasts spilling out. "Better."

His bandaged hand against my bare skin makes me suck in a breath. Arousal throbs through me, and I squeeze and pump his cock with my fist, moving harder and faster. My fingers can't close all the way around his thickness, and I can't even imagine how that knot will possibly fit inside anyone. Is that why he must pay sex workers? Because no sane woman would put herself through that?

Yet my friend Aspeth has been through a rut with her husband, and she spoke of it quite fondly, blushing the entire time. It can't be that awful. Boldly, I reach down and grasp his knot with my slippery, lotion-covered hand.

The big Taurian makes a choking sound, his back bowing off the bed.

I immediately draw back, my impression that of intense, almost painful heat radiating from his knot. "Should I not have—?"

He wheezes, trying to catch his breath. "Sensitive . . ."

"So I shouldn't play with it?" I lightly tease a finger along that hard, violently red bulge at the base of his cock. Even his balls, flushed and huge, are nowhere near as tight-looking as that knot.

The Taurian's head goes back and he sucks in a breath. One heavily bandaged hand tightens on my breast—in an exciting, possessive way, not a bad way. He rubs his wrapped hand over my nipple, teasing back and forth even as his hips lift in another silent entreaty.

His knot might be sensitive, but he doesn't seem to mind me playing with it. I take my time, tracing along the edge of it where it meets his shaft, then along the underside, where it pulses against the base of his cock. I tickle it with featherlight touches and give it a squeeze, which seems to elicit the most reaction from him. It's probably like my clit, then. Teasing touches are well and good, but I need a proper rubbing if I'm going to get off.

"Just like that," he encourages.

"Just like what?" I ask innocently, pulling my hand away. He growls, and I feel powerful. "You didn't want *just* my hand, did you?"

"You going to keep toying with me or you going to mount me, woman?" He brushes my nipple with his mitt.

I'm feeling playful, though. I push his hand away and slowly make my way down the side of the bed. I should probably hurry things along because we could get caught at any moment, but I like the edge of danger. It helps drown out the hum of the dead man's presence. I drag my fingers along his legs, brushing over his hooves as I circle the bed and then move to the other side. I want him aware of where I am, because I imagine he doesn't like to be startled, but I want to keep teasing. "I'll give you two choices," I say in a flirty voice. "You can have my hand, and I'll even throw in my tongue. I'll wipe all that lotion off and mouth you good. Or you can have my cunt."

"Cunt," he says immediately, and gestures to his thighs. "Come sit on me. I'll make you feel amazing."

I'm a little surprised at his choice. If it's just about getting off, most men would take a hand and go on about their day. That he wants my body means he's interested—even slightly—in my pleasure, too. Maybe it's a Taurian thing to be a generous lover. If so, I've been seeing the wrong men all my life. "I'm warning you, I'm a heavy woman."

"You say that like it's a problem. I like thick thighs." He angles his head, as if he wants to get a look at me, even though there's no way he'll be able to see my face through those heavy bandages.

"And what about that big knot of yours? Is that supposed to fit?" I drag my finger over the heated band of flesh, enjoying the hiss he makes.

"Just take what you can and enjoy yourself." The big Taurian manages a roguish grin. "I know I will."

I roll my eyes at that one, but I'm still amused at his confidence. It's hard not to be attracted to that, and I'm enjoying this diversion probably far more than I should. "I'm coming up, then. Tell me if I hurt you."

He holds a bandaged hand out to help me up, but I gently nudge it aside, and that makes him laugh anew, just as I figured it would. He's a lot of fun to toy with, this Taurian. I climb up the side of the bed, glad that it's low to the ground. My thighs brush over his and then I rest my slick, lotion-covered hands on his stomach as I straddle him and keep my hips high in the air.

His enormous prick pushes straight up to the sky, and I lower myself onto it just enough for the head to graze my cunt, and then I lift up again.

He groans, head jerking to the side. "Mucking tease." The words are harsh but his tone is affectionate. "You just want to make me suffer."

"It's my job to torture those at the hospital," I flirt. "I like to hear the begging."

And I drag my slick cunt along the head of his cock again. His hips surge upward—as I knew they would—but I shift my weight away again. He makes a ragged sound in response.

"Ask me nicely," I purr at him.

His big hands go for my breasts. "Please, Sarya."

Hearing the strange name makes me wince. I change tactics, seating myself atop him with a wiggle and letting him sink the tip in. He's by far the biggest lover I've ever had, but I'm slick as hell, and his cock is slippery from the lotion. It's a tight fit, but not an unpleasant one.

"More?" I ask, trembling with the strain of holding myself aloft over him.

"More," he agrees, rubbing bandaged fingers over my freed nipple. "Damn, but your tits are big. Gorgeous. I'm a lucky male."

"Perfect for those big hands of yours."

"Aye, you're more than perfect."

I slide lower onto him and he makes another one of those ragged sounds. I make one, too, because by the five hells, he's thick. I have to go slowly so I don't feel as if I'm impaling myself. To his credit, this stranger doesn't try to shove his way into me. He lets me take my time seating myself upon him, and when I've taken all I can, I reach a hand between us and his knot isn't even in my body. Maybe if I had more time to prepare myself, I could fit him, but this'll have to do.

"Still good?" I manage, breathless.

He nods, those dangerous horns with their ribbons bobbing. "Ride me."

I do, rocking over him slowly and then with increasing speed. I'm in charge, and I go as slow or as fast as I need to. He's so big that even with me seated on him, our bodies don't meet. I can't grind my clit against his body to get myself off, which is a problem. But I'm a pro at making sure I get my own, and so I carefully take one of his hands and position it between us, so when I bear down, he rubs against my clit in just the way I need.

"Such a good girl," he growls at me. "Look at how well you're taking my cock."

"Not well enough," I whine, riding him even more frantically.

"Next time. Next time I'll knot you good, sweetheart. Wait and see."

As if there'll be a next time. Arrogant prick. But his confidence makes me even more aroused, and I ride him harder, my thighs jiggling as I rock up and down above him. "Hush and let me fuck you."

His laughter rumbles through his chest, and he presses his arms against my hips, working me over him. I gasp at the sudden change of pace, but he's fucking me so much harder that it makes me clench deep inside. He's *using* me . . . and it feels amazing. I slide my own hand to my clit and touch myself as he moves me on his cock, shuttling quickly into my body.

When I come, it's with a full-body shiver of relief and a choked sob in my throat. Bliss spreads through my veins and I clench all over, driving out every sensation but that of delicious contentment. With a shuddering gasp, I brace my hands on his chest again as I recover. His strokes slow down and he murmurs soothing things to me, telling me what a good job I did, how my cunt fits him perfectly, how he's never had anyone as good as me before. Typical man stuff, especially from a Taurian who's knot-deep inside a woman.

Now that I've gotten what I needed, though, I'm eager to get out of here. The sooner I can get those windows cleaned, the sooner I'm free for the day, and now I think I can work again. With a pleased little sigh, I reach between us, where his knot is still throbbing. I give it a squeeze and he chokes on air. "Want me to work this for you while you fuck me?"

He responds by driving into me harder, and I'm going to take that as a yes. I toy with his knot as he uses me, but it isn't until I scrape my nails over his knot that he comes with a furious sound, and then he's flooding inside me. I'm a little shocked at the sheer volume of seed he pumps into me, but I remain in place until he's done. If I didn't anticipate how much he'd come, well, that's on me for not thinking things through.

"Mmm," I practically purr. I've had plenty of sex in the past, but that was really, really good sex. I give a wiggle atop him and realize that his knot is still taut, even if his cock is not. "You good or do you need more?"

The Taurian bucks into me once, tension returning to his body, and that's my answer. He's not a normal man, so he needs just a little bit more, it seems. Well, I'm fine with that. I slip off him, ignoring the hands that try to grab me and hold me in place.

"I'll take care of you," I soothe. "Just hold still."

He growls, his fists twisting in the sheets even as he pants. He lets out a ragged, heaving breath, his head tossed back on the pillows. "Just . . . let me touch you a bit more. Play with your breasts. I can make myself come—"

"Hush," I say again, turning my attention to that wet, sticky cock that's only at half-mast. I run a finger along the swollen base of him, unsurprised when he gives a fresh spurt of seed. The ring of his knot looks tight, as if he's still got more to give, and I ponder this. Squeezing it doesn't seem like a good idea.

I lean over him and move my mouth close to that hot, reddish band of flesh and run my tongue over his skin. He tastes of salt and sex, and lotion, but I don't mind it. I'm still feeling loose and pleasant from the toe-curling orgasm I just had, and I want to give him the same. He shifts his weight on the bed, huffing slightly when I tongue him, but it's not a huge response.

"Not as sensitive here as the rest of your cock?"

He shrugs.

Interesting. "So then you won't mind if I do this . . . ?"

I bite his knot. Just a tiny bite, more of a love nip with a scrape of teeth and a suggestion that I can be fiercer.

His response is stunning. A low, feral sound drags from his throat. His back bows off the bed and a geyser of seed pours forth from his cock, splattering all over his body and our surroundings.

This is the release he needed.

I wipe his spend from my face and hair. Then I glance up at the ceiling, but to my relief, there's only one small spot. Well, perhaps no one will notice that. I grab a towel and tidy myself as he catches his breath in huge, gulping bellows, then towel him down.

When I'm done, he shudders and reaches for my hand. "You were mucking *incredible*, Sarya."

"Just doing my job," I tell him cheerfully. Or, erm, not.

"Leave your contact information with the healer. I'll want you again."

Eesh. "Sure thing." I wriggle out of his grasp.

"My name's Raptor."

"Don't care," I joke, but when he chuckles, I realize he has no idea I'm telling the truth. There isn't going to be a next time, but that's fine. I feel excellent. The buzzing under my skin has dulled, and I feel like myself again. A nice, relaxed version of myself. I grab my clothing and begin to dress quickly.

If dead bodies start to bother me again, well, I now know the solution.

THREE

GWENNA

THE UNCOMFORTABLE SKIN-CRAWLING sensation returns just as I finish the last of the windows. I all but race out of the building once Umala releases me for the day. Instead of crossing to the nestmaid quarters where I've lived for the last several months, I head deeper into the heart of the city. The center of Vastwarren belongs to the Royal Artifactual Guild, a three-hundred-year-old guild that specializes in the retrieval of magical artifacts from the ruins of Old Prell far beneath the city. The guild is rich beyond imagining and controls the very heart of the city, but there are some buildings that even they don't visit much. The guild's archives are practically deserted at this hour, with the young archivist at the front desk brightening as I rush in.

Flycatcher yawns, his face propped up by his fists. "Did you bring me cake today?"

"Not today," I say apologetically, shutting the door to the library behind me. Immediately the place feels oppressive despite the magical lighting that illuminates the interior. It's the hundreds of tall shelves crammed full of heavy books that go almost up to the ceiling that make the library feel claustrophobic. This is one of the older buildings in Vastwarren, so the ceiling beams sag and the floors groan with every step, which doesn't make me feel at ease. "Is Aspeth around?"

"Do you mean Sparrow?" he asks me with a chiding look.

"Right, right. Sparrow." I grimace. To me, she'll always be Aspeth, but I know I'm supposed to call her by her guild name now that she's one of the archivists. "Is *Sparrow* around?"

"Yes. She's downstairs." He straightens, drumming his fingers on the desk. "Bring me some cake next time. I'll pay you for it."

The little cakes I've been making in my downtime are the only reason I've had enough money to send letters home. "When I come back, I promise. I haven't had a chance to bake today."

"Next time, then." He gives me a sulky look and goes back to petting the cat sprawled across the desk. "I'll log you in as a visitor."

"Great. Thanks." I move forward, my skirts swishing against the narrow shelves.

"Need help—"

"I know the way! Thank you!" I head farther in before he can ask me to bake anything else. Bad enough that I spend all my time cleaning. If I get a reputation as a baker, I'm going to find myself back in a kitchen for the rest of my days. Never again. I want bigger things for myself.

Thinking of kitchens makes me walk a little faster through the narrow, packed shelves. A cat darts out from behind another shelf, nearly tripping me, and I manage to catch myself before I fall flat on my face. Then I find the circular iron stair that leads down to the lower floors of the archives and head there.

Aspeth's workstation is easy to find amidst the clutter of books, shelving carts, and boxes of artifacts. Hers is the desk covered with all the cats. The archives keep cats around as mousers, but Aspeth is a softhearted sort and started feeding them bits of her lunches, she told me. Now they all hang about her desk, waiting for handouts or petting. Today she's seated at her desk, which is piled high with books and has a lamp on the corner. Two cats are curled around each other to her right, and another peeks down from a stack of books on her left. A gray beast with a huge fluffy tail saunters past me as I stand and wait for Aspeth to notice I'm here.

She doesn't, of course. Aspeth is lost in her research. Her face is bent over something, a magnifying glass held in one hand. I clear my throat and she startles, thunking her head with the glass. One of the cats scrambles away with a yowl, sending papers flying in his wake. I get a chance to see what she's studying so intently. It's a long, pointy pin the size of a finger, made of gold and with a jewel at the end. There is a strange glyph on the prominent head of the pin.

"New find?" I ask.

She huffs, adjusting her oversized spectacles and pushing them back up her nose as she straightens. "I wasn't expecting you today. You startled me."

"I see that." There's a chair parked across from her desk, but when I pull it out, another cat leaps up and runs away. "Is this a bad time?"

"Of course not. I'm just studying an item before it gets shipped out to Lord Emijar." Her eyes gleam with excitement. "It's quite fascinating."

"It looks like a diaper pin."

She leans back. "Well . . . yes. But it's the glyphs on it that are the interesting part. Even something as small as this has magic attached to it. Do you know what it says?"

I shake my head. I can't read a lick of Old Prellian.

"This symbol is the one for 'sickness,' and the one on the other side of the pin is the symbol for '*dohren*,' which was the soul. And to the Prellians, the soul was housed in the gut. The interesting thing is that the sickness symbol is inverted, which means that it's the opposite of sickness— health. And the fact that they're wishing soul health on a diaper pin means—"

"—that someone's baby left some truly heinous messes?"

She giggles. "Possibly! Or it could just be a general blessing. I'm looking for duplicates of this particular duo of symbols to cross-reference and see if there are any other symbol pairings like this. But to think—a spell for good digestion on your baby's diaper. Isn't that *fascinating*?"

Frankly, the most fascinating thing to me is that the Prellians enchanted everything. Even a diaper pin. It means anything found in the network of caverns and tunnels below Vastwarren is likely to be magical in some way, and thus it makes the guild money. "Very interesting. I don't suppose you have a moment to chat, do you?"

"For a friend? Always." She beams at me and rubs her nose, leaving a dusty smear there. Her glossy brown hair is pulled into a tight bun at the top of her head, but several strands have slipped free and she looks a frowsy, scattered mess. It makes me happy, though, because Aspeth is doing what she loves. She's thriving in the cutthroat guild environment. Married to a Taurian guild master, apprenticing to the head archivist, and surrounded by cats as she studies ancient artifacts. I don't think I've ever seen her happier.

Which is why I hate that I keep showing up with bad news.

She blinks owlishly at me. "Is something wrong?"

I nod, a lump in my throat.

Quickly, she sets aside her magnifying glass and the artifact she was studying. A cat wanders over the desk, tail in the air, and she picks it up and moves it to the floor. "What is it?"

I bite my lip, then sit in the chair across from her and lean forward so I can whisper my terrible news. "I found another body today."

Aspeth—Sparrow—gasps, her ink-stained hand flying to her mouth. *"What?"*

Hissing, I wave a hand at her. "Quiet! No one else can know!"

She nods and leans in closer. "What do you mean," she asks, her voice pitched low, "*another* body?"

"Remember how I told you I felt one the other day? That I was tingly all over? And it only stopped when they moved the dead man out of the alley?" When she nods, I continue, rubbing my arms as if I can still feel the thousands of pinpricks. "Well, I felt another. Worse than before this time. I think I even know how he died. Someone cut his throat in the alley behind the guild hospital."

Her eyes are huge and unblinking as she stares at me. "Did you tell anyone?"

"No, of course not!"

"Why not?"

It's frustrating to talk to Aspeth sometimes, because she has a sheltered worldview. As a holder's daughter and heir for her first thirty years, she just naturally assumes that if you tell someone something, they believe you. Better yet, that you won't be blamed. She doesn't see things the way I do. I've been a servant all my life, the daughter of another servant. I know what it's like. I know how when something is missing or wrong, the first ones to be blamed are the staff. "Don't you think that'd be suspicious? Me, the woman who reported a dead body in the alley last week, suddenly finds *another* dead body in *another* alley?"

"Oh." She leans back in her chair. "Yes, I suppose that is bad. But we can't just leave it there."

"I know." I twist my hands in my lap. "Trust me, I know. I also don't know who to tell besides you."

"It's obvious," Aspeth says. "We'll tell Hawk."

Her husband. Hawk is the first Taurian to rise to the rank of guild master and is my former teacher, before I flunked due to last year's mess. Aspeth trusts him wholeheartedly because she loves him and he loves her, but I'm just Aspeth's old friend. He has no such loyalty to me. How do I know that he won't choose to tell the guild instead of keep my secret?

But I suppose we must tell someone. I can't keep working, knowing that there's a dead man in the alley. Several of the buildings I clean are located close enough that his presence will continue to bother me, and I can't very well go around attacking every man in sight and begging him to fuck me as a distraction.

I squeeze my thighs together, a pleasant tingle skittering through my body at the thought of the big pale Taurian I dallied with earlier. It had been very nice, a delicious interlude in an otherwise horrible day. Bad judgment on my part, though. I can't afford to fuck guild artificers or they'll think I'm trying to get into the guild on my back. Ugh. I'll have to avoid him in the future if I run into him. Sarya indeed. What was I thinking? "Do we have to tell Hawk I was the one who found it?"

"Of course not. I'll come up with . . . something. Let me think on it for a moment." Aspeth pulls out a quill and dips it in ink. She pushes aside a cat sprawled on her desk and scratches a note onto a page in front of her. "You're certain it's another dead man?"

I rub my neck, thinking of the uncomfortable, uneasy feeling that had moved all over me. "I didn't go look at him, but . . . yes. It always feels the same."

She nods, writing frantically. "Describe your symptoms to me."

"What? Why?" I just want to forget about the entire thing, not dwell on it.

Aspeth looks up at me, her eyes huge behind her spectacles. "I'm going to search through some of the texts here to see what they mention about such things. When other people have had, ah, the same problems."

My brows go up. "Problems?"

"Sensing, ah . . . things they shouldn't," she says delicately.

We both know what she's talking about. It's something we've considered a dozen times before and discarded, but I'm afraid we cannot anymore. "Let's call it what it is. We think I'm a mancer."

A magic user. An evil person with secret powers. Mancers were outlawed three hundred years ago, and all of them were put to death. Since then, the guild has risen to power. The only magic allowed now is magic found in artifacts, so the Royal Artifactual Guild retrieves magic doodads from the ancient ruins and sells them for large amounts of coin to the noble holders.

Personal magic should be dead. I should *not* be a mancer. I can barely even read.

She blinks. "I mean . . . possibly."

"I don't want to be a mancer," I tell her, twisting my hands in my worn skirt. The anxiety crawling through me is worse than the buzzing feelings earlier. "If they think I am, they'll burn me in the square!"

"No, they won't," Aspeth says confidently. "No one's been burned as a mancer in a hundred years."

That's because no one has been stupid enough to step forward and claim to be a mancer in the last hundred years. I don't want to be the first. "Aspeth, *please*. If we keep pointing out dead bodies, someone's going to become suspicious!"

"I promise you'll be safe, Gwenna. No one will know it's you. I just want to find out what I can so we know what to expect. You know I would never say anything to endanger you."

"Which is why I would really like it if we didn't bring this up," I counter. When her expression turns to hurt, I take a deep breath. I force myself to swallow the worried knot in my throat. Aspeth has kept my secrets in the past. I'm just . . . terrified of what will happen if I'm found out. There's so much at stake. "Until I can figure out how to make this stop, I'd prefer we say nothing."

"But there's a dead man in guild territory. It's not right to just say nothing at all. He's not the first one to be murdered, you know."

"Oh, I know. I've felt them both." My dry sarcasm carries in the small room. At my feet, a cat with long fur rubs against my legs.

"Of course. I'm sorry. I'd forgotten." My friend seems chagrined. She drums an ink-stained finger on her lip, thinking. "Perhaps I'll steer Hawk toward that area and we can accidentally run across the dead man so he can be identified and removed."

"Aspeth, please. . . ."

"I won't say anything about you, Gwenna. I promise." She pushes her glasses up her nose, the lenses making her blinking grotesquely exaggerated. "Anyway, you should call me Sparrow. No one calls me Aspeth anymore except for Hawk."

I'm still not used to her guild name. She's been in my life since I was a girl, and she'll always be Aspeth to me. I know the name means a lot to her, though. "Sparrow. Apologies." Her wide smile is like sunlight coming through the clouds. "And you asked about my symptoms . . . ?"

"I did!" She poises the quill over the paper again, readying herself.

For the next while, I tell her in great detail what it feels like to sense a nearby dead body. I don't know if it's because my sheltered life as a maid back in Honori Hold never allowed me to brush with death, or if there's some sort of latent magic in the very soil here in Vastwarren City that activated this whole "death sensing" power. Vastwarren was built upon the bones of an ancient civilization full of magic, so it'd stand to reason that magic permeates the very air here. I describe to her the sensations, the feeling of dread, and even the vague "memories" that drift into my mind about the dead person.

She's most interested in the physical sensations, making little exclaiming noises as she writes. "It sounds dreadful."

"It doesn't feel good, no."

"How did you manage to stay there so long? Feeling all of that? How did you not run from the building?"

My face feels suddenly hot. "I, um, found a way to distract myself."

She nods, continuing to scribble away. "A distraction to minimize the physical reaction is good. What did you do specifically?"

There is no way in goddess Hannai's green earth I'm going to tell her what I did *specifically*. "Pain. Bit my lip, stabbed my fingernail into my hand, things like that."

Aspeth—no, Sparrow—keeps writing. "And did you have to reach a certain pain threshold? Were there certain applications of pain that were more useful than others? Perhaps we can narrow down what brings effectiveness in case this occurs again—"

"Just pain," I say, blushing. "I wasn't too focused on what kind or how much. There was a lot going on."

"Hmm." She doesn't seem convinced. "Perhaps other stimuli might be listed in the archives. Things like smells, or perhaps even certain visuals. I'm not certain how much the records here go into mancers, but I'll see what I can find. Give me a few weeks to see what I can dig through."

"I don't want to be a bother."

"You're no bother. You're my best friend." Sparrow beams at me. "Give me time to work on this and I'll see what I can find out."

"No rush. I'm not going anywhere," I joke. It's true, though. I've got one month left before recruitment day, and I'll be damned if I give up my chance to become a fledgling again. I'm not spending the rest of my life cleaning windows and tossing chamber pots. I'm not.

My friend looks up, and then her countenance changes to a soft delight as she slides her notes underneath a blank sheet. "Oh! Hawk! I didn't realize you were coming by, darling."

Uh-oh. I jump to my feet, anxious as the big russet Taurian strides into the cramped quarters. "Master Hawk! Hello."

He gives me a distracted smile. "Gwenna. Good to see you."

Is it? He doesn't know why I'm here yet. I watch nervously as he moves to Sparrow's side and presses a kiss atop her head. She leans into him, her mien one of pure contentment. They look good together. Hawk is large and forbidding, while Sparrow is softer. Gentler. She reaches up and nudges the golden ring through his nose, and they share a secretive smile.

It's time for me to leave. These quarters are far too close for me to stay comfortably with a pair of starry-eyed newlyweds. Even though my friend initially married the big Taurian for practical purposes, it didn't take long before they were both in love. Good for them, but I'm not jealous. The last thing I need is a man dragging me down. My ambitions don't include relationships, not right now. I want to join the guild, become an artificer, and make some real coin.

"Well, I should get going," I say, moving away from the desk before they start making kissy noises at each other or something embarrassing.

"I promised I'd cover Kerta's nestmaid shift, and I need to go home and change out of these sweaty clothes. Thanks for the chitchat, Sparrow. I'll get out of your hair."

Her face glows at my use of her name. She gives me a quiet thumbs-up and I know she'll keep my secrets. My relief feels intense, as if I can suddenly breathe again.

At her side, her Taurian husband is sniffing the air. "Did Raptor come by?"

I freeze in place. Damn Taurians and their elite senses. I scrubbed at the mess the big white Taurian had left between my thighs earlier, but perhaps I didn't do enough.

"No, why?" Sparrow glances up at Hawk.

"I'm picking up his scent." His bullish mouth pulls into a frown and he eyes the room, nostrils flaring.

I decide to play dumb. "Is he an oversized sort of bull with a white face and vicious horns?" I wiggle my fingers by my temples in an imitation of horns. "There's a big male like that in the hospital. I was cleaning in his room earlier."

Hawk relaxes. "That must be it."

"Well then, I really had best be going," I chirp in a bright voice. I need to bathe again once I get back to the nestmaid quarters to ensure that no one picks up the scent of Taurians—or sex—on me. "See you soon, Sparrow!"

One more month, I remind myself. I just need to lie low for one more month.

Surely I can manage that.

FOUR

RAPTOR
Weeks Later

I T'S NEVER A good sign when I'm called into the head guild master's office. I like to spend my time on the fringes, because you can get away with a lot more. Unfortunately, it seems that I've caught Rooster's attention in some way. Lucky me. It means he's about to assign me a muck-ton of extra work, or someone important has gotten lost in the tunnels and every single Taurian in the guild is being called to action, even the more recently injured ones like me.

But when I get to Rooster's office, I'm surprised to see that there's no one else waiting except for Hawk. Master Hawk, I remind myself, proud of my friend. Took him a long mucking time to get some recognition, and I'm glad for him . . . but the fact that we're here alone with Rooster means nothing good.

Rooster is seated behind the heavy, ostentatious wooden desk of the head guild master, his short arms resting on the surface. "Please close the door behind you, Artificer."

Well, that's not a bad sign. He doesn't know my name. To him I'm just another Taurian, another set of hooves to send into the tunnels to do the hard work. I glance over at Hawk, who's seated on the other side of the desk, but his expression is impossible to read. I shut the door behind me and then move forward to take the seat next to Hawk, opposite the head of the guild.

"Your wounds look like they've healed well," Hawk says, nodding at me in greeting. "How are your eyes?"

"Good as new," I reassure him with a lazy grin, putting on an air of casualness I don't feel. I rub the bare patch on my skull that covers my head from horns to just below my eyes. "The healers say the fur here will grow back, too. Good thing, as I'd hate to disappoint the ladies without even a sexy scar to show for my troubles."

"A sexy scar?" Rooster echoes, his expression sour.

"Sure." I sprawl my legs out in front of me, making sure to take up as much space as possible. I slouch on the delicate wooden chair, meant for human builds and not Taurian ones, and cross my arms over my chest. "Hard to impress pretty girls when half your head looks like a roasted chicken."

Hawk says nothing.

Rooster's expression grows sourer, his small hands clasped on the desk in front of him as if he's some sort of penitent monk. Even for a human, Rooster's a small, squat type. The desk dwarfs him, and I mentally picture him sitting on a cushion to make himself appear taller. It feels like something he'd do. If he doesn't get up during this meeting, I'm probably right.

The guild master politely scratches the side of his nose, and it makes the healing patches on my face itch in response. "You mention females. I've heard that you headed for the brothels the moment you left the hospital. Is there . . . a problem?"

"No problem. I just like the ladies," I say, voice flat. My tail twitches. Neither knows that I've got the god's hand upon me. That I'm forced to rely upon illegal magic potions that keep my knot from making me crazed at all times and I was out of my potion recently. That I needed a woman while at the hospital. I don't want to tell anyone that I've been obsessively hunting for Sarya since the moment the bandages were removed. No one needs to know I'm infatuated with a sex worker who likely thinks of me as little more than another job.

Because I am.

Infatuated.

I can't stop thinking of Sarya. I'm not sure why. I've hired plenty of sex workers in the past. Another one shouldn't be special. It's that she made me feel . . . normal. Most of the time I feel like a freak. A Taurian male in rut is thought to be irrational and difficult. The moment a bed partner finds out that I have a knot, they look at me differently. Treat me differently. Demand more coin for "extra" work. Like I'm a *problem*.

Sarya didn't act like I was a problem. Didn't act like my knot was an issue, just noted that it was there and it was nothing but another tool for pleasure. There was something about her—her self-deprecating humor, her ease with my body, and how she used me to give herself pleasure. All of that fascinates me. Her gorgeously thick curves helped, too. I don't care what she looks like—all humans are a little bit strange-looking to a Taurian—but I want to see her again. I want to talk to her again. Hear that throaty little chuckle of hers. I just want to get to know her, which sounds ridiculous considering that it's her job to fuck and not chat.

I want to be with her. Just . . . with her.

I can't find her anywhere, though. She's disappeared. Every person I asked in the hospital gave me the stink eye, as if they would never hire a sex worker on my behalf. I'm guessing they're not supposed to talk about it. I've approached all the brothels, too, looking for a tall, busty blonde named Sarya. No luck.

My knot has been aching since I was released, and I should just hire one of the many men or women who service the city's sexual needs. Pay extra to have someone work my knot the same casual way she did. Or just break down and get another potion dose. But I want Sarya. I've never been choosy in the past, but I suppose everyone can have a change of heart, even a lecherous piece of shit like me. Maybe it's not just Sarya. Maybe it's that Hawk, my oldest friend, is utterly besotted with his new human wife. That he has a partner—not just for upcoming Conquest Moons but for every day in between.

I'm envious. I've never had a romantic partner. Sex partner, yes. But romantic? No. Most respectable men and women run for the hills when they hear I have a knot, and the disrespectable ones are just interested in my coin. I'm back to taking cock-deadening concoctions.

Maybe that's why they've called me in. I've been caught. They've realized I've been loading up on potions on the sly. "What's wrong with frequenting brothels?" I ask, since they're both being rather quiet. "Didn't know it was suddenly against the rules."

"It's not," Rooster says in that same delicate, sour tone that tells me he doesn't approve. "But it does make me wonder about your discretion."

"Raptor is the most trustworthy male I know," Hawk says immediately, sitting up as if he wishes to fight in my defense. "Just because he's hiring companions doesn't mean that he can't keep a secret."

So . . . I'm not in trouble. They're just worried I can't keep a *secret*? I arch a brow at Hawk, wondering what the muck this is about. He's busy staring down Rooster, though, as if daring him to take a chance on me. "I know when to keep my mouth shut."

After all, no one in this room knows that I've been pilfering artifacts from Lord Nostrum's expeditions for my own pockets. Been doing that for years and never been caught. I take stuff that only brings a few pennies here and there on the black market. I've gotten good at spotting things, and the person I sell them to never asks questions. It's helped me keep my potion habit going. It's helped me pay off a friend's debts. It's helped keep me afloat when Lord Nostrum decides that he's not going to pay us for an excursion, or our Five ends up with a fruitless run. Is it skimming off the top? Yes. Is it illegal? Yes. Is it hurting anyone? No.

I wouldn't have to do it if cheap Lord Nostrum paid his team every excursion. A lot of the time, he decides that our efforts are not worth his coin and won't open his wallet. It gets harder and harder for him to carry a team that doesn't know if it'll get paid or not. I've been his only long-term artificer, and that's because I'm taking a bit here and there to make ends meet. As it is, I can barely keep ahead on my potion costs. Which makes me think of Sarya again, and the envy I feel at Hawk's contentment.

The guild master exchanges a look with Hawk, and silence falls on the room again.

"We have a problem," Rooster finally says.

I can't imagine how it involves me, but I remain silent, waiting.

"There are thieves in the guild." Rooster's expression is that of a deeply disappointed father.

Is this a setup? "You don't say."

Hawk clears his throat, leaning forward in his seat. "The guild always has problems with a bit of thievery. Snatching a few trinkets here and there isn't what we're talking about. We're seeing Greater Artifacts that are disappearing from guild storage or from the archives before they can be sold, only to appear on the black market a short time later. It's been occurring for the last year or so, and we've only realized it within the last few months. To date, thirteen Greater and twenty-nine Lesser Artifacts have been recorded as stolen."

I whistle, because that's a lot of coin to drift out of the guild.

Hawk nods in agreement with my reaction. "Exactly. And it's coming from someone—or *several* someones—who obviously have access to guild buildings normally off-limits to citizens."

"We do not think it is an artificer," Rooster adds. "They won't be paid until the sale, so a stolen artifact cuts into their personal profit."

"Then . . . a guild master?" I suggest.

"More likely one of the repeaters. Or several of the repeaters. Or even an archivist."

"An archivist wouldn't," Hawk growls. "We've discussed this."

Rooster focuses that pinched look on Hawk. "We are not ruling out possibilities—"

"Not an archivist," Hawk says again, voice deadly.

"I think Hawk is right." I decide to speak up before Hawk jumps over the guild leader's desk to throttle him. "You know how they are. They'd rather study things than sell them. They don't even like the holders having the artifacts instead of them."

Rooster purses his lips, but after a moment, nods. "You are both correct. My apologies."

At my side, Hawk relaxes into his seat again, his wife's reputation (and that of the other archivists) secure.

"Whoever it is," Rooster continues, "we feel they are working with some of the repeaters. Two of the repeaters have been murdered lately, their throats cut, and it seems like a warning of some sort."

"Either that, or they're of no further use to whoever was utilizing them to get the artifacts out." Hawk gestures with a spread hand. "Dead people don't talk, after all."

They both regard me with somber expressions as if waiting for something. "Sounds frustrating, but I'm still not sure what it has to do with me."

Hawk continues. "What we've told you cannot leave the room. Only the three of us know that this is being investigated. We've spread the word that the deaths of the two repeaters were related to robbery. Others in the guild know that there have been artifacts disappearing, but we've told the head archivist that he's to tell anyone who asks that it was shoddy bookkeeping and the items were misplaced."

". . . And? How do I play into this?" I'm still not entirely certain what this has to do with me, but the more Hawk tells me of the plan, the more I suspect it's not going to be something I like. That once again, Taurians are picking up the slack for the rest of the guild. I'm probably going to have to bust some heads on their behalf, get information from whoever I can. Something physical. That's usually what we Taurians are brought in for.

The two exchange another look. Rooster purses his lips again before speaking. "We're going to demote you."

"The muck you are," I growl, getting to my feet. A demotion is a grave insult. It means being stripped of my status and my ability to make coin on the finds assigned to my name. My sash will be removed, and I'll be shoved into the repeater ranks until some guild master takes a chance on me . . . and that won't be likely considering that they'll wonder *why* I've been demoted.

"Lord Nostrum's team—or rather, what was left of it after your accident—has been expelled. Their carelessness cost one man his life and ruined several valuable artifacts in the process. You have no team to return to." Rooster looks down his nose at me. "And it's common knowledge that you haven't a pristine record behind you."

I flinch at his words. Even if it's just Lord Nostrum, I don't like that my team has been destroyed. Some of those men were friends. Some were fools, but even fools don't deserve to lose their lives. To make matters worse, it seems they know my dirty secret. I wasn't aware anyone knew I'd been taking a little off the top. They're right. The scars around my eyes itch and feel tight, and I swear I can still feel the sting of the burn from the fireball that blasted me in the face.

"The fact that we've expelled the others and have kept you will be a sign in your favor," Hawk says. "You're strong and fit and you know what you're doing. Another master will pick you up, if only to ensure that you carry his team into passing."

"Another master . . . but not you?" I eye my friend.

"I'm going to be taking a class of repeaters," he says. "And I'm going to be watching them closely to see what I can find out. We're trying to keep this as quiet as possible, so I'd prefer you don't know who. And we'd like to put you in a nest with another group. Befriend them. Take them out for drinks. Encourage them to confide in you. And tell us what you find out."

Ugh. I can't believe what I'm hearing, but when I eye Hawk, his expression is just as serious as Rooster's. "How am I supposed to make coin while all this is going on? I can't just not make money for a year while I play with the fledglings."

"You'll be compensated."

"I'd better be." I don't work for free. That's just stupid. "How much?"

"You'll be paid enough. It's either that or you leave the guild entirely," Rooster says, and there's a thread of steel in his voice. "Lord Nostrum has released his team. You have no employer. You have been stripped of your rank. You can take our offer, or you can leave Vastwarren and take your chances with other employment."

What other employment does he think I'm going to get? For Taurians, it's farming, farming, and more farming. And if we're not cut out to be farmers, we can be . . . what? Sailors? Work in a mine? So I can scramble for whatever pittance I can eke out for the rest of my life? Or work in the temple back home, spending most of every day in prayer and giving up all my worldly possessions?

To the muck with all that.

Teeth gritted, I glare at Hawk for getting me into this mess. "Just for the record, I hate this idea."

Rooster sniffs, every bit the haughty guild leader. "Just for the record, I don't care."

"Just for the record," Hawk adds, his tone placating, "you're the perfect one for this sort of task. You're good at ingratiating yourself, and the other guild masters will be fighting to get you on their fledgling team. Help us find this murderer—or murderers—and the guild will be extremely grateful. More Taurian guild masters are going to be needed in the future."

There's buttering someone up, and then there's buttering someone up.

"We're going very quickly from 'about to be kicked out of the guild' to 'guild master,' aren't we?"

Hawk tugs at the ring on his nose in agitation. "This problem goes pretty deep, Raptor. The two repeaters who were killed were working in different parts of the guild. They had no connection, except that they were found murdered in the same way. It could be anyone who's next, and even if we ignore the threat to people's safety, the thieves are costing the guild thousands upon thousands of gold crowns. Somehow, they're getting into locked rooms and finding objects that have been discreetly hidden away by the guild. We must find out how they're discovering these items and how they're extracting them. Who their source is. It's a knot with many tangled threads. We need the best to help us."

It sounds like a clusterfuck to me. I glance over at Rooster, whose sour, disapproving look has never changed as he gazes upon me over his tiny spectacles. "You need the best, eh?"

"Hawk reassures me you will be the help we need," Rooster says stuffily.

"I'll agree to all of this on one condition." At Hawk's raised brows, I point at Rooster. "I want *him* to tell me that I'm the best."

There's nothing more satisfying than Rooster's outraged sputtering.

FIVE

GWENNA

Swansday, One Day Before Recruitment Day

Dere Ma,

Tomorrow is the big day. Please say a prayer to the gods that I was accepted as a flegling. The men here that are artificers are all full of themselves, and it's hard for a woman. Evin Aspeth, who had a lot of knowledge about artifacts, isn't taken seriously. I hope I can pass this year. I don't think I can do another year as a repeeter. We don't work for money. We work for room and bord and to pay off our debts for flunking. If we're good, maybe we will get picked to be a flegling next time.

I am sending along a few coins I've managed to make through odd jobs. Buy yourself new shoes—I no yours are always worn out.

Love, Gwenna

THE NERVES ARE starting already, and recruitment day isn't until tomorrow. I've finished my work for the day, and I can either sit in the nestmaid quarters on my bunk with the other women who work for the guild and have them ask me why I want to be an artificer, or I can get out for the night. Lark and Mereden are heading to the King's Onion, our favorite nearby tavern, and suggested we get together for drinks before the big day.

I think getting drunk sounds like the right call. Hopefully I can get drunk enough to pass out so I don't have to stay up all night thinking about what tomorrow will bring. With my black repeater sash slung over my shoulder like a brand, I make my way through Sparkanos Square at the center of Vastwarren's heart and ignore the men who catcall and make rude noises as I march past. They can give a repeater shit, but the moment I have a fledgling sash they'll leave me alone.

Actually, they won't. But it's a step closer to respectability, and I'm used to men making arses out of themselves and me ignoring their efforts to get under my skirts.

The tavern doors open to the smell of beer and sweat, and the overbearing scent of raw onions. I wrinkle my nose as I enter, waving to Naiah behind the bar. Her expression brightens when she sees me, and she points at the back of the crowded room, knowing just who I headed here for. Sure enough, I spot the dark, curly hair of Mereden next to Lark's bright blond, tangled hair. As I approach, I spot their repeater uniforms . . . and Lark's foot propped up on a chair beside a large leaf-green slitherskin with a patched-up shell house strapped to his back. Kipp is here, too. "Well, isn't this a treat?" I call out as I approach, delighted. "All we need is Aspeth and we'd have our Five from last year back together."

Mereden gets up to hug me, the warm vanilla scent of her skin comforting. She's been working in the guild kitchens and smells like pies and fresh bread every day. "There you are," she exclaims, hugging me tight as if we haven't seen each other for months instead of just a few days. "I was about to come after you."

"I had to work late," I tell them cheerfully. "You know what Mistress Umala is like."

She and Lark groan obligingly. They do, in fact, know what Mistress Umala is like.

"Where's Aspe—er, Sparrow?" I ask, looking around for my friend. "Did I miss her?"

"Research project running late," Mereden says, settling on the far side of the table next to Lark again. She sets her hand atop the table and their fingers immediately intertwine. "She said she'd be by later."

Aspeth says that a lot. It rarely happens, though. If a project runs late, it means she's lost in her research and won't look up until her husband,

Hawk, comes to drag her to bed. I'd be annoyed except Aspeth is living the life she's always dreamed of, so I'm happy for her.

Glancing down, I offer a fist for Kipp to bump, as slitherskins don't like prolonged touching of humans, and he taps my knuckles with his knife, which means he's feeling overstimulated enough that even a brief touch will be too much. Lark doesn't get up to greet me, and her foot remains propped up in what I assumed was my chair. Now that I'm closer, I can see the linen bandages turning her foot into what looks like nothing more than a gigantic beige sausage. "What the muck happened here?"

"Tripped on a cobblestone," Lark says with a grimace. "I wish I could say it was something more exciting, like a runaway horse, but no. I was carrying a crate across the courtyard for Master Grackle and my foot caught. You should have heard the snap."

My jaw drops. "Today?"

"Today. Rotten timing, isn't it?" Lark looks annoyed, but not devastated.

I thump into the only empty chair left. I'm the one who's devastated. If Lark's foot is broken, then that means she can't become a fledgling, not this year. All the masters will be selecting their fledglings tomorrow. "Rather convenient timing," I finally manage to say, "what with it being Master Grackle and all."

Master Grackle is well-known amongst all the women who are employed by the guild for just how dismissive he is. I'd rather have a lech for a teacher than deal with one who treats me as if I've got no brain in my skull.

"It's just the fact that I was hurrying," Lark reassures me. "Wasn't as if he tripped me or anything."

"But recruitment day is tomorrow." I'm whining about the obvious.

"I know. Guess that means I'm mucking stalls for another year."

"Not with that foot," Mereden replies tartly, leaning over to brush a lock of stray hair off Lark's forehead. "Until it heals, I'll put in a word for you with the healers. You'll probably have to sterilize tools over a pot of water all day, but you can do it seated."

Funnily enough, neither of them seems devastated about Lark's broken foot. "You're both taking this rather well."

They exchange a look. Mereden is the first one to speak. "We thought we might try for a baby instead. Join the guild later."

Kipp raps his knuckles on the table with approval.

I don't want to ask which one of them is going to get pregnant and how. That's not my business. Mereden and Lark are happy together and have been a couple for a year now. They married last month. Of course they'd want to grow their family. "So neither of you is going to recruitment day?"

Lark gestures at her foot with a shrug.

Mereden just gives me a calm look. "One of the healers at the clinic is leaving to work in a hold, so there's an apprenticing spot open. I have to get the rest of my repeater debt waived, but since I've got holder blood, they're being lenient. And you know how I love healing."

"You're good at it," I agree, my words faint. I'm trying not to be disappointed, but it's hard. When Naiah brings over tankards of the house ale, I grab mine and immediately swig it, ignoring the garnish of onion on the side. "I just . . . I thought we'd all do it together."

"Cheer up," Lark says. "Maybe you'll fail."

"That's not a thing to be cheerful over!"

"But then we'd all be together. Unless there's a baby, of course." And she lifts her and Mereden's joined hands to her mouth and kisses her wife's hand. Mereden just looks radiant with happiness.

I glance over at Kipp.

He looks at me and shrugs.

"Are you going for recruitment, I hope?"

Kipp nods.

The tension in my shoulders eases a little. "That's something, at least. I won't be alone."

He pats the table in front of me as if to reassure me that no, he'll be there.

"I don't know why you're so worried," Mereden says in her calm, low voice. "You'll do just fine. You know Hawk will take you both on right away."

I don't disagree with her, but I have my doubts. Mereden's from a noble family, and Lark has always made her own path. I've been a servant all my life, invisible and unimportant. The least valuable of people. I could be completely overlooked simply because I don't know how to carry myself as anything but a lady's maid or a scullery wench.

It's my worst nightmare.

But I'd forgotten that Master Hawk will need another Five to teach as well. Hawk, who's Aspe—er, Sparrow's husband. Hawk, who was the assistant to Master Magpie last year. Hawk would definitely take me on as fledgling once more, because Sparrow would never let him hear the end of it otherwise. He'd take Kipp, too.

"I'm still nervous," I confess to my friends as I pick up my beer again. "I don't want to empty chamber pots for the rest of my days. You won't abandon me, will you, Kipp?"

He thumps his chest with his small fist and gives me a nod.

It's reassuring, even if I'd rather be there with the other women as well. A former maid and a slitherskin, looking to rejoin the ranks of the guild's students. Who could possibly turn that away?

The thought makes my stomach churn, and I drain my beer, then hold my finger up to call the barmaid over for another.

THE ROYAL ARTIFACTUAL Guild is big on pomp and ceremony. Every year, recruitment day is held in the Great Hall, or so Sparrow has told me a dozen times before. All the masters are present, and throughout the day they'll speak to and interview potential students before selecting the five they'll be teaching for the next year. There are always more student hopefuls than there are masters, so the competition is fierce. I didn't go last year, but Aspeth went by herself and was completely humiliated in the center of the room by Head Guild Master Rooster.

I've decided I'll avoid him entirely, check in with Hawk, and quickly escape back out. I don't want anyone to give him—or me—guff simply because I'm a female. There's a lot of dick-swinging in the guild, unfortunately.

I pack my bag and make my bed in the nestmaid quarters for hopefully the last time, tucking the coverlets in tight. One of the other maids, Jelessa, eyes me with a look of curious disgust, as if I'm a giant spider that's suddenly crawled across the floor. "You know if you give up the whole 'repeater' thing, they'll hire you. A maid can earn a decent living, and meals and a bed are paid for."

"I want to become a fledgling." It wasn't my dream as much as it was Sparrow's, but I've been tempted by the thought of coin. Of never making another bed or emptying a chamber pot ever again. It's a gilded dream, that thought, but I'm going to chase it anyhow. "I could have been a maid back home."

"Aye, you could have," Jelessa says. She doesn't understand me at all, but she hugs me anyhow and gives me a firm pat on the back. "Good luck to you. You're a hard worker. If they can see past the skirts, they'll take you for certain."

I'll make sure they see past the skirts. I'm going to pitch them the moment I leave the barracks and wear my trousers instead. Just in case. I'd rather have my arse hanging out than have them think I'm not serious about things.

My small pack is over my shoulder, and I'm hugged by four other women—all maids living in the barracks—before I make it out the door. Then I duck into an alley, shimmy off the skirt that's over my pants, and head on toward the main guild hall.

Even before I get there, I can see the crowd forming outside. My stomach flutters with anxiety. There are men everywhere. I see men with dark cloaks, men with embroidered cloaks, men with the homespun shirts of farmers and the poor. They crowd at the front of the Great Hall, which looks like a fancy-pants church of some sort on the outside. There's a line at the double doors of people waiting to get in.

I see no women. Not a single one. It makes the hairs on the back of my neck prickle with awareness. Maybe I should turn around and leave. Accept my fate as a maid for the rest of my days. The guild pays better than Lord Honori did, and it's not the worst living.

But I'll die inside. I know I will. I can't do it. Being Sparrow's friend has taught me that if you want something badly enough, you must pursue it, regardless of what people say. Even if I'm not successful, I can at least try. Failing makes me end up at the same spot that not trying does, so why not try? I have nothing to lose and everything to gain.

As I step forward, I'm more aware of the men eyeing me. I keep my gaze ahead as I approach, but I'm waiting for someone to pinch my arse, or brush up against my tit. I'm waiting for the sniggers. The comments that I don't belong. I approach the doors, and a trio of men turn around and give me stares that could boil water.

"This isn't the servants' entrance," one states, eyeing me and ignoring my repeater sash.

"I'm applying to the guild, same as everyone else." I keep my tone sweet, because the last thing I want to do is make a group of men even angrier at me. Pinching men are an annoyance. Angry men are a terror.

They look me up and down, and the one at the front sneers at me, pointing away from the doors. "The back of the line is that way. You want to get in, wait your mucking turn."

"We're repeaters. We get in first."

"Everyone here is a repeater. New students aren't coming until after lunch."

Oh. I lift my chin and manage to sweep away with a crumb of dignity. "Of course."

It's hard to march past the long line of men, all of whom seem to be smirking at me with delight, pleased to see me retreating. I hate that they're reveling in my walking away, even if it's only to the back of the line. It just reinforces my need to prove them wrong. I'm not going to be a maid for the rest of my life.

I'm not. Surely I'm destined for more.

By the time I make it to the back of the line, I'm practically in the middle of the plaza, and the stretch of the queue in front of me feels depressingly long. What if I don't make it to the front before they cut off? What if all the masters have full groups by the time I get there? I try not to think about those things as I wait for the line to shuffle forward. A few men get in line behind me, and one snickers. I wait for someone to shove me or pinch my arse. I know it's coming. The shove comes first, and when I get knocked into the man waiting in front of me, he scowls with an utterly black look on his face.

"Sorry," I say meekly. In this moment, I hate everyone.

Crossing my arms over my chest, I try to ignore the others in line, even as they jostle my heavy pack, which carries everything I own. What am I going to do if I don't get picked? What if I get to Master Hawk and his group is full? What if he is told not to take any women this time around? It's not a guarantee that he'll pick me again. I'm just hopeful. But maybe even that is wishful thinking.

The line shuffles forward and I move in step with the others. As I do, something tugs on my pant leg, right at the knee. I turn to see a welcome, bright green face.

Kipp.

He eyes me in that calm way of his, his shell perched on his back and a weapons belt at his waist. His black repeater sash looks like a ribbon across his tiny shoulder, but I'm thrilled to see him. I could cheerfully hug him in this moment, because I am no longer alone. "Kipp," I breathe, sagging with relief. "You're here."

He pats my leg and then gestures that I should stand with him, a few paces back. I don't mind losing my place in line in the slightest, because it means I'll be with a friend. I let the men move in front of me and ignore their expressions entirely. They don't matter anymore.

Kipp flicks a bit of imaginary dust off his shoulder as I stand in line next to him, in front of a pair of sailors.

I clasp my hands, but I can't stand still. "Are you nervous, Kipp?"

He gives me a look that scoffs at the very idea of nerves.

I wish I could be as confident as him. Even though slitherskins are rather alien to most humans, I suspect most guild members would rather work with him than with a woman. "I'm nervous," I whisper, trying to keep my voice down so the others around us won't hear me doubting myself. "I don't mean to be a bother, but it's obvious I'm not wanted here."

The slitherskin reaches out and touches my hand, giving the side of my finger a reassuring squeeze. I could almost cry at that small, sticky touch. He's confident in me. Why do I doubt myself? I can do this. I might be stout, but I'm strong after years of hauling water for baths and carrying trunks up and down stairs. I'm a hard worker. I might not be as educated as some, but that just means I'll have to be more persistent. I *can* do this.

I won't let them hold me back, because I know what's waiting for me at Honori Hold: lugging chamber pots for Lord Honori and his new wife, and a lifetime of blending in with the tapestries on the walls, never to be seen or heard. Never to have more than a few sorry coins to rub together.

Fuck all that. I want more than what my mother had.

Straightening, I put my chin up as the queue moves forward again.

It seems to take forever for the line to wind along the plaza and up to the main stairs. A few of the men get irritated and leave, but Kipp seems as calm as ever, and I take my cue from his serenity. By the time we get to the doors, the sun is growing hot overhead, my feet hurt, and my stomach is growling. All that goes away the moment the Taurian manning the doors flicks a hand, indicating we can enter now.

We squeeze inside the crowded hall, my pulse hammering wildly. High above, banners embroidered with the symbols of the masters hang from the rafters. The Great Hall feels more ostentatious than the rest of the building, which is saying something. There's an arching, vaulted ceiling and massive windows. Stuffed birds fill the nooks and crannies at the top of the airy room. I'm told they're there as homage to the birds that the guild artificers take as their names, but it strikes me as just vaguely creepy instead of respectful. The floor underneath our feet is a shiny marble that scuffs easily. I know that because I've cleaned the damn thing a dozen times while working for Mistress Umala.

Along the center of the room are impressive statues of famous artificers from the past, the most famous being the enormous statue of Sparkanos the Swan outside in the plaza. Every single one of the statues is of a man.

If I was doubting myself before, seeing all those statues of men—and the floors I've cleaned—just makes me more determined that I'm not going to end up a maid for the rest of my life. I'm going to succeed, damn it.

Kipp moves closer to me as a pair of men shove their way past us, heading for the doors. We step aside, and the slitherskin gestures that I should lead. "I imagine you can't see much, but I'm not having a lot of luck myself." I crane my head, trying to peer over the shoulders of the crowd. I'm not a tall woman, so all I glimpse is a lot of nothing. But then I spot a pair of horns near one of the walls, and I grab Kipp by his sleeve and drag him across the room toward Hawk.

Master Hawk stands near the statue of the legendary Master Owl, Sparkanos's son. Hawk's hands are clasped behind his back and his shoulders seem massive, as if he's taking up all the space between statues. The expression on his roan-colored face is austere, and he gazes at the crowd as if he's assessing it. No one's approaching him, though, which I'm hoping is a good sign. Maybe people are staying away from the first Taurian guild master? If so . . . good. I want a space on his team.

I manage to drag Kipp after me, holding on to his sleeve. I come to a stop in front of Hawk, smooth my repeater sash, and smile at my friend's husband. "Hi again."

Hawk inclines his head. "Gwenna. Kipp. Good to see you both. Are you here to find a master to pledge to?"

Something about the way he says it makes my nerves ping, but I ignore it. I'm sure I'm just reading it wrong. "We were hoping we could be your fledglings again. Serve you."

Hawk's expression turns pained. "Ah. I . . ." He clears his throat. "I wish I could choose you, but I cannot."

A cold chill washes over me and I glance at Kipp. If Hawk won't take us, what do we do now?

SIX

RAPTOR

RECRUITMENT DAY IS always a brutal sort of thing. There are so many hopefuls that crowd into the Great Hall who don't get picked for one reason or another. Perhaps there's a personality clash with a master, or there's a prior obligation of some kind that they think they can still manage while being enrolled. Recruits don't realize just how much work becoming a fledgling entails. You can practically hear the dreams crashing to the ground around you.

It's common for some of the guild members to come and get a good look at the soon-to-be fledglings. I've always crowded inside the hall with all the others to check out the competition. I imagine some get a vindictive sort of pleasure at being one of the few who have passed the tests, and some are probably reminiscing about their time as a fledgling.

I'm usually not all that sympathetic to those who are turned away. It's just part of guild life. You either get in, or you don't. Some try again, some don't. But the woman and slitherskin standing in front of Hawk are so earnest and hopeful that it pains me physically when Hawk turns them down. I knew he would, and yet it's still difficult to see.

Hawk is under instructions from Head Guild Master Rooster to take on five new repeaters so he can keep a close eye on things. I know from talking to Hawk that both of these two were the terrible Master Magpie's students last year and got into trouble when Aspeth did. Aspeth was removed from the guild entirely but was so knowledgeable about Old Prell that the archivists snapped her up. It didn't hurt that she was a holder's daughter, either. Having holders owe the guild is always a good thing. The others on her fledgling team weren't as lucky as Aspeth. They were going to be expelled, but the group had managed to find a few Greater Artifacts, which made the guild quite a bit of coin. There's a guild rule that any fledgling who finds a Greater Artifact is automatically made into a full-on artificer, but that couldn't happen with these students due to the trouble they were in. They were stripped of fledgling status and demoted to repeaters instead of being kicked out entirely.

The little round woman and the lizard must have been expecting to serve with Hawk again. He had a motley crew last year and word got around, especially after Master Magpie was removed from the guild and Master Hawk took her place. Anyone who came from that old fledgling team would have a difficult time getting someone to look past the rumors of stealing to consider them. The fact that it's a woman and a slitherskin? Not gonna happen.

Which makes me want to take them both under my wing. It wouldn't be a bad thing, I reason. I'm supposed to get friendly with all the repeaters anyhow, right? I eye the unlikely pair. I know a bit about them from Hawk's stories of the craziness that happened last year. The slitherskin is named Kipp. He never talks, but he's competent for his small size. Arrogant, Hawk had called him. Good with blades but he knows it. I'm amused that such a tiny creature could be an artificer. I doubt he even comes to my waist. Any knife he wields will be little more than a toothpick. Still, a small size can be useful. He can get into places others can't. I'll be curious to see if he's a liability or an asset.

Is he the one Rooster is looking for? I wonder. I contemplate the slitherskin while he stands next to the human female. If I'm honest, it could be him. There are no slitherskins currently on the guild's roster. It's entirely believable that he's simply going to remain in the ranks of the repeaters and work on getting rich from the inside. If he can get into small spaces, perhaps he's the one sliding into the guild's locked vaults and stealing what's there. It bears watching, certainly.

My gaze moves to the human female. She's a bit younger than Hawk's wife, Sparrow, if I recall correctly. Can't remember her name. She came with Sparrow from the hold, but she was a maid or a servant or something. I've seen her with Sparrow several times and remembered her because she's built just how I like them. She's short, but a tasty treat. Her breasts are overflowing handfuls, and her hips are nice and thick in the trousers she wears. Her waist nips in, emphasizing the exaggerated curves of her form. Her hair is dark and pulled back into a no-nonsense bun at the back of her head, and when she moves, it's with both purpose and skill. There's no awkward clumsiness to her motions, which I find appealing.

Five hells, if it weren't for the fact that I'm already half in love with the missing Sarya, I'd say this one is just my type. I can't stop eyeing that delectable backside of hers. Good thing I'm here only to flirt and get to know everyone. I want to save myself for Sarya, to show her that I'm committed, but I can't seem to find her, no matter how hard I search. I don't want to give up, but I'm getting discouraged. I suppose in the meantime I can devote myself to the guild's secret plan. I can toy with a pretty female, get her to spill her guts . . . but that's as far as it can go.

As I approach, I hear Hawk speaking to the pair. "If it were up to me, you know the two of you would be my first choice," he's saying, and I've never seen the bull look so damned uncomfortable. "But Head Guild Master Rooster has asked that I take on an entirely different roster this year. It's my first time as a master and he wants me to prove myself. You understand."

"Of course we do," the woman says, her tone all business. "Can you recommend anyone in particular that we should approach? Given that we're"—she gestures at herself, and then at her slitherskin companion— "a bit out of the ordinary?"

Hawk tugs on his nose ring. "I'm sorry. I'm not allowed to steer potential candidates. I'm happy to put in a good word for both of you with any master who shows interest, though."

"Right." Her tone is brisk again, without showing a hint of disappointment. I catch an almost imperceptible tightening of her shoulders from behind, as if she's bracing herself for the future. For disaster.

Time to make myself known.

I stride forward through the crowd—which always seems to part when a Taurian is on the move—and stand behind her. Her scent drifts through the air, sweet and clean and oddly familiar, but I can't place it. I lean forward, looping a casual arm over her shoulders, and rap my knuckles on the slitherskin's shell. "Looks like we rejects have to stick together this year."

Half expecting the woman to jump, I'm impressed when she simply looks over her shoulder at me. A flush on her cheeks and the dilation of her pupils are the only giveaways that my nearness has affected her. She flicks her gaze over me and arches a brow of disdain. I feel as if I've been caught by a maid after I've dared to touch a particularly pricey lamp at the master's house.

I love it. Makes me feel naughty.

I grin at her, leaning in and ignoring the scowl Kipp sends my way. "I couldn't help but overhear the two of you."

"Of course you couldn't," she replies, her voice tart. "You're standing practically on my arse."

Is Hawk paying attention to this? When I glance over to catch his eye, he's gone, though. He cuts through the row of statues to go and talk to a particularly sweaty and nervous-looking younger man.

"But it's a very nice arse," I offer, turning back to the woman. When she snorts, dismissing me, I try another tactic. "You're here for recruitment day, aren't you?"

Her eyes widen, just a fraction, as if she's surprised by my words. Why do they surprise her, I wonder? The woman's gaze flicks back to the nearness of my chest as if she's debating my too-comfortable approach. Then, with a delicate pinch of her fingers, she plucks my hand off her shoulder and slithers out of my grasp. "I'm not telling you anything. What with you having no manners and all."

Clutching at my chest, I pretend to stagger. "I'm wounded, lady. Truly wounded. Here I thought I'd spotted two kindred souls." I flick my black repeater sash. "Given that we're all in the same situation."

Her gaze flicks to the guild sash that marks me as a repeater, and then she glances down at Kipp. His mouth is flat and he licks his eyelid, which could mean anything. But she looks over at me again and lifts her chin in that pert way of hers. "Kipp says you're a rude shit."

"He said all that, eh?" I cross my arms over my chest in the classic Taurian intimidation move, enjoying myself immensely. I love it when a woman isn't afraid of my size. "What else did he say?"

"I can't presume to speak for him," she continues in that no-nonsense sassy voice, and for a moment she sounds just as bold as Sarya. "But I imagine he'd tell you to muck off so we can get on with our business."

"You're looking for a teacher, aren't you? So am I." I twirl a finger, indicating the three of us. "Thought we might stay together, seeing as how we three stick out a bit with this crowd."

"Oh." Again, she seems surprised, and her cheeks flush with color. "You want to team up?"

I shrug, feigning casualness. If I'm being honest with myself, she's a lot of fun to tease, and I'm curious about the little slitherskin. Both of them bear watching, and Rooster did tell me to find repeaters who could likely be thieves. A former maid could have a plethora of reasons as to why she'd take to stealing from the guild. Slitherskins tend to be secretive, and they can get anywhere. It's worth cozying up to them. "Figured that I can probably get onto any team I want, if I'm being honest. Repeater or no, everyone wants a Taurian on their team."

"Then you don't need us." That pointy little chin of hers goes up.

Is everything she says a challenge? Why do I love that so? "Thought it might be nice to be with some others who don't fit the mold. Hard to blend with all the merchants' sons and farm boys when you don't have anything in common. Know what I mean?"

Her gaze flicks to my muzzle, and her jaw clamps. She looks as if she's about to protest—or give me a tongue-lashing.

Kipp taps on her leg, which is probably the slitherskin version of a throat clearing. She eyes him and takes a step back. "We need to talk in private for a moment."

"You're leaving?" I tease, gesturing at the crowded hall we stand in. "You'll lose your place in line."

"Just give us a moment," she all but barks at me, and I can't help but grin. I don't know how I'm managing to get under her skin so easily, but by the gods, it's entertaining. With a huffy little look at me, she turns to Kipp and he moves deeper into the room. I'm impressed when she drops into a squat to talk on level with the much smaller slitherskin, treating him like an equal. Few would do such a thing.

I also notice that several of the men in the room are checking out the tight fit of her trousers across her very plump arse. It's a nice one, for sure. Reminds me of Sarya . . . which makes a stab of bitterness shoot through me. Am I so terrible to be around that she's made it a point to avoid me? That's the only reason I can think of that I can't find the woman in any brothel in all of Vastwarren.

The human woman and the slitherskin put their heads together. She's doing all the talking, and the lizard seems to communicate entirely with hand gestures and facial expressions. After a while, she nods and gets to her feet again, straightening. Her gaze meets mine.

I give her a languid smile, toying with my repeater sash.

She marches the short distance to stand in front of me again. "Tell me your name," she demands. "And why you're a repeater."

Hmm. It's not a question I'd thought to answer, actually. More fool me. I thought for certain that any master with a lick of sense would take one look at my tall, muscular form and jump to have me. Explaining myself never came into the picture. I stroke my chin, pretending to consider her words. "I'll give you my name—it's Raptor."

"I know who you are. What's your real name?" she says irritably. "You can't take a bird name until you've passed."

Some of my amusement dims. "I'm not changing names. I've been Raptor for a decade. They're going to let me keep it."

"Oh, are you so certain, then?"

"I am, aye." And I'm going to make sure everyone mucking knows that my name is not up for grabs. "And if anyone asks, I'll tell them that I'm Raptor, and that it's bad luck to say my old name."

"I've never heard of such a thing."

That's because I've just decided it. "It's a Taurian belief."

Her eyes narrow at me. "Just give me your name."

"I promise you, it's Raptor. I'm from the Southwind Plains, but I've been here for fifteen years. What's *your* name?"

"Gwenna. From Honori Hold." She thumbs a gesture at her companion. "This is Kipp."

Kipp lifts his chin at me, the only acknowledgment I get.

"And why are you repeating, my *fine* Taurian?" Gwenna says the word like it's an insult, but the bristly part of me still laps it up like wine. "If you're such a catch?"

"My Five disbanded after they got caught stealing," I say, deciding that most of the truth is probably a good idea. "Since I'm *such a catch*, they just demoted me instead of getting rid of me entirely."

The answer surprises her. "Thieving?"

"Nothing big or I'd be in the tower waiting to be hanged." My grin is cocky and full of reassurance. I wouldn't normally volunteer that I've been caught thieving, but since I'm trying to find a thief, maybe this'll help build camaraderie. "It happens, even in the best-run Fives. But I've apologized properly and they've accepted it, and so here I am."

Gwenna blinks at me, as if quietly digesting this. Then she nods. "If you've been forgiven, all is well."

My senses sound a warning. She thinks thieving is all right, then? Perhaps she's the one I'm looking for after all. That's disappointing. Then again, why am I judging? We all do what we can to get ahead. I nod at her and Kipp both, and Kipp seems less convinced than her. He's still scowling at me. "Shall we work together, then? See if we can find a master who will take on three unexpected students?"

Gwenna moves closer to me, and her expression is full of doubt as she glances around the crowded room, eyeing the potential students around us. "No one's going to take us on, are they? A woman, a slitherskin, and a thief?"

It's an odd collection, and I don't point out that even as a thief, I'm still far more desirable than either of them. I want to reach out and put an arm around her shoulders again, tuck her against my side where she'd fit perfectly, but the slitherskin is eyeing me as if I'm dung beneath his tiny boots. I give them both my most reassuring smile. "Of course someone will take us on. We just look for the most obvious candidate."

She casts another glance around the room. "Most obvious candidate? What do you mean? You make it sound like we're the ones picking."

"We are, in a way." I put a hand on the small of her back, testing the waters. For some reason, I'm dying to touch her. Put my hand on her in some small way to claim her. She doesn't move away from my touch this time, and I gently steer her toward the far end of the room. "It's all about finding the right master for the job."

"And who might that be?" Gwenna asks.

I lean in to whisper to her, even though Kipp is nearby and deserves attention, too. "We hunt for the master who looks the most pained at this gathering. He's going to want to get out of here quickly. Three good students in one fell swoop is a dream come true."

Kipp flips his hand over and moves it back and forth in a dismissive gesture. There's a look of doubt on his triangular face, as if he doesn't believe what I'm saying.

"We *are* good students," I point out. "Three repeaters means we know exactly what we're doing. They can skip all the basics and go straight to the training. We're a safe bet."

"But we failed."

"A lot of good people fail. You didn't give up, which is all that matters." I point to the back of the room, where a few men in guild uniforms and the bright red sashes of masters are clustered together. "Come on. I know just the person."

"You do?"

"Aye, I'm thinking we head for Master Jay."

Gwenna stops in her tracks and gazes up at me. Her eyes are big and soulful . . . and full of skepticism. "Why him? Are you friends?"

That makes me snort. "By all the tunnels underground, no. We're not friends in the slightest. He's a pain in the arse and makes all his students crazy."

"Then why would we want to be on his team?" She looks at me as if I'm mad.

Because once you're done for the day, he doesn't give an arse hair about what his students do, which helps my plans. Because he was on the list of masters that Hawk suggested I'd be able to work around. "Because he'll just be glad to get his team filled. He's got a reputation for being fussy, hence the name Jay."

"Sounds delightful," she says dryly. "And he's going to want a slitherskin and a woman?"

"No, but he's going to assume that I'll carry you both through the tests."

Kipp makes a huffy sound. Gwenna doesn't seem offended at this. She gives me a thoughtful stare. "And will you? If we need help?"

"I can be persuaded."

Her face flames bright red again, and she marches forward, avoiding my hand, and I wonder what it is I said.

Master Jay is an older human man with a head of gray hair and a stern look on his face. He frowns as our motley little group approaches, glancing over at a doughy young man at his side. The younger man has a repeater sash on his shoulder, which is perfect. I put on my broadest smile as our group descends. "Jay. Just the man I was looking for."

"Why?" the master asks warily.

"Because I'm about to offer you an excellent deal to fill out your team. You need students, and unless I miss my guess, you need four of them, yes?" My tone is my most charming, despite all the suspicious glances I'm getting from both Jay and Kipp. It's fine. I'm used to dazzling those who aren't wanting to be dazzled.

Master Jay looks at the soft man at his side with a downright sour expression. "This is Hemmen, who was on Master Tiercel's team last year. I . . . owe Tiercel a favor, and his team is already full, so he'll be joining me." And he looks quite unhappy about it, too.

"Where've you been working while repeating?" I ask Hemmen cheerfully.

"Kitchens," he says, slicking his hair back with a palm. "Last year it was sweeping. Year before that it was scribing."

I can feel my brows crawling up. The fact that he's been tossed around between different departments means he's terrible at all of them. "You've repeated three times?"

"Four," Hemmen says, his tone slow and dull.

Mucking hells. No wonder Jay looks so annoyed. He's been saddled with deadweight. This is good for me, though. "Lucky for all of you that I'm here."

"Careful, if your head gets any bigger, you won't be able to make it through the doorways," Gwenna replies tartly, and she's so mucking cute that I want to squeeze her.

I focus on Jay, who looks unconvinced. "If you take on us three, you only need one more. We'll make a strong team."

Master Jay eyes Gwenna and Kipp, and then turns back to me as if they're not there. "I'd take you, of course, but I'd rather save the rest of my slots. Though I've heard the slitherskin is fast enough."

Next to my legs, Kipp puffs his chest and brandishes the tiniest weapon ever in a show of skill. Gwenna says nothing.

Strangely, I become insulted on Gwenna's behalf. I don't even know the girl but I can tell she won't be the problem of the group. Not choosing her because of her gender is just old-fashioned foolishness. "I'm afraid we're a package deal. It's all three or none at all."

Jay's expression grows even more sour. He studies me, and I resist the urge to flex, showing off my strength. Instead, he glances down at Kipp, and then eyes Gwenna. "You were both with Master Magpie last year, right? Part of that mess that happened?"

"Aye," she says, voice crisp. "Due to circumstances, we were demoted to repeaters."

His mouth tightens with displeasure. "'Circumstances' as in you were there to steal from the guild. Don't act like I don't know."

"'Circumstances' as in we were doing our best to help a friend who was being blackmailed and backed into a corner by someone working with our *master*. All artifacts were turned over to the guild without protest, and we've learned our lesson. We all came here with the intent of becoming artificers, not stealing from the guild, and that hasn't changed." Her back is ramrod stiff, and it's impossible to tell if there's a hint of dishonesty on her face. Thievery is one of the more common reasons people end up as repeaters, so it's not a death sentence, but a repeater caught stealing twice is sent packing.

"You're Sparrow's friend. Can you read or write Prellian? Any special skills?"

"No. I'm here to learn."

"You've a chaperone?"

"Sparrow is my chaperone."

Jay grunts, as if he expected this. His gaze turns to Kipp. "And you're a swordsman." When the slitherskin nods, the guild master gestures at our surroundings. "Prove to me that you can be effective even with your size, because right now it looks like a detriment."

In response, the lizard leaps past the scatter of people and clings to the nearest statue base. He scrambles up it quicker than a blink and hangs over the statue's extended arm, then brandishes his sword as he hangs practically upside down with only his sticky feet keeping him in place.

Jay grunts again, but I can tell he's impressed. He turns back to me. "Fine. If you're all three a package deal, I'll take all three of you. But I expect you to drag Hemmen and the woman through the tunnels if you must." He's staring right at me as he says this. "And you have to find me a decent fifth."

"Easy enough," I drawl. Secretly, I'm pleased. Not with Hemmen— he's a lump—but that so far, we've got four repeaters, and I'll be working closely with sharp-tongued Gwenna. I just need to find one more repeater to round out our team. I've worked with worse in the past. Lord Nostrum used to hire the cheapest teams, and I'd find myself with drunks, lazy fools, and the absolute bottom of the barrel of the guild. I'm used to doing the majority of the work.

Gwenna looks as if she wishes to protest, but her lips are drawn into a hard, thin line, and if there's a comment there, she's biting it back.

I rub my hands together and glance around the room. "You lot stay here. I'll handle this."

I wade back into the crowd, trying to pick out someone who seems decently capable. Tall would be helpful, considering that both Gwenna and Kipp are smaller-statured and Hemmen won't be reliable for anything. No wonder Jay looked so mucking sour. Four repeats in a row. Five hells, that's a nightmare.

Perhaps I should find someone acting shifty. Someone who looks as if they could be the problem that Hawk and Rooster are in search of. I step through the crowd, watching as masters interview possible candidates, and eye the ones who are turned away. Leaning against the far wall, I see a taller human man with yellow hair who might be strong. He also wears a scowl on his face, as if he's been turned down already. He stands near Master Finch, who's well-known for his scrupulousness in his fledgling choices. He won't pick a repeater.

And this one? This one looks far too shifty for the likes of Master Finch.

Well, it can't hurt to ask. I cut across the room and go to stand near the pale man, all casual like. "Any luck today?"

"None so far," he comments, watching the room with that petulant expression. "You?"

"Some." I pause before easing into the rest of the answer, trying not to seem too eager. "I've got a master who will take me and my friends on provided I can find a capable fifth. Know of anyone who's looking to find a spot?"

The pale human pushes off the wall. "Me. Name's Arrod."

"Raptor," I say.

"But your name—"

I put a hand up. "I'm keeping it. I've been demoted, but not for long." I nod at his sash. "What are you repeating for?"

"Truancy. Skipped a few too many classes, and Master Crow flunked me. I've been working as a runner ever since." There's a hot, hungry look in his eyes. "I'll be your fifth."

"Even if I tell you that our group consists of a woman, a slitherskin, and some spoiled boy who's been foisted on Master Jay due to a favor?"

"Even so." He tilts his head, indicating the busy room. "I'm not having any luck with this lot, and even if we fail, at least it's more training."

I admire his attitude. "All right. You're in."

A big grin crosses his face. He rubs his hands together. "The woman. She pretty?"

I suddenly want to plant a hoof in his backside and kick him across the room. "Does it matter? She's going to be your fellow fledgling. You don't stick your dick in that."

Arrod just laughs. "I'm not looking to get married. Just figured it might be nice to have a bit of fun on the side. But the guild comes first, of course."

I'm souring on Arrod the more he speaks. But we do need a fifth, and he's a repeater, which means he bears watching. Despite my better judgment, I wave him forward, indicating he should follow me. We make it back to the small group waiting awkwardly in front of Master Jay, and I introduce Arrod with a flourish. "Our fifth."

Master Jay perks up at the sight of him. "Trained with Crow last year, didn't you? You had promise. Don't muck it up this year."

"No, Master. I won't." He bows quickly and then flashes a grin at Gwenna. A flirty grin, I can't help but notice. She smiles back.

It takes everything I have not to scowl at Arrod. Gwenna, too. I don't know why their friendliness bothers me. I'm waiting for Sarya. I've never felt as connected to a woman as I did to her that afternoon, and nothing else matters. Once I find her, all will be right again.

Let Gwenna and Arrod flirt. It's fine.

It's all perfectly fine. They're all suspects in my eyes anyhow.

SEVEN

RAPTOR

HGM Rooster & GM Hawk,
    Have joined a fledgling group under Master Jay. All are repeaters. All seem
suspicious. Will keep you updated on what I learn.
    —Raptor

PS—I'm not trading out my name. Muck all that.

I MEET UP WITH Hawk at his fledgling nest later that morning, once I've dumped my things at Master Jay's nest. Hawk's wife, Sparrow, is there, seated at the desk near the fireplace, a magnifying glass perched under her spectacles as she pores over a book. Students are filing in, some of them with heavy trunks, as he assigns rooms.

"You. Boden. Upstairs," he calls out. "Room at the top left."

"But I've got six trunks, sir," the human called Boden protests.

"That's your problem, isn't it?" Hawk growls at him, and the students scatter. He shoots me an irked look as I enter. "You lost?"

"I was sent with a note," I say, holding out a piece of folded parchment. "It's to be read in private."

He grunts and turns to his wife. Leaning over her, he kisses the top of her head. "You'll be all right out here, love?"

"I'll be fine." She looks up, her big eyes magnified behind the lenses of her spectacles. "I'm sure if they have questions, I'll be able to answer them."

"Undoubtedly." He caresses her jaw and then straightens, glancing over at me with none of the old, friendly camaraderie we've known in the past. "In my study, then, fledgling."

I follow him in, my expression betraying nothing. If Sparrow notices anything out of the ordinary in our manner, she doesn't comment. A trunk crashes upstairs, and a cat howls and races down the steps. Sparrow exclaims and gets to her feet, and then I'm left alone with Hawk.

The Taurian master says nothing until we're in his study and the door is shut firmly behind him. Then he looks at me and down at the note in my hand. "Is anything on that?"

I unfold the paper, grinning. "It's blank. I just thought it might look better than me showing up with nothing but a smile."

"Good call." Hawk moves behind his desk, then sits heavily and rubs his hands over his face. "I have five repeaters on my team as commanded, and I swear that they're more clueless than entirely new students. How is that possible?"

"You're just lucky, or they were failed for a reason." I sit on the edge of his desk, keeping my tail carefully off to the side, and I eye the study. Last year, this was Master Magpie's domain, and all the tattered furniture is gone, along with the fleet of empty liquor bottles. This room is somewhat spare, with a cat bed by the hearth and a few heavy books on a table next to a large chair. There's a smaller chair pushed right next to the larger one, and I imagine Hawk spending his nights here with Sparrow at his side, holding hands—or holding other things.

Makes me think of Sarya. Damn the five hells, but why can't I find her?

"Tell me about your Five," Hawk says, picking up a quill and an empty sheet of parchment. "I'll relay what I can back to Rooster. Any leads?"

"All repeaters," I drawl. "I latched on to the slitherskin and the woman, since I figured they'd bear watching."

He sits up, frowning, and puts down the quill. "Gwenna and Kipp? I doubt they're our thieves."

"They've been caught stealing before," I point out. "Just because you're fond of them doesn't exclude them from suspicion. Both have plenty of reasons as to why they'd steal from the guild."

Hawk grunts. "I don't know if I believe that."

"You also believed that Magpie would change, and we saw how that went."

His expression darkens and he glares at me. Mental note, Hawk still doesn't like being reminded that he was fooled by Magpie. Good to know.

"I'm not trying to be a prick. I'm just reminding you that we can be fooled by anyone. You said Gwenna was a maid, right? Sparrow's maid? Have you ever known of any household staff that didn't take a little nip from their master's stores here and there? And she doesn't have money of her own, so it'd stand to reason that she'd be looking for a way to make some. Would anyone suspect a woman?"

"I hate that everything you said makes sense. If it's Gwenna, Aspeth will be devastated." He picks up the quill and scribbles again. "Fine. We'll keep them on our suspicion list for now. Who else?"

"Some idiot named Hemmen. Repeated four times already."

He shakes his head. "I know the one. 'Idiot' is right. I doubt he's our man, either. He's not clever enough."

"I also have a tall human named Arrod in my group."

"Arrod. I don't recall him." Hawk pauses, staring into space.

"Says he was failed for truancy. Worked under Crow last year and has been a runner while repeating."

He writes all this down. "I'll confirm this with Crow and see if I can pick up on anything suspicious. I'm also compiling a list of all repeaters who are serving as fledglings this year. See if you can befriend as many of them as possible and find out what you can."

"Will do. I'll run you more notes when I can and tell you what I find out. I'm serving with Master Jay this time around."

"Jay?" The ring on his nose flexes as Hawk's nostrils flare. "You actually went with him?"

"You suggested him!"

"Yes, but I didn't think you'd take me up on it. Was there no one else?"

"It works. He ignores his students in downtime." I shrug. "Figure it'll give us plenty of opportunity to get to know one another."

"Yes, he might ignore you in downtime, but that's because he'll work you like dogs during your sessions. I don't envy you."

"Just buy me a beer out of pity now and then," I joke. "And speaking of, I have to head off before anyone realizes I'm gone."

He keeps writing. "Good luck, Raptor. You'll need it."

"I know." When my friend chuckles, I slip back out of the study and then out of the dormitory that serves as Master Hawk's fledgling nest. Instead of heading back to Jay's dormitory, however, I head out of Vastwarren's heart and down a side street, toward a tavern. I can smell the King's Onion before I even see it, and when I step through the doors and head for the bar, I'm looking for a familiar face.

The barmaid lifts her chin at the sight of me. "What'll you have, friend?"

"Beer. Four wedges of onion." It's code, of course.

"Four wedges?" Naiah asks. She pretends to scrub the bar with her rag, leaning over to get a particularly difficult spot—and to whisper. "You have eight crowns on you?"

"I do."

"I can't guarantee how effective the potions will be if you hold on to four at once. They're the best when they're fresh."

"I know, but I'm going to be fledging for a while, so I don't know how often I'll be able to get away. Just load me up and I'll worry about the details later."

"Four onions, coming right up." She grabs an onion, quarters it, and shoves each wedge onto the rim of the mug, then fills the tankard with beer. "They'll be in their usual spot tomorrow."

Behind a false stone in an alley wall. I nod. "I appreciate it. I'll leave my coin there tonight." I pull a chunk of onion off the mug and chew on it. "You hear a lot of gossip—heard of any repeaters selling things on the black market? Things they shouldn't?"

"No, but I can ask around."

"Do that, but be discreet. And don't tell anyone who's asking. There'll be a reward as long as it stays secret."

Naiah just huffs, slinging the bar towel over her shoulder. "Oh, I can be discreet."

EIGHT

GWENNA

I CAN'T BELIEVE IT'S him.

The big white Taurian from the hospital. The one I rode like a shameless hussy and who gave me one of the best orgasms of my life. The blinded one who's apparently healed up enough that he can see, with only some pink scarring around his eyes to show where the bandages had been. He's as healthy as ever, and he's here on recruitment day. It seems like the most painful of coincidences that I'd run into him again. I clearly did not think things through.

And now we're here together. On the same fledgling team.

Truly, the gods are laughing at me.

I haven't been able to stop blushing all day. I thought for certain that he'd recognize me. That I'd say something and realization would dawn on his face. That he'd know I'm the sex worker who accosted him in the hospital and hopped upon his cock without getting paid.

But he seemingly has no idea that it's me, and I don't know if I'm glad or irritated. It's foolish to be disappointed, but how can you fuck someone and then not realize that they're standing right in front of you?

Even so, this is a good thing. Him not being aware it was me that day makes things easier. Gods willing, he'll never know, either. I certainly don't plan on telling him. Because he'll want to know *why* I was so eager to have sex, and I can't very well tell him that it was because a nearby dead body was troubling me.

It's just another secret to pile onto the growing stack. Bad enough that I'm secretly a mancer. Now the guy I fucked (who can't know we fucked) is going to be around constantly. Ugh.

Once we have our Five—because five is the sacred number designated by the gods, and artificers are a superstitious lot—Master Jay leads us out of the hall and across the plaza. His nest—the fledgling barracks assigned to a particular teacher—is one of the smaller buildings in the heart of the city. Hawk's nest had been a large ramshackle house near the outskirts, but Master Jay is in the midst of all the action. When I step inside, I can see the archives from one window and the hospital from another.

"My quarters are at the far end of the nest," Master Jay explains as we head inside with our bags. To my surprise, there are no stairs leading up. There's the main front living area, complete with a desk and fireplace to provide light and warmth, and it leads into a tiny kitchen. At the back of the house is a garderobe for bodily functions, and across the narrow hall is a set of double doors. Hemmen opens them to peek inside, and then frowns as he looks in. "We're bunking together?"

We are?

"It will build teamwork and companionship," Master Jay says in that sharp voice of his. "I see no need for you to have the luxury of your own quarters. This isn't a vacation. This is you learning a trade. Are we clear?"

Kipp frowns, his hands on the straps that hold his shell to his back. He glances up at me, a question in his gaze. Am I okay with this?

Truth be told, I'm used to sleeping in shared quarters with other maids. I had no privacy back at Honori Hold and none when I was a repeater. But in each case, my roommates were women. It was nothing to change in front of them, or to bathe near the hearth, because there were only more women with the same bits to see mine.

But I'm to have no privacy at all? Bathing and sleeping around a bunch of strange men? I don't mean to be a bother, but I'm also uncertain about bunking with several strange males. I glance over at Master Jay, and he's watching me with a hard stare. This is a test, I realize. The men get no special treatment, and if I demand it, I'll be a problem.

"Well, I hope you like being around a stinky wench, because my bathing will be nonexistent while you lot are around. So no, I have no problem with the sleeping quarters," I say. "And I hope no one snores."

The blond man—our fifth, who goes by the name of Arrod—chuckles at my comment. He gives me a cocky grin. "Nothing could make you unpleasant as far as I'm concerned."

"No one asked you," Raptor says in a gruff, annoyed tone. "We're here to pass the tests, not sniff one another's mucking armpits."

I give Arrod a flirty little wink, because I know how to handle men like him. They're not serious about a woman, just testing the waters to see if they can get anywhere. Fending him off with a bit of casual teasing keeps me from making an enemy. But Raptor scowls deeper at my response, which is baffling. Maybe he doesn't want any hookups while we're fledglings. I understand it—and I'm of the same mind—but there's no need to be stodgy.

"Set down your packs and we'll eat dinner. Tomorrow is enrollment day, and after everyone has been officially recognized as my fledglings, your training will begin." Master Jay turns on his heel and walks out of the room, and it's clear he wants us to follow him.

I eye the line of beds, trying to decide the best spot to claim as mine. Which bunk offers the most privacy? Which bunk is farthest away from the street, just in case a random man dies on our doorstep? Raptor picks up a bag from the corner of the room and puts it on the bed closest to the double doors, and then Kipp hops over to the bed directly in the middle of the five. That leaves one bed between them, and Kipp's expression makes it obvious that I'm to take that one.

Sandwiched between them means I'll be as safe as possible, considering that Raptor is already fussing at Arrod for flirting with me. It's very thoughtful of them, and I set my pack at the end of my narrow bed, claiming it. I flash them both grateful looks for thinking of me.

"Come on," Raptor says, gesturing at the doors through which Master Jay just exited. "Let's go get our lecture. I'm sure it's going to be the first of many. Jay loves to hear the sound of his own voice."

He's not wrong. I'm seated between Kipp and Raptor again as we have a simple dinner in the kitchen of the dormitory house. There's bread and cheese, fruit and nuts, and some roasted partridge meat that Hemmen immediately monopolizes for himself. As we eat, Master Jay drones on about his expectations for our group as we live in the nest and fledge under his command. We are to keep ourselves clean and tidy at all times. No guests for visiting. No overnight guests for certain. No thieving. No fornicating. We are to eat regular meals to keep up our strength, but not too much food so that we gain weight and are unable to compete physically with other teams. No fights in the dormitory. We are all to be amicable with one another and not complain.

I listen for a while, but as he continues to drone on with his expectations, I pay less attention. There's a nestmaid working behind us—a woman assigned to the house for upkeep by the guild itself—and I know her. Marta is a young woman who has a bad back due to a mule kick when she was younger, and as a result, she gets tired easily. It makes me antsy to see the mess that the others are making as we sit in the kitchen. Arrod picks at his food and spills his water. Kipp nibbles on fruit and nuts, but it's Raptor with the best manners. He's meticulous as he eats platefuls of fruit.

Even so, the kitchen is quickly getting disordered, and I have to sit on my hands to not help as Marta works silently behind us, cleaning dishes. If I help her out, I'm establishing myself as a maid and not as a student. I can't help. It pains me to sit back and do nothing, but I'm stuck.

The food is devoured and everyone eventually gets up from the messy table. "I will see you all in uniform in the morning," Master Jay says. "No deviations from the standard. Be ready at dawn."

"Yes, Master," I say, along with Arrod and Hemmen. Kipp nods. Raptor does, too, and I wonder if he's having a hard time deferring to a master as a fledgling after being a full artificer for so long. He catches me watching him and winks, and I turn away, huffy.

I'm *not* thinking about me riding him on the hospital bed, with his cock buried deep inside me. I'm *not* thinking about his big hands squeezing my backside, making me feel dainty. I'm *not*.

Once dinner is over, I change into a sleep shift for bed while in the garderobe. It's the only place I can get a modicum of privacy, but my sleep clothing is intended for coolness and not modesty. It's nothing but thin straps and even thinner linen. After a moment's hesitation, I toss my chemise over the entire ensemble. It's hotter but at least no one's going to ogle my tits.

As I exit the garderobe, I hear the clank of dishes in the kitchen and fight the urge to help Marta once more. She must be exhausted, but if I get caught . . .

"Don't," says a deep voice from behind me.

I turn, seeing the large form of the Taurian standing in the hall. He's leaning against the wall, legs crossed, waiting for me to exit the garderobe, I assume. My face grows hot at the sight of him—his guild shirt is open and loose to his waist. "I don't know what you're talking about."

"I can read the look on your face. I know you want to assist her, but if you do, those other two nitwits on our team are going to think you're the hired help and not their equal. Trust me." He eyes me with lazy insouciance. "It won't kill her to do a few extra dishes on her own, but it'll absolutely destroy your hopes of a career if your Five thinks of you as a maid."

I hate that he's right. I lift my chin and pluck at my chemise. "I was just changing, thank you very much."

"Sure you were, sweetheart." He pushes off the wall and grins. As I move to walk past him, he leans in close to me.

"I'm not your sweetheart," I reply tartly, and head back to the dormitory.

"Little bantam, then." He chuckles to himself.

A bantam. I know what those are. Every servant does. A bantam is a smaller fowl . . . and they're usually quite fierce. I'd think it's an insult, except he says it in that flirty, coaxing sort of way. Even so . . . I don't like it. I fume at being so obvious—and for all the lusty thoughts I was entertaining—as I climb into bed and settle my pack under my bunk. When the scratchy, guild-issued blankets are pulled up to my chin, I stare at the ceiling.

This is all so different from how I'd imagined it would go when I thought I'd be a fledgling once more. I'd tried not to think too much about what it would be like without Aspeth by my side, now that she's Sparrow and working for the archivists. I thought Mereden and Lark would be here. Kipp is, but so are two strangers.

And the big Taurian I fucked. He's here, too, throwing a spanner into the works. Why did I not think things through? He's a guild artificer, so it stood to reason that I'd run into him again. I didn't stop to think what it'd mean if I touched him.

Now he's climbing into the small cot next to mine. The wood creaks and groans as if in pain, and I want to look over and see if he's as uncomfortable as I imagine. But if I look at him, I feel like he'll suddenly know all my secrets.

Those secrets seem to be piling up by the damned hour.

There's a tap on the side of the bed, and I roll over to see Kipp's face hovering near mine. He wears an expression of concern on his small pointy face, and taps my bed again, then gives me a thumbs-up that also seems to be a question. *Are you okay?*

"I'm fine," I whisper. "I just . . . I don't know what I expected for this year. What about you?"

He shrugs. Gestures at both Arrod and Hemmen and rolls his eyes. Gestures at Raptor and shrugs, then flexes. I know just what he means. Raptor he might be iffy on, but at least Raptor is strong physically.

I nod. "I feel the same. I just . . . I wish Mer and Lark were here. And Sparrow. And maybe even Hawk."

He eyes me with alarm.

"I'm not going to quit, I promise. If anything, it makes me even more determined." I make a fist and hold it at the edge of the bed, as if I need to show him just how strong I'm going to be. I hate being a bother, but I need to get over it, I suppose.

Kipp bumps my fist with his tiny one and gives a nod.

NINE

GWENNA

Dere Ma,

I'm a student again—a flegling. Say a prayer to the goddess that I'll pass this time. I am with the slitherskin Kipp again, as well as two human men and a Taurian. We are a strange group for sure, but I'm happy just to be a flegling. I would be evin happier with another woman on my team, but my friends were not able to participate this year.

It feels strange to look at the windows in the nest (that's the dorm) and realize it's someone else's job to clean them. Hope you aren't working two hard.

Love, Gwenna

THE FIRST COUPLE of weeks of classes pass quickly. There was enrollment day, when we signed the Book of Names and pledged ourselves to Master Jay. It was almost a full repeat of last year's ceremony, right down to Head Guild Master Rooster making a pompous speech about how much our lives will change and the esteemed history of the guild. I spent my time people-watching instead, eyeing Master Hawk's fledglings with envy. After that, we exchanged the black sash of a repeater for the pristine white sash of a fledgling.

Then the real work began.

Each day, Master Jay had us perform a variety of tasks all related to one particular skill. The first day was all about testing our physical endurance. He made notes in a tiny book with a charcoal pen and frowned a lot, especially when I brought up the rear of every single jog. Then he tested us on our fighting and bladework. Another day was navigating and our direction sense, along with our general knowledge of the city's layout. Finally, he tested us on our knowledge of Old Prell.

It's safe to say that I performed terribly at the lot, especially compared to the others. Hemmen was awful at everything except his knowledge of Old Prell. Given that he always has his nose stuck in one book or another, I wasn't surprised to learn that. Arrod was excellent at physical things like fighting, and he knows the city well. He's an idiot at bookwork, though. Kipp was great at everything, but I expected that.

Raptor put us all to shame, though.

He flies through every test with ease. In physical endurance he outstrips all of us by far, and he knows the layout of Vastwarren blindfolded (which is another test that Master Jay gives us). He also knows just about everyone in the city, and rarely do we take a few steps without someone pausing to say hello to him and give us curious looks. Raptor's fighting style is less sword work and more smashing heads due to his immense strength.

When I fall behind on every single course that Master Jay designs for us, Raptor slows down to jog at my side.

"We're only as fast as our slowest member" is all he says, shrugging.

Each day, I wait for him to point out that he knows me, that he recognizes my scent from that afternoon in the hospital. That he knows we've slept together. He never says anything, though, and then I wonder: How can he *not* know? Sure, he was blindfolded, but Taurians are so prized for all their senses. What about touch? My voice? Anything? Is nothing about me special or notable?

The more I think about it, the more it irks me, so I try not to think about it at all.

The one bright spot in all of this? No murdered men, no prickling that tells me the dead are nearby and want to speak to me. All is quiet.

By the time the first humiliating week of tests comes to an end on a sunny Fifthday afternoon, Master Jay releases us all. "I'll return on Firstday, bright and early. I expect you all to comport yourselves properly while I'm gone." With a crisp nod, he picks up his pack and heads out of the nest without a backward glance.

"He's leaving for the weekend?" I ask Raptor, stunned at this turn of events as our teacher heads across the plaza and down the street away from our dorm. "Can he *do* that?"

I don't recall Hawk ever taking a day off while we were students, but then again, he was an assistant and Magpie was the one in charge, and Magpie had been a mess. Perhaps they were not the greatest standard to measure by.

Raptor just gives me one of those lazy grins that makes me both irritated and flustered. "It's one reason why I picked him. We work hard during the week so we can have our own time on the weekends."

"Doesn't that seem a little . . . lax?"

"He's got spies everywhere ready to tattle on us. If he hears anything amiss, I'm sure he'll be quick to get us into shape on weekdays." He rubs his muzzle. "You sound very disapproving."

"I don't mean to be a bother, of course," I say automatically. "I just don't understand what's so important that he'd leave his students."

"Not what, but *who*."

Ah. It becomes clear now. He's got a piece on the side. I'm the fool who took too long to put things together. Both Hemmen and Arrod smirk, nudging each other. To his credit, Kipp looks as annoyed as I feel. "What are we supposed to do all weekend?"

"Have a good time," Arrod says, moving to my side and looping his arm over my shoulders.

I neatly slide out of his grasp. Just because I'm short, men think they can tuck me against them. "Surely there's a lesson plan of some kind we can do over the weekend."

"I had no idea you'd be such a stickler," Raptor says to me, amused. He eyes me down his long nose.

"I'm not a stickler," I protest, because the way he says it makes it sound like it's a terrible thing. "But I don't want to repeat again, either. I've had my fill of tossing chamber pots and washing windows, thank you."

And then I freeze, because those were the very chores I was perform-
ing on the day that I felt the dead man in the alley . . . and then had sex
with a stranger.

If Raptor notices my hesitation, he doesn't say anything. He just grins
widely. "If it'll make you feel better, we can pick up odd jobs at the main
guild hall for coin. Lots of fledglings do that when their masters are un-
available."

I can't decide if I like the idea or hate it. While I'm always in need of
coin, I'm also wary of taking on jobs. It'll likely mean nestmaid work,
and it's hard enough keeping the lines clear with my group as it is. I
slapped Arrod's hand away a dozen times this week already simply because he was trying to help me up instead of letting me manage on my
own. I can't be seen as weak.

I also can't be seen as a maid. Frowning, I eye Raptor. "Does everyone do this?"

He leans in close. "Some of us just get drunk in taverns."

There's a cozy tone to his voice, as if he's sharing a secret with me,
and it makes my body react. My nipples prick and heat pulses between
my thighs. "I don't have any coin."

"If you want to go drinking, I'm happy to buy your way."

"I can't pay you back."

Raptor just shoots me another flirty look. "I can think of ways you
can thank me. Maybe a nice hug or—"

Kipp steps in front of him with a frown, putting a hand out. He
shakes his head at Raptor, disapproving, and then holds a coin up to me.
The message is clear—I don't have to sell myself to Raptor just to hang
out with the group. "Why, thank you, Kipp. Glad to see someone in the
group is a gentleman."

"I never said I was," Raptor drawls, and I'm reminded of that day in
the hospital. He was anything but gentlemanly when I rode him.

I push ahead of him, fighting the blush rising on my cheeks. "What
tavern are we going to if we're so determined to do this?"

Raptor looks around our group, eyeing both Arrod and Hemmen for
suggestions. When they shrug and look back to him, he says, "How do
you all feel about onions?"

THE KING'S ONION is bustling for a Fifthday night. Most of the masters don't go out of town like Master Jay, Raptor tells me as we sit at the bar and wait for drinks, but even the strictest of masters will allow his students a little downtime on a weekend.

"They want us to bond," he tells me and Kipp, leaning back against the bar as if he owns the place. Arrod and Hemmen are off finding a table for us. "What better way than to become drinking buddies?"

"I can think of a few ways," I mutter.

"Like what?"

"Saving one another's lives. Working together toward a common goal. Passing the test. Being study partners. And Master Hawk says fledglings don't drink."

Raptor waves a hand at my answers, dismissing them. "You're no fun. Just like Master Hawk."

Kipp huffs, crawling up onto the barstool on my opposite side.

Is Raptor serious? He expects me to be *fun*? To entertain him? "I'm a maid. We're not allowed to have fun. We're expected to blend in with the walls and do the dirty work without question."

Instead of silencing Raptor, this appears to intrigue him. "You're good at observing people?"

I'm not the type to talk myself up. "Decent. Just like any other maid."

He gestures at the entrance. "There's a slitherskin over there, Kipp. You know him?"

Now I'm just irritated. "Not all slitherskins know one another—"

Before I can finish my sentence, Kipp scrambles away, racing for the entrance. The moment he sees the other slitherskin, he starts wriggling, and they fall atop each other in a squirming embrace. Humph. I guess they do know each other.

I turn back to the bar and notice Raptor looking at me with a smug smile on his face. "Oh, shut up."

"I didn't say anything. I'm just questioning your powers of observation." He nods at the barmaid and puts up two fingers. "Drinks are on me tonight."

If he's trying to soften me up after insulting me, it's not going to work. "Great. You call me a liar and then buy me a drink. Wonderful start to the evening."

He grins at me, leaning an elbow on the bar as he studies my face rather intently. "I'm just trying to get to know you, Gwenna."

He knows me very well, he just doesn't realize it. I grab at the mug slid my way, pull the wedge of onion off the side, and take a sip.

"I'm good at figuring out most people," Raptor continues, plucking my onion wedge off the bar and eating it in one bite. "But you? I can't decipher. You've got secrets, and you won't let anyone underneath that shell of yours."

My skin prickles at the accuracy of his words. Raptor is dangerous to get to know, and yet I can't resist a tart response. "I told you. I was a maid before coming here. What secrets do you think I'm carrying? Who's got the dirtiest knickers in the land?"

He laughs, the sound deep and baying, but it's a full belly laugh and it makes me smile in response. Raptor doesn't do anything halfway, I'm realizing. When he laughs, it's with his entire body. When he smiles, it's with pure, unfettered delight. And when he touches you . . .

I take a larger gulp of my beer to drown such thoughts.

TEN

RAPTOR

Gentlemen,

Keeping this brief. Going out with the fledglings on my team this weekend. Am trying to get to know them better. So far I've got a braggart, a lazy loaf, a woman, and a lizard. There's no way this group is passing any tests. Still looking for signs that one is our master thief.

—Raptor

PS—I should get paid extra for spending my weekends pretending to be a student.

GWENNA IS AN intriguing sort of puzzle, and I find her more interesting with every day. She carries herself like a true professional during all the training exercises that Master Jay puts us through, no matter how brutal they might be. She never complains, just does them to the best of her ability. I like that in a person, regardless of gender.

Whereas Kipp, Arrod, and Hemmen seem to be settling into their roles as fledglings, I can't help but feel that Gwenna grows more agitated by the day, as if she can't rest. Perhaps it's that which draws me to her constantly.

Right now, she's staring me down over her beer, practically daring me to try to discover her secrets. I love a challenge, so how can I refuse? I give her a smile and slide my stool a little closer to hers, leaning over. "Tell me more about you."

"Why? So you can use it against me?" She arches a brow. "Don't you think I know someone trying to fish for information when I see one?"

I grin wider, loving that she's calling me out on it. "What's wrong with a little information? Maybe I just want to get to know you better."

I'm surprised when she blushes, her round cheeks turning bright red. "You know me plenty well already."

Not well enough. But if she wants to hold on to her secrets for a while longer, I'll just enjoy the slow unveiling. She takes a sip of her drink, her mouth pink and full.

Lusty, dark thoughts slide through my mind even though I just took my latest potion dose yesterday. I shouldn't be feeling anything.

Maybe Naiah's batch this time wasn't as strong. I'll have to say something to her.

There's a strand of Gwenna's dark hair that has escaped her no-nonsense bun, and it takes everything I have in me not to brush it away. Sarya, I remind myself. You're allowed to admire attractive women but you want Sarya. "Fine. If you don't want to share your secrets with me, share your observations. Surely it can't hurt to tell me what you really think of the others in our Five?"

She takes another sip of her beer and licks the foam off her upper lip. Sarya, I remind myself. Sarya and the way she touched me like she owned me. I want that again. I must stay strong.

Gwenna glances about the tavern, her gaze lingering on Arrod and Hemmen at a table in the back. Arrod is chatting with a barmaid, and Hemmen has pulled out a book. She looks to Kipp, where he's twining himself around the other slitherskin, and finally back to me. "Well, if I'm going off observations from this week alone, I would say that Arrod is spoiled. Probably comes from nobility or a rich merchant family. He's not been told no a lot in his life. I don't expect him to be the type to work harder as the pressure increases."

I look over at Arrod. The human man is fingering his sash as he charms the barmaid, leaning closer to her than he should. He's giving her a flirty smile that I've seen him flash at Gwenna all week long. "Do you think he's handsome?"

"I think he should have been smacked a bit more as a boy," she replies tartly. "Then he wouldn't be so full of himself."

Erupting with laughter, I pound a fist on the bar. She's got him pegged, all right. My thoughts were the same—a man who's gotten by on his charm and money all this time. But if he has coin, is he our thief? Has he always been wealthy, or is it a more recent development? "You think he's trustworthy?"

She considers this for a moment. "Do you mean, do I trust him to carry me out of a collapsing tunnel? I don't trust *any* of you lot to do that."

I lean in so I can lower my voice. "I'd carry you out."

Gwenna puts a finger on my nose and pushes me away. "And you'd demand a kiss for it."

"Taurians don't kiss. We save our tongues for other things."

Her color gets high.

"But we won't speak of that," I drawl, reminding myself of Sarya. "What do you think of Hemmen?"

"I try not to think of him at all," Gwenna retorts. "But if I must . . . he reminds me a lot of Aspeth."

"Aspeth?" I'm startled by her answer.

"Sorry, Sparrow. It's taking me a long time to remember to call her that." She grimaces and stares down at her drink. "But aye, he reminds me of her. She was always creeping off into corners to read, would rather sit in a chair with a book than attend a party."

Considering that currently Hemmen is at a distant table with a beer in one hand and a book in the other, ignoring his surroundings, it's not much of an observation. "That's all you've got on him?"

"Like I said, he reminds me of my friend. He's terrible at just about everything Master Jay sets him to, except that he's knowledgeable about Old Prell. I'm not going to complain about that, because I'm terrible at everything as well, and I am not knowledgeable about Old Prell in the slightest."

"You can ask me. I'm happy to share what I know. You pick up a lot just by being in the field."

She seems surprised at my offer, tucking a lock of hair behind her ear as she studies me. "Thank you. That's very kind. I don't like being the worst member of our team. Bad enough that I'm the only female one. I'd like to be successful at something."

"You're just fine," I reassure her. "Everyone's terrible when they start out as fledglings."

"Yes, but I was a repeater. I should have *some* experience."

"Doesn't matter. If you were good at everything they throw at us, you'd be wearing an artificer sash instead."

She lifts her beer, acknowledging my words.

"And what about Kipp?"

"Kipp is exactly what he seems to be," she says, her tone taking on a defensive note. "He's self-contained and very competent. It's just that we communicate through words and he doesn't, so that's the biggest issue. That and his size. But if I needed someone to carry me out of a collapsing tunnel . . . well, he wouldn't be able to, but he'd do what he could to save me anyhow."

Loyal, affectionate words. Their bond is stronger than she's let on through the week. I consider this, wondering if I need to pry at her more. I haven't found a single shred of evidence that would lead me to a thieving repeater, but we're all still settling into our roles as fledglings. Any smart crook would wait for things to grow quiet before making a move. I need to be patient, too.

She's gazing up at me, that challenging look still on her face.

"And what do you think of me?" I ask, curious. "What are your observations?"

Gwenna tilts her head and takes another sip of her drink. Then she gives a tiny shrug of her shoulders and touches her fledgling sash, and her body language changes to one of fluttery discomfort. "I think you're a flirt and you use your charm like a weapon. But you won't let anyone get close to you. You keep them right where you want them."

I stare down at her. That was . . . far more astute than I'd like.

A smile blooms across her lips and she straightens, her posture growing more erect with her confidence. She likes having rattled me. Lifting her chin, she asks, "How'd you get burned anyhow?"

Just like that, the easy fun of the night is gone. All the patchy fur around my eyes has grown back, and thanks to the guild healers, you'd never know I was injured. I drawl my answer, choosing it carefully so I can watch her response. "I don't recall saying I was burned."

Sure enough, she gets flustered, her face turning red. "Oh. I just . . ." She waves a hand at her own eyes. "I just recognized that the skin around your eyes seemed pinker than the rest of your flesh. I assumed it was a burn."

I grunt, on edge. "My, you *are* observant."

And I wonder what other secrets she's keeping. All my suspicions are focusing on her. If it turns out that Gwenna's the thief, I'm going to be truly disappointed because I actually like her. It's impossible not to like her. Perhaps that's how she's slipped under the guild's noses for so long.

But the thief has been murdering other repeaters. Does Gwenna have what it takes to murder? I don't think she does, but the more agitated she gets, the more I wonder. If she's not the killer, it's possible she knows who it is.

Either way, she bears closer watching.

ELEVEN

GWENNA

WANT TO KICK myself as I go to visit Sparrow the next day. Me and my big fat mouth.

I can't stop thinking about how I let my stupid guard down, and I let myself relax with Raptor. I let myself tease him back and then I tripped all over myself. He's never mentioned that he was burned across the eyes. He's never even acted as if he was injured. Now he's going to wonder how I know. It was obvious he didn't buy into my excuse.

If he knew it was me in the hospital, he'd want to know why I fucked him, and I can't tell him the truth of it. Worse, what if he tells the others? Arrod would never leave me alone. Master Jay might remove me from the team for my relationship with Raptor, even if it was before we fledged. No one can know at all. That's safest.

Sparrow is at her station in the archives, which is completely unsurprising to me. Forcing her to take a day off would be like punishment. She brightens at the sight of me walking up to her desk, a cat perched on a stack of books next to the parchment she's writing on. "There you are! How has the first week back as a fledgling been going?"

"It's interesting," I say. "Master Jay has a very different mindset compared to Hawk. Did you know he leaves the city every weekend?"

She pets the black cat that walks across her paperwork. "I'd heard something along those lines, aye. Hawk says that the other masters aren't thrilled that Master Jay abandons his students, but they watch them for him on the weekends. It seems that Master Jay has a long-standing relationship with a farmer's widow who lives just outside of town. She won't give up her land because she wants it to go to her children when they're old enough, and he won't leave the guild. So they meet up on weekends."

It changes my opinion of Master Jay, which, up to this point, has been rather sour. "That's sweet. I like that they both have a life of their own but manage to make it work together."

She nods, putting the cat on the floor, only for it to jump back onto her desk again. A moment later, a striped tabby joins it, followed by a big black-and-white cat with a stump of a tail. The black-and-white cat takes one look at me and hops into my lap, and I've no choice but to pet the beast. I scratch at its ears idly, thinking about guild relationships. Would I be able to only see my husband (if I had one) on the weekends? I suppose if there are children, it's different, but it makes the week long and lonely.

Sparrow pets the cat closest to her and glances at me. "How is your Five this year? I heard that Lark and Mereden weren't even at recruitment day. What's going on there, do you know?"

It's just the right thing to say to distract me from my troubles. I tell her about Lark and Mereden opting to remain as repeaters, and how they want a baby. How Mereden is going to try to get a position at the healer's guild. Finally I get to the makeup of my new team. "At least Kipp is with me. It doesn't feel so strange as long as he's here."

"And Raptor," Sparrow enthuses. "He's a good friend of Hawk's and very skilled. Hawk speaks very highly of him."

Yet Hawk didn't take Raptor onto his team this year. He said he was supposed to pick new students, but Raptor would have been new, wouldn't he? Perhaps he felt Raptor didn't need his help. Whatever it is, I'm not going to complain to Sparrow. She adores her husband, and both of them have always been nothing but fair to me. "Raptor is a shameless flirt," I tell her, scratching the chin of the cat in my lap. "But he's also excellent at all the tests Master Jay has set before us. I suspect if we pass this year, it'll be thanks to him."

I bite back all my worries about my own skill, because whining to Sparrow will make her feel guilty for my situation, and then she'll try to get involved. She's got a good heart and feels responsible for me, since she brought me to Vastwarren, but I can't bother her with my petty concerns. I just need to work harder, I decide.

"Any more dead men?" Sparrow asks, her voice hushed as she glances around the book-strewn archives.

"I haven't felt anything," I confess, clutching the cat to my chest as I move forward to sit on the edge of my chair. "Have you heard of any other people experiencing what I am? In your research?"

"Yes and no." She purses her lips. "Most of the books I need seem to live permanently on Jackdaw's desk, and I don't love that. I can't get them without making him suspicious, so I've been reading widely and noting down everything I can find that pertains to mancers. Sadly, there's not much. We do know there were different types, and I've been able to dig up more information in regard to that."

"Like what?"

"Oh, all kinds." She pulls out a piece of parchment and studies it. "Like they had different houses that specialized in types of magic. I found an entire pantry list from an old family hold called Dennett that was wiped out in the Mancer Wars, but apparently they specialized in geomancy—that's earth magic. And there was another house that specialized in hydromancy."

"Water mancers?"

"Aye." She runs her finger down her list. "Let's see. Pyromancers, sanguimancers, sarcomancers—those are healers—and here we go. Necromancer. That's you."

Necromancer. A mancer who deals with the dead. Finding out that it has a name doesn't make me feel better. "So it truly is a thing? I'm not crazed?"

"It is absolutely a thing. Widden Hold was in the north and specialized in all things necrotic." She wrinkles her nose. "'Necrotic' is truly an unpleasant word. Just the sound of it is vile. But yes, northerners. Do you know anything about your ancestors?"

I shake my head. Ma grew up the only daughter of another servant woman, and I never met my father. They were both from the northern realms, though, and that's where Honori Hold is, where my mother currently works in the kitchens. It's not out of the realm of possibility that some ancestor of mine somehow slipped undetected through the purge after the Mancer Wars, when all those who practiced magic were killed.

"All books pertaining to magic were destroyed in the Mancer Wars," Sparrow continues. "I'm waiting to get my hands on a history of northern families from Jackdaw's desk, but I don't know that it will say much. It's entirely possible they were erased from that particular history, as all the mentions I've found are fleeting. I'll keep trying, though."

"Don't bother yourself. It won't tell us anything other than necromancers existed, not how to turn the powers off. As long as there are no other bodies found, I'm fine. I'll just devote myself to my studies."

Sparrow nods, her spectacles sliding down her nose. "I'm glad you're with Kipp. He knows what he's doing, and he's loyal to you. He's probably the best one on the team."

I consider this. "Raptor's even more impressive than Kipp, if I'm being honest. He's just as competent, and he makes friends everywhere he goes. It can't hurt to have both of them pull me along as the weaker party."

"Raptor *is* friendly," she admits.

For some reason, her simple praise irritates me. "He's ridiculous. That Taurian would flirt with a statue . . . and then the statue would blush!" Why won't I shut up about him?

"You sound like you don't like him."

"I like him just fine," I protest. I don't want it getting around that I can't get along with Hawk's best friend.

Her eyes gleam. "Aha. You like him too much."

"Of course not." But my face gets hot. Why is it I can always keep my cool unless Raptor is mentioned, and then I blush like a virgin?

A cat winds its way across her desk again, and she nudges it aside, her focus on me. "No judgment here, but do you need a charm?"

"A charm? What for?" I'm not following.

"So you can't get pregnant, of course. There's nothing wrong with getting close to someone, especially if neither of you have commitments, but I'd be remiss if I didn't point out that Taurians are notoriously virile." She taps her lip with a finger, thinking. "Oh, wait. There's not a Conquest Moon."

"You mean that time when Hawk went into a rut and jumped you back in the crypt?"

"Right." She blushes bright pink, her tone formal. "Taurians go into rut only at that time and aren't truly in control of themselves. They aren't fertile unless it's the Conquest Moon. It's when the god's hand is upon them. I suppose you don't need birth control after all."

"It's sweet of you to worry, but it isn't necessary. I'm not sleeping with anyone," I say primly. I'm not averse to sex. Sex is amazing. But I don't want a reputation that I've slept my way into the guild. I haven't touched anyone since that day with Raptor. I open my mouth to tell her there's no way I can be pregnant . . .

. . . and then I stop.

Because I've not had my period. Not in two months. Granted, I've skipped for a month or two before because of stress, and it's certainly been stressful lately.

I also had sex with a Taurian recently.

A notoriously virile Taurian.

Who has a knot outside of the Conquest Moon. Does that mean he's fertile outside of it, too?

Oh gods. Am I *pregnant*? On top of everything else?

I want to run out of the room and throw up, but I don't know if that's nerves or morning sickness. Digging my fingers into my palms, I offer Aspeth a tight smile. "I'm good, but thank you. Master Jay has us all bunking in the same room to build companionship, so it's not as if I'd have time alone with him."

"He does? Ew." She wrinkles her nose, which causes her spectacles to slide down.

"He does," I agree, voice firm to hide my trembling. "And on that note, I should probably return before someone starts looking for me. I'm supposed to be helping out with laundry to earn a few coins."

It's a lie, because I'm refusing to touch any sort of chore out of fear that someone will catch me. But it sounds like something I'd do, and it'll give me an excuse to leave. I drop the cat out of my lap and give Sparrow a hug, because she's obsessed with hugs now.

Then I quickly exit back onto the cobbled roads of Vastwarren. The bustle of the afternoon streets feels like a relief. I take a deep breath, closing my eyes and letting the city's stink wash over me.

It doesn't help.

What am I going to do if I'm mucking *pregnant*?

TWELVE

RAPTOR

Gents,

*One of the fledglings here is being very secretive. My suspicions are aroused.
Will update when I learn more.*

—R

PS—You're lucky I'm such an ingratiating sort.

FLEDGLING GWENNA," MASTER Jay says in a sharp voice as we line up for the day's training. "Tell me, what is the shop behind the fishmonger's stall on the docks? The one with the anchor on the sign?"

The look on Gwenna's face is utterly blank, and I almost feel sorry for her. I'm tempted to give her the answer—the moneylender—but if I do, Master Jay will shit himself. He's a teacher unlike many others, in that he feels the best thing a fledgling can learn is self-sufficiency. It's an admirable thing to teach in a guild that values teamwork, because I've been saddled with terrible teammates far too often.

This is one of Jay's favorite ways to dole out lessons, too. He asks about something benign, and if you don't have the right answer, he knows what area of expertise you're lacking. Can you read this map? No? Then you get to spend the day redrawing the map until you're familiar with everything on it. Do you know the Old Prellian symbol for *below*? If not, you need to spend the day brushing up on the most common Prellian glyphs that an artificer will run into. Do you know the layout of Vastwarren City like the back of your hand? No? Then you're going to walk the streets with a heavy pack on your shoulders until you do.

Poor Gwenna has borne the worst of Master Jay's tasks. She doesn't know Prellian symbols. She's never first on an obstacle course. She's unfamiliar with a lot of Vastwarren. She's not great at anything physical, and that's me being generous.

She composes herself after a moment and then pins a smile to her face. "I don't know what's there, Master Jay. Shall I get my pack?"

"Yes. Find the building behind the fishmonger. Then write me a list of all the buildings along the two closest streets and what times they are open. Wear your loaded pack at all times, and if you take it off, I'll be informed of it."

"Yes, Master." She moves away from the breakfast table, heading across the dorm to get one of the training packs near the front door.

Master Jay stops in front of Hemmen. "Prellian symbol for 'danger'?"

Hemmen rubs his bulbous nose and thinks for a moment. "It's a bird, upside down with the feet in the air."

The correct answer. Master Jay grunts. "You'll be on the obstacle course today. I want you to practice the current setup, running it repeatedly. Kipp will be at your side to run it with you. Do you think you can do the course blindfolded, Kipp?"

The slitherskin taps his hand over his heart twice, a quiet affirmation.

"Good. Partner up, then. Hemmen, watch Kipp to ensure he doesn't remove his blindfold. Kipp, you are to report back to me how many times Hemmen performs the course. I expect no less than fifteen rounds."

Hemmen's face falls. He runs a hand through his messy hair and looks as if he wants to protest, but then nods, defeated. "Of course, Master Jay."

Master Jay gazes at Kipp and they share an unspoken nod. I suspect that Jay is sending Kipp with Hemmen to keep Hemmen busy more than because Kipp needs to work on anything. In a very short period of time, Kipp has quickly become Jay's favorite. I must admit that the slitherskin is extremely competent for all his small size, but I bet it's his silence that makes him Jay's prized pupil. Jay doesn't like back talk.

That leaves just me and Arrod awaiting tasks for the day. Master Jay strides up to us, his hands behind his back as he eyes his remaining students. He gazes at me before turning to Arrod. "What's the symbol that marks a Prellian burial chamber?"

Arrod thinks for a moment. "It's that yellow bird, isn't it?"

"It is not," Master Jay bites out sharply. "You will go to the guild library and study Prellian glyphs. I want you to know a hundred basic symbols by the time this month is over. Do you understand me? We are still in the early days, fledgling. I'm still testing your abilities. You must be competent on your own before you can work as a team."

"Yes, Master. Of course, Master." Arrod nods, giving Master Jay a quick, respectful bow before turning to leave. I catch a hint of a smile on his face. Lazy shit knows exactly how to work Master Jay already. Something tells me that he did that on purpose.

Well, two can play that game.

Master Jay approaches me. "Is it even worth me asking you if you have the city memorized? Do you know what's near the riverside docks?"

"I know there's at least three brothels," I say. "Do you need their names?"

His face turns a mottled, dark shade. "Get a pack and accompany Gwenna. I don't want either of you back until you've mapped those streets. And take the long way."

"Yes, sir," I drawl, pleased.

GWENNA TRIES TO avoid me, little minx that she is. She races ahead of me on the streets, heavy pack bouncing against her back as she walks as quickly as possible over the cobbled, sloping streets. She's been avoiding me the last couple of weeks, and I'm not certain if it's because I annoy her or if it's because she has things to hide.

The more she tries to avoid me, the more I wonder if she's the thief who's been stealing from the guild. But when I picture her working with murderers, I can't see it. I don't know what to think. It'd probably be smarter for me to go spend time with Arrod, because he deliberately got out of the more difficult training and seemed pleased about it, but I find myself chasing after Gwenna instead.

She refuses to turn and look at me. "Go away. I'm busy."

I jog up to her side, an easy thing to do given that her legs are short. "Lucky for you that we're on the same task."

Gwenna shoots me a withering glare, but I find her ferocious manner charming. "I don't see the point of this. We both know that you have this city mapped out in your head. Can't you go find someone else to bother?"

"I could, but they're a lot less fun than you. I'm still trying to figure out why you hate me so."

She marches up the street, huffing as it slopes, and then speeds when we get to a downhill part. After a long moment, she says, "I don't hate you. I just don't want anything to get in the way of me becoming an artificer."

"And you think I'm a distraction? That's quite the compliment," I purr.

The little human gives me another glare. "You are a ridiculous male. Now go away so I can work my task."

"We can work together, if you like. The river docks aren't all that safe for a decent woman alone." It's another reason why I was glad to come with her. The only women who head down to the docks are there to make coins in darkened alleys or brothel beds, and I want to make sure no one bothers Gwenna. Master Jay should have thought of that, but he's determined to treat her the same as the others in our Five. Which is fantastic . . . most times. Sometimes he needs to be aware of where he's sending a young woman alone.

Together, we march along the winding streets for a while longer, and I let her have the walkway while I move through the cobbled roads and dodge carts. It's some time before she glances over at me again. "Can I just say I don't see the point of this task? Master Hawk never made us traipse all over the city looking for specific buildings."

I'm not surprised to hear that. Nothing against Hawk, but he automatically assumes everyone knows the basics as well as he does. Master Jay has been teaching a lot longer, and he's more fully aware that some students have come from a more sheltered background than others. "They have different teaching styles," I tell her. "Master Jay is a big proponent of his students being as independent as possible before they work as a team. How can you be expected to perform tasks for the guild if you don't know the layout of Vastwarren? Knowledge is power, and even if you don't pass this year, Master Jay wants to make sure you're well-equipped for next year."

She shoots me a furious look, as if the thought of failing enrages her. "Just seems utterly foolish to me to waste class time memorizing buildings on the riverbank when I could be digging in the tunnels."

So impatient. It's adorable. "Every fledgling says the same sort of thing, but you have an entire year to learn to be an artificer. Take your time. Master Jay knows what he's doing, much as it pains me to compliment the man."

She considers this. "It doesn't mesh with my experience, I suppose. Magpie took us down into the tunnels early on."

"Magpie was also banished from the guild for her many questionable actions, and her students all flunked or were kicked out. I wouldn't look to her for expertise."

Her expression tightens. She grabs the straps on her pack, adjusting it. "Let's just get this done, shall we?"

As we walk, I watch her expression. I look for nervousness on her part, just in case she might be one of the thieves and doesn't like being shadowed. I also keep an eye on how well she knows the city. One of the thieves we're hunting for would surely be an expert on the layout of the buildings. She could be pretending to be ignorant of her surroundings. Magpie was a bad seed, and her students could be worse. Definitely bears scrutiny.

I traipse through the bustling city with Gwenna at my side. Vastwarren is always crowded, but there's a bit of order to things in the heart of the city, where the guild holds full rein. As we get deeper into the bowels of the city itself, the streets become narrower, the congestion of people thicker. I'm lucky in that as a Taurian, my big frame and menacing horns make most people avoid me. Gwenna isn't quite so lucky—she's nudged and pushed around and has to constantly squeeze past people who won't give way to a mere woman, even one in a guild uniform.

I put up with it for a while, because it's clear she's determined to manage on her own, but when a man shoves her and she staggers into my side, my temper flares. "You want me to carry your pack for you?" I ask, helping her right herself. "Might let you move a little easier."

"You're not supposed to."

"I won't tell if you won't." My urging is a test in many ways. If she's open to breaking the rules in this small way, what else is she open to?

"I can manage, thank you." Her tone is prim as she pushes me away. "Do I look helpless or something?"

I can't help but approve of her answer. "You look soft and sweet."

She scowls, and I grin to myself.

The types of buildings lining the busy streets grow less appealing the closer we get to the river and the docks there. The outskirts of Vastwarren are full of slums and run-down businesses squeezed together as tightly as possible, carving space out for themselves when there's little space to be had. Along this dirty, congested strip are several brothels, many of which I've frequented in the past when I couldn't acquire potions to handle the endless rut that's upon me thanks to my ever-present knot. It's early in the day, so the women aren't hanging out the doors trying to pull in passersby. All is quiet.

I should stop in and ask about Sarya. See if anyone here recognizes her by the description or the name. I should . . . and yet I don't want to leave Gwenna alone. Not in this part of town. I'll just have to return later when Gwenna is safe and back at the nest.

Part of it is probably that I'm currently full of my knot-alleviating potion, and so I'm not feeling particularly sexual at the moment. Flirty, yes, but I'm always flirty. Yet my thoughts turn to Sarya most when I'm aroused, and I feel guilty that I haven't looked for her more. If I'm in love, shouldn't I be thinking of her constantly, instead of only when my knot is full? Then again, it's not like there's been anything between the two of us but sex. It's hard to imagine what books Sarya might like, or what her favorite food is, when all I can think about is her throaty laugh and the way she touched me.

Probably mucking good that I'm full of potion right now. I'll look for Sarya in a day or two, when I'm less potion-drunk.

The river comes into view, and with it, the barges that line the docks, dumping cargo. Cats skitter past as crates are loaded onto the streets and men busily stack them or place them on carts. There's a stink of sewage and dead fish in the air, and it makes my nostrils flare with distaste.

Gwenna eyes all of this and then pulls out a piece of parchment and a charcoal stick to write. "I'm to find the building behind the fishmonger. Have you seen it?"

"All I've seen is your winning smile," I tease. In fact, we passed the building she needs a few moments ago, but if she's determined to do this on her own, I'll let her.

She stops in the street, turns to fully regard me, and there's a scowl on her face. "Quit flirting with me. I don't like it."

"Is it me that you don't like, or the flirting?"

Her eyes narrow. "If I say I don't like the flirting, then you'll say I like you. If I say it's you, you'll try even harder to win me over. There's no right answer to that question."

The astute response makes me throw my head back and laugh. "What if I'm not flirting but telling the truth? Does that change anything?"

"I'd just tell you that I'm not going to fuck you, because we're in a Five together. Same thing I told Arrod."

My laughter immediately dies, replaced by a hot fury. "When did he proposition you? What did he say?"

"Forget I brought it up." She seems more annoyed by my question than ever and scans the buildings around us.

I'm not letting this go. How did I not see this? I rack my brain, trying to think of times that he's been hovering a little too close to Gwenna or spending too much time with her. I haven't noticed anything out of the ordinary, but I'm also not always around her. Is there something happening that I need to be concerned with? I've seen him flirting with her in the past, but she's always shut him down as neatly as she's shut me down. But I know *I* won't push harder . . . I don't know that about him. "Is he bothering you? Do I need to gut him?"

Her mouth twitches in a faint smile. "I can take care of myself."

"I'm sure you can, but I still don't like that you have to." Mentally, I'm composing the note I'm going to send to Hawk. Arrod needs to be watched more closely. What if he's the problem after all and I've been dismissing him as uninteresting? What if he's got a dark side to him?

What if he mucking dares to touch Gwenna? I'll flay the skin from him.

"I appreciate the concern, but like I've told you before, I was a maid. Men think we're easy pickings all the time. I know how to shut them down. I also know better than to end up alone with the worrying ones."

"You're alone with me right now," I point out.

"Am I?" She gestures at the bustling streets around us, even as another person shoves past her and glares at the two of us for standing still. "And for all your very obvious flirting, you're not one of the more worrying ones."

"But there are worrying ones?" I ask as she walks away. "What about Hemmen? Has he been bothering you?"

"Let it go," she says, voice light as she scans the streets. "Like I said, I appreciate the gesture, but it isn't necessary. I can take care of myself. I don't need you or your help."

I decide I'm going to add Hemmen to my list of possible lechers that I'm sending to Hawk. If a man is bothering a woman, he doesn't deserve to be in the guild, working alongside her. I don't care if it means they both flunk and thus our Five fails. As far as I'm concerned, it'd be worth it, especially if they try to touch her. Just the thought makes me utterly fucking furious, and I clench my fists to keep from snarling at the skies.

Is this why there aren't more women in the guild? The thought has never crossed my mind before, but now I'm starting to wonder.

And that idiot Jay put us all in the same room together. I think of Arrod sneaking over to Gwenna's bed in the middle of the night and him touching her . . . My blood boils.

I stomp over to her side. "I'm saying something to Master Jay before he leaves tonight."

"I don't want to be a bother. In fact, I'd prefer you keep to yourself and just leave me alone." Gwenna doesn't look at me as she addresses me, her gaze intent upon the buildings nearby as she looks for the one in question.

I'm wounded at her dismissal. "You know, you don't like me and I'm trying to figure out what I did."

"It's not that I don't like you." She pauses to look over at me, her expression one of exasperation. "But I need to pass this year, and you're not taking being a fledgling very seriously."

I've been deliberately encouraging this line of thought so no one will suspect that I'm watching them. Even so, I don't like that Gwenna thinks I'm not serious about any of this. "What makes you think I'm not?"

"Because . . . well, you're you." She gestures at me.

I don't even know what that means. "What, because I like to have fun? Nothing in the rules says I need to spend my days frowning at the world around us."

"That's not it at all." Gwenna pauses again, clasping the sheet of parchment to her breasts so it doesn't flutter away. "You're good at everything without even having to try hard. You know plenty about Old Prell. You can handle yourself in a fight. You're excellent on the obstacle courses. Heck, you probably already have the city memorized and came just to bother me."

Her answer's a little too close for comfort and reminds me how very astute she is.

"Me," she continues, "I'm not good at anything. I'm not athletic. I'm out of my depth in all of this, and I'm a woman. I need to push harder than everyone else so I can catch up."

Oh. Is that the reason she frowns at me so when I try to flirt? "You want me to help you?"

"Help me with what?"

I shrug. "Whatever you like. I can teach you the basics of Old Prellian glyphs. I don't know many, mind you, but most artificers don't. You just need to know some of the more common ones that you might run across scribed onto old buildings or on walls. I can assist you with training. Whatever you feel you need to brush up on, I can work with you. I don't mind."

She pauses, blinking up at me. "You'd help me with all of that?"

"Of course. It'd probably be on the weekends, since that's our only free time." I rub my chin, thinking. "Well, not this weekend, of course. There's the wedding for Master Siskin and his partner, Tern. Everyone's going . . . well, except Master Jay, but that's just how Master Jay is."

"Not everyone. I wasn't invited to a wedding."

Ah. I suppose I was the only fledgling who was invited. Tern is friendly with the Taurians in town, and I've worked with him several times on a variety of rescue missions. He probably didn't think about my status when he invited me. "You can come with me. No one will think twice if I bring a date."

Gwenna's expression changes to a withering look. "Is this another bout of you flirting?"

Her wariness makes me choose my words carefully. "No, this is me suggesting you show up at my side so we can check out what you're up against."

Some of the tension in her frame eases. "What do you mean, what I'm up against?"

"We see which masters act offended because you're female. We see which ones treat you like anyone else. We see if any repeaters or fledglings are invited and how they act. We chat with the masters and see what they say their teams are good at. In short, we collect information on everyone. Because we're not going to be scouring the streets endlessly. After a few more weeks of preliminary training, we're going to be doing team exercises, and then we'll be pitted against the fledgling teams of other masters. Wouldn't you rather know what to expect so you can train properly?"

She pauses, thinking. "I don't have much in the way of dressy clothing."

"Neither do I. We can linger at the back of the wedding so no one notices if we're shabby. And after the wedding, they're celebrating at a tavern. We can get dinner, a few drinks, spy on everyone. It'll be great fun."

"Mmm." Gwenna considers this and then eyes me speculatively. "And what are you expecting in exchange for dinner and this information?"

"Companionship."

Her brow goes up.

"Of the chaste, friendly sort. I wouldn't expect you to suck my cock simply because you got a mouthful of bread," I scoff. "Any male who does expect that should be hit over the head, and repeatedly."

My cock isn't working right now anyhow, thanks to the potion.

Gwenna's mouth curves in a faint smile. "On that, we're in agreement."

I smile back. Damn, she's prickly, but it doesn't bother me. I understand the reasons behind her crabbiness, and it makes me feel a strange wave of affection for her. It also makes me want to protect her from idiots like Arrod and Hemmen more than ever. I like that she keeps me on my toes. Makes me think. Reminds me of Sarya, but in a completely different way.

Then I think guiltily of all the brothels we passed by and how I didn't go hunting for Sarya. I won't be able to this weekend, either. Or longer.

Not with the wedding and Gwenna needing protection from Arrod and possibly Hemmen. I'm not going to let them trap her or be alone with her. She needs someone intimidating looking out for her. I know she's close to the slitherskin, but he's not very intimidating, and he won't speak up if she's in danger.

It's up to me.

Surely Sarya would understand.

I wonder privately if I'm ignoring my hunt for Sarya because of the amount of knot-deadening potion I've been downing lately. It makes me pleasantly numb in all the right areas, but it's possible it's numbing other things, too. When I find Sarya, I can wean myself off the damned stuff. Until then, it's a necessity.

Focusing on Gwenna, I gesture at the crowded street. "Come on. We're in the right area. We'll work on our mapping, but just slow enough that Master Jay can't give us any new tasks before the end of the day. And once we're done, we can talk about what we're going to practice on weekends."

She gives me a pleased look that makes me feel as if I've just climbed a mountain. "That'd be wonderful. What sorts of things are you envisioning we practice first?"

Her question is innocent enough, but my mind goes to hot, dirty places. So much for the potion deadening everything. I clear my throat, thinking. "Maybe . . . sword work?"

"Oh, you just want to see how tight my grip is, is that it? Or see me work a staff?" There's a tease in her voice.

I stare at her in surprise. "Are you . . . flirting with me?"

"I'm not opposed to flirting," Gwenna says, an amused expression on her round face. "But I like to be the one in control of the situation."

"So I need to wait for you to flirt with me before I flirt back?"

She just gives me another smile and saunters away, down the crowded street. For some reason, I'm reminded of Sarya. Maybe I just like bossy women who put me in my place.

With a grin, I trail after Gwenna. I'll let her do a bit of wandering before I point out she's going the wrong way. No sense in wasting the entire afternoon just to prove a point.

◦◦◦

GWENNA

When we return to the dormitory, I'm in a good mood. If Raptor's
going to help me brush up on my skills during the weekends, I might not
feel so far behind and lost. I might have a chance instead of fretting all
year that I'm not fast enough, not skilled enough, not smart enough. Not
enough, all around.

I'm surprised when we get back to the dormitory and he grabs his
pack, sets it on my bed, and then moves my pack and belongings onto his
old bed, the one closest to the double doors. He also glares heartily at
Arrod and Hemmen. "No one gets near Gwenna when she sleeps. Try
anything, and you're going to find an angry Taurian's fist down your
throat. Understand?"

They blink in confusion, and to be fair, so do I. Only Kipp seems un-
concerned at this turn of events. He just nods at me as if he expected
something like this all along.

Raptor stands at the foot of his bed and gives me a nod, crossing his
bulging arms over his chest.

"M-Master Jay is about to leave for the weekend," Hemmen stammers. "Should we go t-talk to him? Tell him the change in sleeping ar-
rangements?"

"If you like. He won't care. And this isn't just for this weekend. This
is permanent. This is a job, and you treat it like one. If she wants your
fucking dick, she'll ask for it." And he glares at both of them. "I'm sure
Master Jay will agree with me."

I bite my lip, looking over at Raptor. "I don't mean to be a bother—"

He puts a hand up. "Stop."

I go silent. No one's ever stood up for me like that. Normally it's just
a maid's lot to forever be pushing away hands and telling men you're not
interested. Doesn't matter what you look like—if you're a servant, you're
considered fair game by every noble or rich man. For Raptor to lay down
the law for me so I don't have to?

It's rather nice.

I step forward to pick up my bag tossed at the foot of the bed . . . and then I feel it. A thick wetness between my thighs. Eyes wide, I grab my pack and race with it to the garderobe. The moment the door is shut behind me, I hike up my skirts and check my undergarments.

Sure enough, I've started my period.

I've never been so happy to bleed. Collapsing on the seat, I cry tears of pure joy.

THIRTEEN

RAPTOR

Rooster to Raptor: *The entire shipment due to go to the south has gone missing. Tell me you have an update.*

Raptor to Rooster: *When there's an update, I'll let you know.*

I'M ON EDGE as Gwenna goes to bed early Fifthday night, citing a headache. She's still in bed the next morning when I wake up, and I take my time dressing in my uniform, waiting to see if she'll address me. She doesn't, though, just pulls the blankets over her head and rolls over.

We're supposed to go to the wedding of Master Siskin and Artificer Tern later today, but I'm concerned. Gwenna hasn't been herself since she raced to the necessary yesterday and emerged a while later, eyes red from weeping.

Was it something I said?

Kipp is in the kitchen when I head over, and I grab a handful of nuts and several apples, eating as I ponder the problem with Gwenna. "She said anything to you?" I ask him.

He shrugs, settling his large shell in the corner of the kitchen. Last weekend, he'd moved his shell house to a warm corner in the kitchen near the hearth and moved it back to his bed when Master Jay scolded him. I suspect he's going to move it in every weekend. Good for him.

"You know her better than I do. Think I hurt her feelings somehow?"

Kipp huffs, shaking his head. He finishes settling his shell in place, gives it a friendly pat, and then scrambles onto the table. He picks up a handful of berries and sits across from me on the tabletop, regarding me with a serene expression.

"You'd think I'd be better with women, given that I've bedded so many," I tell him ruefully. "But in my life, women have usually just one role, and not a good one. I spend the rest of my time with artificers, either moving through tunnels or rescuing them when they get lost."

Kipp eats a berry, watching me.

"I'm just trying to be respectful of her is all," I say between bites.

He nods once, then continues eating a blueberry like I would an apple.

"If I muck something up, you'll tell me? I'd rather know than have to tiptoe around, guessing."

The slitherskin pops the rest of his berry into his mouth and tackles the next one, nodding again.

"Do you know what's bothering her? Did she tell you?"

He taps his nose and gives me a look.

"Good talk." I knock on the table twice. "Let's do this again."

With my last apple in hand, I exit the kitchen, only to run into Gwenna. She has a bag in her arms and gives me a surprised look.

"There you are. You—"

"If you'll excuse me, I have to go to the necessary." She darts away before I can finish my words, and as she does, a metallic scent trails after her. Blood.

Aaaaaah. Her menses.

Hot relief hits me. That I haven't somehow mucked this up and she doesn't hate me. I don't know why it matters so much, just that it does. I enjoy talking to her. I like her sass and her pert responses. I like that she doesn't make it easy for me.

Sarya crosses my mind, and hot guilt replaces my relief. I've not gone to any of the brothels in search of her recently. I feel as if I'm abandoning her. It's just that being in a Five is time-consuming, and I'm supposed to be watching everyone for Hawk and Head Guild Master Rooster. Add in my concern over Gwenna and the extra tutoring I'll be giving her and . . . well.

I'll go looking for Sarya tomorrow, I decide. The wedding and Gwenna today, the hunt for the woman of my dreams tomorrow. I'm putting off Sarya again, but it's the last time. No more potions for me. The one I took a few days ago is going to be my last. It's messing up my priorities. It'll mean I'll crave sex, but hopefully I can find Sarya before it starts to become a real problem.

I find ways to keep myself busy while I wait for Gwenna to emerge from the necessary without making it seem like I'm waiting on her. Both Hemmen and Arrod have taken the weekend as an opportunity to disappear. Neither one is in the nest this morning. I should be bothered by that—one of the core tenets of a working Five is that you're close and get along. But I'm too set in my ways. I'm older than them and crabby at the thought of babysitting a pair of idiots, especially when one might be our thief.

Hmm.

Now's the perfect time for me to check their belongings to see if they really are thieves. I head to the dormitory room and make my bed, tucking the blankets tightly under the too-small mattress that I wish curses upon every evening. Gwenna's bed is made, and Kipp's is undisturbed except for a circular ripple in the blankets where he'd kept his shell atop the folded coverlets. Hemmen's bed is made, Arrod's is not. I glance around the room, then mess up Hemmen's bed.

Then I get to work "making" their beds again.

I flip the mattresses and feel all along the undersides, looking for holes. I shake out the blankets. I beat the pillows. I peer under the beds. When none of that leads anywhere, I dig through Hemmen's bag, and then Arrod's. There's nothing of interest. Hemmen's bag just has a couple of books in it and a box of old letters, and Arrod's has nothing but clothing and what might be the ugliest velvet hat I've ever seen. Annoyed, I move to shove everything back into Arrod's bag when I notice Kipp standing by the double doors. He has another berry in his hand, casually eating it as he watches me ransack their things.

"Lost a sock," I tell him to explain away my actions. Never mind that Taurians don't wear socks. Or shoes.

He just licks his eyeball with that long tongue of his and goes back to eating his berry. When he finishes it, he turns and walks away. Huh.

I'm tempted to check his bed, too, but whatever he has of value would be in his shell, and it's currently in the kitchen. I toss Arrod's bag back into its spot by the head of the bed just as Gwenna enters the room, wearing a pretty dress and a tightly fitting bodice over a fluffy white chemise. She touches her black hair, which has been braided into a crown atop her head, and her cheeks grow pink as I regard her. "Is my braid crooked?" she asks. "It's bloody hard to braid without a mirror."

"Come here and I'll check it for you," I say, waving her toward me.

She approaches without hesitation, sitting on the edge of my bed. She smells like flowers, soap, and fresh cotton, the tang of blood only a slight note now. I don't mind it, as long as I know she's not in pain. Even so, I'm aware of her tears from yesterday, and I play with how to approach that in my mind even as I unbraid her hair for her. "Let me redo this for you."

"I don't mean to be a bother."

"You say that a lot."

She hesitates. "It's a bad habit of mine. I worked as a maid for a very long time before coming here."

"Ah. So you're more comfortable being invisible." I finish unbraiding her hair and shake it loose.

"Precisely. Invisible is safe in a lot of ways. If you're invisible, no one points out that the shelves need dusting. No handing you chores just because you happen to be standing nearby. No men deciding that because you're a servant, you're fair game."

I bite back a growl.

"It's a difficult habit to break." She tilts her head slightly, leaning into my touch. "I had no idea you were so good at braiding."

"I have three younger sisters, and they liked ribbons braided into their manes," I tell her, my fingers brushing against her scalp. Her hair is softer and silkier than that of my sisters, but it also has a lot less body to it. It's fine and clings to my calluses like cobwebs. "And occasionally there's a tunnel rope that has to be braided to reinforce it."

"Well, thank you." She sits tall and straight. "Where are your sisters now? And your parents?"

"Living in a farming village over in the Southwind Plains. It's called Clover Hollow."

"It sounds very pastoral."

"It is, and that's why I couldn't wait to leave when I was younger." I twine her hair around my fingers as I braid, easily working her smooth locks into a crown once more. "I wasn't cut out to be a farmer. I wanted adventure, so I left for here as soon as one of my sisters mated and her mate took over the farm. My parents live there with them, but they're both older and don't quite get the need for adventure."

"It's hard when you don't want the same thing as your parents," she agrees.

"Is that your story?" I ask. "Why you're here?"

"I'm here since someone needed to follow Aspeth—sorry, Sparrow—because I didn't want her going to Vastwarren alone. She's very trusting, and I worried someone would take advantage of her." Her hands are clasped calmly in her lap. "It didn't occur to me until we stepped foot in the city that I could become an artificer, too. I thought I'd spend my entire life working at Honori Hold. The highest I'd be able to reach would be that I might end up as a chambermaid to whatever lady Lord Honori remarried."

"Sounds . . . dull."

"Oh, it is." She chuckles, the sound soft and rueful. "In a way, coming here has ruined me. Now that I see I can be something other than a maid, it'll break me if I have to go back to it. I'll do anything to stay."

Gwenna says it so casually, so cheerfully, that I pause to absorb what she's said. Anything, huh? Said like a true thief. The part of me that's supposed to be looking for clues about the culprit knows that this is vital information I should pass on. That this makes her suspicious.

But the young Taurian male who left his family behind because they didn't understand why he felt the need to do something other than farming? He knows just what she means.

"I'm going to help you pass," I tell her. "You don't have to worry about that. We'll make it happen."

"I would appreciate it." Her voice is soft again. "My mother's still working in the kitchens, and it's getting harder and harder on her. I'd love for her to come here and join me, but I can't afford it. Not yet."

"And your father?"

"Never met him. Just a visiting lord who thought he could do whatever he wanted with a servant."

I digest that, and decide it makes me angry. "If you ever find out who it is, let me know and I'll cram my big Taurian fist down his throat."

She laughs. "You're eager to punch some throats."

"I really am." But more than that, I like her laughter. I like making her smile, because it feels like I've done something important to earn that instead of her tartness. I finish her braid, and when she hands me a pin, I tuck it into the end to anchor the tail of her hair underneath the plait so it doesn't show. "All done."

Gwenna touches it carefully and then tilts her head back to smile at me. "You did an excellent job."

"Like I said, three sisters." I offer her a hand to stand up, and she takes it. I study her expression carefully. "You don't have to go to the wedding with me if you don't feel up to it. I noticed you cried yesterday."

"Oh." She manages a fainter smile and pulls her hand from mine, crossing the room. "Those were just . . . emotional tears. A lot has been on my mind lately, and one worry was taken off my plate, so to speak."

A worry off her plate? That's suspicious. I keep my voice casual, even though my senses are on alert. "And do you have a lot of worries?"

"You have no idea." She says the words cheerfully, but it feels forced. It also mucking pisses me off, because the more she says shit like that, the more I worry she's the thief after all. She's too likeable to be the piece of shit that the guild's been trying to catch, but she's also making me wonder what's going on.

"You wanna try me?" I give her a teasing smile. "I can be a really good listener."

"They're not your problems." She smooths a hand down the front of her dress. "And this is all I have to wear that's suitable for a wedding. I don't have to go if I'll embarrass you. I really do understand."

I eye her, with her round, pink cheeks and her black, glossy hair pulled into an unadorned braid-crown. Her clothing is plain and clearly mended more than once if you look closely. Her skirt is a dark shade of blue with no adornment, and her bodice is a deep brown with only a frayed ribbon sewn along the scooped neck as a nod to fanciness. She wears no jewelry, but to me, she's stunningly beautiful. Her magnificent cleavage is shown off by the bodice that plumps her breasts and reveals a nipped waist. She's short and curvy, but it's the sparkle in her eye that I can't look away from.

If she's the thief, it's smart for me to get in close and learn all her secrets. Seduce her to find out information. Become her confidant. But if she is the thief, it'll absolutely gut me.

I hold my hand out to her. "I would be honored to have such a lovely date for the wedding."

Gwenna puts her hand in mine with a smile.

FOURTEEN

GWENNA

EVEN PERIOD CRAMPS and intermittently heading to the necessary to check the thick, absorbent cloth I have pinned into my drawers doesn't ruin the fun of the day for me. Raptor is an utterly charming date. He's attentive and considerate and talks me up to everyone we meet. I don't know anyone at the wedding other than Hawk and Sparrow, but after a short time it becomes clear that it doesn't matter—Raptor knows everyone, and he's excellent at smoothing the way.

The wedding ceremony itself is brief, with Head Guild Master Rooster presiding over the two men's union in the main guild hall. Then everyone heads to the King's Onion, which has been rented out for the party. I get stressed every time we head into the streets, waiting to feel the unpleasant buzzing of the dead, but it never happens. We make it to the tavern with no incident. Floral garlands festoon the otherwise bland wooden walls, and a white cloth decorates the long bar. Drinks and food cover a trestle table along the back, and the front of the room has been cleared for dancing, with a fiddler situated in the corner. It's incredibly crowded, but there's a mix of both men and women squeezed into the tavern, and so it doesn't feel as oppressive as the guild-only ceremonies, when I stand out for being female.

Raptor brings me a glass of wine, his beer mug covered in slices of onion. He leans over me, his hand resting lightly on my shoulder, and I could swear his thumb brushes against my bare skin, exposed by my wide-necked bodice. It's enough to make me shiver and grow distracted, but I'm always a little hornier on my period. "Shall I get you something to eat?" he murmurs, looming close. "It might be a while before we can slip away."

"Perhaps just some cheese and bread? Something simple? I don't mean to be a bother," I catch myself saying, and then try to correct it. "Plus, I don't want to flick crumbs out of my cleavage all night."

I skim my fingers over my chest, mimicking a cleaning action.

"I'd be happy to help you with that," he teases, dumping his onions into his beer before taking a hearty swig. I'm a little horrified at all the onions, but it's the theme of the bar, courtesy of some artifact given to the bar's owner by the king. Watching Raptor relish a chunk of onion reminds me that he—and all the Taurians—are vegetarians. No meat, and certainly no cow dairy. Goat's milk is all right, but how am I to know which cheeses look like goat and which don't?

I think for a moment and then change my order. I hold my hand out. "Here, I'll hold your beer. Maybe skip the cheese and get some fruit to go with the bread instead?"

I don't know why I care if I have dairy breath when he's going to have onion breath. . . .

And he says Taurians don't kiss.

And we're supposed to be just friends anyhow.

Even so. I take the onion-and-beer mug from him and hold it, sipping my wine as I watch a couple head out to dance a jig in the center of the floor. I'm pressed up against the back wall of the tavern, surrounded by strangers, but I'm enjoying myself. It's because of my company, I realize. Even now, as he waits to get food for us, Raptor sends me playful little glances and gestures designed to make me laugh, as if we're the only ones in the room.

He did a fantastic job with my hair earlier, and he's given me appreciative looks all day. At one point I caught him staring down my cleavage, but the look on his face was so admiring (and he's so tall it's not as if it could have been avoided) that I stood just a little bit straighter, my chest thrust out. After all, why not? It's not as if this is anything but a pair of friends enjoying a day out.

He still has no idea that we fucked. That I rode on his cock and squeezed his knot. I shouldn't even have such things on my mind, but I can't seem to help myself. It was *really* good sex.

I spot a table emptying out and rush over to it, setting down our drinks. It's got a perfect view of the festivities. Flicking a few crumbs off the wooden surface, I smile at a nearby man as I nudge Raptor's beer over to indicate I'm waiting on company.

Hawk leads Sparrow out onto the dance floor, and my friend is all pink cheeks and glowing happiness. They both stumble over their steps, but neither seems to mind. Hawk pulls her closer, his big hand splayed across the small of her back, and twirls Sparrow around. I'm hit with a note of envy. He adores her. She adores him. It must be nice to be besotted and in love.

"You're looking at them as if you want to dance," Raptor says, suddenly appearing at my side.

I jump in my seat, startled, and then shake my head. "I'm about as good a dancer as a three-legged dog."

"What a coincidence. My dancing tutor was a three-legged dog." He sits and holds out a shiny, steaming roll of bread crusted with nuts.

I pluck the roll from him and smirk. "It was not. You're just saying that because you want to see my arse hopping about on the dance floor."

"Me? I would never." Raptor pretends to be offended, then ruins it with a grin and a big bite of his own roll. "The food's decent. Always a good thing at this sort of shindig."

"Do you go to a lot of weddings, then?" I nibble delicately on my own roll. The top of it is honeyed and my fingers get sticky. I resist the urge to lick them. That'll seem obvious, and I'm on a slippery slope with Raptor as it is.

"No, but there's usually one or two every year. You spend a lot of time in the tunnels with someone, working side by side, and it makes sense that your thoughts lead to love."

I make a face at the thought of falling for Hemmen or Arrod. "Does it?"

"I'm sure it'll lead to love for you if that's what you're looking for."

He finishes his roll with the second bite and takes his mug in hand. "No one will be able to resist your charms for long."

"I'm looking for a job, not to charm anyone," I reply tartly. "Not every woman needs a man in her life."

"Needs, no. Wants?" He shrugs. "If you *want* one, that's different. If we were at your wedding next year, I wouldn't be surprised. That's all."

"And who am I marrying in this fantasy of yours? Who am I spending tireless hours with? Arrod? Hemmen? I truly don't think I'm Kipp's type, so that rules him out."

Our gazes meet, and it feels as if time slows.

I shouldn't say it. Shouldn't mucking say it.

"You?" I blurt out, even though I shouldn't say it.

Raptor gives me a wry look. "Alas, my heart is spoken for. But if it wasn't, you'd be irresistible to me, aye."

I laugh and take a big drink of my wine, but I feel shredded on the inside. He's spoken for? And I fucked him? Mucking *hells*. All five mucking hells. I'm a home-wrecker on top of everything else.

FIFTEEN

RAPTOR

GWENNA GOES SILENT, and I hate that I've ruined the mood. Not that I should care, but I feel it all the same. It's right that I tell her. She deserves to know that my heart is Sarya's, and that our flirting can't go anywhere. Even as I think it, I wonder if I'm a fool. If I'm far too hung up on a woman I met for only a brief moment in time and didn't even get to look at.

And yet . . . I can't stop thinking about her. Being with her just felt so right. Like I'd met the perfect woman, the one I'd always been meant to find. Perhaps that's what makes it difficult to be around Gwenna. I get the same feeling when I'm around her. That if I'd let myself, I'd be utterly besotted by her tart tongue and her sparkling smile. That if I'd only met her first, it'd be a very different story.

I hate that realization.

Almost as much as I hate hurting her. She might be the thief, but she's still a person I'm wildly attracted to, a person I like being around. A person who impresses me with her wit and intelligence. I change the subject, handing over the bowl of fruit I've brought along with me from the refreshment table. "Any more observations to share with me, my sharp-eyed female?"

She sets the bowl down between us to share, then pulls apart her roll with delicate fingers. Gwenna arches an eyebrow at me. "Why do you want to know?"

"Because I like hearing all the juicy details." I shrug and pop a slice of peach into my mouth. "But more than that, I just like learning what you've observed."

"Mmm." She eats a fluffy bit of roll, her gaze moving to the dance floor and avoiding me. "Hemmen has bad dreams and talks in his sleep."

"Interesting. I didn't notice that."

She shoots me a sharp look. "That's because you sleep like the dead."

Another observation, and a true one. I steal another slice of peach, because I love fruit. "Can I help it if I need my beauty rest?"

"I'm just saying, if we get robbed in the middle of the night, I'm not trying to wake you to save us. That's all."

Chuckling, I eye the roll she's mangling. Is she imagining it as my neck? "I've noticed you never mention Kipp in your observations."

"That's because I like Kipp, and I'm not selling him out to you."

"Is that what you think you're doing? Selling them out to me?"

The side-eye she gives me is magnificent. "If Kipp has secrets, I'm keeping them. He's earned my trust, and I've earned his."

I prop an elbow on the table and lean in, my hand on my face. "And how do I earn your trust?"

"Didn't know you wanted it."

"I do. I like you."

"Not enough to tell me that you're married."

"Oh, I'm not married. I wouldn't be here at a wedding with another woman if I was. But I met a lady not too long ago who charmed me, and I've been looking for her ever since. And I thought we were friendly enough for me to point that out without hurting your feelings. Obviously, I was wrong, and I apologize. I wasn't trying to make you feel foolish by withholding information."

"I don't feel foolish." Her shoulders go up, her back straightening again. "I was just . . . surprised. You're allowed to love whoever you like, and I shall be more than happy to come to the wedding."

It's my turn to feel awkward. "A wonderful thought, but I'm not certain that will happen anytime soon. I haven't seen her in a while and . . . well, I doubt she thinks about me at all."

Her expression turns sympathetic. Gwenna nudges the bowl of fruit toward me, as if I need comfort. "I'm sorry. It's her loss if she doesn't want you. You're a good male."

"Flatterer."

"And a better one when you shut up and take a compliment."

I laugh, pleased at her tart rejoinders. She's such fun to chat with.

She smiles and pops a finger into her mouth, sucking it clean of the honey on the roll, her gaze on the dance floor. If I watch her sucking on things, I'm really going to have a hard time keeping my focus on Sarya, so I stare out at the dancers, too.

"They look good, don't they?" Gwenna asks. "Sparrow and Hawk?"

"They do." There's nothing but berries left in the bowl, so I dump them all into my mouth, since they're too tiny for my big hands to fuss with. I watch my friend smiling down at his owlish wife, her glasses hanging off her small nose, and I feel a stab of pure, unadulterated envy. They get to spend every mucking day in each other's arms, and I haven't seen Sarya in weeks. Might not ever see her again.

Might be nothing but endless potions in my mucking future.

"Oh, look. There's Mereden and Lark. I'm going to go say hello." Gwenna pops out of her seat and moves along the edges of the dance floor to greet her friends, and I'm left with nothing but berries and some sour thoughts about the woman I can't seem to forget.

A woman I'm also starting to resent for just how difficult she is to find.

SIXTEEN

GWENNA

I'M A CONFLICTING mix of emotions. I'd been having a wonderful time with Raptor, and loved chatting and sassing and even flirting with him. It had all been terribly romantic, but then my heart hurt at hearing that Raptor is obsessed with some other woman. I don't know why it bothers me, given that we can't exactly be together. We're in a Five, and we're supposed to be business companions only.

I should just be thrilled that I'm not pregnant and call it a day. And while I am incredibly, happily relieved that I'm not carrying his child, I worry I'm becoming far too obsessed. I cannot afford to fall in love with anyone before I've established myself with the guild. It'd be smartest to put some distance between the two of us. Starting tomorrow, I decide. I'll thank Raptor for the lovely day, and then find ways to stay busy when I have the opportunity to be alone with him. It's the right call.

Even if I do feel a little lonely. That's just the wedding mood calling to the romantic side of me.

I push aside those thoughts and focus on my friends. It seems that Mereden is friends with Siskin, who has a brother who works in the healer's guild. Mereden and Lark are both beside themselves with excitement because they've been visiting the orphanage and have fallen in love with a pair of children. "There's an older brother who's five," Lark gushes as Mereden clutches her hand tightly. They sit on the far side of the dancing, with Lark's foot propped up on a nearby chair and a cane under her arm. "And a little girl who's two. They're just the smartest kids, and we love them both."

"As soon as we get permanent housing, we're applying to adopt both of them," Mereden says, her voice soft and shy. "Which means as soon as I'm accepted to the healers, things will really move forward."

"You're not going to work at being an artificer at all?" I don't know if it's disappointment I feel or happiness for her. In my head, I was still mentally placing Mereden and Lark into our Five, along with me and Kipp and . . . well, Raptor. I blush just thinking about how presumptuous and awful I am for swapping out my best friend, Sparrow, for the man I have a crush on, but Sparrow's happy in her job.

"I'm still doing it," Lark says, gesturing at her foot. "Soon as this starts behaving. And Mereden will fledge, too, but we want to have a family. If one of us must stay with the kids while the other fledges, that's just how it goes. She's going to work at the healer's guild for a while until I can bring in coin. We've talked about it, and when she's working, we'll have a nanny until I finish being a fledgling."

They share a giddy smile.

I want to be excited for them. I do. But everything is changing so fast. I don't know what to make of it all. "I can't believe you've already picked out children. I thought it'd take a while for some reason."

"We visited the orphanage and just fell in love," Mereden says, leaning her head on Lark's shoulder. Their hands remain intertwined, as if they'll never let go of each other. "It was impossible to say no to those sweet faces. Every day we have to wait to get them home feels like torture."

"And your father? What does he think of all this?" I ask, because I know Mereden's father is noble. Not the heir, but one of the spares. I'm guessing they were expecting her to make an advantageous marriage.

Her expression tightens. "We, ah, haven't told my family yet."

"We might have to if we can't get income soon," Lark says, glancing over at Mer. "We're still figuring things out, obviously."

"I'll be on the lookout for odd jobs," I tell them. "Seems we're all in need of a bit of coin these days."

Lark lifts her chin, glancing up at Raptor, who's still across the room. "What's the story with you and him?"

"Other than us being fledglings together? There is no story."

"I don't know." Mereden sits up, craning her neck to get a glimpse. "He does keep looking over here a lot for someone who's just a friend."

"It's complicated," I tell them. I don't know what else to say. I'm not sure I want to tell them that it's complicated because I was feeling sick from sensing a dead body so I fucked him to distract myself and it turns out he doesn't know it was me and he's also pining over some other woman. That seems like far too much. I just smile brightly and gesture at the food spread. "Have you tried the rolls? They're amazing."

A SHORT TIME later, Raptor and I head out from the tavern. Our easy mood from earlier is gone, and our conversation as we head back to the dormitory is sparse. I'm thinking about how happy Mereden and Lark are, and Sparrow and Hawk, and the newly married couple of Siskin and Tern. I didn't come to Vastwarren to seek out a relationship. I came here for a job. But seeing so many people so happy and paired up makes me feel lonely. Hormones, I suspect, and I want to squeeze my crampy abdomen with relief and delight.

Raptor holds the door to the nest open for me, and I step inside, then wait politely for him. We stare at each other in the doorway, and then he gives me his best smile and cocks a thumb to the kitchen. "I'm going to grab a drink of water to wash the onion out of my mouth. Want anything?"

"No, I'm going to change and write a letter to my mother." I want to carefully fold my dress and bodice so they don't wrinkle, and I'll need to change if I plan on lounging on my bunk and writing.

He nods and retreats, and I head for the dorm sleeping quarters.

I'm not surprised to see they're empty. The sun hasn't even set yet, so there's plenty of day left. Hemmen's probably at the library, and Arrod is, well, doing whatever it is Arrod does on weekends. Kipp's bed is made but his shell is gone, and I suspect he's in the kitchen if he's in the house at all. Privacy is hard to find, and I decide not to waste it.

With quick motions, I flick open the laces at the front of my bodice and give myself room to breathe deep. My breasts bounce as they're freed from their cage, and I scratch at the skin underneath the thick material. I sling my pack from its spot on the bedpost to the center of my bed. I have two changes of uniform, my traveling dress, and a nightgown, and I'm not sure what's best to wear at the end of the day. It feels silly to wear a uniform, but my traveling dress is equally uncomfortable, and yet I don't want to get into my nightgown so early. It feels like it'd be an invitation, and one I'm not inclined to extend if Raptor already has a woman.

I ponder for a moment longer, and then pull open my bag to get a uniform after all. It's not as if I have a ton of choices. Perhaps when I start making artificer money, I can afford a lounging sort of dress. Until then—

I stare down at the strange item in my bag. What the mucking hell is that? It looks like . . . a tube of some kind but decorated with what look like Prellian glyphs. As I stare down at it, uncomprehending, the glyphs begin to glow and shimmer golden.

Quickly, I shut my bag again and take a step backward. Then another. I run into the side of Raptor's bed, and it hits the backs of my knees. I flop onto it, staring at my bag in horror.

How do I have a working artifact? How is that possible?

It's in my bag, so someone clearly placed it there while I was gone. They wanted me to have it . . . or they want me to get into trouble. Do they know I'm a mancer and they're going to blackmail me in some way?

I . . . don't know what to do.

Do I hide it and pretend like it's been mine all along? Any artifact is worth a small fortune, even one that doesn't work. I'm penniless, but I can't sell something like this. I don't have the right contacts, and I don't want to anyhow. I want to be in the guild. I don't understand why this artifact is here. Is someone trying to get me kicked out for stealing? Do they know that I was flunked last year because of stealing? Aspeth tried to take the blame for it, but I know my name was tossed around as well.

Or is that what whoever put it in my bag expects me to do? Do they want me to hold on to it, and the guild enforcers will search the dorm tomorrow and find me guilty? Is this a setup?

Where do I hide it? Who do I turn it in to?

Before I can figure out what to do, the doors to the dorm room open and Raptor steps inside. His gaze drops to my cleavage, spilling out of my loosened bodice. "If that isn't the prettiest sight I've seen all day. I'm flattered, but I'm also taken."

SEVENTEEN

RAPTOR

THE GODS ARE torturing me. Somehow, I've fallen out of favor with Old Garesh, and now he's getting back at me by putting a gorgeous, curvy little human wench into my bed. Gwenna's tits are practically falling out of her loosened bodice, and they're big and juicy and heaving, her cleavage deep enough to sink my muzzle into, and I'm so mucking tempted.

So mucking tempted.

I've never been the type to lust after a woman and not follow up. Thanks to the god's hand ever-present upon me, I've always been highly sexual. But all of that was before Sarya. Sarya, Sarya, Sarya. I'm resenting her absence. Does she not *want* to be found by me? Is she avoiding me? Have I been assuming things between us all this time? Was I just another client to her?

I run a hand down my face, frustrated. I can't afford to be so easily distracted by a pretty fledgling. Forcing myself to look away from her (magnificent) tits, I focus on her face . . . and realize just how pale it is. "You all right?"

"No, I don't think I am," she says in a faint voice.

"What's wrong?" I gesture at the doors behind me. "Should I get a healer?"

Gwenna wrings her hands. "No healer. Don't bother anyone. I . . . Can I trust you, Raptor?"

My senses go on alert. All the lust I've been struggling with goes cold. Here it is, then. The information I've been sent here to seek out. Mentally I'm already composing a letter to send to Rooster and Hawk right after this. But I keep a smile on my face to reassure her even as every part of my spirit grows hard and tired. "Aye, you can."

With a trembling finger, she points at the bag on her bed.

I open it and gaze down at the tube inside. It's Old Prellian, and the glyphs immediately start to glow the moment the item is exposed to light. It's either a carrying case of some kind, or a telescoping spyglass. Whatever it is, it's valuable beyond imagination. And it's in a fledgling's hands.

Precisely where it doesn't belong.

I'm immediately disappointed. I don't know why—I'm here to find the thief, after all. I should be overjoyed that we can give up this farce of me being a fledgling.

But the fact that it's sweet, sassy little Gwenna doesn't sit right with me. She doesn't seem like the monster who's been responsible for all the atrocities that have been happening. It's one thing to steal, and it's another to murder your accomplices. "You stole this?"

"What? No! It's not mine," she immediately hisses, a look of outrage on her face. "Someone put it in my bag while we were out!"

I eye her, because of course a thief would say that. "How do I know that you're telling the truth?"

"Hannai's tits, why would I tell you to look at that thing if I was the thief? Why wouldn't I just hide it away?" She glares at me, her entire body trembling, and looks on the verge of tears.

Gwenna could just be an excellent actress, but something about all of this feels sincere. In the weeks since we've become fledglings together, she's proven to be a hard worker and trustworthy. Yet I can't overlook this. I remain calm, and even though my mind isn't made up, I'll let her think it is so I can win her trust. "All right, then. Let's say you're not a thief. Someone just came into the dormitory and dropped a priceless artifact into your bag. The question is, why?"

"I don't know." She presses shaking fingers to her lips, thinking. "There's got to be some sort of reason behind it. Someone wants me gone from here. They're clearly trying to frame me."

"But why you? You're just a fledgling."

"I don't *know*." Gwenna gets to her feet, clenching her fists. "I haven't been in the tunnels since last year. I don't have access to anything in the archives. Where would I get something like *that*?"

From a connection in the city, obviously. Her friend in the archives, Sparrow. But Sparrow would never do such a thing. And Gwenna seems incredibly upset at the sight of the artifact. She could have hidden it away in a loose floorboard or under the garderobe sink (the spot where I hide my illegal potions) and I would have never known. Instead, she's bringing it to me. That's got to count for something. Because I've got a soft spot when it comes to her, I put my hands in the air. "All right, all right. I believe you."

"Why would I show it to you when I could just mucking sell it to someone and get it off my hands?" she continues, practically hysterical as tears pour down her face. "If I'm caught stealing again, I'm destroyed. They'll send me away—"

"Shhh," I say, moving forward and capturing her smaller hands in mine. I'm growing more and more convinced that she's not involved. No wonder she's panicked. She doesn't know what's going on. Doesn't know that I'm here to hunt a thief. She just knows she's been given an artifact she shouldn't have. "It's going to be fine, Gwenna. We'll get rid of it."

"What if someone comes looking for it?" Her hands are shaking like leaves in my grip. "It can't just have been misplaced."

"We'll take it to Hawk and Sparrow. They'll know what to do with it." And we'll turn it over to the right hands.

Gwenna nods jerkily. "I'm sorry. Truly. I shouldn't be involving you in this—"

"Nonsense. I'm a friend. Friends help each other out." Even as I say the words, my mind is racing. It's the weekend, so anyone could have come into the fledgling dormitory. Everyone knows that Master Jay takes off on the weekends. The nestmaid could have planted it here. A courier. Kipp is in his shell house in the kitchen, but he could have acquired the item at some point and decided to leave it in Gwenna's bag while we were at the wedding.

There's no sign of Hemmen or Arrod, either. Those two are under suspicion as well.

I want to believe Gwenna's telling the truth, I really do. But if she is, that means someone else related to this particular nest is in on things, and that means it all needs watching. I glance down at Gwenna's expression, but she's just as miserable as before, her chest heaving.

Surely it's just coincidence that Gwenna's practically got her tits out. It's not necessarily a distraction. But if it is, it's a mucking good one. If I wasn't full of knot-withering potions at the moment, I'd be all over her right now. Perhaps that was the goal?

Or am I now thinking in conspiracies, too?

EIGHTEEN

RAPTOR

One Week Later

Hawk (and Rooster),

As you both suggested, I continue to monitor the situation here in the nest.

There has been no further mention of the artifact that one of my Five claims was planted in their bag. Master Jay is unaware of the situation, and no one else is acting out of the ordinary.

If it is indeed a plant, someone is bound to come looking for it. I will remain vigilant. Furthermore, I'm going to find a way to remain at the targeted student's side for every moment. If they're the thief, I'll find out.

—Raptor

PS—I'm having to do obstacle courses alongside the other students. My pay for this undercover job had better be mucking worth it.

NINETEEN

GWENNA

Dere Ma,

Classes are continuing. I haven't had a chance to work at any odd jobs to make coin. I'm sorry. As soon as I have some I'll send it home. We are not in the tunnels yet. Master Jay wants us to learn how to do obstacle courses by hart, and that means running them blindfolded. If you don't here from me for a few weeks, it's because I fell flat on my face in one of our drills and hurt myself. Just kidding. Please don't worry. It's all part of the job. I'm looking forward to the weekend when Master Jay gives us time off.

Love you and miss you, Gwenna

IT HAS BEEN the longest week of my life.

I can't sleep. I can't eat. I can't concentrate. Every time I close my eyes, I see that stupid mucking artifact tube lighting up, and I fear I'm going to be caught. That someone's going to find out that I was somehow involved and I'll be imprisoned and booted from the guild for good.

If I am, it'll be the destruction of all the dreams I've cultivated over the last year, all the hopes for a better future. I've allowed myself to imagine what life would be like if I wasn't a maid, and I want it so badly I can taste it. I can't help but feel that I've been targeted because I'm a woman attempting to join a guild primarily full of men. That has to be the reason, doesn't it?

I'm uneasy. Even though we gave the artifact to Sparrow and Hawk and explained the situation, I'm still worried that I'm not going to be believed. That no one will care about the former maid crying foul and just get rid of me. Sparrow reassured me that it would all be handled and my name would be kept out of it, but I know it's out of her hands.

And of course this week Master Jay decides we need to start doing obstacle courses as a team. I have some experience with those from last year, but last year my team consisted of four women and Kipp, and I could hold my own with the others. This year, I'm the only woman, and it's far more difficult to keep up with the men in my group as we climb over massive stones and crawl through narrow training tunnels and sling ourselves over short walls.

Raptor makes us all look bad. Even the most physical of challenges look effortless for him, and he frequently must wait for all of us to catch up—or he pulls us through the remainder of the course.

Master Jay hates it when he does that. "They need to learn to run it on their own," he barks at a bored-seeming Raptor. "Quit helping them succeed when they cannot! You aren't doing them favors!"

Raptor just ignores that. "Being a team is about more than how well someone can climb a wall."

I kinda love him for saying it, especially since I'm short and the wall gives me the most trouble out of our team. Kipp is shorter, but he can just scramble up the side of it. Me, not so much.

I'm feeling a lot of things for Raptor right now—most of all, gratitude. He's been at my side all week, no matter what we're doing. "I'm here with you," he tells me. "No one is going to try anything while I'm around. And if they do, I'll handle it."

I've never had a male protector before, and it's so nice. Even if I'm the last one to finish the obstacle course, Raptor waits for me. If I head to the kitchen to draw a bath in the small copper tub, Raptor stands guard at the door. He checks my bag for me every time we return to our rooms. So far, there's been nothing, but I still get anxious every time we return to the dorm and I see my bag hanging on the end of the bed.

"Once more and then we're done for the day," Master Jay calls out as we drag ourselves to the front of the obstacle course again. "And this time I had better not see Raptor helping anyone!"

"Oh, he won't see it," Raptor mutters as we prepare at the starting line. Arrod stifles a snort of amusement, and Kipp wriggles in place. I put one leg forward, leaning in so I can be ready. My waist is sore from the rope attached there and me constantly being jerked forward over the course by the others in my Five. No one's complained, but I've caught a few frustrated looks that Arrod and Hemmen have sent my way.

Is it them, I wonder? Is one of them trying to get me out of training? I eye Arrod and Hemmen with uncertainty. If it is, it makes no sense. If I'm removed, our entire Five fails out. It's only after we pass the team exam that we're assessed as individuals. They need me until then.

Master Jay blows a whistle. "Begin!"

Fighting back the groan rising to my lips, I race forward with the others. My legs throb, but at this point we've run the obstacle course a dozen times today. I'm hurting but I know the motions by now—over this heap of rocks, under a set of fallen logs acting as a roadblock. Over a stack of old bricks that form a wall, dive into a too-shallow tunnel that requires we belly-crawl to the other side. Over the next obstacle. Into another crawl space. By the time I emerge from the last crawl, the others are ahead of me by quite a bit. When I get to my feet, the rope attaching us together jerks me off balance and I plant, face forward, into the muddy pit that I'm supposed to use a balance beam to get over.

I push myself up out of the mud without complaint. I need to get faster. I know I do.

"Who the muck was that?" Raptor growls as I get to my feet. I look up just in time to see him grab Arrod by the collar and shake him. "Was it you, you mucking brat? Do you think that's funny?"

"Raptor!" Master Jay says sharply, racing onto the obstacle course. "Stop it!"

He snarls at the teacher in response, and then drops Arrod and stomps to my side, his hooves like the beat of a heavy drum on the ground. Looming over me, he offers a hand.

I take it, a little surprised at his reaction. I'm even more surprised when he takes the hem of his tunic and untucks it from his belt, then uses it to wipe the mud from my face. ". . . Thank you?"

"Fucking pricks," he grumbles. "Are you all right?"

"I'm just fine." A little embarrassed that he's fussing over me in front of the others, but I like it, too.

Master Jay blows his whistle again. "That's enough today. I've seen all I can take. Be ready at dawn on Firstday, and if everything goes well, we're going to start with our first forays into the basic tunnels soon. Take the weekend to prepare yourself, as I'm not going easy on you from here on out."

And he looks at me pointedly.

Raptor catches that, too. He steps in front of me as if to protect me, and his hands go to his hips. "I'm working with Gwenna all weekend," he tells our teacher. "No need to worry."

Master Jay eyes the two of us and then grunts. "Good. You should probably work with Hemmen, too. He could use some assistance as well."

Hemmen doesn't look happy at being called out. "I don't think—"

"No," Raptor says, just as quickly. "I already promised Gwenna. Someone else can work with him."

Kipp pretends to study his boots. Arrod clears his throat and glances away.

"It's fine," Hemmen says. He pushes his messy hair back from his face. "I'll just go to the library and study more."

"Excellent idea," Master Jay says. "I want no failures in this class."

No one says anything to refute that. We don't want to fail, either. In silence, we untie ourselves and leave the obstacle course, following Master Jay back through the heart of the city to the nest. My boots are full of mud and my clothes are sticking to my skin, but I'm not going to complain about any of it. I'm ready for the day to be over. A nice, quick bath by the hearth and a chunk of bread and some cheese for dinner, and I'll be back to normal. Maybe I'll even borrow one of Hemmen's books and see if I can brush up on some Old Prellian. I try not to glance at Raptor too much as we walk. He's at my side, his body full of tension as if he feels the need to protect me. I don't know what to do with that. It's sweet and makes me want to smile far too much, so I keep my face averted.

The walk back to the nest takes forever. The obstacle course is along the side of the large wall that separates the Royal Artifactual Guild from the rest of busy, overcrowded Vastwarren. Master Jay's particular dormitory is on the edge of the central square, so it's a fair bit of walking. By the time the massive statue of Sparkanos the Swan comes into view, I'm exhausted. It takes me a moment to realize the others are slowing their steps, and a rumbling growl starts low in Kipp's throat. He moves to my side and puts a small hand on my leg to get my attention as I almost walk into Master Jay's back.

The guild master stands in place for a moment, staring at the nest with his symbol flag hanging above the door. Every window in the dormitory is open, trunks and gear spilling into the street as a frantic Marta, the nestmaid, wrings her hands. What looks like a dozen of the guild enforcers with their green sashes are moving in and out of the dorm.

"What's the meaning of this?" Master Jay squawks.

A man with a gold-bordered green sash and a large symbolic patch on his sleeve holds out a piece of parchment. "We have orders to search all of the fledgling nests."

My blood goes cold. I bite back a gasp, but I feel faint.

"Did this come from Head Guild Master Rooster?" Master Jay sounds indignant and confused. He strides forward, snatching the letter from the guild enforcer.

The enforcer just crosses his arms over his chest. "It came from the head of investigations in the enforcer department, which has full approval from the guild and the king himself to perform independent searches. We are following up on an anonymous tip about students stealing artifacts."

"My students would never!"

"Then you've nothing to worry about," the enforcer drawls. "Now let us finish conducting our search."

Master Jay throws his hands up in frustration. Hemmen makes a whining sound in his throat, dropping to the cobblestones and sitting down, the picture of exhaustion.

"What do we do, Master?" Arrod asks.

Master Jay paces back and forth, then shrugs. "We sit out here and wait until they're done."

Great. I'm not going to breathe until then. My thoughts keep whirling. I was right. I was right all along. Someone's trying to get rid of me. I have no doubt in my mind that whoever dumped that artifact in my bag is responsible for the anonymous note to the enforcers. I just hope that they didn't somehow plant another artifact during the last few days. The thought makes me want to vomit.

A heavy arm loops around my shoulders, and I'm dragged backward a half step against Raptor's big body. He leans over me, so big he blots out the late-afternoon sunlight. "Calm down. They're not going to find anything."

"We don't know that."

"We do. We gave it to Aspeth, remember? She's going to stick it in a box in the archives and tell them it was misplaced in their records and not to worry." He rests his muzzle atop my head in a friendly manner and, when I don't relax, leans in. His muzzle moves near my ear and he continues. "If you stand here all white-faced and stiff, they're going to suspect something is wrong. Try being a little more relaxed."

Oh sure. Relax while enforcers turn our nest upside down looking for an artifact I know was planted to get me in trouble. *Relax.*

Relax and hope no one dies nearby and I start hearing the dead babbling.

Raptor presses lightly on my shoulders, and I drop them, releasing some of the tension in my body. He's right about one thing—if I look guilty, I'm going to make them wonder. I turn to the slitherskin, who has set his shell on the ground and perches atop it with an inscrutable expression. "What are your plans for this weekend, Kipp?"

Kipp looks over at me and then proceeds with a flurry of gestures that I can't make out. Something about dancing. Or fishing. I'm not entirely sure which. But I nod brightly, as if he's told me something charming.

"What do you want to practice this weekend, Gwenna?" Raptor asks, keeping that lazy arm around my shoulders. "Any particular skills you feel the need to brush up on?"

"All of them?" I manage to sound like my normal sarcastic self with that and relax a bit more. "In all seriousness, I need help with a great many things, but I'm open to suggestions."

Raptor squeezes my upper arm. "Could probably work on your strength and endurance before anything else. As a woman, you're going to need every advantage possible when it comes time for the test."

I bristle at his words, though I know he's saying it from a place not of sexism but of brutal honesty. I do need to be as good as I possibly can at everything. Better than good. Excellent. Because no one's going to cut me any slack at all. "I don't mind working on fitness."

"I do love it when a woman wants to get sweaty with me."

Shoving his arm off my shoulders, I step out of his embrace. "Don't be repugnant."

Kipp huffs with amusement.

Arrod joins our group, a curious look on his face. "What are you three talking about?"

"Sweating together," Raptor drawls. "You weren't invited."

Kipp huffs again, his lizardy version of laughter.

Arrod isn't deterred by Raptor's commentary. He just grins at me knowingly. "Is that how it is, then?"

"Is that how what is?" I ask, voice icy.

"Getting a little extra *tutoring* in?" He gives me an obvious wink.

"You're disgusting," I tell him. Then I turn to Raptor. "You are, too." I turn back to Arrod and point at him. "But you're worse, because I know you mean it, and he doesn't."

Kipp falls off his shell, clutching his sides and wheezing in that silent slitherskin laughter of his.

By the time the search is done, the sun has almost completely set, and Master Jay is furious at how long it's taking for the enforcers to move the trunks and boxes of goods back into the nest. "I have somewhere to be," he says, voice as shrill as his namesake. "What are the results?"

"You're clean," the enforcer captain finally says. He twirls a finger at his men. "Wrap it up, boys. We'll move on to the next one."

I manage to remain stone-faced at this announcement, though my insides have turned into a puddle of mush. They found nothing. I eye everyone around, but no one seems guilty or annoyed. Kipp is watching with a bored expression as the men pick up trunks. Hemmen is cleaning under his nails with the edge of a knife, and Arrod is busy flirting with Marta, the nestmaid, who looks fluttery with delight at his attention. I'll warn her about him.

Once I give myself a moment to collapse in sheer relief, that is.

TWENTY

RAPTOR

Rooster:

Our nest was searched recently due to an anonymous tip, which is ironic. Someone's investigating my team at the same time I am. Nothing was found, given that we handed the artifact over to you. Makes me wonder what their goal is, though.

Still monitoring the situation. I have it all under control.

—R

I PLAN ON WAKING Gwenna early the next day for training, if for nothing else than to see the sleepy, grumpy expression on her face when I rouse her. She's normally the one who wakes up earlier than all of us, and says it's been brought on by years of working in a household and rousing before dawn. So today I get up while it's still dark outside and give her bed a quick shake.

She doesn't fling her arms out or bolt upright like most would at such an unexpected interruption. Rather, her eyes fly open and she looks around, her body still. I wave a hand at her in the darkness.

I'm rewarded with the charming scowl I'd hoped for. "It's dark out." Her voice is a low whisper. "What do you want?"

"I think we should get out of here for training before someone else tags along." I thumb a gesture at the two bunks at the far end of the room, indicating Arrod and Hemmen.

Her eyes widen and she sits up, nodding. Gwenna grabs her bag and pads away to the garderobe, no doubt to change into her uniform. I dress, too, but it's easier for me because I don't care if the others see me naked. Once I tuck in my guild shirt, I fasten the lightweight fledgling sash to my shoulder. It feels odd, given that I've been used to wearing my regular artificer sash with its many pins denoting the discoveries I've made. I'm eager to have it back.

When I'm ready, I glance over at the other beds. Kipp's bed is empty and neatly made, and I suspect I'll find him in the kitchen again. Beyond his bed is Hemmen's bunk, with its occupant snoring and clutching a book to his chest, two others by his pillow. On his other side is Arrod, who sleeps sprawled on his belly, still dressed in last night's clothing. Guessing from his appearance, he reeks of alcohol and late-night choices.

Good. If he's nursing a hangover, it means he'll leave me and Gwenna alone. I don't want either of them tagging along.

I shut the doors to the sleeping quarters with a gentle hand and head for the kitchen. I run into Gwenna in the hall, and she quickly deposits her bag just outside the room before marching back to the kitchen. I follow her, amused at her authoritative manner. She bustles about in the kitchen, slicing bread and fruit. Then she hands me one plate and adds a bit of honey to hers. "We'll eat a quick bite first, if that's all right."

The plate she gave me is full of fruits and nuts and a huge chunk of bread. I grin at her because she's already memorized what a Taurian likes to eat. She'll make a good mate to someone someday. Then I squash that thought because she wants to be an artificer, and most men won't want their wife to work. They'll expect her to make a home and produce babies. She needs to marry an artificer if she marries anyone, I decide. Someone who understands the job and won't expect her to put aside her wants and needs for him. She needs a Taurian, who will appreciate her generous curves and tart tongue.

But when I mentally go through the list of Taurians in the guild, I find myself growing jealous at the thought of one of them getting Gwenna's smiles.

Sarya, I remind myself. You want Sarya.

I'm starting to wonder if I do, though. I don't know anything about her other than she was bossy in bed and didn't pause at my knot or my size. She might hate animals, or she might eat nothing but red meat. She might be one of those types that interrupts a person all the time, or insists on being right in every conversation. I don't *know* her even though we had intense, explosive sex.

Perhaps I've been chasing after the wrong woman all this time. But it's not as if I should be chasing Gwenna right now, either. She's a fledgling in my Five and off-limits until we graduate.

Perhaps my cock needs to calm the muck down. But it's my nature to constantly be thinking about sex, given that the god's hand is always upon me. The potion quiets some of the constant need, but when it wears off, my thoughts veer in sultry directions, and right now, I'm appreciating Gwenna as she slices a bit more bread, her arse outlined deliciously by her guild pants.

"Kipp's asleep," she whispers as she takes her plate and sits next to me at the table. "I cut him up some breakfast, too. Hopefully he'll get to it before the others wake up."

I grunt and eat my food, staring at my plate because I want to watch her eat and I know I shouldn't. If she licks her fingers once, I'm going to grab her and pull her pants down.

And mucking hells, where did that idea come from? I shove the last of my bread into my mouth and gesture at the hall. "Hitting the necessary first."

I go into the garderobe and stare at the last bit of my potion, considering. Do I take it? Or do I continue to have filthy thoughts about the wrong woman? In the end, I put the potion back in its hiding place under the sink and splash cold water on my face instead. I'll be cranky as all hells, but I won't be numb below the waist, at least.

Soon, Sarya. I promise.

We meet up in the hall, and I watch her brush crumbs off the corners of her mouth as we approach the front of the dormitory. "So where are we heading today?"

I've thought about that for a bit. I open the front door, glancing over at her. "We'll see if we can get on one of the obstacle courses and take it at a more forgiving pace. . . ."

I trail off as the door opens and reveals Hawk, his fist up as if he was about to knock on the door. He blinks at the two of us and then grins. "Well, this is fortuitous."

"Is it?" I ask. I'm curious as to what's going on and why he'd be on our doorstep so early, but I'm also slightly annoyed, because whatever it is, I suspect it means I'm not going to get to spend time with Gwenna.

And I don't trust anyone else to watch her closely enough to keep her safe.

Hawk doesn't notice my shitty mood. He just grins and cocks his head, indicating the buildings behind him. "I need several strong backs to dig out Drop Seventeen. No one's injured or in the tunnel, but the path is collapsed and there's a team scheduled to descend there on First-day. Head Guild Master Rooster is paying double time to any Taurians who want to make a bit of coin, and I thought of you."

Ah. Normally I'd be glad, because these kinds of jobs are how Taurians make coin on the side. We're the backbone of the guild and do all the heavy lifting. But digging in the tunnels means that Gwenna can't go. Then again, why not? If I'm there to supervise her, what's the harm? "I'm a fledgling," I point out to him. "Does that matter?"

"Not to me. And if it bothers Master Jay when he returns, I'll tell him it was my idea," Hawk offers. "I've also got Osprey and Gyrfalcon, but I could really use more."

I nod to my friend. "I'll go . . . but I need Gwenna to come along."

Hawk does a double take. "What?" His gaze flicks over to her and then to me. "I don't think—"

"If you say she can't come because she's a fledgling, I'll remind you that I'm one, too." I give him my most cheerful grin. "And she's not going to wander off, because she's got a brain. She needs experience in the tunnels, and what better time than for her to go with several veteran Taurians?"

Gwenna's mouth drops open. "You want me to dig?"

"No, I want you to hold the lamp and our canteens and basically observe," I point out. "I promised I'd keep you at my side all weekend, and that means now, too."

Her jaw snaps shut and she glances over at Hawk. "I don't want to be a bother. . . ."

"You always say that, and you never are," I reassure her before Hawk can reply. "And if it's a problem, Hawk will just have to find others to help him. My priority is spending time with you and helping you get ready for the tests. That hasn't changed. This will be excellent on-site training, if you ask me."

And I look at Hawk, daring him to object.

He crosses his arms over his chest. "Oh, do I get to speak now? Since you've already decided everything?"

I grin at my friend. "She won't be a problem. Gwenna's excellent at hiding in the fringes."

I'll keep her safe . . . and keep an eye on her. If she's the thief, she won't have time to plot. And if she isn't, then it's for the best that she stick with me anyhow. Really, this is better than an obstacle course.

When Hawk throws his hands up, I know I've won. "Come on," Hawk says. "There's a lot of digging to be done between now and Firstday."

TWENTY-ONE

GWENNA

"ARE YOU CERTAIN this is a good idea?" I race after Raptor as we head into the designated "drop" area at the far end of the walled-off guild quarters.

"Why wouldn't it be?" Raptor strides ahead of me, a pack, a shovel, and a pickaxe strapped to his broad back. A few steps ahead, four other Taurians are walking together, all of us headed for the same location. They all take huge steps, and I'm forced to jog to keep up with them.

"Because Master Jay is going to lose his mind if he finds out we've been noodling about in the tunnels! We're not allowed!"

He pauses and I practically run into him. "Incorrect."

"What's incorrect?"

"The rules state that fledglings are not given work permits for the tunnels. No one will let you work without a work permit, so it's moot." He takes the two enormous canteens that are slung over my arm and pulls them over his head, shouldering their heavy weight easily. "And you're not working anyhow. You're *observing. I'm* the one who's working."

And he gives me a dazzling smile that makes me all flustered inside.

"I just don't want to get into trouble," I protest again, but my words are fainter this time.

"No one's going to fail you for coming with us," Raptor reassures me.

"You're going to have five chaperones who will all report back to Master Jay that you touched nothing and simply held the lamps and some water for us. It's not a bad thing for you to come down here, get some experience being in the caves and all that."

"I've been in the caves before," I remind him. Last year's disastrous training involved us going down into the tunnels multiple times, only for us to get into all kinds of trouble.

"Yes, and you were with Master Magpie. The less said about that, the better, frankly. This will be different." He casts me another easy look. "I'll take care of you. No worries."

I'm not worried about him not looking out for me. I'm more worried about what I'm going to feel when we go down into the tunnels. Every other time I went down into the Everbelow—the vast warren of tunnels and ruins that carve out Vastwarren's underbelly like cheese—I'd be buzzing all over from the dead I'd sense. At first, I thought it was nerves, but now I know it was a lot more.

I'm also worried that I'm going to feel things too strongly and need to distract myself again or else I'll give away my worst secret—that I might be a necromancer. But I can't tell Raptor any of that, so I just nod and trot after him, clutching my fears to my chest.

We pass another secure walled area, Hawk flashing his authorization to let us through. Our group consists of Hawk, Raptor, a big older Taurian named Osprey, and two younger Taurians I don't recognize. They don't blink an eye when I join them, probably noting my fledgling sash and marking this as some sort of training.

Then we're in what's called the drop zone and I'm reminded of just how ugly the heart of the city truly is. You would think that digging for artifacts in an ancient, buried city beneath our feet would mean that we're traipsing through marble ruins and old buildings. That's what I thought, at least, when Aspeth first described things to me. Instead, the actual work area entrance looks like nothing more than a bunch of holes dug into the earth with scaffolding built around them. The entire field is covered in mud and tracks, and big gaping holes are scattered about, with rope-and-pulley systems for lowering artificers into the ruins.

I always thought it'd be more dramatic than that, but no. We're tossed in like a bunch of bloody miners and expected to just wander about below as if we know what we're doing. Sometimes the guild strikes me as utterly ridiculous.

Half of the Taurian team heads down first, and I'm in the second group. We wait for the basket to return and then climb in while a repeater turns a crank and lowers us to the appropriate level. The basket lurches along, swaying as we're dropped down the tunnel, and I force myself to pay attention to my surroundings. As we go down deep into the earth, the sunlight above disappears, replaced by the dim glow from various artifacts lodged along the sides of the pit we descend. Sparrow told me once that artifacts that provide light are rather common, and so the guild uses them to illuminate the tunnels. I watch as we approach a glowing teacup and then pass it, followed by a small glowing stone of some kind, and then what looks like a candleholder with no candle. All the while, the basket creaks and continues to jerk downward.

Raptor leans over to me. "You nervous?"

"Just wondering if the repeaters have ever dropped a basket too far," I whisper back.

"Aye, and a Taurian was sent to clean that mess up, too."

I jerk to look at Raptor in shock, but the twinkle in his eye tells me that he's joking. I pinch his arm to let him know I don't find that funny, and his grin grows even broader. He leans in close to say something else, but I don't hear it, because the basket drops into a large, echoing cavern, and then the buzz of a thousand long-dead bodies hits me like a slap to the face.

I'm dimly aware of Raptor sliding an arm around my waist even as the buzz grows greater and greater. My skin breaks out in a cold sweat, my guild shirt sticking to me immediately. It's like we've dropped to a new level and I'm in close enough range to feel everything now. It's stronger than ever before, and I don't know how to make it stop. Nor do I know how I'm going to stay down here all day with them, pretending that nothing is wrong.

The basket creaks to a stop, and the entire thing sways. A bolt of fear flashes through me, and I clutch at Raptor to keep my footing.

"Easy now," he soothes. "I've got you."

I suck in a deep breath, noticing that the sharp, sudden fear chased the worst of the prickling sensations away. A distraction. That's what I need to get through the day. No one needs to know that I'm struggling.

One of the big Taurians pulls a hooked rod out of the oversized basket and uses it to latch on to an iron circle sticking out of the rock over a tunnel. A big 21 is painted on the side of the wall next to an arrow pointing deeper into the earth, showing our destination. The basket is tugged over to the lip of the tunnel and we all climb out—or rather, Raptor hoists me out and sets me down on solid ground.

Once the basket is sent back up, an oil lamp is lit and the three big Taurians stare at me.

"She gonna pass out?" one asks. "Looks pale."

"Just a bit of motion sickness. She's fine now, aren't you, Gwenna?" Raptor rubs my arm, the one more distant from him, and it still feels as if he's keeping me hauled against him. He probably is, just in case.

"I'm good," I manage. "It was dizziness, but it's gone."

It's not gone. The unnerving sensation is building back up, and I manage a bright smile for the others even as they shoot me disapproving looks. I focus on their sashes instead. Two artificers with a great many Lesser Artifact pins on their sashes. Raptor's wearing the same unadorned pale white sash as mine, that of a fledgling. I wonder if this is humiliating for him.

The Taurian whose name I don't recall holds out the oil lamp, set carefully atop a shoulder-height walking stick (my shoulder, not theirs), and I take it from him. "If I've got the lamp, should I be in the front?"

"You can be at the rear," Osprey says. "We can see just fine in near darkness."

Of course. It's another reason Taurians are so prized in the Everbelow. I nod and take the canteens that Raptor hands back to me, slinging them over my neck. "Lead on, then."

Raptor shoots me another worried glance, but when our party takes off and I gesture that he should follow, he does. I trail behind them, putting a hand on one metal canteen to stop it from banging against my gut. It scratches me, and I realize there's a hard metal shard sticking out of the side. It's no bigger than a hangnail, but it's enough to hurt when it bites into my hand.

It's also enough to distract, so as I walk, I push my hand against the shard, over and over again. It keeps the buzz at bay, and I'm able to concentrate a bit more.

It's been nearly a year since I've been down in the tunnels, and from what I've heard from others, there's a variety of shapes and sizes. Some of the older, more excavated tunnels have walls that have been smoothed down from all the artificer traffic moving through them, while others seem to be carved from jagged rock. Some are tight, with little headroom, and some are big enough that one could drag that ridiculously huge statue of Sparkanos through with no problem. This particular tunnel is closer to the latter, with a high ceiling and a practically roomy size. The floor is worn down and slopes deeply the farther we go in. The blackness around us gets more and more intense, and the air grows colder, and I'm reminded of just how deep into the earth we are. If it wasn't for the lamp I'm holding and the fact that I've got three strong Taurians walking in front of me, I'd probably be a little panicked right now.

But the dead feel no nearer, and the tunnel isn't getting smaller, so even the intense darkness at the edges of the light becomes normal after a time. The Taurians talk cheerfully amongst themselves as if I'm not there, discussing what the harvest is going to be like in the southern plains due to this year's drought; the Greater Artifact that was uncovered by an artificer named Pelican, whom no one seems to like; the best place to get corn cakes in the city.

It's all so completely normal that I relax. Stab my hand with that sliver of metal again and again, and relax.

Soon enough, we reach the crumbled part of the tunnel and reunite with the others. The buzzing feeling is less awful here, so I'm able to slow down the hand-stabbing a bit. The big tunnel is blocked off by what looks like a jumble of rocks of all sizes, and I wonder what caused the cave-in. The others in our group—Hawk and another Taurian—are gazing at the rocks, assessing the situation. "We've got big pieces to move, so that's both good and bad. Good in that they'll be easier to take care of, bad because they're heavy," Hawk says.

"Heavy for puny humans, you mean," brags a Taurian, and flexes his bicep. The others snort with amusement.

I clear my throat.

They look over at me, startled, and the one flexing his arm immediately lowers it. Raptor just gives me an utterly amused grin. "Yeah, not all humans are bad. Some of them are rather adorable."

"Oh gods, you're just as bad as the rest of them," I say, waving a hand as if to shoo him off.

They laugh again, and Hawk points at the largest boulder. "We'll start there. Who's got the wand?"

Osprey pulls it free and holds it against the tunnel wall, drawing a massive circle. As he does, it lights up and creates a portal. Sunlight spills in from the portal, and on the other side, a bored-looking repeater jumps to his feet and straightens the black sash on his shoulder. He's standing in what looks like a rock quarry, and as I watch, the portal seems to tilt, facing what looks like the edge of a gigantic hole.

"Ready over there?" Osprey calls.

"Ready—send through as you please. The portal's in place."

Osprey turns back to Hawk. "There we go."

"All right. Let's get moving. Be on the lookout for signs of a man-made collapse. Scorch marks, unusual debris, or even broken artifacts."

"You think this was deliberate?" Raptor asks.

"We're going to rule it out" is all Hawk says.

I shiver at that and jab my hand again.

Raptor glances back at me, no doubt making sure that I'm all right. I give him an overbright smile and step back as the Taurians gather around the largest boulder, debating how to maneuver it. "If we pull it free, it could cause more of a rockfall than already exists," says Osprey.

"If it does, then this tunnel is no use to us anyhow. Besides, I've never met a Taurian who got bested by a mere tunnel collapse." Hawk's words are challenging, meant to fire them up.

Raptor just rubs his hands together. "Let's earn ourselves some coin, aye?"

TWENTY-TWO

RAPTOR

GWENNA'S PRESENCE IS quiet and unobtrusive as we haul rocks from the collapsed tunnel and shove them through the portal to the quarry. Her silence is a bit unusual to me, but perhaps she's just not used to being around so many loud Taurians in their element.

For all that it's hard work, I enjoy clearing tunnels. It's one of the rare occasions when multiple Taurian artificers are called together, and we're all close friends. Hawk talks about his students and what it's like to be a master for the first time. Gyrfalcon brags about the latest find his Five made, Osprey provides sour commentary to deflate Gyrfalcon's ego, and Shikra is silent, but he always is. He's a hard worker, and I catch him smiling at a few of Osprey's terrible jokes, so it's not as if he's miserable.

They rib me about my fledgling sash, but I know it's all in good fun. They can't know the real reason why I've been busted down, so I just joke that I got caught with my hands where they shouldn't be, and when Osprey opens his mouth to make a crass joke, I point at him and silence him before he can offend Gwenna.

Not that I think she'd be offended. It's hard to know what will bother her and what won't. I do know we wouldn't be making these kinds of cracks in front of Hawk's wife, Sparrow, or any of the women who work as nestmaids. Gwenna seems like she has a tough hide and can take a joke, but I also know she's alone in a tunnel with five Taurians, and that can make anyone uneasy.

The rocks don't crumble as we pull them free, and the ceiling's collapse isn't nearly as bad as we thought it could be. The farther we dig, the more the rocks turn into what look like old bricks, common for the endless ruins in the tunnels. Sure enough, once the broken bricks are cleared away, the cause of the cave-in is determined—a new shaft has opened above, the now-removed ceiling leading into what looks like another open chamber. It's a siren call to an artificer, and all of us are eager to explore. "Could be something good up there," Gyrfalcon says. "If someone wants to lift me up, I can take a look."

"Can't," Hawk says. "Our orders are for clearing the tunnel alone. Excavating and artifact hunting are for the team that comes in after us."

"You're no fun."

"It's because I'm in charge. You don't get to be fun when you're in charge."

I chuckle at that, and glance back at Gwenna. She's still holding the oil lamp in place, the canteens at her feet. At my attention, she gives me a small, seemingly distracted smile. Maybe she's growing tired. We've been here for a while now, and a Taurian's strength is many times greater than a human's, especially one with a smaller stature like her. "Let's save the fun for some other time," I drawl, turning back to the others. "Some of us want to get dinner soon."

We finish clearing. Osprey shuts down the portal and thanks the repeater on the other side, and the last of the water is drunk, the empty canteens handed back to Gwenna. My stomach rumbles and I stretch, trying not to seem too obvious as I check on my human companion. Is that sweat on her brow? "Can we take off?" I ask Hawk. "We need to check in with the rest of our Five."

It's a lie—I couldn't care less if Arrod and Hemmen fall off a cliff, and Kipp won't worry about us. But I can't shake the feeling that I need to get Gwenna out of here.

Hawk nods, studying the walls of the cleared tunnel ahead of us. "I'm going to stay behind and make sure things are stable before heading up."

"I'll join you," Osprey tells him, and the others don't look as if they're ready to go just yet. Likely they're going to pressure Hawk to explore that new cavern the moment we leave, but I don't care. I can't get paid for a discovery like that anyhow.

I take the oil lamp from Gwenna and hand it to Osprey. She's got the empty canteens around her neck again, her hand pressed to one of them as if to hold it in place.

"Do we need to see our way out?" she asks, voice shaky.

"I can guide us back to the drop point," I tell her. "Do you need the light? Are you frightened?"

"I'm all right. I just don't want to get lost."

"I can hold your hand," I offer. "Or you can hold on to my belt. Just not the tail. Wouldn't want you getting the wrong idea."

My joke doesn't land. She reaches forward, feeling for my arm in the low light, and then clasps my hand tightly in her sweaty one.

"Come on," I tell her, keeping my voice soothing with encouragement. "It's been years since I've been lost, and this tunnel's so basic even Hemmen could navigate it."

That earns a small, trembling laugh from her.

We head for the drop, the long, wide tunnel echoing with the clop of my hooves on stone. Gwenna is silent, her hand tightly clutching mine, and I wonder at what's bothering her. The dark? The tunnels? Some students can't hack being underground. Given that she's been in the tunnels in the past and never voiced complaint, I didn't think it would bother her. Spiders?

Or is she still rattled from yesterday's search?

"You want to talk about it?" I ask her in the darkness.

"No."

"I can tell something's bothering you."

"I also just said I don't want to talk about it."

"Fair enough." There's a faint wink of light up ahead from the tunnel shaft, and I gesture to it despite the darkness. "We're almost there."

She doesn't respond, but her hand clenches tighter around mine. She continues to hold on to me as I jerk the bell chain to let the person above know that we need a ride. When the basket drops to our level, we get into the lift. I let go of her hand to ring the bell to let him know we need to go up, and the entire thing sways wildly due to the imbalance in our weights. She clutches at the side of the basket with both hands, and I can smell her fear-sweat.

"It's fine," I tell her, bracing my hooves. "I just need to move toward the center. Happens all the time with a Taurian in a lift. . . ."

It's then that I notice her hands. Both are rigidly clutching the side of the basket lift, and one is covered in blood that she's smearing all over the side of the basket.

TWENTY-THREE

GWENNA

THE BASKET SWAYS, and even though I know it's not going to tip over and dump me into the depths of Vastwarren, I can't help but reflexively reach for it. My hands grip the side, and the cut one sends a searing bolt of pain up my arm.

It's more than welcome, because ever since they opened that tunnel, my skin's been crawling like mad. Whatever's up there is long dead and won't stay quiet in my head. I hear disembodied whispers floating through my mind, speaking in languages I don't understand. I can feel the presence of their bodies, just like I can feel the oppressive fog of the many dead still lost in the tunnels.

"Gwenna," Raptor says, his voice dimly breaking through the cacophony in my head. "What happened to your hand?"

Right. My hand. I squeeze the injured one tightly, making it hurt, and some of the fog clears away again. "It's nothing."

"You're bleeding."

"I was just trying to focus." I squeeze it tight again and again, trying to chase the fog away entirely so I can focus long enough to get out of the drop without having a nervous breakdown.

He grabs my wrist, forcing me to stop, and immediately the voices whisper in my head again. I whimper, even as he looms over me. "Why are you doing this?"

"Figured . . . you wouldn't be into fucking right now. . . ." I wanted it to be a joke, but I'm not thinking clearly or Raptor isn't in a laughing mood. I'm dimly aware of him staring at me like I've lost my mind. Maybe I have. "It's fine. I'm not on birth control."

"What are you babbling about?" The basket sways, and he instinctively puts an arm around me.

I lean in close, liking that far more than I should. "Taurians are fertile. Aspeth told me. Shit. I used her old name. Sparrow. Sparrow told me."

"You're babbling."

"I know." My thoughts are all over the place, drifting away, and trying to focus is like trying to catch a handful of fog. "Sorry. You know that Taurians are fertile. I don't have to explain it to you."

"A Taurian is only fertile when the god's hand is upon him, Gwenna. When he has a knot." He leans over me, smelling my breath. "Are you drunk? Because you sound drunk."

"Not drunk." Though I do feel like I'm drunk, a little. Mostly just foggy, as if there's too much going on in my head and I don't know where to focus.

The basket rises to the surface, and the worker waiting nearby hooks it with a staff and drags it to the edge of the platform. Raptor lodges his arm tightly around my waist and carries me over onto solid ground like I'm a satchel. Then he eyes the great many pits that dot the area, sighs, picks me up again, and heads out of the drop zone.

"Sorry," I mumble.

"Did you breathe in something strange? Eat a mushroom? Lick some strange moss while we were down there?"

"Nope." I giggle, my head clearing a little. "Why, do I sound like I was licking moss?"

"You were asking about knots. Most Taurians are only fertile during the Conquest Moon, when the knot rises."

"Oh, did yours go away? I didn't realize." Him carrying me is making things worse, I think. He moves through the streets at such a rapid pace that I'm bobbing back and forth, swaying far more than I did when I was in the basket. "Can—can you put me down?"

But he's already coming to a halt, his feet slowing. Raptor stares down at me. "What do you mean, did mine go away?"

"I don't mean anything," I tell him, a little faint from all the jostling. At least now I can breathe. The voices are going quiet, and all that's left is the awful itching sensation on my skin that makes me want to tear it off. That takes longer to fade, I've learned.

He puts me down and then grabs my arm before I can move away. "Sarya?"

Shit.

TWENTY-FOUR

RAPTOR

I CAN'T BELIEVE WHAT I'm hearing. How the muck does Gwenna know that I have a knot? Only a sex worker could tell her the truth— or maybe Naiah, who supplies my potions—but the women I go to know that I pay extra for their silence. There's only one way that Gwenna would know that about my body. . . .

I close my eyes and put my hands on her hips, ignoring her startled squeal as I grope her in the street. I've imagined getting Sarya in my arms again so many times. I still know what she felt like, and she felt like . . . this. I open my eyes again just in time for Gwenna to slap my hands away. "A tall, busty blonde, eh?"

"I have no idea what you're talking about," Gwenna says in a prim voice.

"Admit it. You're Sarya." I've cursed that blindfold and my healing eyes a dozen times over since that fateful day. I'm practically giddy with relief that she's stumbled over her own words and shown herself to me. If she truly is Sarya, this is the best possible outcome for me. I haven't been neglecting locating the woman I'm obsessed with. She's not a figment of my fevered imagination. She's been right here under my nose the entire time.

And considering that I'm wildly attracted to Gwenna, this is perfect.

"I don't know what you're talking about." She puts her nose in the air, glaring up at me. "Now, if you don't mind, I'm tired and hungry and I'd like to go home."

"First, tell me that you're Sarya." I move to stand in front of her, blocking the street. "There's no point in lying any longer."

"I don't know what it is that you think I'm lying about," she maintains, but her cheeks are bright pink with color. Far better than the bleached white they were down in the caverns. She's bothered by my words.

She's bothered because she's been caught in a mucking lie. How has she hidden who she is all this time? How has she not said anything to me?

Unless there are more secrets she's hiding from me . . . like being the thief.

Surely not. I can't picture her as the thief in question. I can't picture Gwenna—or Sarya—working with a bunch of cutthroats, opening up necks the moment a foolish repeater is no longer needed. It doesn't match what I know of Gwenna. She can be a little jaded at times, sure, but who isn't? And she cares for those she views as her family.

Gwenna's cagey responses just irritate me. I point a finger in her face. "You and I are going back to the nest, and you are going to do some serious explaining."

She swats my finger away from her face with her good hand. "There's nothing to explain! Just leave me be."

As if I could possibly walk away from a mystery like this without getting to the bottom of it? After learning that she's Sarya?

She might not be the thief, but it doesn't mean she's not working with him. Or her.

I fight the incredible urge to throw her over my knee and spank her. Then again, that might not be irritation making me want to do that. It might be pure lust. I'm off my potion, so I'm going to be impulsive and turned on. There's a small part of me that feels an overwhelming sense of relief that Sarya isn't missing or hiding from me. That she's been here all along.

That the charmingly tart human I've been fighting my attraction for is the woman I've been dreaming about, even if she lied to me.

But there are a few too many lies for me to be comfortable. Not when my task is to ferret out the truth of the conspiracy going on. I say nothing, just turn things over in my head as we walk across Vastwarren's heart and return to the dorms.

When we get to Master Jay's nest, Gwenna immediately heads for the necessary. I glance in the sleeping quarters, but they're empty. Checking the rest of the house, I find only the nestmaid, busy chopping vegetables. "Get out," I tell her. "You're done for the day."

The woman turns around, her mouth opening. "I don't—"

"Out," I say again, putting a growl in my voice. The woman nods, terrified, and races out of the kitchen, wiping her hands on her apron.

As she races away, Gwenna enters, a towel around her hand. She frowns at me as if I'm the problem. "What did you say to Marta?"

"I told her to leave."

"She has work to do. It's not her fault you're in a shitty mood." She moves to the counter, eyeing the unfinished vegetable chopping on the counter. "If someone complains they weren't fed, she's going to be the one who gets in trouble."

"No one's here but you and me," I point out. Even Kipp's shell isn't in the corner it usually inhabits. "Which means we're going to talk about what's going on."

"There's nothing to talk about." Gwenna picks up the discarded chopping knife with her good hand and attacks the vegetables.

I move to her side and pluck the blade out of her grip, ignoring the glare she shoots at me. "I want to know what your game is."

"I cannot even begin to know what you're talking about," she says with a huffed laugh.

"Probably because you've been lying to me so much you can't even keep your own stories straight." That earns me a dirty look, which confirms that I'm on the right track. "Give me your hand."

She shoots me an indignant glare.

I gesture that she should hold it out. "Just let me see it. I'm not going to sit here and watch you chop up vegetables while you're bleeding and in pain."

Her jaw clenches, her expression mulish. Well, I can be stubborn, too.

I hold my palm out, waiting patiently. Eventually she slaps her hand into mine. I gently pull the towel off, and I'm not entirely surprised to see that she hasn't tended to her wounds. "Why didn't you put an ointment on this?"

"Why are you fussing over me?"

Gwenna is being unusually grouchy, and there's a distracted look on her face, as if she's having trouble concentrating. Her pupils seem a little wider than normal, her gaze a bit glassy. Is something else bothering her? As the most experienced on the team, without Master Jay around, it's my duty to look after her. At least, that's what I tell myself, since I'm going to fuss. I pick her up, settling her backside on the counter next to the cutting board. "You sit right here and wait for me to get the salve. If I come back and you've moved, I will hunt you down and pin you to the ground until you let me doctor your hand."

Her jaw drops and she makes a sound of protest . . . but she doesn't get off the counter.

Good. "I'll be right back."

I head across the kitchen, pulling open the cabinet that every nest is stocked with—herbs and potions for headaches and muscle aches, bandages for wrapping twisted ankles, and a tea that helps the too-tightly-wound sleep at night. I pull out a small jar of ointment and a roll of bandages and move back to Gwenna's side.

This time, she doesn't protest, just extends her hand toward me.

I tend to her brutalized palm, saying nothing as I wash her hand with water and then dab the herb-laced ointment on her skin. "Did something happen when we were down in the caverns? Something that caused this?"

She doesn't answer.

"If there's something dangerous down there, it affects more than me and you, Gwenna. Tell me."

"I did it to myself," she says after a moment. "No need to fuss."

She tries to pull her hand away again, but I refuse to release her. "I'm not done. Hold still." I finish with the ointment and then carefully wrap the bandages around her hand. "If you did this to yourself, why?"

Again, she hesitates. "Focus. I needed to focus."

I've heard of people injuring themselves to block out mental anguish. Is that what this is? "What did you need to focus on?"

She's silent again.

"You're quiet."

"You're not listening to me when I say anything, so why should I try?"

I hesitate. Is it possible that I'm wrong? Is it possible that she's not Sarya and I'm racing off with the idea like a fool? I pretend to fuss over the bandages and close my eyes to focus. "Say my name."

"I'm not doing anything for you when you're behaving like an arse." Her tone is indignant, but there's no question in my mind that it's Sarya after all. With my eyes closed, there's no mistaking it. How did I never see this before? Have I been so blinded by the thought of a tall blonde that I never saw the woman right in front of me?

Mucking hells, I don't even like blondes.

Gwenna being Sarya brings new complications, though. In addition to the pile of lies, it poses a problem that we're both fledglings on the same team. We're both supposed to be concentrating on getting ready for the future tests (and I'm supposed to be finding a thief). I know I can pass the guild tests again, but it'd be unfair of me to distract Gwenna from her studies.

Even so, I need answers. "Why'd you fuck me? That day when I was in the hospital?"

"No idea what you're talking about," Gwenna says, voice crisp.

I want to pluck her off the counter and shake her until the truth comes out. "Give up on the bullshit and tell me the truth already. We both know that you're lying."

"I don't know why you think I'm lying."

I grit my teeth. I grab her chin and force her to look me in the eye, and then I recall something else she said earlier. *Figured you wouldn't be into fucking right now.*

"Do you still want to fuck?" I demand.

Gwenna goes still. Her eyes go wide as she gazes up at me, but her pupils betray her. They dilate, growing larger, and I can feel her breath speed up.

Well now. That's interesting. "You want me to touch you?"

"I didn't say that!"

I stroke my thumb along her soft jaw. "So I shouldn't touch you?"

Her lips part, and when my thumb grazes her lower lip, she captures it in her mouth and sucks on the tip. When she releases it, she gazes up at me with hot, hungry eyes. "I didn't say that, either."

Mucking hells, this woman is going to be the death of me. I bite back a groan, leaning in and nipping her tiny ear. I'm careful with my teeth, but I let them graze over her lobe. She gasps and clutches at my shirt, and just like that, any potion I might have had left in my system is completely obliterated. My cock swells, and the band of flesh at the base of my shaft prickles with awareness.

"Tell me to touch you," I demand. "Tell me to make you feel good."

"Touch me," Gwenna breathes.

Our eyes lock and I release her jaw, grabbing the waist of her pants. I put my hand on her belt, and then very slowly undo the knot that clasps it to her waist. She doesn't tell me to stop. She doesn't tell me that she doesn't want this. She just continues to meet my gaze, and when I loosen her belt enough to slide my hand into her pants and between her legs, she makes a hungry little noise and spreads her thighs farther apart.

I have permission, which is all I needed.

I cup the mound of her sex, loving her gasp. She's not quite wet enough for me yet. "You want me to pet this pretty little cunt of yours until you scream?"

She nods, her eyes growing heavy-lidded.

"Tell me that, then."

Gwenna growls low in her throat. "Pushy bastard."

"Never said I wasn't. But tell me to finger you and I'll make you feel so damn good you'll weep with joy."

She rolls her eyes and reaches for the ring through my nose, lightly tugging on it. Even that makes my cock twitch with awareness. "Quit talking. You're cooling my ardor."

"Am I? I don't think I am." I stroke a finger through her folds, exploring her with a light touch. As I do, more wetness seeps from her core and dampens my skin. "Feel that, love? All that glistening slick doesn't come out unless you like what I'm doing."

And just to make a liar out of her, I slide my middle finger into her, and she's already slippery enough that I glide in like butter.

Gwenna gasps again, turning her head slightly and rolling her body to move against my touch.

"So pretty," I croon. "Such a soft, dainty little thing—"

"I am not dainty—"

"Hush. To me you are. You're nothing but a dainty doll of a woman I want to bend over this counter and fuck with my knot until you scream."

She bites her lower lip, rocking her hips against my hand again.

"But maybe that's for later," I whisper in the ear she's presented to me. I'm having to hunch over just to maneuver close to her ear, but it's not uncomfortable. Having her up on the counter helps, and I keep that in mind for the future. Because this is absolutely not going to be the last time I touch her, I decide.

She's made the mistake of showing me that she's interested, and now she's never going to shake me.

"How does my finger feel inside you?"

Her breath hitches and she moans.

"Ah ah," I chide. "I don't think that's a word. I'm afraid I need to hear more."

She tugs on the ring, pulling my nose down. Again, our eyes lock. "Are you going to touch my clit or do I have to find someone else to do it?"

I want to laugh with pure delight, but a growl escapes my throat instead. Sexy little thing. "You want me to touch your clit for you? Make you come?"

"*Yes.*"

"Say my name."

"Raptor." She breathes it out, oh so prettily.

"Good." I place my thumb between her folds and slip it through her increasingly wet channel until I find the bud of her clit. It's a prominent one, and I bet it'd look so pretty against my tongue. I stroke my thumb pad over it ever so briefly. "Better?"

She moans, her entire body shuddering. By the five gods, I wish she was naked so I could admire the bounce of her glorious breasts. I bet they jiggle the entire time she's being fucked. I want to see that so damn badly that my knot aches just thinking about it.

But I want her a little more talkative. I still my thumb. "You didn't answer me, Gwenna. Is that *better*?"

"You prick," she wheezes, squirming against my hand. "Move."

"What shall I move? My thumb or my finger?"

"YES," she snarls at me, pressing her nose to my much bigger one.

She's so needy and charming I can't stand it. I stroke my middle finger in and out of her a few times, letting it build up, and then I take on a much slower pace, occasionally teasing her clit to feel her jump against my hand. I'm making it impossible for her to climax, and she realizes it, too. "Raptor," she pants. "I need more."

"So do I," I all but purr even as I finger her. "Tell me that you were Sarya and I'll make you come."

Her expression changes to one of anger, and she squirms against my hand again. "Fuck you."

"You want me to stop? Tell me to stop." I skim my thumb over her clit again, and then drill my finger deeper into the sucking, needy well of her cunt. "Tell me to stop touching you and I will."

"Make me come."

"Tell me what I need to hear."

She growls again, furious. Gwenna lets go of my nose ring and plants her hand over mine, trying to use me to work her cunt, and I grab her wrist, grinning. I love how bossy and demanding she is. She's not telling me to stop. She's wanting that orgasm. I can read her like an Old Prellian glyph.

I work her with my finger, adding a second one and driving both into her with quick, hard strokes. I grin down at her as she rides my hand, panting. And then I stop again.

She all but screams in outrage.

"Fine." Gwenna spits the word at me, her eyes snapping fire. "It was me, all right? I told you I was Sarya and I climbed on top of you and used you for sex. That what you want to hear?"

My suspicions are confirmed, and I can't stop grinning. I never told her that Sarya climbed atop me. It truly was her. "I do feel better hearing that, aye."

And I cup the back of her neck, holding her even as I finger her and work her clit just the way she wants. Her mouth drops open, and when she comes, it's not with a noisy cry but with a choked little sound, followed by a sigh of pure satisfaction.

I decide I like that better than any theatrics.

My knot aches and throbs, and I want nothing more than to bury my muzzle in the crook of her neck . . . and then bury other parts of me in her body. But there's a very real potential problem. I'd expect a sex worker to have birth control handled, but Gwenna isn't a sex worker. "Is there a chance of a baby? Between us?"

"No. I already had my period." She wrinkles her nose, glancing up at me even as she pushes my hands away and fastens her pants once more. "But I did want to ask. Sparrow says that Taurians only have a knot during the Conquest Moon. Or is she wrong?"

"Tell me why you fucked me that day and I'll tell you all about my knot," I drawl, watching her with a possessive gaze as she straightens her clothing. The more she moves, the more confident I am that she is indeed Sarya. There's a brattiness to her that shields her vulnerability, and it's that same thing that attracted me to the mysterious woman I'd touched in the hospital bed.

Her expression grows shuttered, and she hops down off the counter. "That's my business and not yours."

"Don't tell me I'm going to have to finger all your secrets out of you," I tease, and lick those selfsame fingers as she watches me. Her taste is magnificent.

"Fuck right off."

She flounces out of the room, and I watch her go with a grin. Oh, this is going to be *fun*.

TWENTY-FIVE

GWENNA

Dere Ma,

Sorry I haven't ritten. Training isn't great. Our teechur is very fond of drills and I am not fond of them at all. I haven't bene sleeping well. I'm just stressed because it's important to me that I pass this year. Please don't worry about me. I will send more money when I can.

Love, Gwenna

THERE'S A JITTERY feeling in my stomach all weekend as I keep busy and avoid Raptor. We were supposed to work together, but the tunnel job is completed and I latch on to Marta instead, offering to help her cook up some of the meals she was supposed to make yesterday.

Raptor sits in the kitchen, sharpening his weapons, and never leaves me alone for a moment. He's the source of my stomach flutters for sure. He watches me closely, and whenever our eyes meet, he gives me a lazy smile, as if he knows all my secrets. Well, he knows one for sure. He knows that I'm the one who had sex with him that day . . . he just doesn't know why.

I can't stop thinking about yesterday, either. When he hoisted me onto the counter and then proceeded to work my pussy with his hand until I came. In that moment, I'd have blurted all my secrets, and the thought of losing my mind simply because he touched me is terrifying. If he finds out that I'm a mancer, is he going to go straight to the guild to demand a bounty of some kind? I don't know if I can trust him, so I can't say anything.

Only Sparrow knows my true secret.

I'd been doing a good job of hiding things while in the cavern, or so I'd thought. But then they'd opened up that new room, and a flood of fresh sensations washed over me. There were dead up there. A lot of them, all very long deceased but still echoing in my head and crawling under my skin as if they wanted something from me.

I can't stop thinking about that, either. How am I supposed to be an artificer if I can't even go in the blasted tunnels?

After our round in the kitchen, I avoided Raptor for the rest of the night and went to bed early. Today I'm chopping vegetables and making overly chatty conversation with a bewildered Marta, despite doing my best to avoid her for the last several weeks. "I can help out as long as the others aren't around," I explain to her, dicing onions with my good hand. "But the moment they return, I have to go back to ignoring you."

"I understand," she says in a soft, gentle voice. "You have to be seen as one of them."

Her words make me want to weep with the acceptance in them. "When we're done here, though," I continue, my voice low, "I'm going to tell everyone, especially Mistress Umala, what an amazing job you did. How comfortable you kept the nest. If I pass, I'll be an artificer, and an artificer that suggests you get a pay raise holds a lot of weight around here."

"I'll do the same," Raptor adds in behind us, reminding me that he's listening to everything we discuss.

I shoot him a dirty look. "Don't you have something better to do?"

"I do not," he says, and runs his blade over the whetstone on the table again.

KIPP RETURNS EARLY in the afternoon, setting his pack and his shell atop his bed. Marta is cleaning Master Jay's rooms, so I sit on the end of

Kipp's bed and turn all my efforts to one-sidedly chatting with Kipp while he gives me the slitherskin equivalent of a bewildered stare. Through a few gestures and lots of questions from me, he tells me that he spent all weekend delivering letters. I've seen slitherskins moving about the city as couriers, so this doesn't surprise me. I've never known Kipp to do it, though. "Are you saving up for something?"

He gestures at something on his brow and then licks his eyeball.

"I don't follow."

"He's saving up for a lady friend," Raptor offers, sprawled on his bed next to Kipp's, his hands behind his head. "They have little ridges on their brows. That's what he was indicating."

"Oh!" I want to shoot Raptor another annoyed look for listening in, but Kipp practically squirms, his hands going to his tiny lizard cheeks as if he's mimicking a human's blush. "That's very sweet of you, Kipp. Are you going to take her on a date? If you want suggestions, find out what her favorite food is and take her some of it."

"That's a wise choice," Raptor comments. "What's your favorite, Gwenna?"

"I love a tall glass of shut-your-trap-and-mind-your-own-business."

Raptor laughs.

Kipp huffs with amusement and goes back to gesturing wildly, extolling the virtues of his lady friend, who works as a messenger in the lower parts of the city and apparently has gorgeous skin. It's so sweet.

Both Hemmen and Arrod return just before dusk and flop down in their bunks, not speaking to the rest of us. Hemmen pulls out a book and lights a candle to read by, while Arrod takes a nap. Kipp and Raptor start a discussion on the best kinds of blades, and since I know nothing about knives, I retreat to my bunk and work on stitching a subtle breast dart into the front of my fledgling uniform so I don't look so very boxy when I wear it. It's a terrible thing to be vain, but I'm not a looker in the face, and I'm not rich. Tits are all I have.

As we settle in for another week, I stare up at the ceiling in bed that night, hating how out of control I feel. It's because Raptor thinks he has the upper hand on me, I decide. He thinks he can push me around and I'll allow it, and I have been allowing it, because I'm worried that he'll find out the truth. It's clear he's not going to leave me alone, and while I wouldn't mind another glorious fingering (truly, I wouldn't mind that at all), I don't want him to continue to have the upper hand.

I need to gain control of our relationship again, such as it is. If nothing else, we need to be on equal ground. I have to stop getting flustered every time he addresses me, because others are going to guess that something is going on. But how do I get on equal footing with him again?

An idea floats into my head. An obvious one.

I could touch him like he touched me. Make him come.

He'd like that, of course. But then he wouldn't have one over on me any longer.

And if I'm being honest with myself . . . I'd like touching him, too. Every time he gives me a look from across the room, I feel as if I'm the only person he's noticed that day. That no one else matters but me. It's made me wet for hours.

It could backfire spectacularly, me touching him . . . but . . . Raptor knows how to be discreet. And if he doesn't keep this to himself, well, it tells me all I need to know about him.

I glance over at his bunk. He's a few feet away from me, sleeping on his back with the blankets at his waist. Kipp isn't in his bed, which is good, because he's a light sleeper. I lay where I am, quiet, and listen to the sounds of Arrod and Hemmen sleeping. Good. They're both fast asleep.

I can do this now, before I have the chance to talk myself out of it.

Sliding out from underneath the covers, I sit up and put my feet on the floor. After two quiet breaths, it's obvious no one is waking up, so I tiptoe the short distance over to Raptor's bed and kneel beside it. He's enormous, his big body taking up so much space that the bed seems inadequate and downright uncomfortable for someone his size. Even the blanket doesn't look sufficient.

I have no idea why that fascinates me so much. Why I can't stop thinking about him. Why I increasingly search out his amused comments or his wry laughter. I can't afford to have a crush on a fellow student. On anyone, really.

I tell myself that I shouldn't be doing this, even as I reach for the blanket and peel it back, just a fraction.

A big hand reaches out and grabs my wrist. Raptor's awake.

"You'll get in trouble if you get caught, little bantam."

Oh, I know that. But he's not telling me not to touch him, either. I pull free from his grasp and give him my best saucy look. "So be *quiet*."

The darkness hides his face, but he gives just the faintest huff that tells me he's amused by my response. He releases my wrist and his hand goes to his stomach.

I could stop now. Or . . . not.

My hand goes under the blanket. I find the waist of his pants, the worn-out ones that he always sleeps in, with the patches on the knees. I walk my fingers along the band, giving him a moment to acclimate himself to my touch, and then slip my hand under the fabric.

Immediately, my knuckles brush against the hot, heavy head of his cock.

A gasp rises in my throat, and I bite down on my lip to keep it at bay. Quiet, I must stay quiet. I'd just forgotten how very large he is. My hand feels as if it's being scorched just by proximity to his heat. I run my fingers along the head of him, unsurprised to feel that he's dripping pre-cum already. How long has he been lying here, listening to me try to sleep? Or did he guess what was going through my mind? Whatever it is, I'm in this moment now, and I know what I want.

With my good hand, I tease his cock a little more, letting my fingertips lightly drag over his length, learning him again. It seems like he hasn't forgotten that day in the hospital, and while I haven't had it on my mind too much, I remember his knot more than anything. I curve my hand around the thick length of his shaft, stroking it. I'm going to need lubrication if I want to give him more than just a dry hand job.

I contemplate my options.

Giving him a dry hand job is the easiest, but I also want this to be memorable. I could finger myself until I'm wet and use that as a lubricant, but that might take a while and involve too much rustling of clothing. Plus, one of my hands is bandaged.

Actually . . .

Now that I think about it, I wrapped my hand again and reapplied salve just before bed. It's still wet underneath the bandage because I applied far too much. Pulling my hand free, I ignore the slight shift of his body—I'm sure he's wondering if I'm losing my nerve—and unwrap my injured hand. I run my fingers down my palm, getting a lot of the herbal salve on my other hand, and then rub the two together. A moment later, my good one is back under the blankets, and this time when I grip him, my hand is slippery and glides over his shaft.

I hear him suck in a breath.

Reaching forward—because he's so enormous that I'm having to stretch—I press the back of my injured hand to his muzzle to keep him quiet as I work his cock with my good hand. I start with long, firm strokes, until he's so rigid that there's absolutely no give to his cock. Once I've got him good and teased, I toy with his balls a little, and the hot ring of flesh at the base of his cock, before starting a quick pumping motion under the blanket.

The room is silent except for the occasional wet sound of my hand on his skin, and I glance over at the other two, who are fast asleep and oblivious. One of Hemmen's ever-present books is over his face, and Arrod continues to snore. I fight the urge to laugh, especially when Raptor arches his hips, trying to rock into my grip. He's got my other wrist now, holding me tight but careful not to touch my self-inflicted injuries. All the while, I jerk his cock with a bit of smug precision and my own arousal growing by the moment.

His muzzle goes to the back of my hand again, and the ring in his nose presses against my skin as he holds me tight. His hips lift again, and his tail swats against the side of the bed, far too loudly.

I work him harder, using my thumbnail against his knot to push him over the edge.

To Raptor's credit, he doesn't make a sound when he comes. There's a wave of tension through his large body, and then heat spurts all over my hand. I continue to work him, dragging my fingers through the mess to milk everything he has. When he gives one last shudder and grips a handful of my hair, I know it's time to pull away. I've made my point.

As I do, though, I drag my hand up his chest, making sure to leave a messy trail. It's like I'm marking him as my territory, and I drag one cum-wet finger around one of his nipples, and I could swear he shudders all over again.

Then I give him a pat and get to my feet, picking up my bandage and heading quietly out of the room and toward the garderobe.

The moment I get into the hall, I run into Master Jay.

My eyes widen at the sight of him. "M–Master. It's late."

"It is. I've just returned from outside the city. Why are you up?" He eyes my hands, covered in an absolute mess, gripping my wadded bandage tight.

Oh, fuck me. I can't think of anything except the mess on my hands that's now more Taurian semen than salve. "Ah, my bandage came unwrapped in my sleep, and I made a mess with the salve while trying to fix it."

He glances down at my hands, then at my flushed face, and grunts. "Are you going to be too injured to participate this week? We will be heading into the Everbelow soon, and I need everyone at their best."

"It's just a small injury. Should be better in a day or two." Please, please don't ask to see it.

He studies my face and then grunts again. "See that it is."

Then he turns and leaves, heading for his quarters, his traveling pack still on his back.

I don't breathe until I've washed up, rebandaged my hand, and returned to bed. Raptor hasn't moved from his spot, but a brief time after I lie down, he quietly gets to his feet, no doubt to go clean up.

Before he does, though, he moves to the side of my bed. I keep my eyes closed, even when he brushes a finger over my mouth.

It's wet. Tastes like seed.

I suppose I deserved that. I smile even as I lick the taste of him off my lips. Perhaps he felt like branding me, too.

TWENTY-SIX

GWENNA

WE LINE UP in the morning for our weekly check-in. Normally Master Jay asks us how we spent our weekend, quizzes us on whatever he thinks we're needing work on, and then sends us off on a task or two. Today, though, he does none of that. He simply eyes us as he walks back and forth in front of our lineup at the fore of the house. He paces and says nothing.

Is it possible that he guessed what I was up to last night? Or did someone snitch on me? Did the room smell like sex? Did Raptor say something?

No, I think. Raptor wouldn't. If nothing else, I can trust that Raptor wouldn't say anything about our fooling around. It's a gut feeling I have.

Master Jay strolls past our lineup, and I wait for him to nitpick something. To ask me an obscure location in the city. To ask me what a specific Prellian symbol is. Or he'll just decide that I look too out of shape and make me run an obstacle course alone. Instead, he pauses and eyes all of us. "What did you do this weekend, Kipp?"

Kipp gestures, indicating handing out letters and running the streets.

Master Jay doesn't follow. He stares at Kipp and then looks at me to interpret.

"Courier," I say, and I lose a little respect for him. Truly, how difficult is it to attempt communicating with Kipp? Even if he'd guessed incorrectly, I'd have had respect for that. Didn't even try, though.

The guild master just eyes me instead. "And you?"

I have no idea how much I'm supposed to say. I gesture at Raptor. "Shadowed him."

"I was pulled into a tunnel excavation," Raptor says, his voice carefully bored, as if he's determined not to show any emotion to Master Jay. "Gwenna held a lamp while I worked."

The teacher grunts and goes down the line. "And you, Hemmen?"

Hemmen's eyes go wide and he gives us panicked looks. "I, ah, went to the library to read."

"Arrod?"

"Met up with some old friends. Had a few drinks. Nothing special."

Master Jay clasps his hands behind his back and turns around, pacing down our line again. "So out of a team of five, I have four different answers. Why is it that no one spends their time together other than these two?"

He gestures at me and then at Raptor, and even though I try to betray nothing, I can't help but think of that slippery hand job I gave Raptor last night under the blankets, and how Master Jay caught me as I went to clean up. Is he going to confront us in front of the group?

"It's clear to me that you are all still acting as individuals and not as the Five you should be," Master Jay says, looking us each in the eye. "It is crucial that you are a team. Your first test will be all about how you function as a Five, and right now I'm not seeing success at all. If you want to join this guild, it's important that you know how to work as a team. I think we'll start with the obstacle course for the first half of the day."

I bite back a groan, because I hate getting sweaty. Well, that's not true. I hate getting sweaty for the wrong reasons. An obstacle course is absolutely the wrong reason, as far as I'm concerned.

"I'll get the belt rope," Raptor says cheerfully, almost like he's pleased that we're going to be jumping over walls for the next several hours.

TWENTY-SEVEN

RAPTOR

Raptor to Rooster: *No updates other than to say I'm keeping a close eye on the woman.*

Rooster to Raptor: *You think she's the one, then? Should we take her in for questioning?*

Raptor to Rooster: *I didn't say she was. I just said I'm updating you. As for the woman, don't worry, I'm all over her.*

IN JUST A few short weeks, Gwenna's improved on the obstacle course, and I watch with pride as she maneuvers over a low wall with a sideways full-body roll. Even though she's short, she knows how to move. Hemmen, on the other hand, is rotten. He's got no stamina at all, and by the time we get halfway through the course, I'm being forced to drag him by his belt to the finish line.

"I just don't see the point," Hemmen whines. "I can be the group's scholar."

"Are you an idiot?" Arrod scoffs. "You're a repeater. This can't be new to you. You know you have to be physically fit enough to explore the tunnels."

"Maybe I'm not cut out for it." Hemmen sprawls on the ground like a dramatic child. "Maybe I should be an archivist instead."

"You have to be invited to join the archivists," I point out, standing over him. "And you signed up to be a fledgling again. You can't quit now or you muck things up for all of us."

"I don't care." Hemmen seems on the edge of tears, which is downright embarrassing. I want to grab him by his shirt and shake sense into him.

"It's all right," Gwenna soothes, moving to sit next to Hemmen. She's roped between me and Kipp, which means that it tugs a little on my waist and completely hauls poor Kipp over toward us. "It's difficult for everyone right now. We'll get better with practice. We just have to stick with it. You don't want to be a repeater forever, do you?"

"Maybe." His tone is sulky, but he's responding to Gwenna at least.

"You don't," she reiterates. "Think of all the terrible things you had to do as a repeater. I had to change chamber pots and do laundry all day long."

"I had to help repair the streets," Arrod says suddenly, volunteering information. "Mucking cobblestones always come up out of the street in the worst weather. It's never when it's sunny and nice out. It's always when it's snowing or when it's so hot it can roast you in the street."

Kipp moves to Hemmen's side and gestures. Looks like digging.

Hemmen manages a faint smile at that. "I didn't have to dig them, but I did have to help out with latrine duty."

"See? Hideous work," Gwenna continues. "And none of it paid. Even if an obstacle course isn't fun—and trust me, it is *not* fun—it's a stepping stone to getting us to where we want to be. And if you want to complain, we will all join in on the complaining . . . but don't give up."

"I guess." He still sounds like a brat to me, but I eye Gwenna with new appreciation. I know Hemmen irritates her, but she's managed to soothe his feelings so quickly that I'm in awe. I'm not good with people, because the moment someone complains, I want to throttle them. But I appreciate Gwenna's calm demeanor. We need Hemmen, whether we like it or not.

"Come on." Gwenna gets to her feet, dusting off the seat of her pants. My gaze goes there, admiring that plump, rounded backside. "Once we're done with this, I'll buy you a drink. Deal?"

"That's enough of the obstacle course for today," Master Jay says suddenly. "You can loosen the ropes. I've a better idea for team building."

A SHORT TIME later, our group steps inside the King's Onion tavern, and my mouth waters. Naiah glances over at our uniformed group, but she doesn't let her gaze linger on me more than any other customer. Instead, she throws her bar towel over her shoulder and offers us a cheerful grin. "Welcome! Can I get you lot a drink or two? A fried onion?"

"What are we doing here again?" Arrod asks. "Surely there are other mucking bars in this damned city."

I watch as Kipp heads to the bar and climbs up on one of the stools. He pats the bar, and Naiah gives him a friendly smile and pours him a bit of beer into a shot glass. Kipp holds it with both hands, and his tongue snakes out to lick the foam cap off the top.

Master Jay strides to the bar and gestures for Naiah to come serve us. "The best Fives are those that spend both good and bad times together. Work and play. I want you all to get to know one another well, and perhaps we should start with friendly fun instead of the brutal parts of the job."

It's a nice thought, but it also doesn't sound much like the Jay I know. Some teachers are strict with their fledglings about drinking, but Master Jay has always done his own thing. And yet . . . is this too convenient? Does this mean he's got something going on I need to investigate as well? Do I need to notify Rooster about him, too? My mucking dance card is pretty full as it is.

The others seem excited, though. Gwenna sits at the bar next to Kipp, and Hemmen pulls up a stool on the other side of her. I resist the urge to growl at him, but he doesn't know we're a thing, so I can't get mad. It must remain a secret, at least for now. Reluctantly, I take a seat on the other side of Kipp, and Arrod sits next to me.

"Why does everyone come to this bloody tavern?" Arrod asks, wrinkling his nose at the beer put before him. "The brew is nothing special."

"Free onions." I reach over and pluck the wedge of onion off his mug and pop it into my mouth. I love onions. I could eat them all day long.

It's one reason why this is my favorite tavern, but one reason amongst many. There's a Taurian-friendly menu, the beer is cheap, it's close to home, and I can chat with Naiah when I need potions. I'm here a lot.

Arrod makes a face, wiping the spot where the onion was on his mug. "Just between you and me, if you want to impress the ladies, maybe you don't shove a ton of onions down your gullet. Makes for terrible kissing."

"I'll take my chances." I'm amused that he's giving me advice on women—him, a human nobody all of ten years younger than me. Then again, he might have a point. Gwenna and I haven't kissed, and I wonder if my scent would offend her if I did eat as many onions as I wanted.

I glance down the bar at her. Gwenna has clearly overheard our conversation and takes the decorative onion wedge off her mug and bites down on it, giving me a challenging look. "Real women aren't afraid of a little flavor."

And she winks at me.

Even though it's just her baiting Arrod, I'm filled with a strange sense of pleasure at her response. Like she's going out of her way to make sure I'm aware it doesn't bother her. Like she's got my back. I appreciate that.

Kipp hands his onion to me. It's no more than a sliver, but I eat it all the same.

"Why are we here?" Hemmen asks, slouching on his stool on the other side of Gwenna. "What sort of training can we possibly get in a tavern?"

Master Jay gets up from his seat and puts a handful of gold crowns down on the bar. "This should cover my students. Get them as much as they want today. Make sure they have a good time." He turns to us. "Some of my best memories with my Five were getting drunk together. Bonding doesn't always come in a tunnel or on a job. Sometimes it comes in a place like this."

Arrod grins. "Now, this is the kind of schooling that's more my speed."

"I thought you might enjoy this." Jay's expression turns stern, and he eyes each one of us in turn. "I don't want to see you back before sunset, and I expect everyone to be ready to go again first thing in the morning for Prellian glyph lessons."

Old Softy's going easy on us. Glyph lessons in the morning? He's practically inviting us all to show up hungover.

Jay walks away, patting me on the shoulder. It's a subtle reminder that even though we're given free rein today, I'm the most senior on the team and expected to look after the others. It's fine. I'm not in the mood to get sloppy anyhow. I'm distracted with other things, like watching Gwenna lick a drop of beer from the side of her mug.

"That's it? We just get drunk today?" Hemmen gives us a confused look. "I don't understand."

"It's about us becoming friends," I say. "Getting to know one another. Like he said, we need to start thinking like a Five at some point." At least until I determine if one of these fledglings is the thief. If they are, it means they're fucking over the chances of the others, but it's a risk we all take when we sign on. Can't be helped.

Today should give me a good chance to watch everyone, especially if tongues get loose from too much beer.

"Well?" Arrod asks. "What do we do now? Share stories? Arm-wrestle?"

"I know a drinking game," Gwenna says.

It's my turn to be surprised. "You do?"

"Don't act so astonished." Her nose goes in the air. "Learned it while I was a maid. The staff gets bored and likes to kick back just as much as anyone else."

Kipp puts his empty shot glass back on the counter and gives the world's tiniest belch.

Naiah is there right away. "Another, sir?"

Kipp knocks on the bar, and she immediately fills his drink. She moves on to Gwenna's mug, and then Hemmen's barely drunk beer, and Arrod drains his mug before handing it back to her.

Then Naiah gives me a look, moving down the bar. "Refill for you?"

I gesture at my beer. "I'm good, thanks." I'm also declining a refill on my potion. It's a gamble, but I want to see where things lead with Gwenna, and if I take a dose of potion, it's going to kill my dick dead for most of a week straight.

She just arches a brow at me. "Light drinker today."

"I'm interested in keeping all my senses sharp."

"Smart male." She grins and heads down the bar, checking in with her other clients.

Am I? I might be an idiot when it comes to Gwenna. I haven't been spending my time watching to see if she's the thief. I haven't been spending my time *team building* with her. I've been spending my time wondering when I can get her alone so I can finger her delightful cunt again. If Rooster and Hawk know just what I'm doing with her, they'll take me off the case.

I can't let them know that I'm fooling around with her, because I sure don't intend on stopping.

I need to find this thief, and I need it to not be Gwenna. I turn to the object of my fascination. "What's this game?"

"We need an extra mug of beer," she says. "And a coin."

Hemmen starts to pull one out of his pocket and then hesitates. "I get it back, right?"

Kipp rolls his eyes and slaps a coin down on the bar and gestures at all of us, indicating that he doesn't need it back.

I indicate to Naiah that we need another mug, and then Gwenna takes it and sets it at the far end of the bar. "All right. Now we need a table. And everyone sets their mugs down in front of them. The goal is to get the coin into the mug in the center. If you do, you pick who drinks next. . . ."

FOR THE NEXT several hours, we enjoy drinking on Master Jay's coin. I eat platter after platter of fried vegetables, onion and potato mash, and fresh bread slathered with an apple jam. I eat so much food that I'm certain this wasn't part of the plan, but it helps me stay sober as I drink along with the others. I try to get some bread into Gwenna, too, but it doesn't work. She's absolutely sotted by the time the sun gets closer to going down.

The good news is, Master Jay was right—drinking together has definitely brought the team closer. As I look around our messy table full of old mugs, half-eaten plates, and splashes of beer, everyone seems to be happy. Kipp's resting against Arrod's shoulder, one eye closed, and I can practically smell the alcohol fumes coming off him. Gwenna has her face propped up by both her fists, and her eyelids are heavy. She watches Hemmen intently as he drunkenly goes on about an old master that kicked him out of the messenger corps.

"It worked out, though," Gwenna says to him. "You're here and you're learning to be an artificer. They make loads more money than scribes. Looooads more."

"Money isn't everything." Hemmen pouts. "I wanted to be a scribe."

"Well, I wanted to be a princess," Gwenna retorts. It's cute, because she says it like *prinshess*. "My ma always said we wish in one hand and shit in the other and see which one fills up faster."

Kipp makes a croaking sound that might be a laugh. Arrod laughs, too, but Hemmen still looks upset.

"More rolls for everyone," I say, plucking a plate of them off Naiah's tray as she passes by. I hand them out to the group. "If anyone vomits in the street, you'll have to clean it up in the morning, and trust me, you will *not* feel like it."

"S'that a guild rule?" Hemmen asks. He takes a bite out of his roll, though.

"It's a Master Jay rule," I lie. "Just eat."

They all take bites, and Gwenna watches me, licking jam off her lips. My cock pricks as her pink tongue swipes over the corner of her mouth, and then she gives me another sensual smile. Ah, gods. If I have to fight her off tonight because she's drunk, that's going to be the cruelest irony ever. I want her touch, but I also want her to be aware of what she's doing. I'm not interested in a partner who has regrets the next day. I drop a second roll in front of her.

"Master Jay's strange," Arrod complains. "Always leaving town all the time. S'like he's hiding something."

My senses prick. I say nothing, just watch the others.

Gwenna licks the jam off her roll (gods damn me for watching that so closely). "He's got a lady friend with a farm on the outskirts. That's all it is."

"So you say. Just seems wrong that he's abandoning students when he's supposed to be training us." Arrod takes a half-hearted bite out of his roll and continues talking around his mouthful, spraying crumbs as he does. "I just thought a teacher would be more . . . hover-y. My last one was. Never gave us a moment's peace."

I make a mental note to watch Jay more closely and to tell Hawk about it. It's probably nothing but the grousing of a fussy drunk student, but I have to check into everything. I'll have to search his rooms when he's gone, too. Not that I expect to find anything, but it can't hurt to look for secret compartments or magic residue. I don't want the others to be suspicious, so I put on my best knowing smile. "You're all fussing about Jay, but I promise he's one of the better teachers. A good artificer is independent anyhow. Do you really want your teacher making every decision for you? Or do you want your teacher to give you the tools so you can make the decisions for yourself?"

Gwenna squints at me. "Second one. I think."

"Exactly. We can do the basics on our own. Like deciding who's going to take what position when we rope together."

"Position?" Gwenna licks her roll again, and I swear she's doing it just to muck with me. "What kind of position?"

Hemmen chortles and takes another swig of his beer. "In the tunnels. You know: sword, shield, navigator, healer, and gearmaster."

"Right. Those positions. I knew that." Her cheeks are flushed pink, and tendrils of dark hair are escaping her neat bun, making her look disheveled and ripe for fucking and . . . and I might need another dose of potion from Naiah's stash after all if this continues. I can't think straight.

"Kipp should be our sword," Arrod says. "He's bloody talented. Never seen anything like it."

Kipp preens at that, straightening and patting Arrod on his clothing as a thank-you.

"What about the big horking Taurian?" Hemmen asks.

Arrod shakes his head. "Got it all thought through. He can be our shield."

They both eye me, and I shrug. "I've been both positions in the past. Just happy to serve in whatever way is needed."

"Shield," Arrod declares. Then he eyes Gwenna and looks over at Hemmen again. "What about the woman?"

By Old Garesh's nutsack, this is not going to end well. I can already see Gwenna stiffening.

"She can watch our supplies and make our meals," Hemmen declares. "You know, woman stuff."

Gwenna jumps to her feet and throws her beer in Hemmen's face. "The fuck I can!"

Arrod roars with laughter, wheezing so hard he falls out of his chair and takes Kipp down to the floor with him.

"All right," I say, getting to my feet. "That's enough beer for now. Let's head back."

TWENTY-EIGHT

GWENNA

Dere Ma,

Sorry it's been a few days. I don't have coin to send home this time, but I think of you constently. I miss you. Classes have been taking up all my spayre time. Master Jay is very different than Master Hawk. He likes to talk a lot and he is a big beleever in something he calls repetetif lerning. He makes us do the same drills over and over again so they feel like second nature.

He's fair tho and hasn't treeted me any different than the men. He is a great teechur and I'm not saying that just because the guild reads our letters. We are doing well in our lessons. The Taurian—his name is Raptor—is extremely skilled and is helping me practiss so I can keep up with the others.

I hope you're taking care of yourself. Don't let Cook bully you into making all the bread. She just doesn't want to get up early because she's fooling around with the stable boys at all hours. You can tell her I said that!

Sending love, Gwenna

ALL IS QUIET for several days. An intense storm has hit Vastwarren, turning the streets into rivers and the cobblestones into slippery dangers. Master Jay decides that we're going to learn best indoors, and so we take to the guild library with the other fledgling teams. Every master has the same idea, and the library is overcrowded with people. It's a struggle to find a table, so we have to show up early to claim seats. The air is humid and unpleasant due to the rain and the crush of bodies in the library, and I'm covered in a fine sheen of sweat all week and miserable.

I'm not the only one who's suffering. Arrod groans like a petulant toddler every time a book is put in front of him, as if we're torturing him instead of asking him to learn some Prellian glyph basics. Raptor's in a cranky mood, too. I don't know if it's the humidity in the library or the proximity of so many people, but his mood becomes increasingly irritable as the days go on. He's snappish to all of us, scowls at Master Jay constantly, and isn't fun to be around in the slightest.

It doesn't make me want to flirt with him, either. He's never quite unpleasant to me, but there are times that I want to snarl at him for being a prick.

On Fifthday morning, the three humans and Taurian in our group head over to the library to meet Kipp, shaking out wet cloaks and hanging them on hooks near the doors. Despite the early hour, the library is full of fledglings, and I can hear Master Tiercel droning on about Prellian architecture. A librarian rushes past with a cart full of books and what looks like a crystal globe set atop the cart. The crystal globe flashes and the librarian parks the cart and begins to shelve books in their places.

"I wish someone wanted to get wet," I comment as we swipe our muddy boots on the rug at the front of the library.

Raptor jerks, startled. He shoots me a dirty look.

"What? If they wanted to get wet, they wouldn't be in here, hogging all the tables."

With a scowl on his face, he plants his big hands on his hips and scans the room. "I don't see Kipp."

"He said he was going to wait at the table," I say as both Hemmen and Arrod look to the Taurian. "Why else do you think he came ahead, Cranky?"

Raptor mutters something under his breath that sounds a bit like "least he's coming," but I don't know what he's referring to. I shoot him an irked glance and then make my way across the crowded library, dodging pushed-out chairs and carts full of books waiting to be reshelved. There are no candles in the library to brighten it. The large windows are full of gray skies, but someone has pulled out a series of small globes that are full of a greenish magic illumination. The fist-sized lamps are lifted onto the wall sconces by hooks, and the room fills with a murky, sickly shade of light.

One of the men pushes his chair back just as I walk past, shoving it into me.

I ignore him. Just like I ignore the one who slaps my arse as I move past.

Raptor doesn't, though. He's two paces behind me, and the moment after my arse is squeezed, he lets out a roar. I turn just in time to see the student lifted bodily out of his seat, hanging by his collar. He hauls the terrified fledgling into the air. "Slap my ass," he snarls, the broad blaze down his muzzle pressed to the tinier human nose. "Go on, I mucking dare you."

Should I tell him to stop? I don't want to, because I love that he's standing up for me. I love that he's doing something about the harassment I've dealt with every day since arriving in Vastwarren City. Perhaps I shouldn't be so gleeful about it, but it's nice to see someone realize that their thoughtless actions have consequences.

"S-sorry," the student mumbles, utterly pale.

Raptor shakes him again. "Are you apologizing to *me*?"

The fledging turns wide, frantic eyes toward me. "Sorry! Sorry!"

"Just don't let it happen again," I say magnanimously. I move to Raptor's side, and when he gives the man another shake, I tap his arm. "You can set him down now."

He looks over at me, and I could swear there's a tinge of red in Raptor's gaze. He looks . . . unhinged. All this because some fool spanked me? Or is there something else going on?

I move away from the table full of fledglings and their scowling master (who did not step in, I cannot help but notice). Arrod and Hemmen go ahead, but I turn and wait for Raptor. After a moment, he drops the quivering fledgling back into his seat and stalks away, moving to my side. Once he gets to me, he reaches out. For a moment, it seems as if he's going to put an arm around my shoulders, but he changes his mind and brushes a piece of lint off my fledgling sash instead. "You all right?"

"Are you?" I ask. "It's not like you to lose control like that."

His eyes narrow, and he scowls at me as if I've personally offended him. "It's fine. I'm just tired."

"I don't know if I believe that. You seem cranky lately."

"I said it's *fine.*"

I blink. "Did you just *snap* at me? Because you can fuck right off with that."

He scrubs a hand down his face. "No, I—I didn't mean to be short. I'm not mad at you. I'm just . . . not myself lately."

"Are you all right?"

"It's nothing I can't handle." He sounds tired.

"Is there anything I can do to help?"

He stares at me long and hard. For some reason, this makes me blush, as if his mind is going to filthy places. That must be my imagination.

"I'm going to take that as a no," I say brightly. "Come on, then. Let's join the others."

We cross the packed library, heading to the same table that we've occupied for the last two days. Kipp has his shell on the table surface and sits atop it. Arrod and Hemmen are pulling out chairs next to him, and Master Jay is already there, waiting on us. I hurry over to take my seat next to Kipp, smiling at my small friend. Raptor takes the seat at the other end of the table, scowling at all of us as if he doesn't like his chair. I don't understand his mood.

The moment we're seated, Kipp gets up. He heads to the stack of books and hands out learning volumes created by the archivists to help fledglings master the basics of the intricate Old Prellian glyph language. I should be happy to be inside and warm, but truthfully, I'd rather be on the obstacle course. I can't read worth a lick, and even the simplest of sentences takes me far too long. It's embarrassing, and I stay quiet so the others don't discover just how poor at reading and writing I truly am.

"Turn to page thirty-seven," Master Jay says, circling the table. "We'll start with where we were yesterday and see how many of the eight hundred and twenty-two common symbols of Old Prellian you've retained."

I flip my book open, trying to find the right page . . . and then stop. A bright splash of red lettering on a previous page catches my attention and I turn back to it. Jagged lettering in vivid scarlet has been scrawled across the artifact-printed book on page twenty. It takes me a moment to realize what it says.

GWENNA IS A THIEF.

I slam the book shut, panicking.

"Is there a problem, fledgling?" Master Jay asks.

I panic again, because if I tell him what it says, he'll wonder what's going on. Do I hide it? Is mine the only book with this message, or has it been written across every student text in the library? "Sorry, thought I saw a bug." I force myself to open the book again, my expression neutral, and turn farther ahead in the book, deliberately avoiding horrible page twenty.

"Good." Master Jay hooks his thumbs in the pockets of his jacket. "Now, let's review what we learned yesterday. The Prellian language is considered a feminine language. That means that all non-sentient objects will have female pronouns attached. . . ."

I'm itching to turn back to page twenty, but I don't dare. The writing on the page was so bright, so lurid, that it's sure to grab Master Jay's attention . . . or anyone else's. I peek over my book at Raptor. He's watching me, his gaze intense. I don't know if that means that his book has been vandalized or if mine is the only one. I turn to Hemmen, but he's reading his book intently.

When I turn to look at Arrod, however, he's staring at me, his eyes wide.

Shit.

I stare down at my pages again, the words and symbols blurring before my eyes. I can't concentrate. I'm scared of being kicked out, but more than that . . . I'm starting to get angry. Why the fuck am I being targeted? Is it all because I'm a woman?

If so, that's an absolutely shitty thing to do, framing me as a thief just because they don't like my gender. I haven't even been in a mucking tunnel yet. Well, in any sort of official capacity. I haven't tried *anything*. They just don't like that I'm here learning.

They want me back in the kitchens. Because that's the only place good enough for a woman.

The more I think about it, the more I fume. I grit my teeth, but that page in the book is taunting me. I can't take it any longer. While Master Jay is talking about how to recognize an *ottin* sun glyph from an *ehld* circle, I turn back to page twenty and rip the damned thing out of the book. I wad it into a ball, and immediately Kipp snatches the ball from my hand and shoves it deep into his shell.

I'm both grateful that he's assisting me and horrified that he knows just what I'm doing. It's clearly in his book, too.

Master Jay stares at me, open-mouthed. "That book is intended for all students, not just your use, fledgling!"

"I'm sorry. There was another nasty bug on the paper. Big one. I panicked." I flutter my lashes at him and give the teacher my most "helpless female" expression. "We weren't on that page, were we?"

"There are a lot of bugs in the library," Raptor drawls. He leans back, eyeing Master Jay. "Should something be done about that?"

The teacher frowns. "An infestation can be a problem. Let me speak with the archivist working today."

He walks away, steps crisp, and the moment he's gone, Raptor snatches Hemmen's book from him.

"Hey," Hemmen protests. "I was reading that."

"You can have it back," Raptor replies. He flicks through the book and a flash of lurid red catches my eye. The Taurian rips out the offending page and then hands the book back to Hemmen. Kipp snatches the page from Raptor.

We all turn to Arrod.

"I didn't see anything," Arrod says, sliding his book down to Raptor. "Nothing at all. Is it true, though?"

I say nothing. I *am* a thief, aren't I? I stole a ring for Aspeth last year. Our Five got demoted to repeaters for breaking into the caverns. I can't even protest the statement.

Raptor just opens the book, rips out the graffiti, and then holds it out to Kipp to take. "Do you think it's true?"

Arrod studies my face. Then he shakes his head. "No. She's the one always nagging us about the rules. Wouldn't make sense for her to steal."

I want to kiss him in that moment. "Thank you," I say softly. "For believing in me."

"I believe in you, too," Raptor reminds me, tossing Arrod's book back down on the table with a thump. The Taurian opens his own book and tears out the marked page, tossing it aside. Kipp grabs it, too, then rips a page out of his book as well.

"Don't be jealous," I joke.

Raptor shoots me a wild-eyed stare, jaw clenched, and I wonder at his mood again. Master Jay starts heading back to our table, and Raptor opens his book again, deliberately avoiding the chapter where he tore the page out. "We'll talk about this on the weekend."

Master Jay returns. "It's the weather," he announces. "The archivists say there are a great many beetles coming inside searching for moldy paper. They're aware of the situation. There's no need to be afraid."

I'm not afraid—not of beetles anyhow. But I nod and open my book again, the words a blur in front of my face.

Who's coming after me and why?

TWENTY-NINE

GWENNA

STARTING ON FIRSTDAY, we'll be heading into the tunnels for our first time," Master Jay says later that day as he hoists his weekend pack on his shoulders. "Rest the next two days, study your glyphs, and then be ready. We'll start out in the training tunnels at the top of the Everbelow and work our way downward as we progress in our studies."

"Yes, Master," we all reply, as expected. Well, except for Raptor. He never refers to Jay as "Master," just addresses him directly. I think it stings his pride that he must answer to one of his peers. It makes me wonder again what was so terrible about his actions that they demoted him. Taurians are some of the hardest workers the guild has, to the point that their success makes the humans jealous.

Then again, maybe that's the problem.

I head into the kitchen after Master Jay leaves, preparing myself a plate of food. There's a thick barley soup full of vegetables, but I leave that for Raptor, as I know he doesn't eat meat and cow's milk cheese like the rest of us. There's a heavy bag on a hook hanging by the door. It must be Marta's. Judging from the rectangles pressing against the side of her pack, it's full of books. She must love to read as much as Hemmen does if she makes the effort to carry around such heavy tomes, what with a bad back and all.

Marta smiles shyly at me as she wipes some of the plates clean. "I made extra food for all of you."

"You're so thoughtful. Thank you." I beam at her and fill my plate with slices of bread, cold meats, and a few wedges of cheese. "You take good care of us."

"Just doing my job." She smiles again, her cheerful expression fading as the other students enter the kitchen. She ducks her head and picks up her heavy pack, scurrying out. Poor Marta.

Raptor immediately heads to the big pot of soup, lifting the lid and sniffing. His tail flicks and he sighs in pure bliss. Then he turns to look at us. "Who wants a bowl?"

"The rest of us are going to eat the meat and cheese," I say loudly, gesturing at the food spread on the table for us by Marta. "You need your strength. Eat as much of it as you like."

"But I like soup," Hemmen says.

"And you can eat all of it when it's chicken soup," Arrod says, stepping in. He loops an arm around Hemmen's neck and rubs his knuckles on the other man's hair. "Let the big guy eat whatever that mess is."

"Barley. And vegetables." Raptor takes out a bowl and hesitates, ladle in hand. He glances at us. "You're sure?"

Kipp hops on the table and grabs a handful of nuts, showing what he's going to eat. I glance at Hemmen and hold the plate I've prepared out to him.

He takes it from me, shrugging. "I don't really like barley. I can eat other stuff."

"I'm sure if we ask Marta to make two soups next week, she can," I soothe, making myself another plate. Arrod looks at me hopefully as I do, and biting back a sigh, I toss a little bit of everything on the plate and then hand it over to him. I'm starting to feel like their mother.

I pick up an empty plate for myself and glance over at Raptor. He has the entire soup tureen in front of him and uses the ladle as a spoon. I fix myself a few bites of food and then sit down at the table to eat with the others. All is quiet, the only sounds those of Raptor ladling soup and Hemmen chewing noisily.

"Thank you," I say to the others after a long moment. "For today. I'm not sure why I've been targeted, but it's disturbing."

"If you get booted, we all do," Arrod reminds me, stacking his cheese and meat into his bread as a makeshift sandwich. "We're protecting ourselves, too."

"Who's doing it?" Hemmen asks. "Is it a former lover who wants you gone?"

"You assume I know who it is," I say, indignant. "I've no idea."

"It's some stranger, then? You didn't flirt with someone?" Hemmen continues.

"Now I'm a tease?" I arch my brows. "All because I'm a woman?"

"Gwenna didn't do anything," Raptor says. "They're targeting her because it's easy to discredit a woman. No one wants her to succeed as it is."

"Thanks for that," I comment, the bitter feeling rising in my stomach. Maybe I'll go spend time with Lark and Mereden this weekend or help Sparrow with her projects. I could use some time with women to relax.

"We want you to succeed," Raptor continues, shrugging his big shoulders. "Even if you're a thief, it's in our best interests for you to pass regardless."

He thinks I'm a thief anyhow? That hurts. I keep my voice flat as I respond. "Thanks."

"It's not personal. It's just business," Arrod says. "We all want to pass."

"I do, too! I just . . . I don't understand." I spread my hands, frustrated. "If I was a thief, why would I go to so much effort to steal artifacts when I can make money by turning them in to the guild?"

Raptor clears his throat. "It's not the same amount of money."

"It's not?" I'm surprised by this.

He chuckles, shaking his head as he ladles another huge swallow of soup. "Gods, no."

"Exactly how much?" My brows draw together, and I try to imagine vast amounts of coin. As a maid, I know all too well how much cheap things cost. I know the price of a loaf of bread, or how much it'll cost to get a new pair of shoes. I know the price of an apron, or a night's stay at an inn. I don't know how much a fancy-pants mirror costs, or a glowing necklace. "I thought all artificers were rich."

Raptor chokes on his soup, coughing as it goes down the wrong pipe.

"Artificers are paid a small standard wage established by the guild," Hemmen says. "With a healthy bonus for every artifact turned in."

"A very small standard wage," Arrod agrees. "A pittance, really."

"That pittance is four times as much as what I made as a maid," I point out. "You lot don't know how good you have it."

They stare at me. Kipp turns to the others and gestures at me, then makes a cutting motion and shakes his head.

"Aye, I don't think she's a thief." Arrod chuckles. "Not if she thinks the guild artificers are swimming in coin."

Raptor just squints at me as if he's noticing me for the first time.

I'm determined not to feel foolish at their reactions. It's not my fault they don't appreciate the difference between making one gold crown a year versus four. They've never bought three-day-old stale bread at the market just to make their pennies stretch because Ma needed a warm cloak for her morning walks to the hold's kitchens. "This is all beside the point. Someone's lying about me because they want me out of here. How do we find who it is?"

"It could be someone sitting at this table," Raptor drawls.

Startled, I look at Arrod and Hemmen. It never occurred to me that it might be one of them. Kipp wouldn't sell me out, because I know him too well. We were fledglings together last year, and I know how crushed he was when we were removed and thrust into the repeater ranks. He was even more hurt than Lark and Mereden, who also took it badly. I trust him.

I trust Raptor, too, strangely enough. He didn't say anything about the strange artifact that was planted in my bag. Still hasn't said anything about it, even now. That leaves Arrod and Hemmen. Arrod is smart but lazy. Hemmen is bookish and even lazier, but he's also repeated four years in a row. Does he want to make it five? If so, why?

"Don't look at me," Arrod protests. "If I was the one trying to get you in trouble, I wouldn't write it in a bloody book. I'd go straight to Master Jay."

"I wouldn't write in a book, either," Hemmen adds. "It's terrible to deface something that takes so long to print. You're ruining it for the next person who wants to learn."

Both have valid points, but they could just be saying that to save face.

I cross my arms under my breasts, my appetite gone, and stare down at the half-eaten food on my plate. "What do I do?"

Kipp pounds his fist into the flat of his hand and makes a frantic motion, like he's catching a bug.

"He's right," Arrod says. "Obviously we have to set a trap."

"And how do we do that?" I ask. "Whoever this is already knows where I'm going to be at all times."

And they might know that I'm a mancer. They might already be plotting to use that information against me.

The thought terrifies me. What if they turn me in to the guild enforcers? Will I be burned in the square as a message to all? It's hard to think straight or control myself when I feel a dead body nearby. Hot panic tightens my lungs, and I want to tear my tunic off and rip away my corset so I can breathe.

"It has to be one of the other fledglings," Arrod says. "They're the only ones who would want to take you out of contention. No one else cares if a woman is an artificer or not." He shrugs, glancing at Hemmen and then Raptor. "So we figure out how to trap the fledgling in the act."

"How do we do that?" Hemmen asks. He looks skeptical.

I am, too. I also can't help but notice that Raptor says nothing. He's just listening quietly to the others. That unnerves me, because I want to know what he's thinking. For some reason, him believing in me matters more than all the others.

"Whoever it is who wrote on those books clearly has access to the library," Arrod points out.

"We all have access to the library." Hemmen shrugs. "I go there all the time."

We all stare at him. Kipp thumps his tail on the table in a decisive manner.

"What?" Hemmen asks, confused. Then he realizes what he's said. "It's not me! I don't want to repeat again, either!"

"But you are at the library all the time." Arrod exchanges a look with Kipp.

"I like to read!"

"You could stake out the library," Raptor says, finally speaking up. "Watch out for people who spend a lot of time there. Talk to the archivists working and see if anyone borrows multiple copies of the same books other than the masters teaching classes."

Arrod snaps his fingers at Raptor. "That's an excellent idea. We'll do that. Since there's five of us, we can set up shifts."

"Splitting up is what the accuser wants," Raptor continues. He leans forward, pushing aside the now-empty soup tureen. "You and Kipp and Hemmen should all stick together. Keep an eye on one another. If the accuser strikes while you're all together, then we know it's not one of you."

Hemmen eyes the Taurian. "And what about you?"

Raptor leans back in his seat. "I'm going to be with Gwenna. I'll keep her away from the library all weekend and we'll focus on training. She's still not very strong or good with her Prellian letters, and now more than ever, it's important that she pass. I'll work with her. More importantly, I'll keep her safe."

No one argues.

THIRTY

RAPTOR

Hawk (and Rooster),

I suspect our thief is one of the repeaters in my Five. Gwenna has been targeted twice now in a ploy to discredit her. Hemmen is likely, as he seems reluctant to participate in much of the training. He spends a lot of time at the library, one of the sites where we've had an incident.

Arrod, I just don't trust. He's too friendly with Gwenna. It makes me suspicious.

Kipp seems trustworthy, but he's also extremely attached to Gwenna.

At any rate, I'm on it and will keep you updated when I've narrowed things down more.

—Raptor

PS—My reward had better be mucking worth all this hassle. Jay is a pain in my tail.

GWENNA IS QUIET throughout the weekend.

It annoys me. A lot.

I don't know what to make of this newest twist. I'm not a deep thinker, and so I don't understand the reasoning behind scrawling messages inside books. Every time I ask Gwenna what she knows, she insists she knows nothing. I trust her. I do. But if she is innocent, why get quiet and withdraw from the rest of us?

I hate her silence. I hate it because I want to fix it and I don't know how.

I try to make her sass me all weekend. I smack her training sword out of her hand over and over as I teach her the basics of sparring. She's mucking dreadful at combat. She's a little better on the obstacle course that I make her run while roped to me, but I purposefully keep my pace brisker than I should because I want her to tell me to slow down. I want her to bellow at me or say something sharp and cutting. I want her to be *Gwenna*.

She doesn't, though. She just squares her shoulders and tries again without complaint.

It pisses me off.

Maybe I'd be more sympathetic if I wasn't potion-dry. As it is, I'm starting to regret that I don't have another dose waiting for me. I thought by now Gwenna would be under me every night—or, since we're both fledglings, we'd be hiding in a closet somewhere with me between her thighs. That my knot would be well and truly milked on a regular basis.

But we haven't touched again since she gave me that hand job last weekend.

It's irritating me. It's not her fault that it's irritating me. I know I'm impossible when I'm on edge. Most Taurians are known to be moody leading up to the rutting frenzy of the Conquest Moon. I have the hand of the god upon me at all times, though. My knot never goes dormant. I am endlessly needing, endlessly searching for relief.

And I get cranky.

I'm aware of it. I can't help it, but I'm aware of it.

It's one reason I never stay on any particular team for long. I end up snapping at someone and making an enemy. Or two. Or three. Other Taurians understand it and tolerate my moodiness more than others, but I've burned a lot of bridges with humans.

I should take another potion. Be done with it. Deaden my cock, improve my mood, and focus on finding the thief. It's just that . . . I want Gwenna to touch me. And I don't want to be numb to it when she does. Taking the potion feels like a betrayal of the woman I want.

And I do want her. More than anything. Even if she's the thief. I've concluded that if she is, it's because she's being forced to do something against her will. Maybe she got pulled into a bad business deal. Maybe she's being blackmailed.

My goal is to find out what's going on so I can help her. Not just because I like her. Not just because the guild needs the leak plugged. I want Gwenna's eyes to shine when she looks at me. I want her eager and excited to touch me, her savior. Am I shit for wanting that? Maybe.

But I want it just the same.

I run her through frantic training on Sixthday. The others stake out the library, taking turns at watching over things. They return to the nest to eat a meal, then head back to the library again that evening. "We've got a great spot on the roof next door," Arrod says, shoving a full loaf of fresh bread into his pack for later. "We can see everything that happens down below. If someone goes through the front doors, we'll see them. If someone heads around to the back alley, we'll see them. No one's getting in under our watch."

"Good," I tell him, and secretly I'm glad that Kipp, Hemmen, and Arrod are all heading out again. It'll give Gwenna the freedom to touch me if she pleases. I'm thinking with my cock, for certain.

But that night, Gwenna is quiet once more. She's silent through dinner, and if I prompt her, she'll speak, but otherwise seems lost in thought.

I'm not getting touched tonight. I fight back my frustration, because I imagine she's scared and worried, which is far more important than the incessant throbbing in my knot.

Gwenna goes to bed early. I decide to as well, since we'll be up at dawn to work on more training. She's silent, but I stare at the ceiling, drumming my fingers on my stomach. My mind won't stop churning. Finally, I roll over and look at her.

She's awake, curled into a ball under the blankets, but her eyes are open.

"You okay?" I ask.

Gwenna hesitates. "I don't know."

"Do you . . ." *Want me to fuck you until you can't think straight?* ". . . need to talk?"

She bites her lip in the darkness. "I want to see Sparrow tomorrow. Can we do that instead of training?"

I'm a little wounded that she doesn't want me to comfort her. That she wants her friend instead. "Just for a little while. You do need to practice."

"I will."

I grunt and turn back to staring at the ceiling. My cock throbs mercilessly, and I know sleep is going to be difficult tonight. Perhaps tomorrow while she's chatting with Sparrow, I can slip out and see if Naiah can get me another potion. But then I'd be leaving Gwenna alone, and I promised I wouldn't. I'm just going to have to bear it.

"Did you mean what you said?" Gwenna's soft voice floats through the darkness. "About keeping me safe?"

"Aye. Meant every bit of it."

"Thank you."

My mood improves, despite everything.

THE NEXT MORNING, Gwenna puts on a dress and bodice, and it throws me off. I'd hoped my knot would calm down after a good night's sleep, but I'd dreamed about Gwenna and her luscious tits. Gwenna and her slick cunt rubbing against my greedy hand.

And now I wake up and see her tits rising like two bread loaves from the top of her corset as she strolls into the kitchen.

I immediately turn and veer down the hall. The garderobe is unoccupied, which means I'm free to slam the door shut behind me, jerk my cock from my pants, and fist it furiously until I come, barely able to swallow the groan that rises from my throat.

It's as fast as it is unsatisfying. By the time I wipe my hand clean on a towel, my cock is rising again. I jerk myself off once more, thinking about Gwenna's magnificent breasts and how she'd worked my knot when she'd touched me. She hadn't acted like it was something to be worried over, like it was a problem that needed solving. It was just part of me. I'd never felt so mucking accepted, and I had no idea I'd find it so damned sexy.

I jerk off twice more before my knot is spent. My cock aches and my hand cramps, but at least I can walk now. I toss the towel into the laundry for the nestmaid to deal with and head back out to join the others eating breakfast in the kitchen.

To my surprise, only Gwenna is there when I return.

"You all right?" she asks, slicing up some bread and putting the pot of honey beside my normal chair.

"Something I ate," I lie. "Where are the others?"

"Returning to their library stakeout. They came by to get food and that was it." Her mouth crooks up in a reluctant smile. "They're having far too much fun with this. Kipp is absolutely in his element."

Are they? That's suspicious.

"Hopefully he'll keep the other two in line." I force myself to walk casually past her chair to the other side of the table. Everything in me wants to nuzzle her soft hair and push my nose against her neck. I'm desperate to breathe deep of her scent. To run my hands over her soft skin. By Old Garesh, today is going to be difficult if I don't get ahold of myself. I thump into my seat.

The moment I do, she sets the sliced bread in front of me. "No butter, just the way you like it."

And now she's taking care of me. My cock surges once more. Gods help me. "We're stopping by somewhere before we go to visit Hawk," I bite out. "No complaining."

Her brows furrow. "I didn't say anything."

"You were thinking it. I can tell."

She throws the piece of bread in her hand at my head. "Clearly you woke up on the wrong side of the bed this morning!"

She's wrong. Waking up implies that I slept, and I didn't sleep much. Not with her so close nearby, and dreams of her tits hounding me every time I closed my eyes.

THIRTY-ONE

GWENNA

RAPTOR IS IN the worst mood this morning, truly. He's utterly insufferable over breakfast and answers every question with a surly response that makes me wonder why I even bother. The moment we're finished eating, he practically stomps his way across Vastwarren to the King's Onion, of all places. He parks me in a seat by the door, all but bellows that he won't be a moment, and then puts his head down with the barmaid and whispers to her.

A very pretty barmaid that I know well—Naiah. She smiles broadly at Raptor, her expression more welcoming than anything she's sent to me or the others in the bar. I hate that I'm noticing. I hate that they're talking so intently and she smiles.

I hate that I'm jealous.

The two of them don't talk long, at least. Perhaps they notice me glaring at them from afar. Then Raptor returns to my side with a rueful smile, as if he realizes what a shitty thing he's just done, and tries to put a hand on the small of my back. I shrug him away and walk briskly ahead of him. "Let's hurry. I want to get there before Aspeth leaves and heads to work."

"Sparrow."

I wince. She was Aspeth to me for over fifteen years. It's difficult to remember the change, but I know she's so very proud of her new name. "Sparrow," I agree. "My apologies."

We head over to Master Hawk's nest. Hawk and his fledglings live at the far edge of the guild streets, in a more modern house with a second story and a gabled roof. Hawk's symbol flutters from a flagpole above the front door, and I'm filled with a curious yearning. How simple things were last year, when we were Magpie's students. I've been Master Jay's student for longer, but I felt more at home with Lark, Mereden, Aspeth, and Kipp.

Now I've got Arrod and Hemmen, who annoy me; Raptor, who I want to alternately kiss or strangle; and Kipp, who I'm terrified of disappointing if I fail this year.

We pause at the front door, and inside, I can hear bellowing. "Your right arm! Your *other* right arm!"

I glance up at Raptor. "Should we knock?"

He huffs with amusement and pushes his way inside. Immediately, a fluffy black cat scurries away deeper into the house. We move in, with me following a step behind Raptor. As we do, two other cats trot down the stairs, and another is curled up on the desk near the fireplace. I don't recognize any of these cats. Sparrow's big orange cat, Squeaker, sheds like crazy, but I wasn't aware that Sparrow or her husband had acquired more of them. I watch incredulously as another comes toward us and rubs against my skirts, purring.

"Where did all these cats come from?" I exclaim as I follow Raptor.

"Pick up your weapons," Hawk bellows from a nearby room. "Get your packs. We're going on a hike."

"It's Sevensday," a man protests.

It's silent after that, and I can just picture the glare Hawk is shooting in his direction. A moment later, five students with fledgling sashes come marching toward the front door, a heavy pack on each back and a wooden sword in each hand. I know from experience that the packs are filled with rocks and Hawk is probably going to make them walk up and down the streets of Vastwarren to work on their strength and stamina.

Hawk emerges after the final student, shutting the door to the training room behind him. He looks surprised to see both of us, his gaze flicking to Raptor and then to me, and then back to Raptor. "This is unexpected."

"Is Sparrow here?" I ask. "I wanted to visit."

"She's in our quarters. Go knock on the door. I'm sure she'll be thrilled to see you." He gives me a faint smile. "You've picked a good day to visit. Lark and Mereden are coming over, too."

They are? "That's lovely. I've missed them so much."

And then I burst into tears.

THIRTY-TWO

RAPTOR

IT TAKES EVERY bit of my strength not to wrap my arms around Gwenna as she cries. The untamed bull inside me is furious at her distress, and part of me wants to pull her against me and comfort her. Unfortunately, a bigger part of me wants to push her up against the wall and rut her, so I don't dare touch her. I focus instead on the potion Naiah's going to have for me later.

I still feel like a monster, though, as I watch her cry and do nothing to help her.

Hawk shoots me an alarmed look—he doesn't like women crying any more than I do. Before he can say anything, Sparrow rushes out, her arms wide. "Oh, Gwenna! I didn't realize you were here! Are you all right?"

"I'm fine. I swear it." Gwenna sniffles hard and manages a cheery smile that doesn't match the tears in her eyes. "I just desperately needed to visit a friend."

Sparrow gives me an indignant look as she pulls Gwenna into her embrace. "You're safe here."

I'm offended that she'd dare to suggest that Gwenna isn't safe with me. My hackles prick and I resist the urge to growl at Sparrow—or push her away from Gwenna and comfort her myself. Hawk clears his throat as I glare. "I was just about to run my students up and down the streets. Want to join us?"

I hesitate, but surely Gwenna will be safe at Hawk's nest. "No one else is here but the students, right?" When Hawk nods, I point at Sparrow. "Both of you stay here. Don't leave her alone. Not even for a moment."

Both women glare at me.

"Come on," Hawk says to me, clapping a hand on my shoulder. "We'll just go up and down the street. The house will stay in sight at all times."

I grunt acknowledgment and accompany him after his students, even though I don't want to leave Gwenna behind. I remind myself that whoever is trying to frame her won't try anything in front of Hawk. I also remind myself that Gwenna might be the framer.

I don't like her tears regardless.

"You all right?" Hawk asks as we walk. His students are already several paces ahead, jogging in a perfect line as they make their way up the steep street.

"I'm managing." Hawk doesn't know that I've been taking potions lately. He thinks I'm addicted to women. He doesn't know the real reason behind it. He knows my mood can be changeable, though.

"Any . . . luck?"

I know what he's referring to without him having to clarify. "Nothing more. Arrod and Hemmen and Kipp are staking out the library to watch for any suspicious characters while I keep an eye on Gwenna."

"I don't think whoever it is will go back to the library again," Hawk muses, turning to watch his students.

I keep my eye on the door to his nest. "I don't, either, but it gives them something to do. Whoever it is who's involved, they're a good mucking liar. I can't make out who it might be. Arrod's an excitable idiot, but he's not a bad sort. Hemmen is a complainer, but I doubt he'd scrawl anything in a book. He seemed offended at the thought."

"And Kipp?"

I huff with amusement at that. "Not Kipp. He'd stab my eyes out before he'd let anyone accuse her of anything."

"Kipp is a good sort," Hawk agrees. "Arrogant little shit, though. You're still certain that our thief is in your Five?"

"To be honest, I'm not certain of anything anymore. Any strangeness with your Five?"

He shakes his head. "Model students. They're all very determined not to repeat again, and work twice as hard as they need to on anything I assign them. I haven't found a single thing to be suspicious of." He pauses, and then adds with a grin, "Except for their inability to tell their right from their left."

"Mmm." I glance back at the door to his nest again. It bothers me to leave Gwenna alone with Sparrow, but surely she'll be all right in there. I can't imagine anyone would target her while she's visiting a friend. Unless it's all to distract me from Gwenna being the person I'm hunting for. I still haven't ruled that out yet. It feels unlikely, but is it only because I'm lusting after her? It's hard to trust myself. "I was suspicious of Gwenna, but I don't know that she's a good enough actress, especially when she's targeting herself."

"It's not her. She's too loyal. Good heart."

"But she *is* a thief," I remind him. We all know the story of how Gwenna had stolen something from the Everbelow and Sparrow tried to cover for her.

"She did it to save my wife. That's different. She's had many other opportunities and never stolen a thing." Hawk turns and gives me a curious look. "Why are you so focused on her?"

Because I'm worried I'll get blindsided.

I keep that to myself and only shrug. "I'm not."

I am, though. Focused and obsessed and annoyed with myself because of it.

"It might not be the thieves targeting her anyhow," Hawk comments. "More likely that it's an old lover of hers who doesn't want her in the guild."

The thought scorches my brain and blisters with the force of my hot, searing jealousy. Another lover? Not that I expect her to be chaste, but she's mine now.

Mine.

Gods, I need that potion right away. I'm acting like a jealous lover myself. I scrub a hand down my muzzle. "I don't know of any lovers."

Other than me.

Hawk shrugs, his attention veering back to his students. "It's entirely possible that whoever is targeting Gwenna isn't the thief we're searching for after all. It could just be someone with an axe to grind against a woman trying to join the guild."

Great. More to consider.

THIRTY-THREE

GWENNA

S PENDING TIME WITH my friends is just what I needed. Sparrow fusses over me the moment she sees I'm crying and leads me to the kitchen. My tears dry almost immediately because I hate feeling sorry for myself. Sparrow makes me sit at the table and pours me some hot tea and then begins to cut up some bread and cheese to make a snack tray. Poor thing is terrible at it, hacking at the cheese as best she can, but it's sweet of her to try and so I don't criticize.

"Tell me everything that's been going on," Sparrow insists, sawing at a block of cheese with what must be the dullest knife in all of creation.

Before I can launch into my tale of woe, a cat jumps onto my lap. It's Squeaker, her fat orange cat from home. Squeaker made the trek from Honori Hold to Vastwarren City with us, and it feels as if she's arrived to comfort me as well. "Well, hello there," I coo to the cat, letting her make biscuits on my thighs before she settles onto my lap. I stroke her fur and immediately tufts of it float into the air. Sparrow fans the cat hair away from the cheese, and discreetly moves the plate a bit farther away so I can continue to pet the cat. I scratch at Squeaker's ears, listening to her contented purring as Sparrow cusses at the cheese that's fighting her.

Lark and Mereden show up before I get far into my story, and then we're all hugging, with Squeaker making protesting sounds (but not getting off my lap). Lark drapes herself around my neck, snuggling me as if she hasn't seen me in ages, and the tears threaten once more. "Are you loving being a fledgling again? I'm so stinking jealous!"

It makes me want to burst into fresh tears. "Actually, no. It's a mucking nightmare."

"Is someone being mean to you?" Mereden asks, offense bristling through her sweet, gentle voice. It's almost comical to think that pleasant and easygoing Mereden is determined to defend me.

"Worse. I'm being set up."

Lark hobbles over to the far side of the table, grabs the cheese plate for herself, and gestures that I should keep talking. "Tell us everything."

So I tell them everything. Well, most everything. I don't tell them about Raptor, because I don't know how things are between us and I don't feel like having my friends hash it out. Instead, I tell them all about someone dropping an artifact into my bag to frame me and then the subsequent search of Master Jay's nest. I tell them about the message scrawled in the books, and how the others are staking out the library to see if they can catch whoever it is.

"Why do you think they're targeting you?" Mereden asks, worried. She steals a piece of cheese from Lark's plate, her gaze locked on me.

"Gotta be the tits," Lark chimes in.

Sparrow hesitates. "Truly, it can't be just that . . . can it?"

"What else could it be?" Mereden asks.

I glance over at Sparrow. I'm thinking what she is—that someone might have it out for me because of my mancer ability. Is it safe to share my secret with them? She shrugs, leaving it up to me.

Do I trust Mereden and Lark with my secret . . . and my life? Because I'll be killed if it gets out.

I look at my friends' worried, earnest faces. I haven't even told my mother about my ability because I'm afraid to write it down. Blurting it aloud feels terrifying. The only reason that Sparrow knows about what I can do is because of the situation with the corpses last year. Otherwise, I'd have kept it a dirty secret, known only to me. "I . . ."

The words don't come out.

"You don't have to say anything," Mereden reassures me. "We're your friends all the same."

"Are you in trouble of some kind?" Lark pushes her fist against her flat palm. "Do I need to bust heads?"

"No one's busting anyone's head," Sparrow frets, even as another cat jumps on the table. This one's a tabby, and she gives it a quick pet before pulling it off. "Not now, Buttons."

Mereden points a badly cut wedge of cheese at me. "Is this about your dowsing?"

I go still.

"You think?" Lark mulls the idea. "It didn't work for anyone else. Heck, it didn't even work for us. It kept pointing us right at dead guys. You . . ."

Her eyes widen.

Mereden gasps.

"That's the problem," I whisper, hugging Squeaker tight even as cat hair wafts into the air around me. "I think I might be a mancer. Worse, I think someone else knows that, too."

THIRTY-FOUR

GWENNA

I DIDN'T SAY ANYTHING. I swear," Sparrow says immediately, a worried expression on her face. "You know I would never speak of it. I haven't even said anything to Hawk."

"I know you wouldn't," I reassure her, but the tight clenching in my gut doesn't go away. Perhaps I've been too careless. Someone's been watching me too closely and they've discovered my ability and want me gone.

"It's true?" Mereden's mouth forms an O. "You really are a mancer?"

She and Lark exchange an uneasy look.

"I don't know." Squeaker jumps out of my lap, and I hug my arms tight to my chest, as if I can reassure my body somehow that everything will be all right. Strangely enough, I wish Raptor were here to hug me. He's so big and strong and reassuring that he'd give the best sorts of hugs. I've never been a hugger before, but I wouldn't mind him holding me close. I hate that Mereden and Lark are gazing at me with distrust. Like I'm something they've never seen before.

"We can't say anything at all," Sparrow reminds them gently. "Not to anyone. This is a dangerous secret."

"Of course not," Mereden replies, composing herself. She smiles encouragingly at me.

Lark just stares, her eyes narrowed with suspicion. "You really are one?"

"Why would I mucking lie about it? Who in their right mind would want to be a mancer?" I hiss.

Lark considers that. "Can you mance anything? Can you heal my ankle?"

"It's very specific magic. Actually, I'm not even sure if it's magic. I just know that I can hear the dead. I can feel them when they're around."

"Ew." Her expression changes from worried to relaxed. "That's a shitty power. You're right. No one would want that."

Mereden keeps her composure, nibbling on a bite of cheese. "Have you always known you could do this?"

I shake my head. "It all really started when we went down in the caverns and I picked up the divining rod. I felt something then, like my skin was crawling. Like I had jitters. I thought it was just nerves because I was frightened."

"We were all frightened," Lark agrees. "I was shitting myself."

"You were not," Mereden chides her demurely. "Be nice."

Lark looks over at me and mouths, "Shitting."

My lips twitch with amusement. "Anyhow, after it happened the second time and it led us to another dead guy, I started to wonder. Then a few months ago, when I was doing repeater work cleaning a house, I noticed that I could feel something coming from the alley. It felt like it did down in the tunnels. Like my skin was jumping and my nerves were lighting on fire. I went out of the building to see what it was, and there was a dead man in the alley."

I rub my arms as if I can still feel the sensations.

"Holy mucking shit," Lark breathes. "That's incredible. What did you do?"

Sparrow chimes in. "She told the authorities, like she should have."

"But then it happened again," I tell them. "Just before recruitment day. I could feel the dead man nearby. He was in an alley again, and this time I could feel things about him. Like memories that weren't mine. What he was thinking. What it felt like when they cut his throat." I stroke a hand over my neck in sympathy. "And I had to leave him there, because I can't exactly go around pointing out dead men in alleys, can I?"

My friends are silent.

"That's all I know." It feels good to get it out in the open, to quit carrying it around like an anvil. "I don't know where this power came from or how to make it stop. I wish it would go away. All I want is to be an artificer so I can make a decent living."

Mereden taps a finger on her lips, thinking. "And this never happened back at the hold?"

"Never."

She continues to think, then glances over at Sparrow. "Is it possible that all the magic in Old Prell is activating it? That all that power below Vastwarren is somehow bringing this to the surface?"

Lark turns to look at her wife. "You aren't more concerned about people being murdered in the alleys? That's two now, right? With throats cut?"

I nod at them. "Both repeaters."

"I'm just saying, for a guild that's supposed to keep us safe, they're doing a piss-poor job of it." Lark leans back in her seat, scowling. "How's anyone supposed to raise a family in this?"

"I don't imagine you're supposed to," Mereden says, soothing her with a smile. "But we're going to do it anyhow."

"But you said you were being targeted," Lark points out, putting a hand on Mereden's leg under the table. "Do you think someone's going to try to murder you next, Gwenna?"

I hadn't thought of that. "Well, *now* I do."

Mereden frowns, her expression unconvinced. "I'm not sure these incidents are connected to your power. Why would someone try to out a mancer as a thief when all they need to do is notify the authorities?"

It's a good question, and one I don't have an answer to.

A calico cat jumps on the table and then makes its way over to Sparrow's side, tapping her politely with a paw. She reaches for the cat, cradling it in her arms like a baby and rubbing its belly. Before I can ask where all these cats have come from, she turns her gaze to me. "What if we give you an artifact? A fake? We could use it as a decoy to try to flush out whoever's harassing you. Or better yet . . . the emergency globes have a tracking spell on them. We can leave one out and see who takes it."

"Anyone involved with the guild would recognize a tracking globe," I point out. "It's a good idea, though."

"If you ask me, you should cozy up to the big Taurian in your Five. What's his name again?" Lark asks.

"Raptor." My face gets hot just saying his name.

"That's the one. Don't let him out of your sight." Lark reaches out and scratches the chin of the cat in Sparrow's arms. "Are you two friendly?"

Now I'm really turning red. I clear my throat, determined to change the subject. "Friendly enough. Sparrow, where are all these cats coming from?"

Sparrow presses a kiss to the cat's head. "These are my cats. Some of them needed homes and I thought, Why not with me?"

"Why are they here and not at the archives?"

"Oh, the cats at the archives are different cats."

"But why so many?"

Sparrow grins wickedly at me. "Because I'm my own woman, and no one can tell me no. And I love cats. And Hawk loves me. So . . . cats."

Fair enough. What would I do if I was married to a big Taurian who doted on me and gave me anything I desired? A mental image flashes to mind, of me atop the counter, Raptor's hand in my pants.

I guess I'm a far more carnal sort than Sparrow, because if I had a big Taurian in my bed all the time, the last thing I'd be thinking about is cats.

LARK AND MEREDEN and I eat all the snacks that Sparrow puts out for us. We pet all the cats, gossip about nothing and everything, and then share a long, wonderful hug when it's time to go. Lark and Mereden leave first, as they want to visit the orphanage before heading home. I linger a little longer, listening to the returning students tromping up the stairs.

"Sounds like Hawk and Raptor are back." Sparrow puts her hand on mine. "I'm still learning what I can about mancers, but I'm trying not to draw attention. Archivist Kestrel has me working on a cataloging project, so it's taking me away from my research, but I promise I haven't forgotten."

"I know you haven't." I give her hand a friendly squeeze. "I'm just worried about this upcoming week. We're going back into the tunnels again. Master Jay wants us to train in the practice tunnels, but every time I go down, I feel all the dead still in the Everbelow. There are so many voices down there. . . ."

I rub my brow just thinking about it.

"You mentioned that the sensation takes you over," she says. "Is there something you can do to dull it? To push it away so you can focus?"

"I've been distracting myself, aye." That's one way of putting it.

"And this distracting, it's been working?" When I nod, she continues. "Keep doing that, then. Whatever it takes, make sure no one else knows your secret. I can't imagine that whoever is killing people wants a mancer, but it never hurts to be safe."

Keep distracting myself with Raptor? Now I'm thinking filthy thoughts all over again.

THIRTY-FIVE

Rooster to Raptor: *Any updates on our situation?*

Raptor to Rooster: *How many times must we go over this? When there's an update, you'll know.*

MY CHAT WITH Hawk was unfulfilling. I can't blame him. It's hard to have a secretive conversation about the state of the guild's thief hunt when he's busy training his students. Nothing else has been stolen from the guild coffers in the last week, though. I don't know if that's a good thing or a bad thing, because it doesn't rule Gwenna out.

And I'm becoming increasingly desperate to rule Gwenna out, because I'm growing obsessed with her.

It's a problem. A Five is supposed to be friendly and loyal . . . but fooling around? Not supposed to happen. Yet when Gwenna emerges from Hawk's dorm with cat hair all over her dress and a sunny smile on her face, I want to grab her and squeeze her tight. I'd much rather see her happy than crying.

"Feel better?" I ask, my voice gruff. She moves to stand beside me, and I put a hand on the small of her back—and this time, she doesn't push me away. It feels like a victory.

"Some? I just didn't realize how much I'd missed my friends until now. It was good to be on a team with them. I miss that."

I feel a stab of jealousy. "You're on a team with me. And Kipp."

"And Hemmen and Arrod, neither of whom I trust all that much. Do you?"

I grunt.

"I know I just need to get over it." Her voice is light, but there's a hint of wistfulness in her tone. "Sparrow loves being an archivist. Lark and Mereden are talking about children. And I just . . . I want the best for them, but I guess I'm also selfish because I want them at my side, too."

"I get it."

"Do you?"

"Every Taurian does. We'd much rather be heading into the tunnels in a Five made of Taurians, but they always split us up. It's just part of the job. I've learned to think of it as doing my duty to the less fortunate."

She chuckles, and the sound goes straight to my cock. "That's one way of looking at it."

"You make family where you can, and you make the best of a bad hand every time. That's all you can do."

Gwenna glances up at me, her dark eyes full of emotion. "Like you are with being demoted?"

"Aye, I suppose so. I hate it. I hate how the others crack jokes about an embarrassing situation. But it's not forever. You must remind yourself of that. And it's not so terrible. You get to meet people you might not regularly sleep next to."

Her cheeks color, and I could swear I pick up a hint of arousal in the breeze. "Oh?"

"Never would have met Hemmen otherwise," I agree, and her wicked snort of surprised laughter makes me smile.

"So Hemmen is my competition? Good to know."

Is she flirting with me? I lean closer as we turn onto a more crowded street. "Sweet little bantam, you should know you have no competition. In this world or the next."

"Keep saying things like that and you're going to get your knot bitten again."

Mucking hell. Here's hoping.

The walk back to the nest is a long one, and by the time we make it back my cock is throbbing. Do I head to the alley behind the tavern to get the potion Naiah promised to leave for me? Or do I hope that the promise in Gwenna's voice is more than just flirting? I'm torn. The last thing I want is for her to reach for me and my cock to be as limp as wet laundry.

I might regret it, but I opt to skip the potion.

When we return to the nest, we're the first ones back. The dorm is echoing and empty, and Gwenna hesitates in the hallway, her hands fisting in her skirts.

I wait next to her, like a lovesick calf. After a moment, I clear my throat. "You look nice today, in a dress. Not that you don't normally look nice. You always look good."

Her lips quirk at my uncharacteristic mumbling. "Thank you. If you don't mind me saying, I feel more like myself in a dress than in a fledgling uniform." She puts a hand to the front of her dress and lets out a ragged breath. "I'm terribly nervous about this week."

"Because we'll be in the Everbelow?" I ask. She was nervous the last time we went in, stabbing at her hand to keep from showing her terror. "You aren't going to hurt yourself again, are you?"

Her gaze seems distracted. "No, I won't. But if I get . . . nervous, will you let me climb you and beg for a kiss? As a distraction?"

"No begging required. You just indicate you want me and I'll distract you so good your toes will curl."

Her breathing shudders. "That sounds very nice to me. I'm going to take you up on that, you know."

"I hope you do." By Old Garesh, I hope she takes me up on it as quickly as possible.

She chews on her lip, then glances up at me. "Maybe I just need practice."

"Or the right weapon in your grip." *Now, let me tell you all about the weapon I want to put in your sweet grip.*

"I'm rotten with all weapons," Gwenna admits. "Master Jay wanted me to practice with you specifically on that, remember?"

I do recall a few sour comments that Jay has made about her prowess, aye. "No worse than Hemmen."

"Well, that's reassuring," she jokes.

"Actually, I've got something for you," I say, indicating she should follow me into the weapons room. Jay will probably lay an egg when he sees what I've acquired, but I plan on having a talk with him anyhow. Just because Gwenna's a woman doesn't mean she shouldn't be given the tools to succeed. Her wrists are more delicate, her build different. If Kipp can use shorter weapons because of his height, she should be allowed to use a special sort of weapon to accommodate her more delicate bone structure. Luckily, I'm two steps ahead of Jay in that department.

Her expression grows wary. "It had better not be an artifact."

I laugh at that, shaking my head. "It is, but it's not magical. I pulled it from the guild's weapons locker, so no one is going to get mad at you for having it. Old Prell had women warriors, and they fought with much lighter weapons than those the men used. Clubbing someone with something takes less skill than using a sword, so I thought a morning star might be perfect for you."

"A morning star?" Gwenna echoes, following me as I head into the training room.

"It's a club that has a spiky, bulbous end. You swing that and no one will get in your way. No need to be precise." I pull it out of the trunk that I've been hiding it in so Hemmen or Arrod wouldn't claim it first. "I found one on a dig once, one with magical charges still. It was the prettiest, shiniest thing I'd ever seen, and it looked like a star on the end of a stick." The image of it still haunts me, and the gut-clench feeling of having to turn it over to the guild to be promptly sold to some fat, rich holder.

"It sounds lovely."

I grunt. "This one isn't. It's ugly as sin, but it's lightweight and beat to hell. There's no magic left in it, and it was left in the training common room, so that means it's free game."

She hesitates. "I don't want anyone to think I'm thieving. . . ."

"They'd have to get through me first," I growl. When she manages a tiny smile, I continue. "I already logged that I was taking it anyhow. Here, let me show it to you."

I move to the trunk and pull the weapon out. It's as light as a baton, the bulbous head of it battered and even dented in one part. The grip has been refreshed with leather bindings, and there are a few fat spikes sticking up from the rounded end. I hold it out to her, expecting her to wrinkle her nose at just how ugly the thing is. It doesn't have the shine of a sword. It's tarnished all over, but it'll kill a ratling just the same.

Gwenna takes it from me, and her eyes widen as she hefts it. "It's so light!"

"Aye, I thought it'd be perfect for you and those delicate wrists."

She gives it a test swing and then smiles widely. "This is incredible." Her gaze slides to me. "My wrists might be delicate, but they still do the job."

"Never said they didn't." By the old bull, I'm still thinking about her hand on my cock.

Gwenna runs her hand over the fat end of the morning star, trailing a finger down its surface. "This is a wonderful present, Raptor. Thank you."

My name. It sounds bloody amazing coming from those sweet lips of hers. How is it I haven't heard her say it very often? That needs to change. "It's not a gift. It's me thinking of my Five."

She teases her finger over the blunt spike on the head of the thing. "Are you always only concerned about your Five, then? When you think of me?"

"Hardly mucking ever. You know I'm thinking of you." I'm practically growling the words at her, leaning one hand on the wall and looming over her smaller form.

"Mmm. I don't know if I believe you." There's a flirty tone in her voice, a playful look in her eyes as she gazes up at me.

"You don't think I'm obsessed with you?" Is she mad? Has she not noticed how obsessed I am? I'm all but slavering for just a hint of her attention. When she moves to toy with the spike again, I grab her hand and press it against my rigid cock. "What does that tell you?"

"It tells me that you've got a big fat cock," she whispers, and licks her lips. "And that you need it played with."

I all but wheeze when she strokes her hand along the outline of my shaft. "I wouldn't let anyone play with it but you, Gwenna. I'd rather hump my fist."

"No need to be dramatic." She slides her hand lower, cupping my sac through my clothes. "I feel like saying thank you to you."

For some reason, those words irk me. "I'm not interested in a thank-you."

"What are you interested in, then?"

"Pleasure." I use my weight to push her back against the wall and press the morning star between our chests. The longer stem of it pushes against her hips and she squeaks in surprise, her eyes widening as she gazes up at me. I take it from her grip and press the handle against the vee between her thighs and then rub it against the fat mound of her cunt, through her clothing.

Her eyes flutter with arousal, and a moment later, her scent permeates the air. "Oh . . . you . . ."

"Me. Aye. I want to see you come first. Then you can work my cock all you like." It's the rutting bull inside me that's taking control, getting possessive and demanding. I want to make her come. I want to make her remember this moment. I want to sear it into her mind.

With the hilt of the morning star in my grasp, I push it against her cunt, parting her folds and rubbing the end of it against her. Her mouth falls open and I brush her lower lip with my thumb.

"Tell me if it's too much. If you don't want this."

Her breath shudders, and then she arches her hips against the weapon.

Ah. Perfect, delicious woman. "That's right, darling. Let me make you feel good."

"Raptor," Gwenna moans, rocking against the hilt. I hold it steady for her, my thumb dipping farther into her mouth, into the wet heat of her. She whimpers and sucks on it, and the breath hisses from my throat.

"That's right. Use me, sweet girl. Use me to feel good. Isn't that what one teammate does for another?"

She grabs my hand, clinging to the one I have on her face, and looks me in the eye as she shatters. Her entire body quivers, the tops of her full breasts jiggling in response to her orgasm. She catches her breath, and then pushes against me.

When I retreat a step, I see the evidence of her arousal—and her release—as a wet stain on the front of her skirt.

"You're very pretty when you come," I comment, feeling smug. No, not smug. Just in my element. Like this is where I'm meant to be, right here with her, watching her come under my hand. This is how it should be.

"Liked that, did you?" Gwenna sounds delightfully breathless, her cheeks pink.

"Aye, you know I did."

"Mmm." She doesn't fuss over her skirts, just smooths a hand over her hair, glances at the door, and then drops to her knees. Setting her weapon down, she reaches for the front of my pants. "Don't knot my mouth, all right? The last thing I want to do is get caught by the others while choking on bull cock."

I'm speechless that she's going to take me into her mouth. It's rare—no sex worker wants to get her face that close to my knot, and most of my lovers in the past have been just that. "You . . . sure? You don't have to—"

She frees my cock and her mouth closes over the head.

A grunt of pleasure escapes me. I want to put both hands on her smaller head and work her over my cock, but I worry I'll lose control. I clench my fists on the wall instead, bracing myself there as it takes every bit of control I have to remain still while she tongues my cock and strokes my balls with her fingers. Her mouth is wet and sloppy and sucking, and it's the best thing I've ever felt . . .

. . . until she pinches the hard knot at the base of my shaft. My eyes nearly roll back in my skull with the sharp bite of pleasure. I snort like the bull I am and my hips jerk, my tail flicking wildly behind me. I rock against her mouth, and when she makes a noise of encouragement, I shuttle between her glorious lips. Her fingers work the base of my cock, soothing and stroking my knot before giving it another sharp pinch.

This time, I come, exploding my release into her mouth. I expect her to jerk away, to recoil as she should, because a Taurian comes with fierce, copious release. But not this incredible woman. She swallows what she can of my seed, and then rubs the leaking tip of my cock all over her chin until she's coated, my release dripping onto her gorgeous tits.

"I feel better," she comments, her mouth rosy and pink and still messy with my seed. "How about you?"

I just groan. Again.

Gwenna uses her skirt to mop the rest of the mess off her face, and then gets to her feet. She grimaces at the sight of her clothing, and then shrugs. As I stand there, my cock throbbing, my knot swollen with the force of my release, she picks up her new weapon and then crooks a finger at me, indicating I should lean down.

When I do, she kisses the end of my nose, right between my nostrils. "I'm going to change. Might want to tuck yourself in before the others return."

Bossy thing.

I mucking love it.

THIRTY-SIX

GWENNA

KNOWING THAT YOU'RE going to feel the dead below the ground doesn't soften the blow of descending into the caverns. I've got my pack on my back, my new weapon slung through a leather loop in my belt, and I'm roped to the others as Master Jay leads us into the practice tunnels.

We're in the very first drop. The shallowest of tunnels, the ones closest to the surface. These are considered the practice tunnels, which new students are brought to so they can get a feel for what being a guild artificer is about before they delve into the deeper maze of the Everbelow. This is as introductory as it gets.

Yet the moment we descend, my skin begins to crawl.

"Note the height of this tunnel," Master Jay begins as our team follows along behind him like ducklings. The weirdest set of ducklings ever, perhaps. Kipp is in the lead, with Arrod and Hemmen behind him. I'm behind them, and Raptor takes up the rear.

Arrod wanted Raptor in the second spot, as befitting a team's shield (to Kipp's sword), but Raptor declined. "You're not going to be able to see around me," he told us. "And I already know what I'm doing down here."

When the others turned away, he pinched my butt. I smacked him, but only half-heartedly. My head is swimming, the dizzying fog starting to creep into my senses and muting the voices of the others.

"The farther in you go, the more likely the tunnels will be a great deal narrower, so keep that in mind," Master Jay continues. "If the fit gets too tight, you are always welcome to widen the pathway . . . with the right permits filed, of course."

"Of course," Arrod pipes up, and I don't know if he's mocking the teacher or just enthusiastic.

"This particular tunnel goes on for two *yents* in this direction and three in the other. It's rumored to be one of the first tunnels dug out by Sparkanos and his people. For all that it's historical, I'm sorry to say that this particular tunnel is devoid of all artifacts."

A sour feeling drifts through me, as if saying *wrong*. I don't know if it's my thought or a dead person's, but a moment later, I feel a throb, like a bug bite, off in the distance. More whispers fill my ears in languages I don't understand. They hiss and chatter, drowning out whatever Master Jay says next, and I blink repeatedly, trying to focus on Hemmen's collar ahead of me. He's got a lantern on a staff, like the one I'd carried for the Taurians the other day.

The light doesn't seem nearly bright enough to push away the darkness around us. Normally I'm not afraid of the dark, but this one has ghosts in it, and they're whispering in my ear. I stare into the shadows, my skin covered in goose bumps.

I don't notice that we're moving forward until the rope gets tight at my waist, jerking me forward.

"Keep up," Hemmen calls back.

"Sorry." I walk a little faster.

"You all have your pickaxes and your shovels, I trust?" Master Jay asks, pausing again as the cavern opens. The rock walls sweep away, revealing what looks like the crumbled remains of a temple pushed off to the side. The strange, pervasive lichen that covers everything down here is all over the marble bricks and the shattered columns, and the ceiling arches so high that it disappears in our lantern light.

A heavy hand clasps the back of my neck, shockingly warm and making me jump. Raptor leans over my shoulder, his muzzle near my ear. "You all right?"

I manage a nod and reach up to brush my fingertips over his muzzle. I touch the ring in his nose, and then his lips before trailing away. I don't know when it was we got so touchy-feely with each other, but right now, I could use more touching.

"Now, let us go over our gear again," Master Jay says, hands clasped behind his back. He looks completely comfortable—if slightly bored—in the echoing recesses of the tunnel. "Normally this would be the responsibility of the Five's gearmaster, but we'll split jobs up in the future as you become more familiar with moving about in the tunnels. Show me your weapons, please."

I hold up my morning star—which Master Jay fussed over earlier today, but only a little, because Raptor glared at him. Raptor holds up his pickaxe, because he's stated before that he's best with his hands. Only, this morning, he looked at me as he said it, and winked, and it took everything I had not to snort with amusement.

Or blush.

"What else is absolutely vital when in the tunnels?" Master Jay asks, his gaze moving down the line of us. "Hemmen?"

Water drips on my head from above—not a surprise, as the stone floors here are wet and there are stalagmites and stalactites along the uneven edges of the walls.

Under the pillar.

It's not really a voice in my head as much as it is a flash of a memory that's not mine. I turn my gaze toward the shattered remnants of a marble pillar close by. The tugging at my senses continues, telling me that it's not that one. That I should look farther up. Up. Up.

Sure enough, there's a stone cornice—the decorated top of a pillar—on a ledge above, heavy with moss and nearly hidden. There's a pulsing there, like an open wound, and I want to rub my arms to whisk away the chill that's set upon me.

"And you, Gwenna?"

I jerk back to attention, pinching my arm. "Mm? Sorry, I was taking a mental count of our foodstuffs," I lie quickly. "But my canteen is full."

"I was asking about your rescue signal stone," Jay says in a sour voice.

"Got that, too." I smile brightly and do my absolute best not to look up at the column that the ghosts keep whispering to me about.

I bite the side of my tongue, forcing myself to pay attention as we finish checking the gear we stuffed into our packs not an hour ago. Hemmen gazes at our surroundings with a hint of disdain, but Arrod looks
thrilled to be in the tunnels. Kipp is stoic, but then again, he's Kipp. He
licks his eyeball once, gaze focused on Master Jay, and I know he's excited. He always licks his eyeball when he's excited. It's the only tell I've
been able to figure out for him so far.

"Do you feel you're ready for the next step?" Master Jay asks us.

"So ready," Arrod exclaims, and Kipp thumps his thick tail on the
ground twice.

"Ready," I agree, hoping my voice doesn't sound as faint as it feels.

"Ready," says Hemmen.

"Let's do this," Raptor drawls. "Before I die of old age."

Master Jay shoots him an irked look, but then smooths his expression
again. "As I said, I have hidden an artifact in the tunnel here. You are to
find it and return it to me, and then we'll discuss how an artifact is properly cataloged. No need to worry about damaging the relic—this one is
powerless. Your goal here is simply to find it and return. Remember that
you must work together."

My breath speeds up. Find the artifact? I could laugh. The ghosts just
told me exactly where it is, and I could end this quickly and get us out of
here . . . but I can't. I can't even tell the rest of my team because they'll
all wonder how I know, and I'll seem even more suspicious than before.

Arrod raises his hand. "How do we know what we're looking for?"

"No artifact hunter knows what they're hunting for when they come
into the tunnels. I aim to duplicate that joy of discovery for you. Instead,
focus on clues in the environment that might lead you to excavate in a
certain spot. Look for ruins, of course, but look for breaks in the rocks.
Look for moss growing over unusual shapes. Raptor can tell you all about
this, I'm sure."

"I thought I was supposed to let them learn for themselves," Raptor
drawls.

Master Jay shoots him a look. "You can guide but not overrule."

"Right. That sounds like me." His tone is full of sarcasm.

"I'll leave you all to it, then. Good luck and good hunting, my fledglings." Master Jay nods at all of us, and then takes the lantern from Hemmen's hand, leaving us in the darkness.

Immediately, the whispers fill the air. I can sense the dead even more now that it's dark. I rub my arms, shivering. Waiting for the feelings to go away. Instead, they just get worse. They grow deeper, seeping into my pores. Into my bones.

"He took our light," Hemmen complains, distracting me.

"I would imagine he expects you to make another one," Raptor comments. His big hand kneads the back of my neck. "I can see just fine, so you're not in danger, but you might want to establish a light source anyhow."

"Right. Who's got the matches?" Arrod says. "Kipp, I hope that's you patting my leg."

Pillar, the ghosts remind me, the thought flaring so intensely in my head that I jump. I dig my nails into my arms and squeeze my eyes shut. That voice was too close and too strong. Like it was hovering right over me . . . touching me. . . .

I need to get out of here. The urge rolls over me like a wave, and then I'm tearing at the rope around my waist, pulling myself free from our group tether. I drop my pack to the ground.

"Where are you going?" Raptor asks as I stumble away from the group.

"Wait, she's leaving?" Hemmen complains. "We can do that?"

"No one is leaving," Raptor growls, even as I turn and head back the way that Master Jay came. I rush forward in the darkness, stumbling blindly ahead.

I don't know where I'm going. Just . . . away from here. Away from the ghosts.

A large arm wraps around my waist, and then I'm hauled up against a massive, muscled body. I bite back the choked scream that rises in my throat, because I'm surrounded by warmth. The living have warmth, I remind myself. Not the dead.

"Sneaking off?" Raptor whispers in my ear. "Like a thief?"

I shake my head violently. "I just . . . need . . . a moment. . . ."

Raptor sets me back down on the ground, but he keeps his heavy arm around my shoulders, pinning me against him. "What's wrong? You're not acting like yourself."

Raising a shaking hand to my brow, I wonder if I can handle this. How am I possibly going to control myself going in and out of the tunnels every day? It feels impossible. "I . . . I . . ." I lean back against his strong chest, sagging in his arms though the voices continue to whisper in my ears. "Are the others nearby?"

"No. They're back in the cavern. I can hear them complaining. Why?"

"I need you to finger me and not ask why."

His breath huffs against my head, even as his grip tightens over my shoulder. His muzzle rubs against my hair. He holds me tight, my back to his front, but he doesn't let go of me. "This is the craziest thing I've ever heard, Gwenna."

"Just call me crazy, then. But I need it."

Raptor groans, and then one big hand is cupping my breast. The other slides down my waist, and I grab my belt, unfastening it so he can have access. When his hand slips into my pants, I whimper, even though he hasn't touched me yet. It's because I know relief is coming. My senses are completely distracted, and I'm so ready for his touch.

When his fingers brush over my folds, breath explodes from me.

"Quiet," he murmurs. "Do you want to call the entire cavern down here?"

I turn my head, biting at the bicep over my shoulder. He palms my breast, then strokes his thumb over my nipple. Then he's touching my clit, and my knees nearly buckle with the shock of pleasure.

"I'm going to make this quick," Raptor whispers. "And then when I get you back to the dorm, I'm going to take you somewhere private and fuck you hard so you can scream as loud as you want."

I moan against his sleeve.

"You like the thought? You want to be stuffed full of my knot, pretty wench?" With quick, skilled circles, he teases my clit and my nipple at the same time as I press against his chest and try not to collapse. "I haven't had my mouth on this fat cunt yet, either. I bet it tastes like the sweetest nectar. I bet it drips so much honey for me that I'll have to tongue it all up."

As he whispers filthy words into my ear, I come hard and fast, my trousers flooding with my release. I gasp and wheeze as I bite down on his sleeve, trying to stay silent, even as he gives my aching, quivering pussy one last stroke and then pats my mound like a well-behaved dog. I don't know how Raptor manages to get me off so damned quickly every time, but I'm grateful for it.

I relax against him for a moment longer, and then straighten, my senses humming. I buckle my belt again and try to adjust my clothing in the darkness. The ghosts still feel like they're in the air nearby, but it's not as oppressive as it was before. It feels manageable.

There's a sucking sound in the darkness, and I realize Raptor is licking the taste of me off his fingers. Heat creeps up my face, and my heart flutters at what he said earlier. That he hasn't tasted me yet. That he wants to do it when we get back. By Asteria, I want that as well. I have no idea where we're going to go so that we can fuck in private, but I'm utterly game.

"Do I need to ask?" Raptor's voice is amused as it floats through the darkness.

"No. Best if you don't," I tell him tartly. "But I'm ready to rejoin the others."

His hand grasps mine in the dark, and I expect him to put it on his arm. Instead, he lifts it to his lips and kisses my knuckles. "You're the strangest woman I've ever met."

"I know. I probably seem like a lunatic to you."

"I also can't stop thinking about you. If you're crazed, so am I."

I smile to myself.

He leads me back to the others. At least, I'm reasonably sure that was the goal. I follow him in the pitch-black, trusting Raptor to lead me forward. I can tell even in the dark when the tunnel opens into the cavern, due to the echoes of our footsteps. There's the sound of a striker, and a spark in the darkness that illuminates Hemmen's and Arrod's faces, with Kipp shooting them a look of pure annoyance from below.

Just as quickly as the spark flares, it goes out again.

"By the bull god's testicles, you still don't have the lamp lit?" Raptor's voice booms so loud in the darkness that I jump. He tucks my hand into his arm, pats it, and then leads me forward. "Here, let me do it."

"Did you find Gwenna?" Arrod asks.

"I'm right here," I chime in. "I just needed a moment."

"If you're scared, you can hold on to me," Arrod jokes.

Raptor growls, and there's a heavy jingle of gear. A scuffle.

"Put me down! I was just joking!"

Raptor snarls. "Apologize."

"I'm sorry, Gwenna! I'm sorry!"

"It's all right. He's just being fussy." I reach out for Raptor and only encounter his lashing tail. It swats at my hand, and I grab it and hold on to the fuzzy tip. "Can we please light the lamp already?"

Another jingle of gear, and the sound of feet hitting the floor. "Give me the strikers," Raptor says.

More jingling.

Light flares into the darkness again, and Raptor's long face is illuminated by the flicker of fire as he adjusts the lamp. He lifts it into the air and gestures at our group. "Go on."

"Go on, what?" Arrod adjusts his tunic, an indignant expression turning his mouth down.

"Master Jay wants you to find an artifact. Probably should get to it." Raptor winks at me.

Arrod and Hemmen look at each other. Then at me. Then at Kipp.

"Our sword should probably be in the lead," I remind them, picking up my pack from where I'd dropped it earlier. "That's you, isn't it, Kipp?"

Kipp gives our group a fierce nod and then picks up the loose end of the rope, eyeing me and then Raptor.

Right. We should tether ourselves again. I take it and loop in at my belt, then hold it out to Raptor.

"Want to do me the honors?" he asks, gesturing at the lantern he's holding aloft.

I put the rope around his waist, and as I do, I notice the raging erection tenting the front of his pants. My face gets hot.

It's a good thing that it's so dark in here.

It's very evident after a while that we have no idea where to begin. Kipp leads us up and down the tunnel, and we examine our surroundings, searching for the very things that Master Jay told us to hunt for—ruins hidden under moss. Rock falls. I desperately want to point out the broken column on the lip higher up the wall, but I also don't want to be the one to call attention to it. Instead, I deliberately avoid looking there and gamely shoulder my pickaxe and shovel as Kipp points out one spot, and then another.

And we dig.

We hammer at the rock. We look for clues. Aspeth—er, Sparrow—mentioned to me once that everything from Old Prell has a layer of the salty lichen that preserves it all. We look for that, but the tunnel here—the practice tunnel—is heavily traveled, and I can see no sign of where an artifact might be hidden. Neither does anyone else.

Raptor refuses to help, too. He holds the lantern and shoots amused looks in our direction. "You four need the experience, not me."

After what feels like hours, we dig at a spot of crumbling rock until we've dug a Kipp-sized hole and find nothing of value. It's the seventh hole we've dug in the last while, and I'm tired and sweaty, and the buzzing from the dead is starting to peck at me again, like a thousand angry birds.

It's that uncomfortable shiver under my skin that makes me speak up, makes me reckless. "Why don't we look near the columns? It's as good a place as any."

"Why?" Arrod asks.

"Because they're ruins," I point out. "Maybe we'll find something near one of those."

"It seems obvious, but I agree," Hemmen says. "We're not getting anywhere right now. Might as well try the obvious."

They immediately turn toward a crumbled column near our feet, and I want to scream in frustration. Instead, I bite my tongue and dig near it alongside them. When we take a water break, I pretend to scan the cavern and then point out the spot that's been bothering me all day. "Oh, look. It's another column."

Instead of looking over at it, they turn to look at me. "How'd you see that?"

Uh-oh.

"How'd you miss it?" I toss back. I mean, sure, it's at least twenty handspans up the cavern, near the tall ceiling and practically hidden by a long stalactite drooping from above. But if one looks closely, one can see just a hint of a shelf of rock, and on it, more of the infernal moss.

Raptor holds the lantern higher, frowning. "You must have good eyesight for a human."

"The best." I keep my tone casual and flirty. "Besides, there's a hard corner under all that moss. Don't tell me that happens naturally in a stone cave."

"Actually, it does with certain types of rock," Raptor says, moving past me. His tail flicks my ear, and it feels like a caress more than anything. I rub my earlobe as he strides over to the spot I've pointed out and holds the lantern higher. "That's definitely a column, though. Good eye."

"Thank you." I'm glad no one else is questioning my ability. It *is* rather far up the cave wall.

He turns to look at our group. "Now the question is, how do we get up there?"

That ends up being easier than anyone expected. Kipp sheathes his sword and adjusts his overlarge, battered shell on his back. Then he climbs up the wall as nimbly as, well, a lizard. When he makes it to the top of the shelf, he disappears behind the column and reappears a moment later with something in his hand.

Something that sparkles in the lantern light.

"Aha," says Arrod, and claps his hands with delight. "Master Jay tried to trick us!"

Kipp crawls down the wall and lands with a triumphant thud. He holds the item aloft, and we all lean in to take a closer look at it.

It's a cube of some kind, made of metal covered in runes. Raptor takes it in hand and turns it over, and as he does, the sparkle turns to a soft yellow glow, with one set of runes lighting up. As he turns it over again, a different word brightens, this one in pale blue.

"Can you read what it says?" I ask, captivated. I've only been close to true artifacts a few times in my life, but each time I'm utterly fascinated by them. They're not meant for common people. They're the domain of the rich and powerful, and even though the cube looks like nothing but a child's toy, it feels special. Valuable.

Raptor turns it over again, and the writing becomes a deep pink. "This symbol is the one for 'mistress,' like lady of the house. And this one means 'activate.'" Arrod reaches over and touches the "activate" rune before anyone can react.

Raptor flinches back as one side of the cube opens . . . displaying what looks like a tiny pair of metal scissors.

Thank the gods.

He glares at Arrod, then peers inside and makes a humph of amusement. "It's got a sewing kit in there and a key. Not important stuff, so I imagine that's why it's being used for training."

Hemmen touches the object and the scissors sink back in again, the compartment closing. He flips it and touches the blue symbol, and a tiny hair comb protrudes. "I thought Master Jay said what we were hunting for wasn't working?"

"Maybe we're not supposed to fuss with it?" I suggest. "Close it up and let's just turn the damned thing in."

We rope together again, and Hemmen takes the artifact, because he insists upon carrying it. Kipp looks slightly annoyed at being passed over, but he shrugs and takes the lead again. Arrod complains as we head back to the front of the tunnel that we didn't get to fight anything, and Raptor explains to him about how you don't want to fight things in the tunnels if you can help it. He also says all of this while keeping a hand on the small of my back and making me incredibly aware of his nearness. By this time, we've been in the tunnels long enough that any wet spot on my pants is long dried, and thank goodness for that.

I'm more than relieved to be free of the tunnels once we make our way back to the surface. We untie the rope at our waists, and Hemmen proudly presents our find to our teacher, who's waiting nearby.

Instead of praising us, however, Master Jay stares at the artifact, and then back at us. "That . . . that's not the one I buried. Where did you find that?"

Well, shit.

THIRTY-SEVEN

RAPTOR

Hawk,

Things are a mess. We found an artifact that wasn't even missing. If you have ideas, I'm open to suggestions. This is taking longer than anticipated.

—Raptor

PS—I've decided I want a bonus. Make sure Rooster knows.

"SHOW ME THE location," Jay insists to me. The other four fledglings are sent back to the nest, with Gwenna shooting worried looks over her shoulder as I remain behind at the drop site with our teacher.

"I told you where it was," I remind him even as we head back to the training drop we just emerged from.

"I know, but it doesn't make sense." Jay shakes his head as we climb into the basket. He nods at the repeater at the ropes, and the boy lowers us down with jerking motions. Jay holds on to the lip of the basket and looks over at me. "You know as well as I do that those tunnels are the most well-traveled of any in the Everbelow. Dozens of students are in and out of them each month. They were cleaned of every bit of artifactual and magical value long before you and I were ever born. And you're telling me that some artifact was just lying there? No one dug for it at all?"

"Seems like." I'm not happy about this situation, either. Those tunnels are hollowed out and useless for anything other than training students. Anything above the old fault line really is. The fact that a fresh, working artifact was just sitting out in the open bothers me.

The fact that Gwenna pointed out the spot bothers me, too. It feels like a setup of some kind, but I'm trying to figure out the reasoning behind it and drawing a blank. If Gwenna's the thief—and after today, it seems bloody likely—then why point right to an artifact that's been stolen? Wouldn't it be smarter to keep your mouth shut?

Or is there something else going on and she's trying to divert away from the real thief? She did run away in the tunnels earlier . . . and then distracted me with pleasuring her. And fool that I was, I fell for it.

I don't like this. I don't like any of this.

We head into the tunnel and stand in the spot our group had rested at. "There," I say, pointing at the barely visible shelf of rock above our heads. "There's a column there. Gwenna saw it from this spot."

Jay holds up his lantern, squinting. "How did she find that in these shadows? I can't see anything at all."

"She's got good eyes." She's also a hell of a liar, because she's had me fooled this entire time.

Jay grunts, then strides across the cavern, toward the wall in question. "Help me up. I want to get a good look at the site."

Lifting Jay up doesn't work until he stands completely on my shoulder, and I brace my arms against the rock wall. He manages to climb up awkwardly, and then lights a candle, holding it out and examining the area. "There's lichen everywhere, but there's also some rotted fabric." He kneels and disappears and I can hear him scraping. "Ah . . . five hells."

"What?" I call out.

"There's a body."

"What do you mean, there's a body?" I think of Gwenna, and how she knew there was something up there. She's involved in some way, and it's obvious she's tricked me all this time. Yet . . . why? Why show her hand like this? "How did we not notice that before?"

"There's lichen all over everything, but an experienced artificer knows that it doesn't grow so thick on rock. It likes rotting things to grow on. I dug through the layer of lichen and there was an old blanket. When I pulled the blanket back, there were remains."

Remains doesn't sound like a new body. "Is it someone we know?"

He makes a vague sound. "No, no. This one is long dead. His uniform—what's left of it—is very old. If I had to hazard a guess, I'd say he's the student who went missing in the caverns back before my time as a fledgling. My teacher knew of him. He'd snuck away from his fledgling class in the night and was never seen again. Never left the cave, but no one could ever find him, either. It's been a mystery ever since I was a young boy. I guess now we know the truth."

If that's the case, it makes less sense than ever. If Gwenna is in league with the thieves who have been attacking the repeaters, what does that have to do with a decades-old missing student? Yet she knew something was there.

What is it that I'm not seeing?

Jay needs help climbing back down from the ledge, and when he's on the cave floor again, he sighs heavily and rubs his brow. "I've got to get the authorities involved. Rooster needs to know about this, and I imagine any family—if there is any left after all this time—must be contacted. Tell the others I won't be back until late."

"I'll take them to the bar," I tell him. "Get some more team building in."

And get some answers out of a very suspicious woman.

THIRTY-EIGHT

GWENNA

"Y OU DON'T HAVE to bring your books, Hemmen," Arrod complains as we all head to the King's Onion. "We're not that boring to talk to."

Hemmen just clutches his books to his chest. "I'm exchanging them with a friend. He's meeting me there."

Arrod nudges him, causing Hemmen to stumble and frown. Normally I'd probably snipe at them—or even tease Hemmen, who's been growing on me. But all I can think about right now is that I'm in trouble somehow. I pointed my team toward the wrong artifact, and now Master Jay is meeting with the guild and Raptor's been silent since returning. It was his suggestion we go to the tavern to spend time together, but he doesn't seem to be in a social mood.

Worse, he's not talking to me at all.

We head inside, and Hemmen and Arrod move toward our regular table. I glance over at Raptor as he heads straight for the bar. He's the one who normally gets the drinks and brings them back to our table, but it feels different today. Wrong. Kipp hesitates, giving me a questioning look.

"You feel it, too, huh?" I purse my lips and incline my head at Raptor. "I'll talk to him. See what is bothering him."

He narrows his eyes at me as if trying to figure me out, and then nods. He pats my leg as if to reassure me, then trots over to join the others.

I glance at Raptor. He leans against the bar, his tail utterly still. Normally it flicks back and forth in a casual sort of way, and wildly when he's irritated. The fact that he's holding it straight tells me that he's deliberately trying not to show what he's thinking. Which means he's probably pissed at me for some reason. I mean, I know the reason. I'm just wondering how he knows that I'm the one who messed things up.

I walk slowly up to the counter and stand next to Raptor. He's chatting with the barmaid Naiah, who turns her smile toward me when I approach. She taps the bar and steps back. "I'll get that tray of drinks and snacks now."

"I'll be here," Raptor drawls, and his tone is more friendly than it has been in hours. Then he glances over his shoulder at me, and his expression shutters again.

Well, that's not a good sign.

I sit on the closest stool and pretend to be calmer than I actually am. "Are you going to tell me what's bothering you, or am I going to have to guess?"

"Depends. Are you going to tell me how you knew that artifact was there?"

"I didn't."

He turns and gives me a sharp look. "You did, and it's clear I'm going to have to get it out of you the hard way. I know how to make you spill your secrets, Gwenna."

Instead of getting irritated at his tone, I get . . . aroused. The last time he tried to get me to spill my secrets, he fingered me within an inch of my life. If this is a threat, it's not working. "Do you, now. . . ."

Raptor's eyes narrow. He studies my face, then his gaze falls to my chest. I glance down, too, and my nipples are obvious through the thin fabric of my guild tunic. So much for subtlety.

"You and I are going to talk in private," he growls at me, leaning in close. "Wait here."

"You're not the boss of me." It would sound more effective as a comeback if I wasn't breathless.

This time he gets in my face, his big nose a handspan from mine. "Wait. Here."

"Or what, you'll spank me?" Gods, I really am the horniest wench around. Distracting him with sex sounds like a fantastic idea, though. If I can get him off, maybe he won't ask how I'd known about that column. Maybe I can get him to focus on other things, and then when I lie about how I had no idea what was up there, it won't seem so damn obvious.

The barmaid returns with the tray of drinks and food. Raptor takes it, shoots me one last glare, and then marches over to our regular table at the back of the tavern. He sets it down, all but shoving Hemmen's books off the table, and then leans over to speak to the others. I wish I could hear what they were saying, but when they all look in my direction and then back at Raptor, they're not smirking. That's a good sign, I think.

Then the big Taurian is stomping back through the tavern, his hooves crashing on the floorboards as he makes his way back to me. The tavern is only half-full due to the early hour—the dinner rush isn't here yet. I get to my feet to meet Raptor, but he turns to the barmaid instead, putting a few coins on the table and giving her a look.

"Room seven" is all she says, scooping up the coins.

Wait, we're getting a room? I open my mouth to protest, but Raptor grabs my hand and heads toward the stairs at the back of the tavern's main room. I have no choice but to follow him, dragged along behind with his tail swatting at me. "The others are going to think we're sleeping together," I protest even as I follow him up the stairs. "I thought we weren't supposed to let anyone know—"

"I told them I'm taking you to the clinic. You've got food poisoning."

I frown, because surely they noticed we're heading up the stairs instead? Yet when I glance one last time back at their table, they're not looking in this direction at all. Following along after Raptor, I try not to frown at his back. Here he's been telling me this whole time that we should be careful not to be seen in a compromising situation together, and today he's dragging me up the stairs. "I thought we were supposed to be cautious when we're together."

"Fuck all of that," he growls, and storms onto the next landing.

With no choice but to follow behind and inwardly cringe at his bad mood, I let him lead me past door after door in the inn part of the tavern. He finds number seven, flings the door open, and then tugs me inside before I can breathe.

I stare at him, wide-eyed, as he slams the door shut behind him. "This isn't like you, Raptor."

"Good," he growls, stalking toward me. "Now we're both pretending to be something we're not."

"What are you talking about?" I lift my chin, determined not to let anything on. Normally when Raptor touches me, I lose all sense of who I am and start babbling anything and everything. I'm not going to let that happen today. I can't. He's far too close to knowing the truth about who I am, and I can't trust him to keep that secret.

I might like him. I might be falling for him.

But I don't know that I can *trust* him, and the realization stings. Will it always be like this? Even if I fall in love and someday get married, will I have to keep secrets? Forever? Or do I just keep adding to the list of those who know my secret, until it feels as if half the city knows that I'm a mancer and it makes it to the wrong ears anyhow?

I'm suddenly so very tired.

Raptor stands in front of me, all looming Taurian. It's times like this that I'm reminded just how very large he is compared to me. I'm barely five feet, and he's so much taller that I don't even reach his shoulder. Instead, I find myself staring at his pectoral area. It's a very fine pectoral area, don't get me wrong, but it tells me nothing about what he's thinking right now.

He tips my chin up with his fingers. "When I chased you in here, I expected you to wear a lot of expressions . . . but sadness wasn't one of them."

I lick my lips, though I'm truly tempted to lick his thumb instead. "What were you expecting, then?"

"Deceit. Because you knew that body was there, and I can't figure out how for the life of me."

A body.

Of course there was a body. I should have guessed, since the spirit of the dead person was pushing me toward that direction. I'm silent. Do I lie and continue with the charade? Or is he going to see right through it?

Do I get brave and confess the truth and let the gods decide my fate? In the end, I chicken out. "What body?"

Raptor looks disappointed for a moment before his expression hardens again. "The one with the artifact. You pointed that pillar out when no one else saw it. What I want to know is how you found that man when he'd been missing for longer than I've been alive."

My jaw drops. He's been dead for that long?

He tips my chin back, holding my mouth open. "Aha. So you do know something. Last chance to tell me or I'm going to be very upset with you."

I push his hand off my face. "Threats get you nowhere."

"Don't they?" Instead of backing off, he strokes my hair, his expression thoughtful. It's both a tender gesture and an unnerving one. He reaches for the bun I always wear at my nape and pulls the biggest pin free. "I know how to make you talk, Gwenna."

He tosses the pin aside, and it clinks to the floor. His gaze never leaves mine.

Am I supposed to be afraid of him? For some reason, I'm not. For some reason, I'm incredibly turned on instead. Raptor might not keep my secret, but physically harm me? Never. "You're talking out your arse."

He pulls another pin free. "I can make you talk," he states again. "And it will be just as enjoyable as last time, when I had my fingers sunk deep into that sweet, wet cunt of yours."

I suck in a breath. "I . . . I don't know what you're talking about."

"Oh please." He chuckles, tossing the next pin aside. As if it has been timed, my hair tumbles free about my shoulders, and he eyes it, raking his big hand through. "I can smell your arousal, Gwenna. Remember that a Taurian has senses far better than any human's."

My pussy clenches at his words. It takes everything I have not to lean forward, to beg him to touch me. "You can smell me?"

"Aye. Smells so sweet and honeyed I want to dip my muzzle into it."

The breath catches in my throat. Goddess Hannai's *tits*. I want that, too. So much. But does he want to touch me or torture me? I straighten, lifting my chin in what I hope is horny defiance. "So what's stopping you?"

He growls, and the sound fascinates me. Raptor takes another step in my direction, and we stand so close that I have to crane my neck to gaze up at him. We stand so close that my hard nipples are practically rubbing against his belt buckle. The look he gives me could curl parchment . . . and it makes my toes curl, too. "You'd like that, wouldn't you?"

"If you licked my pussy? Damn right I would."

Raptor makes a sound that could be a bark of frustration—or of laughter. In the next moment, he snags an arm around my waist and takes two strides over to the double bed. Before I realize what he's doing, I'm face down across his strange Taurian thighs as he sits on the edge of the mattress. One arm anchors my upper body to his lap, and his other hand goes to my arse. "Remember that you asked for this."

"I didn't ask for anything!"

"Tell me what you know." He says it, all calm and collected, even as he rips at my belt, snapping the leather as if it's nothing and tossing it to the floor. I make an indignant sound and he ignores it, grabbing my pants and hauling them down. Seams rip and fabric tears, but he doesn't care.

My arse is exposed.

"You asked for this," he says again, but it's less angry. More aroused.

And then Raptor spanks me.

I gasp, loud. It's not that the spanking is painful. It's noisier than anything, and my buttocks sting from the smack he gave me. It was nothing more than a tap, given Taurian strength, but it surprised me. I didn't think he'd actually do it.

The shock I feel quickly gives way to arousal as his hand lingers on my backside.

"You asked for this," he murmurs, but there's a note of honey in his voice, thick and rich and decadent. He spanks me again, a lot lighter this time, and then caresses my backside. "Look at how pink you get when I smack you."

I squirm against his grip, because if he keeps stroking my arse, he's going to realize just how aroused I am at this. "Piss off and let me go."

"And give you what you want? Absolutely not. Tell me the truth." He smacks me again and jiggles my buttocks when he's done. "We both know you're holding secrets. Tell me what they are."

"Fuck off."

He grunts, then spanks me again. His hand lingers on my arse, and this time, his fingers sink between my legs. He strokes me, and to my shame, I'm incredibly wet. My body makes a squelching sound as he slips a finger deep inside me and thrusts. "Look at that."

Panting, I try to get away from him. Well, sort of. Even in my own mind, I know I'm faking it. I desperately need more fingering, more spanking, more everything. I writhe in place, acting as if I'm trying to get away, when all I really need is for him to throw me down and fuck the hells out of me.

"Oh, no you don't," Raptor growls as I try to escape his lap. "You're not going anywhere until you confess, you naughty thing. You've been leading me on all this time."

"The fuck I have! I—ooh!" My thoughts go sideways when he strokes his fingers into my pussy again, two together this time, and big enough to make me arch with delight.

"You like that?" He no longer sounds angry, but fascinated. The hand on my back creeps around to my throat, as if he's going to hold me in place by choking me, except his grip is so, so gentle. All the while, his fingers viciously thrust into my pussy, forcing wet, erotic sounds into the air around us. His thumb strokes the side of my neck. "You think you can take three fingers?"

I whimper. "You think this is going to get me to tell you anything?"

"Aye, I do." He strokes into me, harder and faster, adding a third finger and stretching me as I claw at his leg and gasp for mercy. "Look at how good you take me. You'd handle my cock so well, wouldn't you?"

Gods, I would. I would love to take his cock. I buck against his hand as he thrusts into me. It feels so good, and yet at the same time, I need more to come. More friction, more of that edge of pain, more something. I'm not the sort of woman who can come on thrusting alone. But oh gods, the way he's stretching me? I'm so *close*.

His hand withdraws. He spanks me again, his fingers wet, and I moan a sound of protest. "You bad girl. You're not supposed to be enjoying this. You're supposed to be answering me."

Funny, he doesn't sound upset. "Guess . . . you'll . . . have to up the stakes . . . hmm?"

Raptor laugh-growls. His hand leaves my throat, but not before he caresses my cheek with his knuckles. "You have me turned so inside out I don't even trust myself."

"Good. Then we're the same."

That sets him off. "We're not. We're not the same at *all*."

He hauls me into the air, and I let out a squeak of distress. In the next moment, I land atop the mattress, my torn pants falling farther until they tangle about my ankles. I've barely gotten up on hands and knees before two massive hands grab my hips and haul me backward. The rest of my pants are ripped away and tossed aside, and then Raptor sits on the floor next to the bed. He drags me to the edge of the mattress, and then his muzzle is between my legs, his hands gripping me and pinning me in place so I can't wriggle away.

As if I want to go anywhere? This is the place I'm desperate to be.

I moan, collapsing on the bed and pressing my cheek to the blankets as his enormous, thick Taurian tongue sweeps over my throbbing pussy. He groans, making a sound of pure enjoyment, and laps at me again. "Secrets . . . tell me. . . ."

He sounds like he's getting distracted, too.

"You're going to have to try harder than that," I pant, and make another horrid whining sound when his tongue strokes deep into me. Oh goddess, is it possible that it can feel thicker than his fingers?

He growls low, as if reminding me that I'm supposed to be talking, but I bite down on my knuckles and give in to the pleasure as he tongues my pussy. One hand slides under me, and then he's teasing my clit as he licks me, and pure ecstasy flares through my body. I lift my hips, driving up against his mouth as he moves me closer and closer to what's surely going to be a mind-blowing orgasm—

—and then he lifts his head, his fingers pausing in their relentless rolling of my clit. "Speak up."

"Argh!" I arch my hips, trying to push my pussy into his face for him to lick again. "You stopped! I'm so fucking close!"

"Good. Tell me what you know." His tongue teases along my folds again, his breath hot against my skin. "And I'll give you what you need."

Now I'm starting to get annoyed.

I push his hands away, only for the one at my hip to lock down tighter. He teases a little circle around my clit, his teeth grazing my buttock.

"Tell me."

"I don't know anything!" I wail.

"You're a little liar and we both know it." He toys with my clit until I'm frantically rubbing against him again, and then he stops once more.

I growl.

"I can give you what you want. Just tell me what I need to know." His finger is poised against my clit again, as if he's going to start rubbing the moment I suddenly spill.

And I'm just . . . frustrated. I can't win. Because I can't tell him who I really am. Even if I could, why would anyone ever want to touch a mancer? Especially one who deals with the dead? Either I lose him now because he can't trust me . . . or I lose him forever if I tell the truth.

A sob escapes me. I bite down on my knuckles again, trying to muffle it, but the damage is done. Even as I choke down the next one, Raptor's hands are gone. In the next moment, his big body presses over mine, all but lying over me in the bed. "Shh. It's all right."

"It's not all right. Nothing is all right," I manage to choke out, even as hot tears sweep down my cheeks. "And I f-fucking hate c-crying over it."

He nuzzles my neck and face, the metal ring in his nose as warm as his skin. "Let me help you, Gwenna. If you're in trouble, I can help. But I need to know what I'm working with."

More tears spill out. I can't tell him. It's not the same as confessing to Mereden and Lark, who already knew that I'd pointed us at two dead bodies back when we were in a Five together. Those were friends. This is Raptor. This is the Taurian I want to touch me, desperately. This is someone I want to look at me with love and affection, and I just know that will change the moment he learns the truth of who I am.

He'll look at me with wariness. Like he doesn't know who or what I am.

And it will *destroy* me inside.

I just cry harder.

"Shh, please, Gwenna." He lifts off me in the bed, then turns me over with gentle hands. When I gaze up at him, my eyes swimming with tears, he leans in and ever so carefully presses his muzzle to my lips. It's a kiss. A strange one, but the meaning is all the same. "I hate it when you cry, little bantam. Please don't. If you're in some sort of danger, I want to help."

I reach up and caress his face, my fingers stroking down his long, beautiful nose. "No one can help me."

"What will it take for you to trust me?" He cups my cheek, nuzzling at my neck again.

My eyes start to fill with tears once more, and I shake my head. I press a kiss of my own on his nose, cupping his face in my hands as I do. "Maybe just don't torture me anymore? If I could tell you, I would."

"Torture *you*?" He nips at my ear, sending shivers up my spine. "Woman, do you think you're the only one suffering? My knot is as hard as iron right now."

I manage a teary giggle. "And your cock is probably just as hard. If only we knew of some way to soften them."

"Aye, they need a good working over."

"Well, I'm happy to help." I stroke my fingers over his face, tracing little tickling circles on his skin. "But only if you want me."

He goes still over me. "Are you saying you'd take my knot?"

"Why wouldn't I?"

Raptor's nose brushes over my sleeve, and I dimly realize that I'm still dressed from the waist up. "Because . . . a knot isn't . . . it's not something every Taurian has all the time. Most Taurians only get their knot when the Conquest Moon is upon us. Every five years, Old Garesh rises again and makes his sons fertile. They rut until their knot is spent."

"But . . . you're different?"

"Aye. Some Taurians are born with the god's hand upon them. It means we have a knot always. It means we're always fertile. We don't go into a crazed rut like most do during the Conquest Moon. We're always in rut. Always ready. Always . . . hungry." He runs his mouth along the shell of my ear, making me shiver. "Some would say we're cursed. Some would say we're blessed."

"Definitely blessed," I blurt out.

He lifts his head and stares down at me in surprise. "You think so?"

"I mean, from what I've seen, it's not something to be ashamed of. You're gorgeous. It's just another part of you." I give him a small smile to make him comfortable. I know all about feeling like you're not enough. All the time I spent as an invisible servant has made me feel as if I'm not worthwhile. That I'm not worthy enough to be an artificer.

Raptor presses a kiss to the side of my neck. He groans against my skin, his breath warm and delightful along my collar. "I've struggled with control, especially around you. I *dream* of knotting you. Sinking deep into your pretty cunt and locking your body to mine. Filling you up and then just spilling my seed in you, endlessly."

Oh. He dreams of knotting *me*? I love that. I love that he always makes me feel seen even when I feel invisible. "Is that what your knot is for? Filling your partner?"

Tension returns to his body, and I can feel him stiffening against me. "Some women don't like it. Most of the sex workers I've hired won't touch my knot. They're worried it's too much, that I'll hurt them. Worse, they don't want to be tied to me. Not like that. A Taurian who knots his mate has to hold them close until the knot goes down."

"How long does that take?"

"Sometimes a half hour. Sometimes less. Sometimes more."

And no one wants to cuddle with him, and it's clear from the bleak look on his face that he wants it desperately. But sex workers aren't paid to cuddle. I can see how they'd find it uncomfortable. Fucking a stranger is one thing. Being pinned to a stranger for a half hour is another.

I understand it . . . and yet I'm angry at them. I'm furious at these strangers for not giving him what he needs. It's my impression that a sex worker will do just about anything if they're asked—and paid—properly. But maybe he can't ask. Maybe he's got a hang-up about his knot and doesn't want attention brought to the fact that he's different. "I'll let you knot me . . . if you want to."

He stares down at me. "You're asking for my knot?"

"Absolutely. If it feels good for you, I want to do it." Then I hesitate. "Does this mean you're going to get me pregnant? Because I want to be with you, but not if it costs me my chance to be in the guild."

He touches his neck, where a tiny bead is on a chain. "I'm wearing the male version of a Prellian pause bead. It stops me from getting you pregnant."

One less thing to worry about. "Then I absolutely want to be knotted."

Raptor watches me with an unreadable expression, and then he buries his face against my neck again, one of his horns swiping dangerously close to my face. "If you're manipulating me, Gwenna . . . you're going to break me. You know that, right?"

I trail my hand along his strange cheek, then up to his horns and along one fuzzy, floppy ear. "All I want is to pleasure you the way you deserve to be pleasured."

He groans again, and then tugs at my tunic. "Take this off. I want to see your gorgeous tits out. I want to see them bouncing when I'm fucking you."

I sit up as he leans back, pulling his clothing off with self-assured movements. I want to watch him . . . but I want to be naked before he changes his mind. Off goes my tunic, followed by the old, tattered corset that I've been wearing under my uniform to keep my breasts in place. It digs into my skin, but there are always other priorities when it comes to spending money, like sending it home to my mother, who never has enough to make ends meet.

Raptor's gaze feasts on my naked body as I sit on the bed, waiting. He pulls off his pants, and then his big, deep pink cock is revealed to my hungry gaze. Just as I remember, his knot is a violently purple shade, so taut it looks painful, and there's a thick vein traversing the underside of his shaft that just begs to be licked. The head of him is slick with seed, and it's clear I'm not the only one who's ridiculously turned on.

"You're small and I'm large, so we're going to have to do a bit of maneuvering to make this work, little bantam." He stands at the edge of the bed and then pulls me down toward him. He's tall, however, and the bed is made for humans, and we still don't line up properly. He growls with frustration. "When we graduate, we're getting a Taurian-sized bed."

I bite my lip to keep from laughing at his annoyed expression. "Or we start sneaking off to Taurian inns instead."

"Good idea for the interim," he agrees, and then twirls a finger. "On your hands and knees, please, my sweet bird."

"Ugh, I don't know if I like that nickname," I tell him, but I do as he asks, getting on hands and knees. I present my arse to him, giving it a wiggle. "This better?"

"Mmm, the view is lovely," he agrees, his hand skimming over my backside and then teasing between my thighs again. "I don't get to watch your pretty tits, but I'll just have to play with them instead."

He leans forward, pressing his cock against my slick cunt, and drags it through my folds. I moan, remembering how good he'd felt before. How has it been so long since we've had sex? Obviously, we need to remedy this, and fast. His other hand goes to my breast, and he teases its heavy weight, finding the tip and toying with it.

"They're not sensitive," I tell him. "You can be a little rougher."

He immediately pinches the tip, and it sends a lightning bolt of heat straight through my body. I bite back another squeal, holding still as he drags his cock against my pussy again.

"Like that?"

"Gods, *yes.*"

"I love how you know just what you like." He slides his cock along my pussy again, then teases the head at my entrance.

I whimper and back up against him, hungry for more. "Please."

"I should be testing you right now," he says, voice hoarse. Slowly, he breaches my body with his thick cock. "But I'm trusting you, Gwenna."

I know he is. I can't say that he's right to do so, because I don't know how he'll feel about the truth. I just moan and push back against him, trying to take him deeper. "I'm yours."

He pushes in, and it's the most overwhelming, most glorious sensation in the world. There's no feeling quite like being breached by a thick cock, and Raptor's is thicker than most. It takes my breath away in the best sense and sends tingles of pleasure all through my body.

"I'm going to go slow," he reassures me in a low voice, one hand on the small of my back. His hand is so big that he makes me feel dainty just with that small touch. "Got to stretch you. By the gods, you feel mucking delicious, though."

I moan, curling my fingers against the blankets. It takes everything I have to keep myself still, to remain in place like an obedient woman while he pushes into me with a downright slothful speed. "Just . . . tell me when I can move."

His big hand moves to my arse, and he gives it a chastising tap. "You move when I say you can move."

Oooh, he's bossy in bed. That makes me ridiculously hot. "Don't be mean or I'll come too soon."

Raptor groans, his hips jerking, and I'm rewarded with even more of his cock. "You tease. How I love that about you."

I tense as he speaks, and it takes a moment for me to realize he's not confessing love. Oh. It doesn't matter . . . does it? I tell myself that it doesn't, just as I tell myself I wasn't eager to hear the words. I can't afford to fall in love anyhow. This is just sex.

He flexes his hand on my buttock, then sinks a little deeper into me. "How's that feel, little bantam?"

"Feels like you should come up with a new nickname," I joke.

He spanks me again, and then reaches forward to play with one of my hanging breasts. "You're a naughty sort when you get cock into you."

"You like it when I tell it like it is," I tease back, and rock against him, testing the waters. There's a lot of him in me—gods, so much—but he's prepared me well, and while I feel split all the way to my core, it doesn't hurt. It feels shockingly good. I move again and love the sound of his breath escaping him. Good. I'm not the type to sit passively while he fucks me. I want to be an active participant. I move my hips in slow, steady motions, enjoying his surprised grunt as he's forced to follow my lead.

We move together amazingly well. I've had sex in the past where we could never find a rhythm together, or where I'd have a man lying over me like a blanket, not like a lover. But Raptor knows just how to move and how fast to move. His strokes start slow and then he moves quicker, until he's hammering into me with sharp, delicious precision with every quick snap of his hips, every stroke of his cock deep inside me. I lose myself in the feel of it, closing my eyes and sinking into the sensation. I won't come like this, but there's nothing wrong with simply enjoying the moment.

Raptor's hand moves from my back, and then he anchors one on my shoulder, the other going to my breast. And then he starts fucking me. *Hard.* Now I'm the one who's gasping for breath as he uses my body, working me hard. I'm never in pain, but the bed shakes, my thighs quiver with the force of his slapping hips, and all the while, he's roughly rolling my nipple between his fingers just the way I like it.

And even though there's no hand on my clit . . . I feel as if I'm going to come. I whimper, because it's almost like my body is coiling in on itself, a sure sign that I'm about to climax. "I'm—close—"

"Then come for me. I want to feel it when you clench around me."

I make a needy little noise as he continues to fuck me. I can't come on command, but now that I know he's not going to take this away from me again, I'm free to sink into the sensations. I close my eyes and lose myself, and the only thing in the world is the sharp thrust of his cock into my body, the big rough hand on my breast, and that ever-building sensation deep in my belly.

When I come, it's not like a lightning strike. It's more of a tidal wave, building and building until I'm swept up along with it. I moan as the first wave of overwhelming pleasure takes me, my body responding with all my limbs tensing and tightening. I clench everywhere, and as the pleasure floods through me, so does gratitude. Gratitude that he's giving me this release, finally. "Thank you," I babble. "Thank you, thank you, thank you."

Raptor's thrusts slow down, and he gives my breast one final squeeze before sliding to my clit. Even as I quiver with the aftershocks of my release, he rolls my clit against his fingertip. "You're nice and wet, my sweet wench. You think you can take my knot now?"

Through a delicious haze, I realize that I've had my release but he hasn't had his . . . and knotting me is what he wants more than anything. I nod, lowering my cheek to the bedsheets as he thrusts into my body. "Yes."

My simple answer makes him pause. "No hesitation?"

"None. Give me your knot."

He takes in a shuddery breath. "Gods, you're perfect, you know that?"

With another thrust of his hips, he pushes deeper into me. The effect is startling—my pussy suddenly goes from feeling pleasantly overfull to absolutely-too-much. My first instinct is to claw my way free and escape him, but I know it'll hurt his feelings. He's being vulnerable, asking for this. And if Aspeth can be happily married to a Taurian who knotted her in a moon rut, I can surely take Raptor's knot.

I breathe through it, relaxing underneath him while he pushes deeper.

"It's a lot, but you're taking it beautifully," he croons at me, teasing my clit again. "I'm almost in. You're amazing, my sweet Gwenna."

His touch sends little flicks of fire through my body, and I find myself rocking against his hand as he works my sensitive clit. I make little whimpery sounds of pleasure even as the sensation between my legs grows tighter and tighter.

With one final thrust, Raptor gives a belly-deep sigh, and his hands flex on my hips. Did I think I was impaled before? It's nothing compared to now. My entire body quivers as I take him, and that delicious edge of pleasure and pain returns.

"How . . . how are you doing?" Raptor manages, voice tight.

I take shallow breaths, adjusting my knees on the mattress. "Well . . . now I know what the sausage feels like when the cook stuffs it."

He makes a choked sound of amusement. "Don't make me laugh. I'll lose control."

"You can lose control now," I tell him softly. "Come inside me, and fill me with your seed, just as you're supposed to."

He groans. "My good mate. My sweet mate."

His mate? I suck in a breath. Why do I love that so much? I shouldn't put too much into his words, as we're in the middle of sex. People say things in the heat of the moment. But . . . his *mate*. It's annoying how much I love that. I want to reward him with words of my own. "Fill me up with your seed, then. Give me everything you've got, my big, strong bull. Knot me and fill my belly—"

His hands grip my buttocks tight, and then he half snarls my name as he holds me against him. It seems impossible, but his knot feels bigger than ever, and I squirm in place against it—and him.

Raptor leans over me and then he's pressing me into the mattress, his big body blanketing mine. He braces his weight on his arms to each side of me but he's still covering me entirely, and all the while, I can feel little clenches in his body that I imagine are spurt after spurt of his seed releasing into me.

He groans and then gives one last push inside me, emptying himself. For a long moment, the only sound is his heavy breathing. If I lift my head, I can see his body over mine, and it reminds me just how small I am compared to him. How he could crush me if he wasn't careful . . . but he is always so good with me.

Raptor takes a deep breath, and I can feel his body quiver.

"You all right?" I ask, voice soft.

"Just . . . feels really good." He tries to nuzzle me but only manages the top of my head. "I'm going to roll on my side and take you with me, all right?"

"All right."

He puts an arm around my waist and rolls us together. I resist the urge to squirm against his hips, which are still locked to mine. This is a new sort of sensation, being trapped against a man as his cock remains inside me, huge and noticeable. It's like I can't quite come down from sex yet, and when he strokes a hand over one of my breasts, arousal burns through me again.

"We probably shouldn't have done that . . . but I can't say I'm sorry." He thumbs my nipple, teasing it into a point. "I didn't hurt you, did I?"

"Don't . . . be . . . ridiculous." I'm breathless as he continues to tease me. "You know I wanted that as much as you."

"This is new for me, though. Knotting someone I like, someone I care for. I want it to be good for you."

"You care for me?"

Raptor huffs. "Is that not obvious, woman?" He reaches up and tenderly strokes his knuckles over my cheek. "I've been in agony for the last few weeks, obsessed with you when I should have been hunting for Sarya. Thinking I was betraying her every time I had a lusty thought about you. Falling for your personality and your strength even as I was supposed to be focusing on Sarya. Wondering how I was going to keep you safe through all the bullshit that's been going on. Knowing that if something were to happen to you, I'd lose control. Lose my mucking mind. That I want nothing more than for you to be happy, and I'll do whatever it takes to get that artificer sash on your shoulder, because what you want has become far more important than anything."

His deep voice is full of emotion.

I don't know what to say. I'm surprised at his confession. Surprised and pleased, my body clenching around his knot even as he drapes himself over me.

"The question is, do you care for me? Because we both know you're keeping things secret." His words are far more accusing than his tone, which is rich and soft with redolent pleasure, and I know they're not meant to hurt me, just to convey a bit of frustration. "You know I'm on your side. I hunted the entire city looking for Sarya because I was obsessed with her. Turns out she was right under my nose."

"The sex is good," I admit. "But sex doesn't solve everything."

"It's not just the sex, Gwenna. Surely you know that by now?" He stops teasing my nipple and slides his hand between my thighs, moving to toy with my clit again. "You think I claim just anyone as my mate?"

I bite back the whine rising in my throat. How does he expect me to have a serious conversation with him when he's going to make me come again like a cat in heat? "You . . . you . . ."

Suddenly my throat burns. It's a sharp knife-slash sensation, and I want to gasp but there's no air.

HELP.

A sharp thought pierces my mind. A familiar, sharp thought.

I know this person.

"Hemmen," I choke out. Oh gods.

At my side, Raptor goes stiff. "That's a damned thing to say when a bull's knotted inside you."

I want to reassure him, but the haze falling over me won't let me. I can feel Hemmen's panic and the pain as his throat is cut. The blood. The gurgling. *Can't breathe. Collapsing.* Then . . . nothing.

I clutch my throat in horror. "I—I think Hemmen is dead."

THIRTY-NINE

RAPTOR

Raptor to Hawk: *I don't think I'm cut out for this shit.*

Hawk to Raptor: *I don't think any of us are.*

HEMMEN IS DEAD.

As I lay there in the blissful aftermath of knotting the woman I wanted more than anything, I find out that one of my Five, one of the fledglings I'm supposed to be watching for possible thievery, has been slaughtered in an alley while I fucked around with Gwenna.

It doesn't matter that hours have passed since that moment. I'm still burning with frustration and anger. I'm still seeing her startled face as I confess my feelings for her and she blurts out another man's name.

As we stand in the alley, talking to the guild's enforcers about Hemmen's violent death, I can't help but glance over at Gwenna. I'm obsessed with her, even as I feel like I've been had. The timing can't be overlooked. The moment I knot her, suddenly someone else dies? It's too convenient. She's distracted me in the best sort of way, my sweet little mate, and I'm the fool who falls for her pretty tears and her caresses every time.

My mate. It's the only word that fits for what Gwenna is to me. I just never thought claiming a mate would be like, well, this.

Now a young human man is dead. I don't even know what to think of it. Hemmen was never my favorite person. He hated hard work and would rather have spent his time inside a library instead of in the tunnels, but I can't fault him for that. It's not a lifestyle for everyone. Even so, I wouldn't wish death on him.

"Where were you at the time of the attack?" one of the enforcers asks me.

"Inside. With the woman." I nod over at Gwenna.

He eyes her, no doubt noting the blanket she has wrapped around her, and the borrowed dress. Naiah lent a gown, since I'd torn Gwenna's clothing in my haste to fuck, but Naiah is nowhere near the same size, and the gown that hangs loosely on Naiah's lean form fits rounded Gwenna like a sausage casing.

Now I know what the sausage feels like when the cook stuffs it.

She'd made me laugh, made me feel so mucking good. Like us being in bed together was as natural as air, as natural as breathing. That it didn't matter that I have a permanent knot, or that I'm Taurian and built differently than her. She never blinked an eye at any of it, and I wonder how much was pretending.

"Can you think of any enemies he might have had?" asks the enforcer, scribbling notes in a small notebook.

"No," I lie. I'll have to talk to Rooster and Hawk about this. I'll tell them what I know—and how Gwenna distracted me at just the right time. "He'd mentioned he was meeting a friend, that's all."

"Some friend," the enforcer says.

I eye the sheet-covered body in the alley. Even now, a thin line of red is bleeding through the fabric, right where his neck is. His throat was cut, just like in the other murders. The murderer isn't Gwenna—as I was knotted in her at the time of the killing—but she knows something about this. And I need to find out what.

Master Jay rushes forward, having arrived on the scene after being alerted by the enforcers. A look of horror is on his face as he drops to his knees next to Hemmen's corpse. "My—my student. What happened?"

Jay looks up at me, and I don't have answers for him. I look over at Arrod instead. They've been questioned by the enforcers already, with no leads.

Arrod takes a deep breath and shakes his head. "We were drinking. Hemmen said he was meeting a friend to exchange books. He was nervous about it. Kept slicking his hair back, you know? Like he does."

Is that something he does? I had no idea. I haven't paid enough attention to Hemmen. I've been too obsessed with Gwenna.

Arrod crosses his arms tightly over his chest and continues. "He got up while me and Kipp were drinking and said his friend had arrived, and he was going to meet him in the alley. Went out front, and me and Kipp finished his beer. We figured that's what he deserved for leaving it unattended." His mouth crumples a bit and then he goes on. "It wasn't until someone started screaming that we realized what had happened. They found Hemmen outside, and his throat . . ."

He trails off, then shakes his head and walks away. Kipp moves to his side, patting his pant leg to comfort him.

"We'll need to ask you some questions, Master Jay," the enforcer says in a polite tone. "I'm sorry about the timing, but it's important."

Jay's expression is hollow, but he nods. I feel bad for the man. He has no idea of the shit that's been going down—Rooster wants to keep it as hushed as possible—and now a fledgling is dead. His grief is obvious, and even though I don't always agree with his teaching methods, it's clear that he feels responsible. Rooster needs to tell him what's going on. It's not fair for Jay to blame himself. Whatever happened with Hemmen, he was involved with the smuggling ring, and now he's paying the price.

Jay looks over at Gwenna, and then at me. "Will you take Gwenna out of here? I don't think murder is good for a young lady's sensibilities."

I want to point out that Jay is training that "young lady" and making her sleep in the same room as four men, that she can drink and belch with the rest of us and knows more dirty jokes than Arrod.

I want to point out that Gwenna already knows Hemmen's been murdered and might be in on it. I want to point out that the last thing we should be worried about is a "lady's sensibilities" when people are dying and the guild is being robbed.

But I want answers from Gwenna first. So I just agree and turn toward her. She seems dazed, her expression unfocused. The thin blanket wrapped around her figure covers the immodesty of her dress. "Come on, Gwenna. Let's get you out of here."

She comes along quietly, and because she seems just as upset as any of us, I put a hand on her neck as I steer her through the streets and back toward our quarters at the heart of the city. Her steps are brisk enough, but I can feel the trembling in her body. She's shaken, perhaps at the thought of getting caught.

She still smells like sex, too. It's making the possessive, rutting-bull side of me go wild. I want to fling her down on my bed and take her again, but I'm not going to let myself get distracted by doe eyes and pretty tits.

I hold my questioning until we get back to the nest, because I don't know who might be listening in. The streets of Vastwarren City are never empty, and gossip spreads like wildfire.

As we step inside the nest, there's the clink of dishes from the kitchen. Gwenna heads there and I let her, releasing my grip on her neck.

"Oh," the woman at the hearth cries, jumping with fright as we enter. Her eyes are red with tears, and she dabs at them. "I've just heard the worst—is it true?"

"I'm afraid so, Marta. Gossip travels faster than we do, it seems." Gwenna's tone is soft and sad. She moves to the other woman's side and gives her a hug.

Marta is startled by the embrace, but quickly puts her arms around Gwenna in return. "I was just making some soup. I thought I'd stay busy. . . ." She pulls away and dabs at her eyes with the corner of her apron. "I was going to make pork stew because that's Hemmen's favorite, but I guess I don't need to now. . . ."

She starts weeping again.

"Hush," Gwenna tells her, putting a comforting arm around her shoulders. "Why don't you get your things and head out for the day? We can fend for ourselves. I don't think anyone's in the mood to eat tonight anyhow."

The nestmaid nods and grabs her heavy pack from its hook by the door. Gwenna quickly sweeps the half-chopped onions and veg into a bowl, clearing the counter. She tidies up the kitchen, not looking at me, until we hear Marta leaving, with the side door shutting behind her.

Gwenna wipes down the counter. "His books were missing. They weren't in the alley. Did you notice that?"

"I noticed that you keep lying to me," I point out.

She stiffens, her shoulders going back.

"First the artifact, and now Hemmen's death." I stride toward her, putting a hand on the counter that she keeps on wiping even though it's clean. "I'm tired of the games. I want to know who you're working with."

"I'm not—"

"You keep distracting me during crucial moments," I growl. I'm just as furious at myself as I am at her. "Tell me one good reason why I shouldn't turn you over to the guild right now and let them prosecute you as the mastermind behind all of this."

She jerks in surprise, staring up at me. "I'm *what?*"

"The thief. A murderer. Take your pick. That's three repeaters who have been murdered now, and an artifact found in your bag. And one in the caverns, along with another body. All of these coincidences keep adding up, and I can only fall for a pair of pretty eyes so many times."

Her mouth drops open.

"Who's your contact?" I press, sensing she's caught off guard. "You're not working alone. Who's doing the dirty work?"

"What dirty work?" She shakes her head.

"Murdering—"

"Murdering?!" She gasps, shocked. "Me?! Are you insane?"

"No, but apparently you are." I lean in close, determined not to be fooled by her false outrage. "Your crew is using students to steal artifacts and then murdering them when they're no longer of any use. We've been keeping tabs on you for a while now. The more you work with us, the easier it'll be. Right now, though, things are looking very grim for you."

She shakes her head again, more vigorously this time. "No—you've got it all wrong. I'm no thief."

Another lie. "Then prove to me I'm wrong. Produce the real thief. Are you just passing information on to them? Are they holding something over you and forcing you to work with them?"

"I'm not working with *anyone*. And I don't know anything about any of this!"

"Yet you were targeted in the books, remember? *Gwenna is a thief.* And an item was found in your bag. And now Hemmen's books are gone. All of this is happening right on your doorstep, and it's obvious you have a secret you're keeping. You're a good liar, but you're not *that* good."

Good enough that she's had me fooled for quite some time, though. I'm fighting back the ache of betrayal, but I want to shout at the unfairness of it all. To think that I was so mucking delighted and relieved to find out that Gwenna and Sarya were the same person all along. That all my problems had been solved. What a joke.

I grab her chin and force her to look up at me. "Tell me your secret."

Her eyes fill with tears, and her entire body shakes. "I can't. I'll be killed if anyone finds out."

Now we're getting somewhere. I fight the surge of triumph I feel, because it's paired with the despairing realization that Gwenna has lied to me all along. "Finds out what?"

She closes her eyes, and then opens them again, resolve on her face. "That . . . I'm a mancer."

FORTY

RAPTOR

"YOU'RE A *WHAT?*"

"I'm a mancer." Gwenna immediately bursts into tears. "A necromancer. But I don't want to be! I'm not even trying!"

I don't think I've ever been as baffled as I am now. I was expecting some big confession, some admission that she'd been blackmailed by an old lover or maybe an old coworker into doing nefarious things. Hearing that she thinks she's a mancer is beyond comprehension. "What do you mean, you're a mancer? How can you be a mancer?"

She pulls away and wrings her hands, an agitated expression on her face as she paces back and forth in front of me. "It started when we came here to Vastwarren. The first time I went in the tunnels, I picked up a dowsing rod. You know they're not supposed to actually work, right? That it's just some silly joke that some masters play on their students? Except this one worked, and it led me right to a dead man holding an artifact. I thought I had done something right. That I'd somehow managed to find an artifact. And then I stole that one and gave it to Aspeth, but that's the only thing I've stolen, I swear."

I grunt, because I've heard the story of this one. Aspeth had one half of a link-ring pair in her possession, and Magpie's students had found the companion to it. The pairing was considered a Greater Artifact find and was confiscated by the guild and sold off.

"But then when I used a dowsing rod again, it led me to another dead person, and I worried that I was doing something wrong." She paces faster, as if moving quickly can somehow straighten her thoughts. "And then I started to hear them."

"Hear who?"

"The dead." She wrings her hands again, staring at the floor as she paces. "At first I thought I was imagining things, that the voices that whispered whenever I passed the graveyard were in my mind. That I was imagining someone calling my name when I was cleaning, only to find out that they'd died yesterday."

Gwenna turns and faces me.

"A few weeks before recruitment day, I found a dead man in the alley. Or rather . . . I didn't find him. He led me to him. I heard him talking. He was frantic. Nothing he said made sense, but he was babbling on and on, and I could hear him no matter where I went in the building, but I couldn't find him inside. I concentrated, and I got an image of the alley behind the house, where the well was located. I followed the voice and I found . . . the body. A young man. A repeater." She bites her lip. "That was the first body."

"First body," I echo, not sure what to think of this barrage of information.

She twists her hands frantically and pauses in her pacing to gaze at me. "The second body was the day I pretended to be Sarya."

I inhale sharply.

"My mother had always said that if you were in pain from a burn on the hand, you should hit your knee with a wooden spoon. It sounds silly, but it distracts you from the other pain. And when I was cleaning windows in the hospital, this dead man kept babbling at me and making my skin crawl. I knew he was in the alley, but I also knew I couldn't say anything. How would that look if I just up and kept pointing out men with their throats cut? They'd suspect me. So I tried to work through it, to no avail. I told myself I needed a distraction."

I rub my mouth. "And so you fucked me?"

"Sex is wonderfully distracting," Gwenna says in a wistful tone. "And it helped me focus enough that I could finish work. And you were nice and attractive, and I thought, What harm could it do? And I had fun. So aye, I fucked you to distract myself and then ran away as fast as I could to escape the dead man's thoughts. That's how I knew about the artifact in the tunnel. The dead pointed me there. And that's how I felt . . . Hemmen."

Her hand goes to her throat, and she rubs it.

"So that's everything," she says in a faint voice. "Sparrow did some research, and she says she thinks I'm what was called a necromancer. They were mancers that spoke to the dead."

Her gaze rests on me, and it's obvious she's waiting for me to react.

I rub my muzzle, thinking. I don't know what to make of the story she's just told me. "You mean to tell me that you've been feeling the dead talking to you? That's your secret?" When she nods, I add, "And that's why you wanted me to touch you down in the tunnels?"

"I needed a distraction. There's so many dead down there, it gets overwhelming." She hugs her arms around herself.

"And seducing me is your best way to get distracted," I say flatly.

Gwenna flinches. "You don't believe me."

"I just wonder at the convenience of it all."

"Oh yes, highly convenient," she says sarcastically. "Let me panic every time I step into the Everbelow, that'll really advance my career as an artificer. Oh, and while I'm at it, why don't I find the most fertile bull I can and demand that he have sex with me. That'll sure show him."

My mouth twitches despite myself. "Excellent point."

"Did it ever occur to you that maybe I just mucking like you, you bloody idiot?"

I smile even broader. "Maybe you do. Maybe it makes us both fools."

"So do you believe me now?" Her expression is worried but hopeful. "Or do you really think I'm some murdering mastermind that could truly have had Hemmen killed?"

"I don't know what to think. Is there any way to prove what you're claiming?"

She throws her hands up, exasperated. "Want to murder someone and have me quiz them?"

I think of poor, unfortunate Hemmen, dead in the alley. "There's been enough death, I think."

"On that, we both agree." Her face crumples. She moves to the table and sits at one of the chairs, covering her face with her hands. "Just . . . tell me what you're going to do with me, all right? All I ask is that if I'm killed for being a mancer, make it quick."

She's serious. She truly thinks that she's going to be killed for claiming to be a mancer of some kind. One that talks to the dead. I eye her small, sad form as she sits at the table, and mentally go through all the things she's told me.

How she'd known the dead man was in the training tunnel even though no one else had for decades. How she'd clutched her throat and blurted out Hemmen's name even as she was on my knot. It explains why she had me touch her in the tunnels. Granted, she could have known that whoever was responsible for the killings was going to cut his throat . . . but that doesn't explain why she gleefully jumped into bed with me that day in the hospital. She had no reason to touch me if she was simply some criminal mastermind hiding her tracks.

And if she was, why would she claim something so terrible? A criminal gets a trial. The last mancer in the kingdom was burned at the stake, no trial at all.

Am I just inclined to believe her because I'm in love with her?

If what she's saying is the truth . . . I don't know what direction we go from here. She was the closest lead we had to finding the thief, and now we've got nothing. If we tell the guild that she's a mancer, what happens if they decide she should be put to death?

The thought enrages me. I won't let that happen.

I move to Gwenna's side and squat beside the table. She's crying again, tears falling silently down her cheeks, and I realize just how much stress she's been under. What would I do if I thought I was a mancer? I wouldn't tell a soul, either. I'd protect myself, just as she's been doing.

And here I've made the situation worse, assuming she was the thief I've been looking for. I'm just as much to blame for this situation.

"Hey." I reach for her hand. "What do they call a Taurian who falls for a mancer?"

"A fool." She sniffs and won't look me in the eye. "Mancers are outlawed."

"Lots of things are outlawed. Doesn't mean people don't do them. I know a potion broker in the city, and they aren't supposed to be creating them, but that's never stopped anyone before."

"I don't know what to do," Gwenna confesses, her fingers trembling in my grip. Her other hand covers her eyes. "All I ever wanted was a job that could afford me enough money to not have to worry about going hungry. To be able to send some home to my mother and help her out. I never wanted any of this."

I'm a monster for making her so worried. All this time, I should have been telling her how I feel about her. How my day is instantly better when she smiles. How it ties me up in knots when she's stressed. "I'm sorry I accused you."

"I guess I have been acting a mite suspiciously." She manages a small smile. "But I'd rather be a thief than a mancer. A thief is just seen as desperate. A mancer is seen as evil."

"You're not evil," I reassure her. "You're the least evil person I've ever met. You're just differently endowed."

She peeks out at me from under her fingers. "Like you?"

I bark a laugh. "Exactly like. And just like me, we'll figure out a way to keep things under control."

Gwenna clutches my fingers tightly. "What do we do now?"

I consider this. Gwenna's secret will only be secret for so long. She's already under scrutiny for the thieving ring, so I need to get her name cleared in some fashion, but that means letting more people know what she's capable of. "We need allies."

"Who?"

"Hawk for sure." I hesitate over the next name. "Possibly Head Guild Master Rooster, since he's in charge, but we'll need to see if Hawk thinks that's wise."

"We can't tell the guild leader! He'll kick me out of the fledglings, and I'll never pass my tests."

"Little bantam, we're down to four," I tell her gently. "There's no way we'd pass this year regardless."

I hate the crushed expression on her face. There must be a way we can fix this somehow. "I'll keep you safe," I reassure her. "You don't have to worry."

"I can't help but worry." She twines her fingers with mine.

"Who else knows about your power? The fewer the better."

She winces, thinking, and rubs her fingertips over my knuckles. "Sparrow has known all this time. Mereden and Lark guessed it from my experiences with the dowsing rod. And you."

As far as I'm concerned, that's three too many people. "No one else."

"Gods, you think I would tell anyone if I could help it? It took me this long just to confess to you." Gwenna shakes her head. "You have my life in your hands, and you didn't trust me until five minutes ago."

"If I could reassure you somehow, I would."

She arches a brow at me. "Give me one of your secrets, then. We'll be even."

I smile at that. "I'm in love with you."

"Wh-what?" Her eyes go wide, and for once, she seems to be speechless.

Her reaction makes me tense inside. I've surprised her that much? "Is it that bad? For me to be in love with you?"

Her expression immediately changes to defensive. "I didn't say it was *bad*. Don't tell me what I'm thinking."

"Then what are you thinking?" I ask, deciding to be blunt about it. "Because I'd really mucking love to know."

She swallows hard, avoiding meeting my gaze.

I tip a finger under her chin, forcing her to look into my eyes. "Well?"

"I'm not good with saying what I'm feeling," Gwenna confesses, her voice small. "All my life, I've been taught to put on a smile and hide what I'm really thinking. So it's hard for me to be vulnerable. To tell you what I feel."

In a strange way, I understand. She's never had the freedom to wear her emotions as plainly as Sparrow. "Try? For me?"

Gwenna gives me a tiny smile. "I love you, too. It's impossible not to love you, Raptor. You're the best male I've ever met, and you've had my back always. Of course I love you. Even saying that sounds weak." She pauses, frustrated.

"Go on." Mostly because my ego is loving hearing all this from her. What male wouldn't love to hear his woman gushing about how great he is?

She pulls my hand from her chin and tangles her fingers with mine once more. Her gaze stays on our joined hands, so different in size but so perfect together. "It feels like . . . you know the chalice at the King's Onion? How it's constantly dropping one onion after another? I imagine that in the morning they have to pick up a massive basket of onions, all the ones that dropped overnight. And just when you think it's got nothing more in there, another onion rolls out. I'm not good with flowery words, Raptor, but what I feel for you feels like that cup. That no matter how deep I dig, I won't hit the bottom of how I feel for you. That there'll always be another onion ready to drop. It's a terrible comparison, I know."

It's a remarkably touching comparison, actually.

She lifts her head and narrows her eyes at me. "Laugh at me, and I'll bloody kill you."

"I would never. Not when you've given me the greatest gift." I lift our joined hands to my muzzle and kiss them.

"I thought me bouncing on your knot was the greatest gift?" She arches a brow, falling back on her playful banter. There's bright red in her round cheeks that tells me she's still feeling vulnerable, though, and I vow that I'm never going to make her feel like less.

"Second-greatest gift," I amend, and smile down at her. "I adore you, woman. You know that, right?"

Her cheeks grow even pinker. It seems she does know that.

FORTY-ONE

GWENNA

I'M A NERVOUS mess as we leave the dorm and head across the square toward the nest that Hawk shares with Sparrow. Neither Arrod nor Kipp has returned, and Raptor thinks they're with Master Jay, comforting him—or getting comforted—and won't be back for a while. This gives us time to talk to Sparrow and her husband.

Gods, this truly is the longest day ever. I'm exhausted from everything that's happened, but we've got a while longer before we can relax.

I cling to Raptor's hand as we walk through the streets. He made me change clothes and wash up before we headed over, and I'm glad he's thinking clearly. I'm in a daze. Every time I close my eyes, I can still hear Hemmen's voice, speaking in the strange unearthly babble of the dead.

And now our Five is down to four. And four is not the sacred number. We won't have enough to pass the guild test to become artificers, much less the individual tests. We've failed this year, all because Hemmen has been murdered. Gods. A coworker has been murdered and I felt his last moments, his fear as he died. A hard knot forms in my throat, and I try not to choke on my emotions. He didn't deserve this. No one deserves this.

I tell myself that if Hemmen is part of this group of thieves, it means he wasn't innocent. It means he was caught up in something he shouldn't have been. But he's dead now, and it seems cruel to get hung up on something like that. When I think of him, I want to think of him as the disheveled student who loved his books so much he slept with them in his bed. Not as a thief.

Not as a dead man, clutching his throat and screaming for help in my mind.

I shiver, pushing away terrible thoughts as we approach Hawk's dorm. My hand is sweaty as I clutch Raptor's desperately, but if he's noticed that I'm on the verge of panicking, he hasn't said anything. He just strides forward, assured, and knocks on the door. Then he glances down at me. "Let me handle all of this, all right? I'll protect you."

Not sure how he can protect me from the truth of what I am, but I appreciate that he's on my side. I nod and brace myself for the worst.

Sparrow answers the door, Squeaker in her arms being carried like a baby. "Oh." She looks at Raptor and then at me, her expression wary. "If you want Hawk, he's with his students. They're talking about . . . ah . . ."

"We know. We were there," Raptor says.

"Oh, good. I mean, not that it's good. It's just good that you know already and I don't have to break it to you." She adjusts her grip on Squeaker. "I'm feeding the cats if you'd like to join me until he comes back?"

We step inside, following her as she heads through the dorm toward the kitchen. As she does, more cats emerge from rooms and follow her, meowing their hunger. I'd laugh at the sight except I don't know that I'll be able to even breathe until this entire situation is resolved. Sparrow sets Squeaker down on the main table in the kitchen and then goes to the counter, where a large boiled chicken sits on a plate. She shoos one of the cats away as it jumps up, and picks up a knife. "Have a seat, you two."

Raptor glances over at me, but I shake my head. I can't relax. He puts his big hand on my shoulder and I cling to it, needing the reassurance. "We're here to talk to both of you, actually."

Sparrow turns to look at us, her eyes wide. Her gaze lands on him and then on me. "Oh, by Asteria. He knows?"

I swallow the knot in my throat and nod. "He knows."

"It's true? She really is a mancer?" Raptor asks.

Sparrow waves her hands at him, the knife flailing in the air. "Not so loud!"

Fighting the urge to bury my head in my hands and moan with horror, I manage a tiny smile. "He figured out something when I knew about Hemmen's death before anyone else did."

"And the body," he adds.

"The body?" Sparrow's eyes grow wide.

"The one she found in the training tunnel that had been there for decades," he clarifies.

"Oh, *Gwenna*." She sounds like she's disappointed in me.

"It's not like I was trying to find a dead man," I hiss. "It just sort of happened."

She clucks her tongue. "How many is that now? Four?"

I bite back a grimace. "More if you count all the people in the crypt where we found the ring."

"Oh dear," Sparrow says, turning back to the chicken. "Oh dear."

"And you knew about this the entire time?" Raptor asks her. He moves toward the table, pushing aside a cat and sitting on the edge. His hand goes toward me, palm up, and I realize he's offering it to me. A warm rush sweeps through my belly, and I hold on to him tightly.

"Well, yes. I haven't said anything to Hawk, though. It isn't my secret to share." She hacks at the chicken's legs, and the cats meow louder, rubbing against her skirts.

"I think we should tell him. He needs to know about this latest development, because right now it looks like Gwenna is working with our thieves . . . unless we point out that there's another reason why she's been tied to all the bodies we've found."

I hold back my anxiety, clinging to Raptor's hand. "I need to know everything that's going on. This whole deal with the thieves? Tell me all you know."

He does, and the more I hear, the more worried and dismayed I become. Raptor's been in on this the entire time, and I never knew. He was watching us, reporting back about us. Only his hand tightly clutching mine tells me that he feels differently about me now than he did when our Five first formed.

Raptor wraps up his story and gazes down at me. "It's why I'm acting as a fledgling. They demoted me so I could help them hunt down the thieves from the inside. I was supposed to be watching my Five, and

Hawk is watching his. We knew someone was working with the fledglings and thought to get the inside information, but so far it hasn't led anywhere."

"You think Hemmen was one of these thieves?" Sparrow asks, delicately pulling chicken free from the bone and dicing it. Or trying to. She's bad with a knife, and the cats are growing impatient. As quickly as she chops the chicken and dumps it into a bowl, the cats are trying to fish the tidbits out to eat. I should go help her . . . but I don't let go of Raptor's hand.

"Aye, that's what we think. If he wasn't the one thieving, he was working with the thieves."

"How do we know?" I ask.

"Because he died the same way everyone else did. We have to assume that they're working together, the thieves."

"It's not Gwenna. If it helps, she can't read Old Prellian," Sparrow offers. "She wouldn't know what objects are valuable and which ones aren't."

"I can barely read Common," I mutter. "And a thief doesn't have to look for specific items, I imagine. They just look for shiny ones. Or ones that are easy to grab. You think whoever's snatching things knows what they're grabbing? They just know they're valuable. That's my guess."

"But why target you?" Sparrow asks. "Why pick Gwenna to try to get kicked out?"

I shrug, glancing up at Raptor.

"I don't know. It's one of many questions we have that don't have answers." He shakes his head. "We need information that no one has."

"Or if they had it, they're dead now," I point out.

Both Sparrow and Raptor turn to look at me.

Oh no. Me and my big mouth.

FORTY-TWO

GWENNA

ROOSTER IS FRANTIC when we arrive at the main guild hall. His clothes are disheveled, there are papers all over his desk, and he tugs at his sash, clearly agitated. "Why is the guild suddenly swimming in bodies? Two in one day? One a current fledgling? Do we need to shut down all the classes for the year? For everyone's safety?"

Raptor looks over at me and rolls his eyes.

I bite the inside of my cheek to keep from smiling, because it's not appropriate. Rooster isn't wrong: two people are dead. The situation is indeed quite terrible. But watching him strut about, pulling on his hair and tugging on his heavy, pin-encrusted sash, is practically comical. I'm trying to picture the small, squat man hunting for artifacts in the Everbelow and I just can't imagine it. Not when there are strong, capable, and delicious Taurians like Raptor.

Of course, I might be biased.

Hawk and Sparrow are in the room with us as we sit in Rooster's office. The guild master's work quarters are quite fancy. There are shelves of artifacts and books; a heavy, ornate wood desk; and a painted portrait of Rooster behind a wing-backed desk chair.

I feel out of place, but Raptor insisted I come with him and, again, let him handle everything. What other choice do I have?

"It's quite unfortunate," Hawk agrees, pulling up a chair for his wife to sit on. "How is Master Jay taking it?"

"Devastated. Absolutely devastated. He's thinking about stepping down. He feels personally responsible, you know." Rooster tugs at one curly end of his mustache.

Poor Master Jay. He's not the only one who's devastated, but it hasn't occurred to me to leave. Then again, I don't feel responsible. Hemmen wasn't exactly the king of sound decisions when he was alive. Likely he got caught up with the wrong people. It's terrible, but it happens. I'm just sad for poor Hemmen. He wasn't a bad person.

"I'll talk to him," Hawk says. "Even if his team is unable to finish out the training year, it doesn't mean that he should give up. He's a good teacher. Makes some of the most self-reliant artificers there are, and we need more of those."

Rooster makes a sound of agreement and sits down again. He picks up a scroll, unrolls it halfway, and then sets it aside once more. He throws his hands up. "I can't concentrate on anything. I'm terribly upset by all of this. Has anyone heard from the archivists? Are more artifacts missing?"

Sparrow delicately clears her throat. "I'm to tell you that Archivist Kestrel is having the repeaters cross-check the inventory, but nothing further has been reported stolen. That doesn't mean that items in storage haven't gone missing, of course. Just that the thefts haven't been noticed yet." She turns and looks at me. "Artifacts were only inventoried in the last fifty years or so. Prior to that, there are no records. We have to assume that things in the deep storage weren't necessarily useful, but we've also had reports of Greater Artifacts in our books showing up in holders' hands without sale records on this end. Somehow, they're getting these items out of the city without paying for them. This thievery must be stopped. If we can't figure out how they're doing it now, it could grow worse. It could destroy the entire guild."

"I feel that's a bit extreme," Rooster says, skeptical.

"Is it? How many artificers do you think will be happy to turn in their artifacts if they know they won't get paid for them?"

Rooster opens his mouth and then closes it again. His gaze turns to me and his expression grows indignant. He straightens in his chair, angry. "Why is *she* here? This is a private meeting, and not one we should have with one of our suspects."

Raptor puts a hand on my arm before I can cringe away or run for the hills. "She's not a suspect any longer. I cleared her."

The guild leader isn't impressed with this simple explanation. "*You* cleared her? She might be involved. We cannot rule anyone out when it comes to these murders—"

"I was knotted inside her at the time of Hemmen's death," Raptor drawls. "She couldn't have done it."

Rooster gasps.

"Knotted?" Hawk echoes.

"God-touched," Raptor says, as if that explains everything.

It does. Hawk's eyes widen and he shakes his head. "Damn. That's rough."

Sparrow makes a startled sound, followed by a quiet "My goodness."

My face gets incredibly hot. I want to pinch his arm for blurting out something private like that, but I remain calm and unruffled. Yes. God-touched. Knots. All very normal conversation.

Rooster's face seems even redder than mine. He flutters a hand over his sash, adjusting it, and then gives me—and Raptor—twin disapproving scowls. "Students should not be fornicating. There are no rules, exactly, but there should be. It's highly inappropriate."

Raptor just looks over at me and winks. "If it makes you feel any better, Head Guild Master, I was told to watch her at all times. I take my job *very* seriously."

It takes everything I have to keep a straight face.

Hawk clears his throat. "Considering that Gwenna was targeted by someone, we have to assume it's the same people who attacked Hemmen. It's also entirely possible that Hemmen was responsible for the graffiti in the books and the artifact that was planted in her bag."

"Both of which Gwenna could not be responsible for, as I was with her constantly when both instances occurred," Raptor points out. His pinky finger brushes against mine, and I want to shower his face with kisses for having my back so ardently in the face of Rooster's blustering scowls.

"Yes, well, now we have one less suspect. If this little gathering is to make me feel any better, it is not," Rooster continues with a sniff. He straightens a pair of scrolls on his desk and then eyes us again. "Why did you request for us to meet?"

My stomach clenches.

"I requested it," Raptor says. "I have an idea, but it requires an open mind."

"I have a very open mind," Rooster declares.

Hawk coughs.

Rooster glares at him and then focuses on Raptor again. "Just tell me what the idea is."

Raptor shifts in his seat, and then leans forward. "We ask Hemmen who he was working with."

"The dead boy?" The guild leader seems confused. "How do we do that?"

"I have a contact in the city who knows a friend of a friend." Raptor waves his hand in the air, as if it's all attached to someone very distant and not at all me, sitting right here next to Raptor. "He knows of a way to speak with the dead safely. If that's the case, would you use it?"

Rooster sits up, all attention now. "Genius. Sheer genius. I love this idea. The sooner we resolve this the better, and if you know someone who has the right sort of artifact to speak with the dead, I think we should use it. We don't even know the kinds of artifacts we're bleeding at this point. Our students are getting frightened. We're on the cusp of los-ing good teachers—"

Raptor holds up a hand. "What if it's old magic?"

The bushy brows of the guild leader go down. "What do you mean?"

"What if someone is using old magic?"

He doesn't seem to grasp it. "Not an artifact?"

"No, artifacts are legal."

Rooster's eyes go wide. "Mancing?"

Raptor nods.

"You can't be serious."

"I'm very serious."

Rooster's eyes narrow. "How, exactly?"

Leaning back in his chair again, as if he has complete control of the situation, Raptor gives a casual shrug. "Didn't ask. It's not important. What's important is that this person is willing to use their magic to help us, but they want assurances of protection."

"We can't protect a mancer," Rooster blusters.

"It was an idea, and the best one we've had so far." Raptor shrugs again. "Getting the mancer to cut through the muck and get answers from the dead? Seems better than remaining stumped forever while this rogue band bleeds the guild dry of artifacts and kills our fledglings."

Rooster wipes his brow, and I realize, to my surprise, he's sweating. "Mancing is outlawed, but I hear what you're saying. I . . . I need to think on this. I must consult the archivists. The advisors. I need to think."

"I'd keep it quiet," Raptor tells him. "If we expose this person, they're going to run from Vastwarren City thinking they're going to be burned at the stake . . . and then we'll never get answers."

Rooster shoots a frantic look at Hawk. "And you approve of this?"

"It seems as good an idea as any." Hawk keeps his expression neutral. "The mancing is the lesser evil in this situation."

"I did some research, actually," Sparrow chimes in. "Prior to the guild's rise to power, people would consult mancers to help them retrieve missing items or even kidnapped people. I think it can be a good power for the guild to have, if used judiciously."

Rooster puts his head in his hands. "I must think on this. On all of it."

"Write the king if you must," Raptor says.

I clench inside. Oh gods, the *king*. Why not just put the stake up in the center of the plaza right now?

"But be sure to point out how many artifacts have been stolen and how many students have been killed while you do so." Raptor gets to his feet. "Give him all the details."

Rooster shoots him a look of pure venom.

Maybe this isn't such a crazy idea after all.

"I need to think on it" is all Rooster says, and then the meeting is over.

FORTY-THREE

GWENNA

Dere Ma,
I bear bad news. One of my fello students recently died and now our
Five won't be allowed to take the tests. I'm going to be a repeeter again.
It hasn't hit me yet. I will probably cry an entire bucket once I move back
in with the other maids but for now, I'm managing. I guess I'd better get
used to washing windows again. I hope you're not working two hard. Say
a prayer to Asteria for luck on my beehaf. I could use it.
Love, Gwenna

WE RETURN TO the nest to wait for Rooster's decision and try to get back to normal.

Except Hemmen is still dead, and our Five is now disqualified. Master Jay is depressed and doesn't even bother with lesson plans for the rest of the week. "What's the point? You'll all be repeaters again, no matter how well you do."

We're left to our own devices.

Some of it's good, I suppose. Raptor's able to show me affection in front of Kipp and Arrod, and when we get back to the dorm the first night, he grabs my bed and slides it next to his, making one large bed for the two of us. The look on his face dares anyone to say something, but no one does. I think we're all too focused on Hemmen's empty bunk.

Kipp tries to get Arrod to practice his swordplay, but Arrod isn't interested. He mopes in bed during the day and spends his nights at the taverns. Kipp goes with him because he doesn't want Arrod to be alone, but Arrod is not happy about it.

I offer to go with them, but Raptor refuses. "You and I are staying here in the dorm, because that's safest right now."

This continues for three days, until I get tired of looking at Hemmen's unmade bed. No one's touched it since that fateful day, and it bothers me to see it in such disarray. The emptiness probably bothers me more, but the maid in me is controlling what she can. I move to his section of the room and begin tidying, first making the bed and then going through his laundry. "We'll clean it and then send it home to his family," I tell Kipp. "It's the right thing to do."

Kipp thumps his tail in obvious agreement. He dives under the bed to help, and then emerges a moment later. He makes a page-flipping motion and then shakes his head, running around in a circle and then displaying empty hands.

"Hemmen's books? He had them with him," I say, the knot catching in my throat again.

It's not what Kipp is asking, though. He shakes his head at me and points a finger at various spots in the room, making the same page flip motion again.

"He says that Hemmen had a lot more books than what he had with him," Arrod speaks up, sitting on the bed I've just freshly made.

"I know what he said," I tell him irritably. I've known Kipp longer than Arrod has. He doesn't need to interpret for me. "I'm just thinking." I glance around the room. Hemmen's laundry is here, and his pack. His extra boots. But there's no sign of all the books he kept with him. At any time, there'd be a stack on his bed, always borrowed from the library. Just as laundry was ever-present on Arrod's bunk, and Kipp's shell is on his, Hemmen would have dozens of books littered about his personal area. He only took one or two books with him to the tavern that day. Where did the rest go?

"Perhaps Marta took them all back to the library for us," I finally say. "She likes to read, too."

"Or maybe whoever killed Hemmen was leaving messages in his books." Arrod jumps to his feet again, oblivious to the bed he just made a mess of. "He always had them with him, remember?"

Kipp folds his hands against his cheek.

"Right! He even slept with them." Arrod snaps his fingers and points at me. "And someone wrote that nasty note about Gwenna in the library's books."

"You think the librarians have something to do with this?" I ask, surprised. I'm picturing the archivists who work at the guild's library, and they're all eighty if they're a day.

Kipp frowns, then looks over at Arrod.

"Maybe not," Arrod says slowly, rubbing the stubble on his chin. "But it seems Hemmen spent a lot of time at the library. I suppose we can ask if he met any suspicious characters there."

"It's as good a guess as any," says Raptor from his spot on "our" bed. "You two should check it out. I'll stay here with Gwenna."

I shoot him a look.

Raptor just winks at me.

Kipp makes that weird lizardy coughing laugh.

"I assume we're going to study," I say in a tart voice as Arrod puts his shoes on and Kipp pulls his beaten-up shell onto his back and gives it a loving pat.

"So much studying," Raptor agrees, tracing a finger on the coverlet.

"Oh gods, we need to get out of here quick, Kipp." Arrod makes a gagging sound like he's a twelve-year-old and not twenty-seven. Kipp races for the double doors, and Arrod is two steps behind him.

I arch a brow at Raptor. I'm not sure why he's implying that we're going to fuck, because there's no time alone. Marta is sweeping the hall, and Master Jay is moping in his study. I haven't felt neglected, though. He holds me close every night, stroking my arm and snuggling me against his larger form. He constantly reassures me that he won't let anything happen to me.

"I'll burn the city down myself before I let them touch a hair on your head," he told me last night as he caressed my cheek.

I don't know how I managed to resist him for so long. Pure foolishness, I suppose. Now he's my own personal obsession. I'm starting to crave his knot, and I ache inside every time he looks at me.

When the others are gone, I sit on the edge of the bed and give him a curious look. "You were quick to get rid of them."

He grins up at me. "They don't need to go where we're going today."

He has a plan. Interesting. "And where *are* we going today, hmm?"

"You and I are heading to visit a friend." He sits up on the bed, swinging his legs over the side.

I'm a little disappointed we aren't going to take this moment to indulge in horny fantasies. I suppose it's not appropriate, but it doesn't mean I don't want it. "What sort of friend?"

"A potion maker."

Of all the things I thought he'd say, that isn't one. "What do you mean, a potion maker?"

"I mean she makes potions."

I wrinkle my nose. Potion makers are charlatans who pop up in every town and village, peddling herbal remedies that never do what they claim. "Why would we do that?"

Raptor eyes me curiously. "I thought you'd be interested in how she manages her magic."

Now he's got me. "She has *magic*?"

"Well, aye. What kind of potion maker did you think we were going to visit?"

"I don't know, some old coot who tells you to drink a bottle of stagnant water with an herb floating in it or tells you to rub lemon rinds on your feet and charges you out the arse for their expertise. That kind."

He waves a hand at that. "Those are fakes. This one makes real potions."

"How, exactly?"

"That's what we're going to find out. You want to go or not?"

"I want to go. Absolutely. This person freely works as a mancer?"

"Oh, I wouldn't say freely. She's quite expensive." He chuckles. "I've been known to imbibe a few of her potions. They're all that's kept me sane over the last few years."

"Potions? You? What for?" I'm surprised. Raptor seems to be brimming with health. He's the most virile male I've ever met.

He grins at my incredulousness. "Such flattery. You know what it's for."

And he pats his groin.

Oh.

"For your *knot*?" Why is that so scandalous? Why am I so titillated?

"Aye. It keeps me in a . . . heightened state, which is not beneficial during longer digs. I get cranky and impulsive and moody to be around. So . . . potions. I've been a customer of hers for many years."

"What happens if you take one of her potions?"

"Nothing . . . which is exactly what I wanted. But I haven't taken one in quite some time. Not since you and I started getting serious."

I blush fiercely. Hannai's rocky bosom, this male makes me act all girlish and giddy with a single look. "Well, just so you know, if you need help with anything"—I twirl a finger at his groin—"I'm more than happy to assist."

"I'm going to take you up on that," he tells me in a silky voice. There's a scrape of furniture from the back of the house—Master Jay's quarters—and then Raptor grimaces. "As soon as we get time alone, that is."

I don't say anything. Time alone is going to be a big problem that's going to get worse. Once Master Jay officially files with the guild that we've been disqualified, we'll be sent back with the repeaters (and me with the nestmaids), and those long rooms with endless rows of beds are even less private than our quarters here. It'll be another half a year (and then some) before I get the chance to be a student again, and the more times you repeat, the worse you look.

I'm probably going to have to work for Mistress Umala again. Ugh. I scrub a hand down my face, forcing those thoughts away. "I don't think time alone is going to be a thing in the near future."

The smile he gives me is faint, wry. "Probably not."

However annoying the lack of privacy is for me, it has to be worse for poor Raptor. "You need a potion, then?"

He rubs his chin. "Not yet, but you might."

Me . . . ?

To my surprise, we head to the King's Onion tavern. Why is it that we keep ending up back here? I glance around curiously, but I don't see anyone in the tavern who looks like a mancer or even a potion maker of some kind. Are we meeting someone who hasn't arrived yet?

Raptor leads me to the bar and pulls out a stool for me.

"Are we stopping for a drink?" I ask, unable to hold it in any longer.

"In a sense." He takes a seat next to me.

Naiah crosses over to us, slinging her rag over her shoulder. Her smile is bright as she flicks a glance at Raptor and then at me. "Afternoon to you both. What are we having?"

"We're having two beers, four wedges on each, Naiah." Raptor inclines his head at me. "I believe you know Gwenna."

Naiah's eyes narrow and she glares at Raptor so furiously that I'm taken aback. Then she composes herself and gives us both a cheery—if puzzled—smile. "I don't think I know what you're talking about. I always give my customers a wedge of onion with their drink."

"You do. But this customer wants four wedges on each drink."

She smiles again, but her expression is more forced. "Got it. Afraid I can't talk for long." She puts one mug under the barrel spout, filling it with beer even as she gives us a sunny look. "Getting a delivery at the back door. Leave your change on the bar, hmm?"

When both mugs are filled, she garnishes them with the onion wedges—gods, this place loves a damn onion—and then walks away.

I eye Raptor as he steals the garnish from my drink and pops it into his mouth. "Should I even ask?"

"No, but drink up." He lifts his mug and drains it in one gulp as Naiah heads farther down the bar. She greets a few customers, refills drinks while I sip mine, and beams at everyone. Eventually she heads into the back room behind the bar, the entrance covered by a thick curtain.

I take one last sip of my drink and then hand the remains to Raptor, who downs it in one swig. He winks at me. "Come on."

I want to ask where we're going, but I get the impression that the less

I ask, the better. We head out of the tavern, and then immediately Raptor steers me toward the back alley behind the inn itself. Down the long alley, there are stacks of crates and two barrels. Outside of a small alcove right behind the inn and next to the well is Naiah, leaning against the inn wall. There's a furious expression on her face.

"What the muck do you think you're doing, Raptor? I should poison your sorry arse for running your mucking mouth."

"Good to see you, too." Raptor grins, utterly unbothered by Naiah's fury. He gently nudges me forward. "Gwenna is my mate. She's in need of assistance."

His *mate*? He called me that in front of an acquaintance? Goodness, are we telling bloody everyone now? It makes me feel vulnerable, and I'm not sure I like that.

Naiah arches an eyebrow at him, and then studies me more closely. "You got this old dog to settle down, then? That explains why business is drying up."

"You need more customers," Raptor tells her.

"Aye, more customers for my *secret* business that no one is supposed to know about and that my clients swear not to share or else I cut them off." Naiah gives him a furious look.

"Don't worry. Gwenna knows all my secrets." His arm drapes over my shoulders possessively. "Even that one."

I eye him with amusement. "He told me about the potions, aye, but I don't know if I buy this. Every village has a wisewoman, and most of the time their concoctions are nothing but kitchen scrapings and lies."

"That's because those people are what we call 'charlatans' and I'm the real thing," Naiah says confidently.

"How did you learn how to make potions? Who taught you?" I'm fascinated. "Does it run in your family?"

"Maybe it does. Maybe we're mancers from ten generations back. Maybe a star fell from the heavens and granted me magic. Maybe I bargained with the fae in exchange for power. Who can say? Certainly not me." She cocks her head and gives a casual shrug. "I would never admit to something so terribly illegal."

Uh-huh. I know a liar when I hear one. "You admit your potions are just herbs and wishful thinking stuffed into a jar."

"Tell yourself whatever story you need. The truth is that my potions always work. Always."

I glance over at Raptor. He nods. "They work."

Naiah just smiles, pleased at his reassurance.

I study her, wondering how she could possibly be the person we need. She's youngish, about my age. Her dark hair is cut to her shoulders, letting her thick ringlets frame her face, and her clothing is the same sort of bland, functional dress and bodice I'd wear back at Honori Hold. If she has coin, she's not showing it. But then again, perhaps that's the point. When I look at her, I don't think *mancer.* I don't think *charlatan,* either. "Are they magic? Truly? The potions?"

Naiah shrugs again. "As magic as any artifact."

"How?"

"I have my secrets, and they're remaining my secrets." Her smile is confident. "You want a potion, that's what's for sale. Not information."

"What kind of potion?" I ask.

She arches a brow. "What kind do you need? I can do most everything."

I cast another uncertain look at Raptor. If I admit that I have magic, is she going to go to the authorities? Not unless she wants to destroy her business, I realize. I suppose if I buy a potion from her, we're both endangered. He's trusting me with the knowledge that he's purchased from her, too. Licking my lips, I finally speak up. "Can you . . . get rid of an ability that someone has? An ability they don't want? With a potion?"

"What kind of ability are we talking about? Like being able to put an ankle behind your ear?" Her expression is teasing but full of curiosity.

"More like . . . magic. Magic that you don't want." I chew on my lip. "Magic you want to get rid of."

Naiah's brows go up, and she glances at Raptor before answering me. "I guess the better question is, why?"

"So you don't get burned at the stake in the plaza?"

She laughs. "Who's going to know as long as you're smart about it? If they ask you to prove that you have magic, just . . . don't?"

She makes it sound so easy. Just ignore your magic. Just pretend like it's not there. Easy for her to say. "It bothers me every time I go into the Everbelow. That isn't ideal for someone trying to become an artificer."

"Ah." Naiah taps a finger on her lips. "I can definitely see how that would be a problem. Let me see what I can come up with. Give me a couple of days and check the usual spot. It won't be cheap, so be prepared."

With that, she gives us a smile and then opens the door, stepping back inside the tavern.

I look over at Raptor. "I can't believe I might resort to magic to fight magic. It feels . . . wrong."

He pulls me in against him, holding me close and rubbing my back. "I know. But when things are different, we need to think differently, too. I was having trouble concentrating on anything while in training as a fledgling, because all I could think about was sex. There's a belief that a Taurian with a knot is in rut, so if you have a knot constantly . . . well, they're not wrong. You do think of sex a lot. You're not crazed and willing to fuck anything with a hole, but you're definitely very *focused* on sex. I had to think of a solution, and it was one of the sex workers who suggested a potion broker. I started asking around and ran into more than a few charlatans . . . and then I met Naiah."

"I can only imagine how annoying the knot is," I say, even though part of me wants to reach down and rub it proprietarily, even now. "How does anyone with one get anything done?"

"You're expected to become a priest, actually. Lots of Taurian women go to the priests of Old Garesh when they don't have a mate or don't want to wait the five years for the next Conquest Moon. A priest-breeder can help Taurian women with that."

That makes me want to hold on to him harder. "I'm glad you didn't become a priest."

He chuckles, his hand trailing over my back. "Aye, me too."

"Can I kiss you right now?"

"You have to ask?"

"Well, yes. You're twice the bloody size of me. I can't just reach over and put my mouth on yours."

Raptor throws his head back and laughs. Immediately, he puts both hands on my waist and lifts me up into the air so our faces are even. My feet dangle several handspans away from the ground. "This better?" he asks.

"It'll do." I lean in and gently press a kiss to his nose. We'll have to figure out how to do the mouth-to-mouth part, but that's for a more private moment when we have all the time in the world. I just rub my nose against his much bigger one instead. "Thank you for always helping me."

"Of course."

"Did you mean what you said? About me being your mate? Even after everything that's happened?"

His expression gets a little cagey as he sets me down. "Hmm?"

"You called me your mate." I flick a finger in the direction Naiah left. "In front of her."

"I wanted her to help you and to not ask questions."

"So I'm *not* your mate."

"Do you want to be?"

"I want to know how *you* feel."

We eye each other.

"I mean . . . I don't hate the idea," he muses.

"You're killing me with flattery here," I say dryly. "Please, stop. A woman can only take so many compliments at once."

Raptor chuckles and drags me in close again, swallowing me into his embrace once more. "Fine, you want the truth? I'm obsessed with you, Gwenna. I want to attack anyone who even thinks of looking at you twice. I want to hug the shit out of you every time I see you. I want to flip your skirts up and lick your cunt until you squeal my name in that perfect way you do. I want to smile at you first thing every morning and be wrapped in your arms every night. I want you to be the most amazing artificer ever because I want your success. I don't care if you're a mancer or a maid or an artificer. I just want to be near you, breathing in the same air and hoping for a smile. If that's not love, I don't know what is. So aye, you're my mate . . . but you don't have to be. If it's not what you want, I'll back off."

I stare up at him.

His ears twitch, his expression uncomfortable. "What?"

"I'm just wondering how long it's going to take you to pick me up again so I can kiss you for saying that, or if I'm going to have to stay down here by your kneecaps."

Raptor laughs, lifting me up and settling my backside in the crook of his arm. I hold on to his closer horn and then lean in to kiss the side of his muzzle. "You sweet, ridiculous male. Of course I want to be your mate. I just didn't know how you felt after everything. The last time you called me your mate, I blurted out Hemmen's name."

"Hearing that was not my favorite, aye." His ears twitch again, and I realize he's embarrassed. "But nothing's changed. Not for me. Not ever. I just didn't want you to feel pressured—"

I put a hand over his mouth to stop his words and kiss his cheek again. "Let's go home so I can show you just how I feel about the situation."

"Sounds good to me."

"You can set me down now."

"Nah, I like carrying you. You're practically pocket-sized." He starts heading down the street, me still in his arms.

I snort, because we both know I am not even close to pocket-sized. More like barrel-sized, but I'll take the flattery. "What happens to us now?"

"We wait for Rooster to decide how he wants to proceed. Or we wait for Naiah to produce a potion. Or we wait for the killer to show themselves. Or for Master Jay to file that we're disqualified. Basically . . . we wait."

I don't know if I like that. We wait for someone else to make a move? "I feel like we should do something more."

"Aye, we probably should. But unfortunately, we're not the ones in charge."

FORTY-FOUR

GWENNA

Despite being snuggled in Raptor's arms at night, I'm still having trouble sleeping. My dreams are filled with more of the senseless babble of the dead, and Hemmen's accusing gaze. Of wandering the Everbelow as hands reach out to grab me and try to pull me into the shadows. I wake up before everyone else in the morning and head to the kitchen. Marta is behind on her cooking. It looks as if she left last night without preparing anything for today. It seems such a small thing to do, and I've spent so much time in kitchens growing up, that I automatically start making the dough for the day's bread. It'll need to proof for a few hours, and she can probably use the help.

Besides, it's not like I'm going to be an artificer anytime soon. I fight back a sigh of frustration and slap the dough a little harder just to work the emotions out of my system. It feels good to do something I know I can manage, so I ready the dough, then start to chop vegetables and soak barley. Raptor really loves a barley soup, and I want to make something comforting. Maybe I'll ask to be the nestmaid at another residence. Maybe I'll ask to be Hawk's nestmaid.

Maybe I'll just toss my pride out the window. I snort at that.

Marta comes into the house at dawn, surprised to see me in the kitchen.

She pulls her shawl off her shoulders and hangs it on a hook by the door. "Oh. What are you doing up?"

"I couldn't sleep," I tell her, shaping the last of the bread rolls and setting it on a pan to rise. "So I thought I'd help out. Are you caught up on the laundry?"

"I am, but it's good that you're awake. I intercepted a messenger as I was coming in." She holds a scroll out to me. "I told them I'd pass it along."

I peer at the name written on the binding. It says **RAPTOR** in shaky lettering. "I'll wake him up. Should we notify Master Jay?"

"He actually just left." She gestures at the back hall. "Got a summons and headed out."

Figures. "Probably mad that all these horrible goings-on are cutting into his time alone with his widow woman. I'll tell the others."

She gives me a grateful smile, her expression turning slightly worried. "I hope the messages are nothing important."

"Aye, I hope that, too." At the rate we're going, though, I don't think that's the case. I'm tempted to read the letter myself, but I'm tits-poor at reading, and it's not my business anyhow. Is this more of Rooster's thief hunt? Or something else?

When I enter the dormitory room, it's quiet and dark. The room has no windows to let the light in, and there are no candles lit. I tiptoe over to the bed I share with Raptor and tap his arm.

He immediately hauls me down onto the bed and nuzzles my throat. His hand goes for my breast, and he makes a disappointed sound when his fingers skim over tight corset instead of loose tit. "Here I thought you were waking me up properly," he whispers, nibbling on my throat. "Should I let you go or should I pretend that we're alone?"

Oh gods, I would truly love to pretend for a while. I shake my head in the dark, though. "You've a letter."

"By the bull god's bollocks," he mutters, but he gets up from bed.

I straighten my clothing as he dresses, and when he opens the doors to let light in, I move to his side.

I hold the scroll out, and he frowns at the seal on it as he takes it. "It's not from Rooster."

"No?" I don't know if I feel relieved or worried to hear that. The guild leader hasn't made a decision, then.

"No. I don't recognize the writing." He flicks the wax seal open and unrolls it, skimming the letter in the dim light of the hallway. Then he groans louder. "I should have known."

"What is it?"

Raptor rolls the missive up again and shakes his head. "Rescue effort. All guild Taurians are needed. It doesn't say what happened, but it can't be good."

"That's unfortunate." I've heard from Sparrow that the Taurians are called in constantly to help when a team needs a rescue in the tunnels. It happens often that someone gets lost, someone gets too hurt to continue, or a mining shaft collapses. "May I come with you? Like last time?"

Raptor pulls me close and kisses my forehead. "This time, no. I knew it wasn't dangerous last time. This time, who knows. It could be a bad ratling infestation and they need more warriors. It wouldn't be safe for you. Best that you stay here and wait for Rooster's response."

I make a face at that. "I know you're right, but I hate it."

"I do, too. I'm going to have to leave you in the care of Arrod and Kipp. You think that doesn't bother me?" He cups my face in one big hand. "Because it does. It bothers me a lot. At least Master Jay is here."

"Actually, he's not. Marta said he was called away this morning. Kipp is skilled, though."

"I have weapons that are bigger than Kipp is."

"There's also Arrod. He's . . . well, he's enthusiastic." I grin up at him. "If that counts for anything."

"Just take care of yourself. Don't go anywhere with strangers. Don't get separated from either one of them. Take the maid with you if you must go somewhere."

"The maid has a name," I chide him. "She's a person. And just . . . be safe, yes?"

"You make it sound like there's a delightful incentive to be safe."

"Oh, there is. The best incentive." I grin slyly up at him. "We find a nice, quiet room, lock the door behind us, and work on our team building."

"Now you're talking." He tilts my face up and then stoops down. His muzzle brushes against my lips, and I find it achingly sweet that he goes out of his way to give me a kiss. "I'll be back as soon as I can. Let's go wake up Arrod and Kipp and give them the good news."

ROOSTER'S RESPONSE COMES in after lunch.

Because of course it does.

Raptor is gone, his gear pack strapped to his back, an extra weapon at his belt. He'd disappeared down the street, heading for the drop zone in the early-morning sunlight. I sit with Kipp and Arrod, picking at lunch as Marta cleans dishes at the sink. I don't have any appetite, and I'm glad I haven't eaten much, because the moment I see the missive, my gut clenches and a sour taste rises in my throat.

The slitherskin at the door is a faint orange-pink color, with a bright yellow belly and vivid green eyes. She has a little frill on her head past her brows, and Kipp doesn't greet her with the usual belly-rubbing that means two slitherskin are talking to each other. They just exchange shy looks. I wonder if this is the lady friend. He hands her a coin and brings the parchment over to me.

I run a hand over the note.

It looks different than the missive that came earlier. The parchment is thicker, the wax seal ornate and showy, with the imprint of a rooster in a circle stamped with the guild's logo. The lettering along the edge of the parchment is neat and tidy, and it has Raptor's name on it.

Not mine. Just Raptor's. Rooster doesn't know how involved I am.

I glance up at Arrod and Kipp, who are watching me. The only sound is that of Marta moving about in the kitchen down the hall. "I don't know when he'll be back."

"You should read it," Arrod says encouragingly. "What if it needs to be answered right away? And it's not like Raptor would mind, because it's you. He loves everything you do."

Kipp makes a chirping sound that I interpret as agreement.

I clutch the scroll and bite my lip. Raptor wouldn't care. I know he wouldn't. It's just . . . do I want to see what Head Guild Master Rooster has said? Or can I wait?

I . . . can't. I tear open the parchment and stare at it with shaking hands. The writing is pretty, but the lettering is cramped and I have to read slowly, my lips moving as I do.

> Raptor,
>   I have decided. We will not resort to illegal methods to solve our problems. The guild's reputation is above reproach and we will not do anything to harm that, despite the costs. What we lose now might be nothing compared to what we would lose if we were to dabble in unsavory choices. I will notify you on any updates to our situation, but until then, we wait for the criminals to show themselves.
>   Head Guild Master Rooster

It's a no.

I . . . don't know how I feel about that. Limply, I hold the parchment out to Kipp, since he and Arrod are both practically squirming with anticipation.

Arrod takes the letter and reads it aloud, with far more skill than I did. "I don't understand what he means," he says after a long moment. "What illegal methods? What problems? I thought the guild was looking for Hemmen's murderer?"

I eye the two of them and then our surroundings. It feels too open to talk about mancers and thievery right here. We need privacy. I grab Arrod by his sleeve and gesture that Kipp should follow, and head into our dorm's sleeping quarters. Once the three of us are inside, I shut the doors and lean against them. "The guild has a thief. Or multiple thieves."

"And this is who Hemmen was involved with?" Arrod asks. "The thieves?"

"It seems so. Whoever is stealing artifacts from the archives is using repeaters and then murdering them when they're done."

Arrod sits on the edge of the nearest bed, his expression shocked. "Are . . . are we next?"

"Are you working with thieves?"

"Not that I know of! But how do I know if they're a thief or not?" He jumps to his feet, pointing at me. "Wait! The messages in the books—are you a thief?"

Kipp blows out a breath. He shakes his head and hops up on the bed, gesturing at Arrod to look at him. He signs a few things and then glances over at me. The look on his face is full of reproach as he turns back to Arrod, waiting.

"Sorry, Gwenna," Arrod says. "I panicked. I know you're not a thief."

"I'm not. If I was, why would I tell you about all this?" I clutch the message meant for Raptor. "I certainly wouldn't flunk myself by killing Hemmen. So that's another thing that makes me wonder. Someone wants us to fail. Us specifically."

"Well, maybe it's because we're repeaters," Arrod says.

I blink at him.

Kipp gestures that he should continue.

"I mean, if they're using repeaters, and Hemmen was one—you know he repeated four times already, right?—maybe they were trying to make us fail so Hemmen could repeat again."

I open my mouth . . . and then shut it again. It makes a bizarre sort of sense. "Why target me?"

"We're on a team with a girl," he says, his tone dismissive. "If you wanted to fail us, it's not that hard to figure out who the weak link is."

The hiss that Kipp makes echoes my own. "That is the rudest—"

"I'm saying what the thieves would think! Not me! I mean, I did originally think you were weak because you were a girl, but you work hard and you don't complain, and you were better at hiking than Hemmen was." Arrod shrugs and then gestures at the letter I'm holding. "What's the illegal stuff that Rooster doesn't want to do?"

I eye Kipp, whom I know and trust.

I regard Arrod, whom I don't know well, and don't know if I can trust. But if they're protecting me, they're supposed to know something, right? I decide to go vague. "Raptor says he knows of someone who could talk to dead people. They could help us speak with Hemmen."

Kipp's expression remains unfazed.

Arrod brightens. "Like a mancer? That's a really good idea. I had no idea they still existed. You think we can find one?"

"Mancing is illegal."

"So is gambling on Sevensday, but you don't see anyone paying attention to that law." He shrugs. "You think a mancer would help us?"

"Rooster doesn't want us to try," I remind him, but even as I say the words, they make me angry. Head Guild Master Rooster knows he's safe. No one's going to target him. Meanwhile, every repeater is going to be wondering if they're the next target. Someone else could die. More priceless artifacts could be stolen from the guild, irreplaceable things that could make a big difference to the artificers who get paid on the sale of objects.

These thieves could target me again. They could target Kipp or Arrod. If Arrod's theory is right, they wouldn't because we're "failures" already. Hemmen's dead, so he can't repeat again, but what if Arrod's wrong? What if there's another reason, and the guild continues to watch and wait until some other innocent gets their throat cut?

Because I don't think Hemmen was a bad guy. I think he was naive and got himself caught up in a bad situation. I think perhaps he needed whatever money these thieves offered him, and he probably needed it desperately. I can't hate on anyone for chasing coin.

If Hemmen had known his death was a possibility, I doubt he would have gotten involved. All he wanted was to read books.

And Rooster wants to wait until another repeater dies, another repeater who might be desperate for income after failing to become an artificer. Another repeater who needs saving from themselves.

I'm tired of waiting for someone else to decide what I should do. "This is stupid. We have the means to get answers, and the guild won't let us."

"You think they're afraid?" Arrod asks. "Because I'm mucking afraid!"

"It doesn't matter."

"It matters to me! I don't want to sit around and wait for someone to cut my throat just because they think I'm connected to Hemmen." There's a panicked look on his face. "If a mancer has the answers we need, why wouldn't we ask them to help?"

"Because mancing is outlawed."

"It's a stupid law, because we deal with magic all the time!" He gestures around us. "It's in every object we pull out and that's fine, but not if someone tries to help us stop a murder because it's coming from a person? Do you know how ridiculous that sounds?"

Oh, I know. And it makes me upset, too. I glance over at Kipp, gauging his reaction. He seems equally distressed, and I wonder if I should trust them with my secret. Mucking hells, it's starting to feel as if I'm blabbing it to the entire city, but what other option do I have? Wait for someone else to die? Wait for someone else to solve all my problems?

Or do I finally take charge?

I think for a moment more and then put my hands on Arrod's shoulders. "Calm down. We're going to fix this."

"How?"

"I need to go visit Sparrow at the archives." I pause and then add, "And if either of you mentions any of what we do this afternoon, I'm going to deny it all and say you were drinking. Understand?"

Arrod's eyes go wide. "Deny what?"

Kipp studies me and then points a finger in my direction.

I nod. "It's me. I'm the mancer, and I'm not waiting for the guild. We're going to get Sparrow, and then we're going to talk to Hemmen and get the answers we need."

"Oh, thank all the gods," Arrod breathes, relieved.

FORTY-FIVE

GWENNA

HOURS LATER, WE'VE met up with Sparrow at the archives. She's hard at work, surrounded by no less than four cats sprawled across her desk as she pores over a large book with cribbed handwriting, her glasses perched on her nose. The archives are bustling, with most of the other archivists currently documenting a large haul that one particular Five just brought in for cataloging. Her husband is busy training his fledglings, and she's surprised to hear that Raptor's been pulled for a retrieval mission. "That's strange that they'd call a repeater and not a guild master."

I shrug. "It came with an official-looking wax seal on it. Maybe they thought Hawk was busy? Either way, we need your help."

I explain to her the situation—that Rooster refuses to use my mancer abilities, that he'd rather wait until someone else is dead, and that we're going to take matters into our own hands. Before I can even finish, she's nodding her head and grabbing a book off her desk. "Yes, of course I'll come with you to brush up on your Prellian glyphs," she says loudly. "Anything for a friend."

"That's not why we're here—" Arrod begins, frowning.

Kipp pushes against his leg while I elbow him. Seriously, and this guy is going to keep my secret? I'm doomed. But that's a problem for me to worry about in the future.

"Right, sorry," Arrod whispers and gives me a conspiratorial wink. "Glyphwork."

Oh boy. "Are you sure this is a good time, Sparrow? I don't want to be a bother. . . ."

"Follow me," Sparrow says, ignoring my words of protest. "I know just the place we can study. It'll help you think to be outdoors and enjoying the afternoon sunlight. I know I always study best with a delightful breeze on my face."

It takes everything I have not to snort with amusement at that. A breeze on her face? Please. Sparrow is very much an indoor sort of woman, and she absolutely hates the wind when she's trying to read something. But if someone else notices the strangeness of this declaration, they don't say anything. They're too busy unpacking and talking amongst themselves as we head out of the archives, following Sparrow.

She marches with authority down the street.

I follow her, doing my best to wear an "I'm about to study now" expression on my face. We head through the central plaza at the heart of the city, past the statue of Sparkanos the Swan, and then head away from the guild buildings entirely. We pass several nests and the training grounds, and when we get to the outer wall, I eye Sparrow. "Where are we going exactly?"

"You need his body, right? He's going to be with Romus's people."

"Oh, mucking hells," Arrod moans from behind me.

All five hells indeed. Of course he's at the god of the dead's temple. All the dead go there to have blessings said over them and to be interred in one of the god's sacred houses so they can be welcomed into one of his five realms. It just didn't occur to me that when I said I'd be speaking with the dead, I'd be going to their house. My skin prickles with goose bumps.

I rub my arms, shivering despite the warmth of the sunshine. I wish Raptor were here.

A small hand touches my knee. I look down at Kipp, who's trotting at my side. He glances up at me and gives me a reassuring lizardy nod. Even if my lover—no, my *mate*—isn't here, I've still got friends at my side. "Thank you, Kipp. I can always count on you."

He gives a reassuring little huff and nods again.

We approach the temple of Romus, Lord of the Five Hells. Sparrow takes the lead, and we step inside. The moment we do, my skin prickles with awareness, as if the dead in the vicinity are suddenly becoming alert to my presence. I dig my fingernails into my palms and pretend to admire the temple. All buildings of Romus are created in the same manner— there are rows of benches like church pews, all facing the murals of the five hells. In front of each mural is an altar, along with the offerings for each realm. Worshipers give offerings to each realm to push them away, and there are no offerings in front of the Hell of Release, because everyone wants to pass through its gates. The Hells of Misery, of Despair, of Penitence, and of War are all flooded with offerings of rotten foods and aversion symbols. Near the doors to the temple stands a nun in front of a stand with a basket of old vegetables. "Rotten turnip for hell?"

I'm tempted to purchase a few myself just out of superstition. It's tradition, after all.

In her heavy archivist robes, Sparrow flounces up to the nun and gives her a haughty look down her nose. "My friends and I have come to pay our respects to one of the deceased. Where can we sit with him and pray for his Divine Release?"

The nun points to the back of the temple. "You'll want the head priestess. She's in charge of purifying the bodies."

"My thanks." Sparrow nods at her and then flicks a hand at us, indicating we should follow close behind.

A shiver moves up my spine as the faint nonsense babble of the dead begins to whisper in my ears. I don't recognize the voices, but then again, the dead never sound familiar. We follow behind Sparrow, bowing to the nun as we pass by her. "She's a little scary like this," Arrod comments. "Mistress Sparrow. I thought she was an archivist."

"She's got holder blood," I tell him.

"Ahhhh. That explains it."

It really does. Even though she's working as an archivist now, Sparrow can put on the invisible mantle of a holder as easily as breathing. She takes on an air of unquestionable authority, as if it's her gods-given right to go wherever she pleases. And it works, more often than not. I'm grateful that she's helping us, because I probably would have flailed the moment I got through the doorway and felt the presence of the spirits inside.

Then again, maybe not. Because I'm determined to see this through. Hemmen deserves for his Five to come through for him. Those who have died deserve justice, too. If I can help them, I will. I've sat quietly for too long in my life, and I promised myself I wouldn't let anyone get in the way of my becoming a guild artificer.

Sparrow heads past the murals of the five hells, pushing aside a curtain in the back. There, another nun comes out to greet us, this one in the tall sunburst-shaped headdress of the god of the dead. She's an older woman, but her expression is kind. When Sparrow explains what we'd like to do, she simply nods and leads us down the hall.

"The dead are given a natron massage and then rest in the god's arms for ten days before we send them on," she says. "You can sit and pray for him, and you will not be disturbed. I must warn you as I warn everyone, however, that he will not look the same as he did in life. His mortal flesh has been rubbed with sacred oils, and even now, there might be some bloating and a faint smell. This is all part of the god's natural way of reclaiming his children, so do not be alarmed." Her sweet smile never falters. "But perhaps do not touch anything."

"Of course not," I say brightly, even though I'm intending to do just that.

We're led into the inner chamber. The god's arms, as the priestess called it. The dead are brought here for the ten days between the moment of death and the god taking them into his arms and leading them to one of the five hells. The double wooden doors open and then an intense smell of incense and rot wafts through the air. The feeling of death overwhelms me, and I dig my nails into my palm so hard that hot pain shoots through my hand. Kipp makes a choked sound that he tries to muffle, and it takes everything I have not to cover my mouth from the smell.

"As I said," the priestess continues, "this is all very natural, but it is not easy for the living. You can sit on one of the benches here." She gestures at a series of hard marble benches lining the walls of the room.

The interior of the chamber would be lovely if not for the stink. I'm familiar with the rites of the dead, but back at Honori Hold, I rarely attended them. There was never an official ceremony for any servant who died, and the servants were never invited to the death rites of anyone important. Even though I've known about Romus and the temple rites all my life, this is my first time experiencing them. Add in that the dead are throbbing in the air around me, and I feel like I'm choking as we're led into the waiting chamber. It'd probably be a very pretty, serene place to visit if not for, well, all the death. The ceiling is nothing but fragile painted glass, full of colors and light. It streams in from above, sending down a kaleidoscope of colors onto the gray marble floor. Wreaths of dried flowers cover everything, along with boughs of heavily scented leaves. There are three marble biers in the center of the room, and to my surprise, there's more than one dead man. There are three.

Of course. It stands to reason that there'd be more than one person paying for a god-blessed funeral in the entire city. This . . . just wasn't part of my plan. But there's nothing to be done for it.

Each marble bier is spaced apart from the others, the dead person covered with thick, heavy sheets. The fabric of the sheet is adorned with Romus's blessing symbols, and as we step deeper inside, I can't help but notice that each of the marble biers that the bodies rest upon are tilted, and a bowl for catching liquid is set at the foot of each bier.

I don't want to know what the muck *that* is for.

"We shall pray right here," Sparrow says, indicating that we should all sit on the bench she's chosen. "And while my friends say their goodbyes, might I have a word with you, Holy Mother? My father—Lord Honori of Honori Hold—could use a bit more guidance from the god's people. Our last priest of Romus died when I was twelve and has never been replaced, and I am deeply concerned about his spiritual health."

The priestess's eyes widen. "Lord Honori?" At Sparrow's nod, the woman all but blushes. "Truly, it would be an honor to offer advice to anyone in a holder's family. What are your concerns exactly?"

"My father has a new wife and son," Sparrow continues, and discreetly closes the door behind her, shutting herself into the hall with the priestess and leaving me, Kipp, and Arrod with the dead. It's a clever distraction, and I'm grateful for it.

Kipp makes another choked sound in the silence of the room.

"It's a lot, isn't it?" I press my sleeve to my nose to muffle the scents.

My skin is crawling, but I ignore it. "I need to be close to do this, though. Maybe . . . maybe you and Arrod watch the doors from the other side?"

The slitherskin all but runs for the door, cracking it open and slipping back out. Arrod remains steadfast at my side, but it's clear from the way he holds himself that he's not breathing through his nose. "I can take it. It's just a bit of rot. Do what you need to do."

I nod at him, my heart fluttering with anxiety.

Time to begin.

The moment I unclench and relax against all the sensations that have been threatening to overwhelm me since we got close to the temple, the strange power washes over me. It's like being sucked under water. My skin prickles so hard it feels like it's trying to come off my body, but I force myself to relax, to allow the sensation to move through me without fighting it. I open my eyes slowly. . . .

Three spirits shimmer into place in the air around us.

They're not people. Not really. More like foggy blobs with vague people-like faces. It's as if they don't know how to hold themselves to-gether without flesh, and so they slip and slither in the air, with only the barest sense of limbs or a head. There are eyes, though, frightening in their darkness, like two holes punched in parchment. And all three sets of eyes are focused on me.

The babbling of the dead fills my head even as the spirits reach for me, drifting forward.

They can't do anything to you, I remind myself. *They've been here this whole time. They're just now realizing that you can see them, that's all.* I force myself to relax, to study each of the amorphous faces to try to determine which one is Hemmen. The babbling in my ears gets louder, their words nonsense, and they take on a more desperate edge with every moment that passes.

"Any luck?" Arrod asks from his spot at the door.

I ignore him and focus on the three spirits in front of me. "Let me talk to Hemmen."

Two of them surge forward, trying to get my attention. They reach for my face and hair, their strange words more frantic, even as one of the spirits hangs back. Somehow, I sense that's the one I'm looking for, but I'm not going to get anything done with the other two flooding the room with chills and strange, incomprehensible words. My head throbs and I feel dizzy, and I know it's from them overwhelming me. "Please stop," I whisper. "I can't handle this. Not all of you at once."

They continue to talk, ignoring my words, and their tones take on a frantic edge, which makes my heart beat faster. I need help. I need . . . something. A guiding hand. A mentor. Help. I can't do this alone.

Strangely enough, I think of Raptor and the impressed way he always regards me, like I've managed to surprise him repeatedly with my clever-ness. I imagine his heavy hand on my neck. Not steering me, not de-manding, just reminding me that he's nearby and he's with me. And even though he's not here right now, imagining that weight helps me focus.

If I want to do this, I must manage it on my own.

I take a deep breath. "I can't concentrate if you all talk at once. Let me speak to Hemmen first, and then I'll talk with each of you, I promise."

The babbling dies down to a low, unhappy murmur, but the spirits slide backward, retreating to their biers and hovering in the air, waiting. Their dark eyes watch me fervently, almost hungrily, but I ignore them and focus on the third one, the least defined, the one with the most blurred edges. "Hemmen? Will you talk to me?"

He drifts forward, and there's no urgency in his strange babbling thoughts as they flow into mine. Instead, they're filled with different emotions. Reticence . . . shame.

"I'm not upset," I say softly. "I want to help you. It's not right that you were taken advantage of like this. I want to fix it. I want to find the person who did this so it won't happen to anyone else. Will you speak with me?"

The spirit of Hemmen moves closer, all smoke and black eyes, and the smell of rot grows stronger. I fight the urge to cough and concentrate on what should be his face.

He speaks again, but I shake my head. "I can't understand your words. We'll have to communicate another way." I hold both my hands out, palms up. "Can I ask you yes or no questions? If it's a yes, touch this hand." I curl my left hand into a fist. "If it's a no, touch the other one." I wiggle the fingers on my right.

Hemmen's ghost reaches out and touches my left hand in what feels like the barest of whispers.

Yes.

I want to weep with relief, but I need to concentrate. His touch is unpleasant, skittering over my skin like insect legs and filling me with revulsion. I fight the urge to shake my hand to flick away his touch and concentrate.

"The guild suspects that there is a ring of thieves working with repeaters to steal artifacts. Were you part of this?"

He touches my hand again. *Yes.*

A wave of sadness rushes over me. "Oh, Hemmen, why?"

He hesitates, his spirit fluctuating wildly. One of the other spirits tries to push in, touching my hand, and I shake it off. "Wait your turn." I turn back to Hemmen's ghost. "I'm not judging you. I just wish I understood. Were they blackmailing you? The people you were working with?"

More sadness ripples through the room, and I realize it's coming from him. He touches my right hand. *No.*

"But they offered you something you wanted . . . ?"

Yes.

"Books? Riches?"

Yes.

His hand lingers on mine, and a new image flashes through my mind. Hemmen, delirious with joy at the thought of having his own personal library, of all the books he could buy and the leisure time he would have to enjoy them. This is what they offered him, I realize. This is a fragment of his memory, being sent over to me.

"You stole for them?"

Hemmen touches my left hand again. *Yes.*

"What did you take? Artifacts? Books? Or something else?"

He hesitates, then drifts backward slightly, unsure how to answer.

Right. I purse my lips, focusing. I want to ask him how he got in to steal from the archives, but something tells me that he won't have the answers I need, not with being constricted to yes or no. There are still more people at work, though, and I need to find out who else could be in danger. "Do you know who it was that killed you?"

He hesitates again, and then drifts his hand over mine. *No.*

I frown at that. "Did you see their face?"

Yes.

"But you don't know who it is?"

No.

It makes no sense to me. I stab at an answer. "Do you think they hired someone to kill you, then?"

Yes.

Oh. Now we're getting somewhere. "Do you know who it was who might have sent that person?"

Again, he taps my hand. *Yes.*

"And do I know this person?"

Yes.

A chill goes down my spine. "Am I their next target?"

He hesitates, then taps no. He gestures at himself, and then at me. Then at himself again.

"You were the one targeting me?"

Yes.

I'm confused. "Why would you do that? I was in your Five. My future was tied to yours."

Hemmen's ghost reaches out and, to my surprise, caresses my breast.

I rear back. "What are you doing?"

The spirit becomes agitated, and he gestures at the right hand that I've pulled away. He's trying to say no. When I put my right hand out again, he taps it. *No. No.*

Then he reaches for me again, my skin shivering as he tugs at my bun of hair. I don't understand. . . . "Wait. Because I'm a woman? That's why you targeted me?"

Yes.

"So I was an easy target, then. You . . . wanted us to fail? Our Five?"

He taps my hand. *Yes.*

I'm starting to figure this out. "Because the thieves needed you as a repeater? Is that why you've repeated so many times?"

Yes.

So Hemmen was working with them for a long time. I ponder this, even as another ghost tries to push its way forward, his touch sending ice down my spine. "Stop it," I tell the other ghost. "You won't get your turn if you keep harassing me."

It prattles frantically at me but retreats backward, going to hover close to the bier at the farthest side of the room. I can feel its agitation in the air, and it makes me want to leave. I want to flee, but I force myself to stay behind, to calmly get answers from poor Hemmen, who only wanted to be lazy and read books all day and ended up in over his head. "Can you help me find the person who did this to you? The one you say I know?"

Yes.

I try to think how to approach this next. He can't tell me the name. "Maybe a word game? Does the name begin with an 'A'?"

No.

"A 'B'?"

No.

I continue down the alphabet until I get to the letter where he says *Yes.*

Instead of brushing his fingers over my skin, he sinks them into my palm. Images flash through my mind, bleeding over from Hemmen into me. Frost coats me from inside, and I feel like I'm drowning. I make a choked sound, falling backward off the bench as Hemmen's flurry of memories pushes through my head, one after the other. Suddenly, I know exactly who it is and how they're working. I know how they're slipping through the cracks and moving about unnoticed.

"Gwenna! Are you all right?" Arrod is there, grabbing me and helping me to an upright position. He slaps my cheek lightly. "You're like ice. Are you well?"

"I'm all right," I breathe, even as the ghosts retreat to the back of the room. The impatient one moans, but Hemmen just looks sad and lost. I wish I could comfort him, but I have to think about the living. I jump to my feet, despite how wobbly I feel. "We have to hurry. Raptor is in danger."

"What? How do you know?"

I know because I've just been shown absolutely everything.

FORTY-SIX

RAPTOR
Earlier

I EYE THE REPEATER in front of me with a scowl. "What do you mean, we need to go to a different drop?"

The student shrugs. "That's what I was told. How should I know? I just pull the lever. I was told the rescue party was coming and I should send them to Drop Twenty-Seven."

I glance over at the others as we wait for the lift. At my side, Stork consults his message, the same as mine. He's a tall, gawky human, but with a mane of peppered gray hair and a stern expression. I've worked with him before, and he's got no time for anyone's nonsense, which means I appreciate him. "My message says Drop Seven."

"Mine says Drop Seven, too." I hold the note out to him to compare. "Maybe whoever was scribing it was rattled and didn't know which drop to write down."

Stork eyes both and then shrugs, glancing over at the other human who's been rounded up to make our rescue team. It's Master Jay, which strikes me as damned strange. The man's in mourning for his student and rarely takes on rescue missions, but he was requested for this particular rescue mission, just like me, Stork, Buzzard, and Shikra. Three Taurians and two capable humans. It's a good team, I must admit, even if it's not all Taurians as the note suggested it would be.

"Well, it's not the first time we've been given bad instructions, and I doubt it'll be the last," Jay says. He shoulders his pack and then ties it at the front of his waist to keep the weight of it in the center of his back. "We can check Seven, and if everything on that level seems in order, we go down to Twenty-Seven."

No one else has an opinion. Buzzard examines his weapons, Stork just looks impatient to go, and Shikra is unruffled, but Shikra is always unruffled. "Fine. Ready the basket for Seven first, and then we'll hit Twenty-Seven."

The repeater frowns. "But—"

"We'll make sure both are clear," I all but growl at him. "The more time you waste up here is time we're not rescuing someone, understand?"

I'm in a bad mood. It's not that I've left Gwenna with Kipp and Arrod, which bothers me, but that everyone seems incompetent today. Should have taken that potion, I chide myself again when my temper flares. It would let me remain calm and collected while we work, instead of my thoughts focusing entirely on my vulnerable mate. I didn't take it because I was anticipating some alone time together, and now I'm going to suffer. Nothing to be done except make everyone else suffer along with me, I suppose. I glare at the repeater again, and he flinches back, even as he changes the settings on the pulley.

There are ten total drop stations, each one with a platform and basket to lower up and down. The numbers correspond with how deep we have to go in the Everbelow, and it makes no difference to me if we're in Seven (which is close to the surface but notoriously unlucky) or if we're deeper in at Twenty-Seven. It's all just part of the job.

We pile in, our packs on our backs and a rope tethering us at the waist. Seven isn't a long drop, so I lean against the edge of the basket and mentally check off my gear—axe, foodstuffs, more rope—but my thoughts drift back to Gwenna again. I wonder if she's heard from Rooster—

The basket lurches. The pulley creaks, and we all jerk our heads up to look above just in time to see the repeater changing the drop setting. He loosens the rope, giving it more slack, and the basket careens down.

"It's supposed to go to Seven," Stork calls up, even as we lurch farther down, so quickly that my hooves lift off the bottom of the basket.

"I have my orders," the repeater calls, and then disappears as the basket lurches in a free fall. I clutch the side, and Shikra grabs the ropes, reaching for a ledge as we try to stop our speeding progress. Then the basket abruptly jerks to a halt, and we sway wildly in the middle of the dark cavern, the ropes creaking.

We manage to pull the basket over to the closest ledge and quickly get out. There's a heavy metallic stink in the air and a scent that reminds me of old garbage. The tunnels always have a strange, vaguely sulfurous smell to them, but today it seems especially pungent.

The fact that we've landed at Drop Twenty-Seven isn't lost on any of us. "What the muck was that?" Buzzard asks.

Shikra gazes up the cavern, back where the rope dangles, cut. "That was the work of a repeater who's going to get my fist in his face when we get back up there, that's what."

"Anyone recognize him?" I ask, flexing my arm and rotating it. I hit the side of the cave wall as the basket careened down, but I can still use the arm, so all is well.

No one volunteers a name.

"No one?" I say, then sigh with frustration. I'm starting to think we've been fooled by a uniform. I know I didn't bother to look closer. Too many years of just blindly assuming that whoever is running the lift is also employed by the guild. It's my own damn fault. I've been distracted. I should have known that whoever is behind all of this—framing Gwenna, killing Hemmen—has their claws sunk in deep. I flare my nostrils and I could swear the stink around us becomes stronger. "I think we need to assume that we're walking into a problem, my friends."

Stork squints in the darkness. "Where are all the lights?"

"Lights?" Shikra asks. "What lights?"

"The ones that should be down here to light the way for humans," Stork replies, putting a hand out in the darkness. "There aren't any."

He's right. I'm so used to low lighting due to my excellent Taurian vision that I didn't even notice. There's normally an array of magical items scattered on high shelves or hanging from hooks along the descent to light the way down, and to provide lighting for the more trafficked tunnels. They're small, unimportant objects like cups or paperweights or even children's toys, but they save the guild quite a bit of coin on lamp oil. Normally the cavern is peppered with them, but today it's empty. There's not a speck of light down here except for what's coming from far above at the top of the drop.

"It's entirely possible that they've been moved to a more trafficked tunnel," Master Jay says, his voice faint and growing stronger. "Twenty-Seven has been closed to exploration since last year."

"And you're just now pointing this out?" Buzzard huffs with irritation.

"Like you, I thought we were going to Seven." Jay clears his throat. "And . . . I admit I have not been myself lately."

Silence falls. I immediately feel guilty that I haven't given more thought to how Jay is taking the death of his student and the failure of his Five. I've been so wrapped up in Gwenna that I haven't noticed just how much Jay is suffering. I go to his side and give him a comforting slap on the back, which is about as close as a Taurian gets to hugging another man.

Jay stumbles forward in the darkness, and I have to catch him.

"Here, I'll light a lantern," Stork finally says. "This is starting to smell like a trap."

"That's funny, because I smell ratlings," Shikra adds.

Buzzard grunts. "I smell them, too. Their scent is thick in the air. This begs the question: Who is it that wants us down in this particular drop that's not being used and is full of ratlings, and why?"

I scratch at my jaw, wondering how much I should admit. They deserve to know, since we're in the thick of it, I suppose. "I might have an idea."

Everyone turns to me.

We stand in the sputtering light of an oil lamp as I explain about the thieves targeting the guild and the dead repeaters, and my role in all of it.

Jay looks affronted. "How did I not know any of this? How was it that I wasn't informed that my students were under scrutiny?"

"How did you not think anything was awry when they put this big lug on your team and let him keep his name?" Buzzard gestures at me. "That didn't clue you in?"

Jay clenches his jaw, and I feel bad for the man. He's getting it on all sides. I step in to take the blame and put it where it belongs. "Rooster was keeping things quiet because he didn't know if teachers were involved as well, since it has to do with repeaters. It was easier to keep it as a small investigative group."

"But at what cost?"

I have no answer for Jay. If it had been a more widespread hunt—or a faster one—would we have lost Hemmen? Or would we have found even more murdered repeaters on our doorstep because the thieves knew they were being hunted? "Just know that the guild is taking this seriously."

"Well, if there's a gang of thieves, I'm guessing we've found how they're removing their loot from the city." Stork holds his lantern up and eyes the yawning tunnel ahead of us. "Easy enough to bribe a repeater in charge of the portals. Easy enough to sneak through a tunnel that's out of use."

"Unless there's ratlings. Which there are." Buzzard flicks the ring in his nose, his long ears twitching. "I can smell them everywhere."

"Which means we know why they sent us down here," Stork continues. "We're either in the way of their plans, or they want their tunnel cleared out. Or both."

"Something tells me we're not expected to arrive back at the guild hall and tell everyone what's going on," Jay says in that somber voice of his. "If we try to make it back out through the lift . . . what then?"

Buzzard gestures at the open drop zone. "Too dangerous. If it was me, I'd drop something on anyone who tried to climb that rope."

He's right. "Then we fight our way through the tunnel?"

"Unless you know of a better option? We've got two ways out of here, and I'm willing to bet that they've engineered things to ensure we go the way they want us to go."

"But they'll be found out. Someone will come after us."

"When? Who knows we're down here?" Stork asks. "I filed with the guild that we were sending five in response to the request, but that can be easily removed from the records if there are repeaters working against us. Which there seemingly are. Will your Five know how long a rescue mission takes, Jay?"

"It might be several days before they worry. They know rescues happen, just not how long they take."

I rub a hand down my muzzle. Well, the good thing is that if we die, Gwenna will know. And if I die down here, at least I'll be able to say my goodbyes, even if they're done as a ghost. Somehow, that doesn't make me feel better.

"Let's head in. We've got a skilled, capable group," I say to them. "I don't want to think of another Five coming down here hunting for us and getting slaughtered by ratlings. If anyone's going to survive, it's this Five. Might as well put it to the test."

Buzzard slams a big fist into his hand, his expression one of grim approval. "Now we're getting somewhere. I'll take the lead."

"Sword?" Jay asks.

"Don't need one. I've got hands."

"Taurians in front, then?" Shikra says to me. "We're the best down here in the darkness."

He's not wrong. Stork has to hold a mucking oil lamp to see anything, and Jay probably hasn't slept in a mucking week. "Aye, we'll take the lead."

"Let's see what they've brought us to play with," Buzzard says, unhooking from the rope tying us together and striding forward. It's an unspoken rule amongst Taurians—in battle, you detach from the Five so you're not dragged down. Good for us, less good for the humans.

Shikra knows it, and hesitates before unhooking himself, too. "I fight better unencumbered."

I do, too, but I see Gwenna's face in front of mine when I think about untying myself, and how devastated she'd be if I got Jay killed. I imagine Jay's widow-woman farmer, too, and Stork's woman—surely he has one somewhere—and how they'd react. Despite the urge to protect my own hide, I shake my head. "I'll remain with the humans. Let's stay together. Make sure nothing gets past the front lines."

Stork readies his blade, and Jay pulls out a heavy mace. It makes me think of Gwenna, and I smile to myself. I'd forgotten that Jay was an expert with a mace. I should ask him to give her lessons when we get back—

Then the smell of ratlings grows heavy in the tunnel, and my hackles rise. "Stay behind me," I say to Jay and Stork, clenching my fists in preparation for a battle. "And if things get bad, run for the drop. Take your chances with the rope."

FORTY-SEVEN

GWENNA

FOR THE FIRST time in my life, I am going to be an absolute bother. To *everyone*.

"I'm telling you again," I say to the repeater at the drop. I'm trying to keep my voice calm, but I'm failing. "Someone has set up a trap, and we have a team that needs a rescue."

He looks at me dismissively. "Shouldn't you be making someone dinner somewhere?"

I resist the urge to curl my fingers around his throat. "Shouldn't you be doing your mucking job? Where is Raptor's rescue group?"

"Just like I told you before, there's no rescue group down in the Everbelow today," the repeater tells me in the same bored way he's told me twice already. "Check the documentation."

I have. There's a clipboard in the main Drop Distribution Office that shows who is scheduled to go where each day, and there's absolutely nothing that shows a rescue effort, and nothing that might indicate where Raptor is. There's a mistake somewhere.

I know he's in the tunnels. I know it just as surely as I know how to breathe. And I'm not giving up until someone listens to me.

"I've checked the documentation," I say, impatience rising in my voice.

"And no one is listed there. Someone's made a mistake, which I can show you if you let me go down in the tunnels."

"Can't," he says. "You're a student. You need your teacher with you. Bring him, and we can get you the appropriate passes."

The urge to choke this man is rising by the moment. "I can't find my teacher," I manage to grind out. "But I can prove that I'm right if you just let me down there."

"No."

"Then get the head guild master," I bellow, stabbing a finger in his face. "People are in danger! A rescue is needed!"

He looks shocked that I'd point a finger in his face. "If you keep acting like this, I'm going to have to have you removed."

I scream in outrage.

Sparrow, Arrod, and Kipp pull me back. "Now, now, Gwenna," Arrod says. "I'm sure there's a logical solution to this."

I try to calm myself, even as the repeater pulls his supervisor over and they both whisper, no doubt discussing how impossible women are. "What's your logical solution?"

"Well. Hear me out." Arrod pauses and looks over at Kipp.

Kipp gestures, indicating a knock over the head and then dragging the unconscious man away.

Arrod is shocked. "Mucking five hells, Kipp! I was thinking we'd distract him!"

Kipp shrugs.

"Unless you have the appropriate passes, you all need to leave," the supervisor says, coming over to confront us.

I put my chin up, deciding to bluff my way through. "Guild law states that students are free to move about in guild territory. Unless you're arresting us, we're not leaving. And I'm not mucking leaving until you either get me the head guild master, or you let me go down in one of those baskets to see what's happening." I stab a finger at him. "Every moment we waste could mean someone else's death, and that's on you."

"Women," he scoffs, stalking away to get reinforcements.

Kipp makes the conking-over-the-head gesture again.

I'm tempted. I'm sooooo tempted.

"I appreciate the sentiment," I tell Kipp, but I know trying to take over one of the drops on our own is a bad idea. I've been eyeing the pulley system, thinking that perhaps it'd be like a well and bucket, but it's far more complex and involves multiple levers and cranks. "But I don't think we'd get down very far without their assistance. Like it or not, we need their help."

Arrod considers this, arms crossed as we whisper a short distance away from the nearest lift. "We could just tell them the truth. Maybe they'd give us a pass then?"

I scoff at him. "What, we tell them a dead man informed me that my Taurian lover has been dumped into an old tunnel filled with ratlings so they can clear it out for the thieves to use because we've caught on to their old method of stealing? That truth?"

"Well, when you put it that way, it does sound a bit ridiculous." He taps his foot, thinking.

I think, too, even as I scowl at the repeater operating the closest lift. Would bribery work? A nice lunch? An offer of kisses or a boob touch? I'm not keen on the thought of either, honestly, but I'm also getting desperate, and we've been standing here for a while. I'm deeply conscious of every moment that passes, imagining Raptor in pain, bleeding, dying. . . .

I'm just about to flop down on the ground and insist on staying where I am when Rooster appears, in full guild regalia. He's accompanied by five guild enforcers, and they approach with a menacing air. The supervisor of the drop immediately points at me. "She's the problem, sir."

"What's going on here? What is the meaning of all of this?" Rooster strides forward, sash clinking heavily with metal pins. Despite his short stature and rounded belly, he manages to convey an air of authority. "Who do you think you are, trying to go down a lift without the proper authorization?"

Oh good. Someone who can finally fix things. "Thank the gods you're here," I say to Rooster, striding up to him. "I need in that tunnel, and quickly. If all of us could go down there, that would be just lovely—"

He raises a hand in the air. "I don't know what authority you feel you have, demanding things. Bad enough that we've got a rogue group down below—"

"Wait, what rogue group?"

"Drop attendants reported that a Five forced their way in early this morning—"

My jaw drops, and I interrupt before he can finish. "That's a lie! It's a rescue effort! I saw the missive Raptor received this morning!"

"There's no rescue effort at the moment," Rooster says with a frown.

"Well, someone is lying!"

"And how do I know it's not you just being hysterical?"

"Because I want Raptor back alive, damn it! The people who sent him there don't! They want him and the others to clear out the drop that's full of ratlings so they can route the stolen goods through it via a secret tunnel in the archives!"

"There's a secret tunnel in the archives?" Sparrow asks, shocked.

"Behind some crates. It looks like a shelf full of old scrolls, but it can be moved aside. It comes out to Drop Twenty-Seven, which has a hidden passage that heads out of the city. That's how the thieves are moving about." I point at Rooster when he opens his mouth. "And before you accuse me of being a thief, if I was, why would I tell you all my secrets?"

"Then how do you know all this?" Rooster asks. "If even the rest of the guild isn't aware of such passages?"

I can't say. I can't tell him that dead Hemmen's ghost showed me everything. I make a wordless sound and look to Sparrow for help.

But Rooster's eyes narrow. "You're the mancer, aren't you?"

His voice is low enough that the repeaters won't hear him, but it still feels too public, too loud. My tongue glues itself to the roof of my mouth.

"That's why you were in that meeting. That's why Raptor wouldn't name who it was. Still won't name who the mancer is. He's protecting you."

I hesitate, and then step forward, moving in closer to him. "I promise you that I just want to save Raptor. Please, help me get him out of the tunnels, and you can burn me in the plaza later. Just please, please trust me when I say that he's very much in danger. Him and the others with him."

Rooster stares at me long and hard. Then he gestures at the supervisor. "I'm going down with this woman. I want three enforcers to come with me."

"Best bring all of them, sir," I say, relieved. "There are a lot of ratlings."

Kipp pats his sword handle and lifts his fist in the air.

"Yeah, what about us?" Arrod asks. "Kipp and I are ready."

Rooster points at them. "You two stay here under supervision. If your friend is lying, all of you are going to be locked up for a very long time."

"It's not a lie," I say, antsy. I move closer to the basket, and the enforcers file in, Rooster putting his hand on my elbow and guiding me in after them. With a creak, the door on the basket is shut and we're lowered a jerky handspan, then another.

The supervisor leans over, as if inspecting our progress downward. "She's right, you know. It's not a lie."

Then he nods at his repeaters, pulling back.

Before we can ask what he means, the basket flies down the shaft, the ropes cut. It swings against the walls and then careens down into the darkness, and I fly up into the air, barely able to grab onto one of the ropes before my head hits something hard and I fall unconscious.

FORTY-EIGHT

GWENNA

"WAKE UP."

A hard slap across the face snaps me awake. I jerk, startled, and stare up at Rooster's round face and his crappy little mustache. He's got blood trickling down his nose and a cut above his eyebrow, and his clothing is torn. He holds up an oil lamp, looking me over.

"Good," he says in a flat voice. "You're alive. Can you sit up?"

I honestly don't know. I stare up at my surroundings, and a bit of dust drifts into my eyes. It's dark, but I can see a few dim lights far, far up on the ceiling. It takes me a moment to realize that those are the lights from the drop, and we're somewhere at the bottom. Then I remember the look on the supervisor's face, the way the basket we stood in tumbled in free fall, and then . . . nothing.

My head throbs, but I don't feel the skin-crawling, gut clenching sensation that tells me that there's someone newly dead nearby. Just lots of old, old dead, but they aren't bothering me too much due to the other aches and pains in my body, and I can ignore them at the moment.

I manage to sit up, wincing. "Everyone's alive."

"That's what I'm checking," Rooster says, and then pauses. "Wait, you mean . . ."

I nod, pressing my palm to my throbbing temple. "I'd feel it if they were dead."

He lets out a long breath. "Thank Romus for his mercy, because I can't get Karref to wake up." He gestures at one of the enforcers, tumbled on the far side of the basket. "I'll let him rest, then."

I glance up again, at the tall, impossibly tall, shaft. "The thieves tried to kill us. How did we live through that?"

"The baskets are padded underneath. Lots of pillows to cushion things in case something broke. Or, you know, was deliberately broken." Rooster limps over to one of the other men and taps him on the cheek. "Wake up, Jenkins."

Jenkins groans, but that's a good sign, I suppose.

I try to get to my feet while Rooster wakes the other enforcers. Leaning on my hand sends a shooting pain up my arm, and I bite back a gasp and roll the other way to avoid using it. When I get to my feet, I'm a little achy all over my back, and my head throbs like I've been binge drinking for days, but I'll survive. My arm is the worst of it, and I cradle it against my chest as I gaze back up at the drop shaft, looking for sunlight. There is none, which means the drop has been closed over.

Mucking bastards. How are they going to explain away this one? I wonder. An accident that just happened to take out the guild leader? Do they have another person they plan to place as the guild leader, then? Or was this just a spur-of-the-moment decision?

One by one, the men are roused, except for Karref, who has taken a nasty hit on the head and won't awaken. He's breathing, but it's clear he needs a medic. Everyone else is a bit shaken but able to move about. Rooster's still limping, and one of the enforcers had to pop his arm back into its socket.

"What now, sir?" the nearest enforcer asks.

Rooster shakes his head. "I can't believe they've betrayed us like this. Broke the lift deliberately. Did anyone bring a rescue beacon?"

No one did.

"We weren't planning on going into the Everbelow, sir." The enforcer cradles his bad arm against his chest. "What drop are we at?"

"If we've fallen to the bottom of Shaft Seven, then . . . Thirty-Seven or Forty-Seven."

Whispers fill my mind, along with a mental image of a different area, higher up. "This isn't the right spot."

Rooster and the enforcer turn to look at me. "How do you know?"

I tilt my head, exasperated. Seriously? "How do you think I know?"

No one makes a sign to ward off evil, which I'm relieved to see. Instead, Rooster approaches me, holding the oil lamp aloft. "You know where we are?"

"No, but I can ask."

"You can?" The guild leader looks dumbfounded.

I nod reluctantly. "When I'm down here . . . the dead whisper at me. I can't understand them, but they send images, too. I'm able to tell from those."

Silence falls in the tunnel.

Stating my ability aloud in front of everyone is . . . awful. It's like being stripped naked in front of a crowd. I stare at their faces, the enforcers wearing a mixture of confusion and fear, and Rooster's grim, determined expression. I hate that I can't blend in with the crowd, but if me tearing off the mask means that I can save Raptor and his companions, I will.

I only hope this doesn't turn into a lynch mob.

"You truly can talk to the dead," Rooster states, as if reaffirming it. I nod.

"There are dead people here?" The enforcer sounds horrified.

"Not everyone got out of Prell alive, Smythe. Of course there are dead here," Rooster snaps.

"But . . . I thought when you died you went to Romus, and he sent you through the five hells."

"The newly dead loiter," I say reluctantly. "Until the ten days pass and the ceremony is performed. But there are still voices down here. I think they must have something they want to share, and that's why they linger."

"Ghosts." He sounds horrified.

"Not really. Just people like you and me. I haven't felt any malice from anyone. No one's trying to scare us. I think they just have things they want to say so they can be at peace." I shake my head, resisting the urge to scratch at my skin as the babble of the dead washes over me. "This only started happening to me once I came into the Everbelow as a student. I think it has something to do with all the magic here. It's only been happening for a few months, but I've never felt threatened. Just like . . . they've found the one person who will hear their whispers, and so they won't be quiet."

"Well, let them mutter at you and see if they can find out where we're at, exactly." Rooster's mouth is a flat line of disapproval. "We can't stay here forever and hope for a rescue. Not if someone's attempting to take over the guild."

"And not if there are ratlings nearby," Smythe adds helpfully.

"Yes, thank you," Rooster snaps at him. "We haven't forgotten."

I close my eyes, concentrating on the low hum of voices. I don't know why there are sometimes images mixed in, but maybe it's that some ghosts are just stronger than others. *Show me*, I tell them. *Show me where I am.*

I get a mental flash of the basket descending past one tunnel after another, and I count them. One . . . two . . . three . . .

"Thirty-Seven," I say, even as ice-cold sensations wash over me. It's the ghosts, and now that I'm paying attention to them, they're all over me like moths drawn to a flame. "We're at Thirty-Seven."

"And where was Raptor's crew?"

"Above." My voice grows faint as more oppressive feelings sweep over me. The ghosts aren't done talking, and I have no choice but to listen. They babble in my ears, voices frantic. Cold touches brush all over my skin.

One ghost is insistent, drowning out all the others. The voice gets louder than all the rest, and I shake my head, but it keeps pushing, shouting in that strange, unearthly babble of the dead. With it comes a flurry of images, and I realize whoever this ghost is, he's trying to show me something. I relax . . . and dozens of images flash through my mind.

The room grows deathly cold. My teeth chatter. More images crash through my mind, flooding in like a surging tide. Tunnel after tunnel, some empty, some not, races through my thoughts. I see where the dead are lying, I see artifacts half-buried, I see—

A hand smacks me across the cheek, jarring me back to the present. "Ow!"

"Stay with us," Rooster says, his face looming over mine.

I jerk backward, touching my cheek. "Why do you keep slapping me?"

"You sagged and looked as if you were going to fall over. And then your eyes rolled back in your head, and all we saw were the whites."

"And you shook," Smythe adds, giving me a wary look.

"Oh." I rub a hand over my face, trying to scrub the flood of thoughts from my mind. "I just . . . I'm not very good with this yet. One of the ghosts is more persistent than the others. He's pushing a lot of things into my mind. It's hard to focus."

"Are you all right?"

I nod. "I . . . I think I know a way out."

"You do?" Rooster is shocked.

I touch my aching head, as if that will somehow help my thoughts clarify. I'm shown the same image again, of a thin wall between the tunnels. They're like a warren hollowing out the ground, the tunnels of the Everbelow, and this one snakes on for a stretch and then comes very close to another tunnel.

A tunnel where they've been digging in the wrong place to find the artifact trove that's very close nearby. It's an old collapsed temple, and as I stare into the darkness, it forms in front of my mind's eye. "Oh."

"What?" Rooster demands. "Is it ratlings?"

I shake my head. I don't know if what I'm being shown is still there, or if it's an old memory long past and has been cleaned out. But the spirits seem to think it's all still there. In fact, they're urging me to go, their thoughts pushing and full of insistence.

"Why do you want me to go and find the treasure? Isn't it your people's?"

"I'm sorry, did you just say 'treasure'?" Rooster asks, but his voice is faint. I'm too focused on the dead in the air around me.

A cold, spectral hand brushes over the torn sash on my shoulder. Ah. It's not the ghost of some ancient Prellian, but an artificer who died in these tunnels and wants to show me what he was never able to claim.

"We have to get Raptor first," I say to the air around me. "Does our tunnel cut to his? Or another?"

The vision cuts away, showing me the tunnel up from us, and then hordes of ratlings, biting and chewing on flesh. I scream, clawing at my clothing, as the vision fades.

I jerk back to myself just in time to see Rooster raising his hand again. "Do not!"

"You were jabbering," he says, frowning at me.

"I was being shown the way. The tunnels are parallel to each other for a while, but this one rises up deeper in, and the one above us lowers, and so there's a place we can break through."

"And that's what made you scream?" Rooster asks, doubtful.

"No, I screamed because it's full of ratlings, and I think that's what killed the ghost who's helping me." I shiver, rubbing my neck with my good hand. "But that means there's probably a lot of ratlings in there yet, and that's why the thieves sent Raptor and his group in. They want it cleared out and made safe. That's where we need to go."

"I don't know that any of us have experience with ratlings," Smythe says, his hand on his sword belt. "We're enforcers in charge of keeping people in line, not animals."

"Ratlings were people once," Rooster comments. "Cursed people, condemned by the gods. But it doesn't matter. If we want out, we must go through that tunnel. And if you're not ready for ratlings . . ." He pauses and eyes our group. "Get ready."

FORTY-NINE

RAPTOR

I T'S NOT GOING well.

I've never seen so many ratlings in a single tunnel. When we do run across one of their nests, they're always clustered in large packs, but this feels like an entire city. Ratlings don't fight fair, either. They climb all over us, biting and scratching and trying to get under clothing and behind shields. One falls and two more take its place. Which is common with ratlings, and yet most times a group can get their backs to a wall or move to a narrower tunnel to mitigate just how many attack.

We have neither such advantage. And the ratlings just keep coming and coming.

"Keep going," Shikra calls out, bashing another ratling to the side. Another latches on to his leg. "We're making headway down the tunnel!"

"Not enough," Stork calls back, stabbing at one ratling that breaks past the others. He and Jay are still behind me, but they're faltering. Stork is older, and Jay doesn't have the stamina that a Taurian does.

Five hells, even Taurians aren't enough to clear this tunnel. Buzzard had surged into battle with enthusiasm the moment we saw the first ratlings, but he's gone quiet except for his heavy, labored breathing. Shikra has been using his shield to bash away the worst of them, and I'm grabbing ratlings and breaking necks, bashing heads against walls, and causing whatever damage I can. My goal is to prevent any ratlings from getting past me, but it's an impossible task. Jay and Stork pick up the slack, but we're all exhausted, and it feels as if the ratlings have been coming at us for hours with no sign of stopping. There's sweat in my eyes—or it might be blood—and I'm covered all over in bites and scratches, but I keep going.

Because there's no alternative. If we stop, even for a moment, we'll get overwhelmed.

"Forward," Buzzard manages to choke out, slinging another ratling off his arm as it bites at him. "Keep. Pushing. Forward."

"Watch yourself," I warn as three more ratlings get past him. Shikra grabs one, and I snag the other two off the floor. They squirm frantically in my grip, and I bash their heads together. Both go slack, and I toss them aside. "Too many are getting through."

Buzzard doesn't answer. He staggers, and then a moment later, he goes down. Immediately, more ratlings swarm him.

I bellow in outrage, hot fear racing through my veins. Surging forward, I drag Jay and Stork behind me as I move to Buzzard's side. Shikra sidesteps, but he's got so many ratlings on him that he can't assist. I pull Buzzard back to his feet, flinging the child-sized ratlings away, only for new ones to scramble forward. We need a miracle from the gods at this point. We need—

A loud banging echoes in the tunnel. The ratlings scatter, red eyes shining as they retreat.

"What the muck was that?" Buzzard manages, leaning heavily on me. There isn't a handspan of skin where he hasn't been gouged or bitten, and he's covered in blood. More worrisome are the wheezing breaths he takes. Ratlings are no longer than my forearm, and they can't overtake a Taurian, but they're vicious and use their claws and sharp teeth and can wear even the strongest bull down until he collapses. Buzzard is at that point, and there's no safe spot for him to rest.

Before I can answer, the heavy clanging sound fills the tunnel again. And again. The ratlings shriek their terror and retreat, surging backward like a tide.

"Whatever it is, we need it to continue," I say grimly. "Is there another team down here somewhere?"

"Doubtful," says Stork, his face covered in sweat, his longer gray hair plastered to his skull as he wipes his knives clean of blood.

The clanging, echoing sound repeats, and it seems like it's coming from the floor. As the ratlings scurry back, I take another step forward, letting Buzzard lean on me. It sounds right below our feet—

Not a handspan in front of my hooves, a pickaxe breaks through the stone floor.

"We're through!" calls a man on the other side. "Thank the gods!"

A rescue!

"We're coming over to you," I bellow. Moving toward the hole, I see it's not nearly big enough for a rescue. That can be quickly changed. I stomp on it with my hoof, and the rock crumbles a bit more, the hole opening wider. Below, I can see several human men in enforcer uniforms and holding pickaxes, their feet surrounded by broken rocks.

Shikra sees what I'm doing and moves to my side to assist. With the help of the pickaxes and our heavy hooves, the hole grows big enough for the humans to slip through. They untie from our lead, and Stork is the first one to go through, followed quickly by Jay. The hole needs to be widened a bit more before Buzzard's heavy, limp form can be lowered through, and then it's just me and Shikra on this side, while the ratlings watch from the nearby shadows, their eyes red and gleaming with anticipation.

"Hurry," Shikra says. "You go first and I'll follow through."

Normally I'd protest, but I've got Gwenna waiting for me above, and I want to get back to her more than anything. I leap in, just as the ratlings jump on Shikra once more. He fights them off, stumbling toward the hole, and then jumps through, carrying three ratlings with him.

"Quick," says a familiar voice. It's Rooster. "Light it up before they all come through!"

The men hurry, and as we're shuttled to the side, I watch the enforcers—why are there enforcers in the damn tunnels? Or the guild master?—race forward with a large pack. They place it directly under the hole in the ceiling of the tunnel, and then Rooster tosses his oil lamp atop the pack.

It goes up in flames, and a puff of black, oily smoke rises through the hole.

"That should stop them for a while, but we should keep moving,"

Rooster says, watching the pack burn. "I hope someone else has a light. If not, the Taurians will need to lead the way."

"Lead the way? Why wouldn't we go back the way you came?" Shikra asks, getting to his feet. He's moving a little slower than I am. Exhaustion is apparent on his face. "Why not head for the drop?"

"The drop has been compromised," Rooster says, voice succinct. He looks a bit banged up, but better than those of us who were fighting for our lives. "We're lucky in that we have a guide."

"A guide?" I ask, helping Buzzard stand. I'm worried about the old bull. If we can't go back the way we came . . .

"A guide," Rooster says, and then looks around. "Where did she go?"

She?

Oh no. A cold ball of fear forms in my gut as he gestures farther down the tunnel. Sure enough, there's Gwenna's small form, her back to us as she stares off into the depths of the tunnel.

"Gwenna?" I ask. I'm surprised she didn't let me know she was here.

She turns slowly, and even in the low light, I can see just how big her pupils are, how pale her skin. She blinks at me, not seeing anything, and then turns back down the tunnel, pointing. "They say to go this way."

"Who?" Jay asks, frowning over at me.

"The dead," Rooster replies. "It's a long story, and better told when we're safe. For now, let's just follow her. She won't lead us astray."

The head guild master knows about Gwenna's powers? That . . . can't be good.

FIFTY

RAPTOR

OUR PARTY FOLLOWS Gwenna as she moves through the tunnels. The lantern is behind her, yet she can seemingly see well in the dark. She paces ahead of our group, her eyes focused on nothing at all, and sometimes pauses, touching the wall.

"We'll come back to this," she mutters as she moves on. "Not today. Not right now."

A bit farther down, she brushes her fingers over another part of the rock wall and then turns to our straggling group of tired, injured, trapped people. "We have to get through this wall here."

"And that leads us back?" Rooster asks.

"No, but it's where we need to go." Her gaze darts over me, and I straighten, wanting her to say something. But her head jerks and she turns, as if pulled away, and then nods, closing her eyes and rubbing her arms. "This is the only way."

Stork and Shikra and one of the enforcers take up pickaxes and get to work.

Jay remains nearby, bandaging some of the worst of Buzzard's wounds. "How do we know she's not leading us on a chase?" Jay whispers to our group. "This seems like nonsense, fairy tales."

"She won't lie to us," I insist, offended that he'd even suggest such a thing.

"I thought the same about the guild once, and yet here we are," Jay says, shaking his head.

It doesn't take long for them to hammer through the new wall, which is astonishingly thin. Gwenna isn't surprised by this. She simply nods as if she knew it all along and steps through to the other side ahead of us.

"Wait," says Rooster, reaching for her. "There could be ratlings—"

"No ratlings," she says in that distant voice of hers, and continues forward. "Come. We've still got a ways to go."

She drifts onward through a new tunnel that climbs steeply and twists in unexpected ways. I share an uneasy glance with Stork, because this isn't a tunnel that's been used before. To call it a tunnel would be giving it too much credit. It's more like a fissure in the rocks—my hooves struggle to find purchase, and each step feels dangerous. The passage is tight, and at some points we have to turn sideways to go through and climb over a tumble of rocks. Stork breathes heavily when we're forced to squeeze through a very cramped crevasse. I probably lose a layer of skin as we do, and angle my head oddly to get my horns through the narrow rocks, but it opens again soon enough. Getting Karref's limp body through takes some finagling, but no one is willing to leave him behind.

A short time later, I smell moisture in the air. And then I hear running water.

"Almost there," Gwenna says in that drifting voice, as if she's not quite with us mentally, even if her physical body is. I'm worried about her, but I trust her to lead our party forward. If anyone can find a way out, it's Gwenna with her strange powers.

I just don't want anyone using this against her.

We get down on our knees to crawl through the last portion of the cave—we Taurians on our stomachs and unconscious Karref dragged on a cloak—but once we're through to the other side, I see moonlight ahead.

"Incredible," Rooster says, pulling himself through the narrow hole. "She truly did find a way out. Where are we?"

"By the river that cuts through the woods," Master Jay says, moving to stand beside him. "I can hear the water rushing nearby. How she knew that cave was there . . ."

"No one says a word of this," I growl at them. "No one. Understand?"

Exhausted men nod at me.

Satisfied, I stalk forward to talk to my female.

Now that we're free from the caves—and any possible ratlings that would have followed us—I want to talk to her, to find out if she's all right. Buzzard is settled with the wounded enforcers near the stream. He doesn't look good, but he's conscious. Karref has been roused and is leaning against one of the other enforcers. Everyone else is on their feet—battered, but on their feet.

"What do you mean, you had a rescue signal stone this entire time and never used it?" I hear Rooster demand of Shikra. "Why not?"

"Who's going to come rescue us?" Shikra asks, his voice dripping with derisiveness. "The same ones who left us there to rot?"

That silences the guild leader. Good.

I frown as I head down the muddy side of the hill toward Gwenna. The passageway had led us to a very narrow, shallow cave—more of a tumble of rocks on the side of a hill nestled against the bank of the river. The others rest near the cave mouth, but Gwenna doesn't seem to be staying put. She keeps wandering away in that strange, drifting way of hers.

"Gwenna." I catch up to her, and she doesn't turn. "Gwenna, are you all right?"

When she doesn't respond, I touch her arm and force her to turn around. Her skin is like ice, her pupils huge. She stares through me without seeing me.

I want to shake her, but she's a small, fragile thing, my human mate, and the last thing I want is to hurt her. What did she say before? That distractions were the only thing that pulled her out of it? I contemplate kissing her, but I'm mucking terrible at it, and I can't kiss her like a human does. I consider for a moment, and then glance around to see if anyone is looking our way. When they're not, I reach out and brush a hand over her front, and then pinch her nipple through her corset.

She jerks with a gasp and reels. Her eyes blink hard and then her pupils contract. Shivers rack her body. "Oh. Oh, Raptor. Look at you. You're all bloody." Her ice-cold fingers reach up to touch my muzzle. "Are you hurt?"

"I'm fine," I reassure her, caressing her too-cool cheek. "What are you doing here?"

"I came after you. I . . ." Her throat works. "I think I'm going to be sick."

Then she turns and vomits at my feet.

I kneel beside her as she gets the worst of her sickness out of her gut, and when she's done, she shivers wildly.

"Gods, I feel disgusting." She wipes the back of her hand over her mouth and then sags against me. "Talking with the dead for too long makes me feel . . . rotten inside."

"Rooster knows. Garesh's balls, everyone knows your secret." I stroke her sweaty hair back from her face.

"I didn't have a choice. I couldn't stay home safe if you were in danger. We had to come find you. It was the only way I could get them to let me into the tunnels to find your party. They'd wiped you from the day's roster. The messages were a trap—"

"I'd figured as much." I keep my voice soft, humbled that she'd put herself in danger to protect me. "You saved our lives, little bantam. How did you know where to find us?"

"I went . . . went to the temple of Romus to speak with Hemmen's spirit. He told me everything. Said that they were planning to get the Taurians out of the way so they wouldn't be bothered in the tunnels. And Rooster sent a missive, too. Didn't want to use a mancer and set a bad example. Goodness, is it cold out here?" She shivers violently.

I drag her closer to me to share my warmth with her smaller form. "Come lean against me. I'm not going to let anyone hurt you, sweetheart. Don't you worry."

To my surprise, Gwenna begins to laugh. She looks up at me, her eyes a little wild. "Do you know, when I first realized I had powers, I was terrified because I thought the guild would kill me on sight? But after today? After this afternoon? I've realized they need me."

I bite back my frown. "Need?"

"Yes." She blinks rapidly, then tucks her cheek against my filthy shirt.

"Do you know how much treasure the dead just showed me? It's going to take years to dig it all up."

"Huh." I rub my hand up and down her back. I'm still worried. Mancers are illegal, and far too many people know about her powers for my comfort. The urge to protect her is fierce, and I hold her close. If Rooster tries anything, I need a plan. I'm not letting them hurt my mate.

No one is sure how safe the guild is now.

"Spies could be everywhere," Rooster frets, pacing and wringing his hands as the rest of us relax by the riverbank. "What if they're not just the lift operators? Not just the repeaters? What if this is an absolute coup?"

"It won't be a coup," Stork insists. "No one likes a thief."

But Rooster isn't so sure. He's also worried about the rest of Gwenna's friends who'd arrived at the lift with her—Archivist Sparrow, along with Kipp and Arrod. Upon hearing those names, Jay becomes agitated, too. "What if they've been hurt?"

"They're smart. They'll figure out how to stay safe," I reassure him. Well . . . Kipp's smart, at least. "And Master Hawk isn't going to let anything happen to Sparrow."

Rooster points at Gwenna, who's been sleeping in my arms for the last several hours. "Wake her and ask her to speak with the dead. See if she can feel them."

"She's tired and drained," I growl at him. "She needs to rest."

"Yes, but this is an emergency."

I lower my voice and lean in. "For someone who didn't want to use mancer powers, you're sure quick to pounce on them now."

That silences him. He goes back to pacing.

In the end, one of the enforcers, named Hopkins, goes into the city. He's got family in the lower side of Vastwarren, and he's going to visit them and gather forces to go to the city guard. From there, they'll head for the guild quarters and see just how bad the damage is.

The rest of us wait by the riverside.

In truth, I thought the night would be endless, but I'm exhausted from fighting, and it's nice to just sit and hold my mate close. Gwenna sleeps on through the night, lightly snoring in my arms in a way that I find utterly adorable, and which causes Stork to frown in our direction. Like I care what he thinks. Jay seems thoughtful as he sits with us, washing his wounds and offering to tend to mine.

I snarl at him, as any good Taurian would. If anyone's going to fuss over me, it's going to be Gwenna.

It's dawn before we hear horses approaching. I gently set Gwenna down on the ground as she sleepily tries to focus. I kiss the top of her head, and a surge of love for this small, determined female fills my heart. "I won't let anyone touch you," I tell her, pulling her close to my chest. "I'll fight every last one of them if I must. Don't worry."

She leans against me, fatigued. Through the haze of exhaustion on her face, fear flickers. "But what—"

"No buts," I tell her gently. "You've been mine since the first day we met, and nothing today is going to change that. You think I would let you be in danger? That anyone here could keep me from my mate now that she's safe in my arms? I'll handle this, little bantam. You don't need to worry at all."

I mean it, too. My protective instincts are surging—a stronger sensation than my mucking knot, that's for certain—as I make sure she's settled and comfortable. Then I move to the front of our group, and my hands curl into fists. If I must fight to shield my mate and my companions until my last dying breath, I will. If I have to fight all of Vastwarren to protect Gwenna, I'll gladly do so.

If I have to fight the gods themselves to keep her safe . . . bring it on.

But when the horses arrive, it's Master Tiercel, Hopkins, and two other guild masters. "It's all over," Tiercel says, riding forward. "You're safe. I've got a wagon full of medics heading up here. I heard there were wounded?"

Rooster pushes forward. "The insurrection—"

Tiercel holds up a hand. "Fizzled into nothing. Master Hawk has arrested all of the lift operators and is holding them for questioning."

The guild leader blusters. "That . . . that's very good. But why isn't Hawk here to report on this to me?"

"Have you ever seen a Taurian on a horse?" is all Tiercel says, and I laugh despite myself. Count on Hawk to swoop in and save the day. Someone probably threatened a hair on Sparrow's head, and he cleaned house.

Which is good, because it means we can finally rest.

FIFTY-ONE

GWENNA

I WAKE UP IN the softest hospital bed, a down pillow tucked under my cheek. I'm facing a window, and the panes are absolutely filthy. I bet no one's cleaned them since I was here months ago. It figures that I was the only one having to clean the damned things.

I roll over in bed, feeling like one big bruise. Everything hurts. On the bed to my other side is Raptor, his big Taurian body practically overflowing the much smaller hospital bed. His eyes are closed, bandages up and down his arms, and one across his muzzle. The moment I roll over, he turns to look at me.

"We've got to quit meeting like this," I murmur.

"I don't know. Every time I wake up with you next to me, I consider that a win."

"I don't know if it's much of a win if we're in the hospital," I say, rolling onto my back. Immediately I wince as pain shoots up my arm, which I notice is wrapped so tightly it looks like it's wearing a corset. "Gods, everything hurts. Are we injured?"

"You, my delightful mate, are dehydrated and exhausted from being in the caverns, and you fractured your wrist. Me, I lost some blood and got bitten a hundred times by ratlings, so they're filling me full of the worst herbal concoctions possible to ensure I don't get sick."

He sounds so grumpy and put out that it reminds me of teenaged Aspeth every time someone tried to get her to put down her book. I look over at Raptor, frantic. "Wait—Aspeth—Kipp—Arrod—"

"Everyone's safe," Raptor continues. His mouth lifts in a smile. "You think I'd let you lie about if they weren't? I know you better than that."

I relax, because he wouldn't, in fact, let me sit around if my friends were in danger. He'd be the first one to wake me up. "What did I miss?"

"A lot, it seems. Hawk took control of the situation. Once they dumped your group, they decided to take Sparrow and Arrod hostage. They tried to get Kipp, but he was too fast and scaled the walls to get away from them. You know he can move sideways on a wall?"

"His little feet are sticky," I remind him.

"So weird, slitherskins." He shrugs. "Anyhow, Kipp went and got Hawk, and their plan was foiled before it even began."

Mmm. I think of the passageway the ghost of Hemmen had shown me, and the faces of the guilty parties. I also think about how Rooster now knows I'm the mancer, and how even now they could be preparing a pyre in the plaza to burn me on. "And what do you think of everything that happened?"

"Hmm?" He eyes me.

"About me. About what I did." There's a nervous quiver in my belly. It's the first time I've openly used my powers in front of him—in front of anyone, truly—and I'm worried that he'll be disgusted. That he'll see nothing but a mancer in front of him. That he'll find me freakish and want nothing to do with me.

But Raptor just grins in that confident, sly way of his. "Are you kidding me? The dead were showing you exactly where to dig, aye? When we graduate, we'll be the most successful team the guild has ever seen."

"When *we* graduate?"

He snorts. "Yes. Did you think I'd leave my mate behind to be in someone else's Five? Not bloody likely. I'm staying with you." He runs a hand down his muzzle and gives me a heated look. "Plus, you might need more distracting the next time you go down in the tunnels. I aim to be the only one who ever 'distracts' you."

My cheeks heat at his words, but I'm glad to hear them. "I plan on you being my only distraction as well. What comes next, then?"

Raptor sends me another heated look, but settles back in the bed, as if deciding we're both too injured to do more than talk about "distractions." "I spoke with Rooster and Hawk earlier. They're trying to round up the culprits so we can have a magistrate called in to sentence them."

Makes sense, and I'm relieved that it's already being handled. I'm so tired of all of it. "Thank the gods it's all settled. Is that why the windows are dirty, then?"

Raptor eyes me, curious. "What do you mean?"

"The nestmaids," I say, the uneasy feeling returning. "They've been arrested, right?"

"Why would the nestmaids be arrested?"

"Because Mistress Umala is the one behind it all. She and Marta are involved. Those were the names Hemmen gave me when I contacted him. They communicated through borrowed library books. When he died, Marta hid them all so they wouldn't get caught."

"Mucking hells." Raptor jumps out of bed, stark naked, and looks around for his clothing. After a moment, he wraps the sheet around his waist and points at me. "You stay put. I'm getting a message to Hawk or Rooster. We've got to tell them about this."

"I thought you said they'd rounded everyone up!"

"Everyone that they knew of! The drop workers! This is different! You're certain it's the nestmaids?"

"Positive." I think of how sick I'd felt when I'd gotten to *M* in the alphabet and Hemmen had indicated yes. It all made sense. "No one notices a nestmaid coming or going. They're always on the fringes, listening. They work closely with repeaters. And they have access to every single guild building."

He curses again, his hooves slamming on the floor as he races out of the room.

I slip my legs over the side of the bed, wincing as every muscle screams in protest. Something tells me that I'm going to be needed very soon.

I wonder what Rooster thinks of my abilities now that he's had a chance to sleep on it. Is he going to find my ability to speak with the dead monstrous? Or is he going to see the potential uses it has for the guild?

Gods, I hope it's the latter. I've never had to persuade others to my side before, but now it seems that it's a skill I need to learn.

JUST AS I'D suspected, Marta and Mistress Umala are quickly rounded up, and I'm retrieved from the clinic and brought to the guild headquarters with an escort. Raptor and I are given fresh uniforms, and even though I ache all over and want to sleep for a week, I try to look strong and unbothered as we wait in Rooster's office for the two women to be brought in. There are a half dozen guild masters and guild enforcers crammed in with us. Raptor remains at my side, snarling at anyone who stands too close to me.

And, okay. I kind of like that he's hovering. I'm still feeling anxious over the whole mancer situation.

Marta is brought in first by the enforcers. Before anyone can ask her a question, she weeps, crumbling before the stern faces in front of her. "I just wanted money to send home to my mother. I didn't know anything about people being killed!"

"Give us names, and we could be lenient," Rooster demands.

Marta quickly spills, naming Mistress Umala as well as three other maids I've met and worked with before. I'm saddened to hear that, because I thought they were nice women. All young and poor, all wanting to work hard enough to make a better life for themselves.

"And your group targeted Gwenna? At Mistress Umala's instruction?" Raptor demands.

Marta looks up from her hands, and the expression she shoots me is puzzled and somewhat apologetic. "It wasn't personal. It's just . . . she's a woman. Women don't become artificers."

It's the same sort of thing every man here has said before, but hearing it come from another woman—another woman in the same situation I've been in in the past—stings. "That's not for you to decide."

"And will you show us the tunnels you were using to funnel the artifacts out of the guild treasury?" Rooster continues to write notes on a piece of parchment as Marta weeps.

"I—I never handled anything," Marta stammers, twisting her hands. "I just sent notes and connected people."

"And tried to frame me," I point out. "With Hemmen's help."

"It wasn't personal," Marta says again. "Why won't you understand that?"

"Because it feels personal to me," I mutter, but quiet down when Raptor puts a calming hand on my arm.

Marta's questioning continues for a while longer, but it becomes evident that she's been used more for spying and passing notes along than for actual stealing. Rooster says he'll consider her sentence, and then she's taken away to the guild's jail to await her fate.

Mistress Umala is brought in next, and she's less than helpful. She stares down her nose at everyone, sneering every time she's asked a question. She responds to nothing, her composure unruffled as the guild masters lob question after question at her. *Who is working with you? What exactly have you stolen? How were the artifacts transported? How did you know what to steal?*

"I know nothing" is all she says, tone haughty. "Do with me what you must."

"We intend to," Rooster says bluntly, and Umala is taken away.

The day grows long, and we remain clustered in Rooster's office, the air overly warm and stuffy. The maids Marta named are interviewed, and all point the finger at Mistress Umala and one of the repeaters who works at the drop site and has for years. Several of the drop site repeaters are interviewed, and all of them indicate the same people. They're eager to name names, but when it comes time to discuss the logistics, no one will offer up specifics. I can see Rooster growing frustrated as he demands information on the tunnels used and gets nothing in response.

After what seems like the hundredth interview, Rooster rolls up the parchment he's been writing on and shakes his head. "The rest will have to wait until morning. I want extra guards on all the prisoners. We'll let them sleep on cold floors and give them gruel to eat and see if they feel like admitting more in the morning."

Everyone starts to file out of the room.

"Hawk, you stay. Raptor, you as well. Gwenna. Smythe. We need to talk."

Oh gods. Here it is. I clutch at Raptor's hand tightly, trying not to physically tremble. This is it, I realize. This is where Rooster tells everyone that he's decided that I'm dangerous and I'm to be thrown into the dungeon, too. That I need to be burned at the stake as a message to all other mancers in the city.

Once most of the room has been cleared, those of us remaining stand awkwardly. Raptor remains at my side. I'm nervous, but I'm also glad for his support.

Rooster leans back in his chair and rubs his face. "This is a gods-damned mess."

No one says anything.

Smythe looks over at me, and then at Rooster. "Gwenna has been an incredible help. We wouldn't have made it out of the Everbelow without her assistance."

"I'm aware" is all Rooster says.

My tongue feels glued to the roof of my mouth. I should say a million things to defend myself. Explain why I'm useful to the guild. Why I'm necessary. Why I can bring in riches. Why I would never want to use my powers against anyone. But I can't seem to speak. How can I possibly change his mind when mancers have been outlawed for three hundred years?

"We're not getting much from Mistress Umala," Rooster says casually, returning his quill to its inkpot. "You said you would be able to find the passage they were using, Gwenna?"

I nod. "Hemmen showed it to me."

"Before?" His brows go up.

I clear my throat. "After."

"Ah."

"Gwenna is a good person," Raptor begins, a warning growl in his voice.

Rooster waves a hand in the air impatiently. "I know that, fool. The question is, how do we hide the fact that we have a mancer in our ranks? Feeding us information?"

We glance around at one another.

"I don't know of any mancers," Smythe says in a slow voice. "I didn't see anything that couldn't be explained away by, uh, luck."

I blink at him, surprised. I'm touched at his loyalty. Support from a stranger isn't expected, but I'm grateful for it.

"I agree," Rooster says, clasping his hands and eyeing our group. "It's obvious to me that Gwenna is not a mancer. There has not been a mancer for a hundred years. Instead, it is clear that Gwenna must have known all of this because she was, in fact, working with Mistress Umala."

I make a sound of wordless protest. "I would never—"

Rooster raises a hand in the air. "Working with Mistress Umala," he continues in a firm voice, "as a double agent. That is how she knows about the tunnel. And their plans. And how to get out of the cavern. They simply started the story of her being a mancer to throw us off. It's nothing but fairy tales. Because of her involvement, there will, of course, be a hefty fine to be paid. But I'm certain that once she becomes a full-fledged artificer, she will be able to pay it back. Am I understood?"

I don't know what to say. My ability is to be . . . swept under the rug? And paying the guild back? Considering I know where a bounty of things are in the caverns . . . it won't take long. I stare at Rooster.

He gives me a knowing look back. Oh. He knows that it won't take long, either.

"Just as it should be," Smythe says after a moment.

"Nothing but a nasty rumor," Hawk agrees.

"You will, I trust, show us the passageway that the guilty parties were using?" Rooster inquires.

I nod. "Of course."

"And if anything else should arise—some sort of assistance that the guild might need in the future in locating someone or something . . ." He arches a white, shaggy brow.

"Of course," I say again, breathing a bit easier. So that's the way of it. I'm to get a slap on the wrist and be available for the guild if they should need my help in the future. "I am absolutely loyal to the Royal Artifactual Guild, sir."

"Good. See that your conduct remains unimpeachable, fledgling." He waves a finger at us. "All of you can go. Tell Master Jay that I need to see him at some point. There's the matter of one of his students being unfortunately killed. We need to speak of a replacement, as it's not fair to the rest of his Five for them to be condemned without ever getting to a test."

Raptor squeezes my hand with excitement. "I'll pass it along, sir. I'm sure Master Jay will know of someone who will want to join our Five, motley though it may be."

"Just . . . see that they're not involved in a thieving ring this time?" Rooster looks tired. He runs a hand over his curling mustache. "I've had my fill of thievery for quite a while."

"Haven't we all?" Hawk mutters.

Rooster waves us out, and Raptor all but drags me through the door. "Let's go before he changes his mind," he murmurs.

"Do you think he will?"

"No, because he likes coin far too much, and he sees a lot of coin when he looks at you. But I'm also not keen to press our luck." His hand slides to the small of my back, and he guides me out of the main guild hall.

Smythe walks at our side, silent. Once we're outside, he turns to me and gives me a polite nod. "Perhaps this is inappropriate, but . . . thank you for saving my men. I feared yesterday would go a very different way."

My heart warms. To think that someone's grateful that I can talk to the dead. It's so strange. "I appreciate you keeping my secret."

His brows go up. "What secret? I don't know anything."

Before I can get flustered, he gives me an obvious wink and turns and walks away.

Raptor pulls me a little closer. "You look tired. Shall we—"

"Gwenna!"

I turn to see Sparrow racing toward me, her archivist robes flapping around her legs as she runs to my side. She flings her arms around me and holds me tight, rocking back and forth. "I'm so glad! I've been so worried!"

Should I laugh? Should I cry? I want to do both. It's terrifying to hear how so many people were also worried about me, but at the same time, I'm safe now, I think.

"We're not done yet," I tell her, hugging her back. I've never been much of a hugger, but since Sparrow loves them, and I adore her, I guess I have no choice. I let her hug it out, patting her shoulder awkwardly until she gives a happy little sigh and releases me. "There's still more to do. I need to show them the tunnel, and the rest of the thieves are to be rounded up. I should probably consult with Hemmen again before they bury him, to see if he has more names—"

She shakes her head. "You need to go home and rest. That's what you need."

"I've been saying that as well," Raptor calls out from nearby, amused. "Gwenna's not a very good listener."

"Piss off," I tell him affectionately. "My friend needed a hug."

"When do I get mine?" he replies.

"Later. In private." And I give him a suggestive wink. Gods, I'm feeling better by the moment. Well, as long as I don't touch my wrist, or any of my bruises, or think about how mucking tired I am.

Raptor just grins at me, his smile wide. "You might want to take your innocent little wife home, Hawk," he drawls, striding toward me. "Or she's going to see me do some absolutely filthy things to my mate."

Sparrow lets out an alarmed squeak and releases me as if I'm on fire. "We'll catch up tomorrow! Come and visit if you can find the time! I'll be at the archives!"

She races away, waving a hand, and moves to Hawk's side. Amused, Hawk just shakes his head and puts an arm around his wife before leading her away.

Hands on hips, I eye Raptor. "'Absolutely filthy things,' eh? Out in public? You shameless Taurian."

"It was a lie," he drawls, pulling me to his side and then heading down the street once more. "If Sparrow started talking, we'd never get away. It made them run, didn't it? And besides, I'm far too wounded to handle much touching tonight. I think the ratlings bit off every bit of skin on my lower body."

I cluck my tongue, letting him loop his arm over my shoulders. It's good to be snuggled up against his side. It feels like it's where I was meant to be. "They have good taste, those ratlings. I guess I'll have to wait for you to heal before it's my turn to bite every bit of skin below your waist."

"Well, when you put it that way, I wouldn't mind a bit more biting in certain . . . locations."

"Of course you wouldn't." I snort with amusement, and then the reality of what we've just gone through hits me. It takes everything I have not to sag against him, to keep putting one foot in front of the other. "Is this really over? Am I truly safe?"

"Rooster's not one to pass up an opportunity, sweetheart. You showed him firsthand how valuable you can be to the guild. Does it mean staying quiet about your ability? Yes. But think of all the good you can do. Think of all the treasure you can find. I know Rooster's thinking of both." He chuckles and squeezes me against him. "I'm just so mucking proud of you."

"You are?" My voice catches. I don't think anyone's ever said that to me. Not even Ma.

Raptor looks around, and then grabs my hand, sprinting toward the nearest alley. Surprised, I trot alongside him, and when we get into the shadows, he pulls me up against the nearest wall, my feet dangling, and presses his muzzle to my mouth in a tentative kiss.

I make an excited noise, cup his face, and make him kiss me again. Is it a little awkward? Yes. Is his tongue much bigger than mine? Yes. Is it the best kiss ever? Also yes. He licks into my mouth as if he wants to devour me, and it sends a bolt of heat straight between my thighs. Moaning, I grab his horns and—

Hot pain flashes through my wrist. I jerk backward. "Shit!"

Raptor recoils. "What'd I do wrong?"

"It's my wrist." I cradle my hand against my chest even as he lowers my dangling feet to the ground.

"Oh, thank gods." At my annoyed look, he explains. "I thought I'd been too enthusiastic and nearly choked you with my fat tongue. Your mouth is quite small. Hot and delicious and wet . . . but small."

"For what it's worth, I would never complain about the size of your tongue," I tell him loftily. "But perhaps a dark alley isn't the best spot to kiss."

"You're right. It's far better for under-the-skirt touches." He grins at me, and then winces, holding up a bandaged hand. "But perhaps that needs to wait, too."

"Surely there's some part of you I can ride that isn't too beat up," I tease.

He taps his long nose with his bandaged hand. "I know just the seat for you, sweetheart."

Heat scorches through me, and I want to wriggle with arousal. I'm forgetting all too quickly about how tired I am, especially in light of his playful flirtiness. "Your knot must be aching something fierce right now," I coo at him. "I'm happy to be of assistance."

Raptor just gives me a long, hard look that makes me shiver with delight.

I wait for him to do something, to say something. If he pushed me against this wall and jerked my pants down, I wouldn't turn him away. I know he must be hurting, as it's been days since we've touched, and I know he gets uncomfortable when he's aching. Instead, he sends a thoughtful look down the alley. "Come on."

"Where are we going?" I take the hand he holds out to me and follow him.

"To a secret hiding spot. Naiah never gives me her potions in person. She always deposits them in a hidden location."

Oh. His potions. The ones where his knot—and the rest of him—goes down for days on end. Is he going to take that now? Not the ending to this evening that I had in mind, but if he needs it, he needs it. I'll be a supportive partner no matter what. And maybe it's best that we rest anyhow.

I guess.

Raptor heads deeper into the alleyway, following it until we're far from the King's Onion and very far from our assigned nest at Master Jay's dormitory. He scans the stonework, and then releases my hand. A moment later, he pulls a heavy brick free from the wall and sets it on the ground. Then he gestures that I should look for myself.

I peek inside. Even though it's dark, I can see what looks like two small bottles, and a tiny scroll of a note. With a glance at Raptor, I reach for the note first. "Two potions?"

"Yours and mine, aye. I thought Naiah would pull through." He grins down at me, proud. "Now you have options."

Options. It's not what I'd expected. I pull the tiny scroll open and squint at it, but it's too dark and Naiah's handwriting is too tiny. "I can't read it."

"Allow me." He takes the note and studies it for a moment, then begins to read. "'As requested, the potion to remove a mancer's power is enclosed within. Do keep in mind that this potion is magical, and will remove your magic from you, like cauterizing a wound. It won't be painful, but the effects are permanent. I cannot reverse it. My payment is due within a sevenday.' Signed, Naiah."

He pulls the bottles free from the hidey-hole and offers me a round one with a pale liquid inside. "Mine is a dark potion. This one is yours."

"I see she's labeled it very helpfully." There's a tiny frowny face on mine. Charming. I turn it over in my hand, thinking. "It's permanent?"

"Aye. I don't know how it works or how Naiah manages to make her potions, but she's never wrong. If she says it's permanent, I believe her." He studies me. "You know I'll support you whatever you choose."

"And if I take this now and we forget all about me being a mancer? And we lose all the riches I've been shown below because my memory is terrible?"

Raptor shrugs and rolls up the note, tossing it back into the hidden nook. "If it makes you happy, I'm all for it. I don't mind doing things the hard way, as long as we do them together."

I consider it.

I consider it very hard. Life would certainly be easier if the dead weren't mumbling in my ears every time I went into the Everbelow. I wouldn't be distracted by nearby murders—though hopefully that fades with time. I would be just like everyone else, succeeding in the guild on my own merits, or failing because of the same thing. I would be normal. Safe.

Or . . . I could keep my powers. Ensure that our Five—when we pass the tests—will be successful. Help the guild with retrievals when someone is stranded or lost deep in the tunnels.

I can be a boon to the guild.

Or I can blend in with the crowd.

I hold the potion out to him. "Think Naiah gives refunds?"

Raptor snorts. "She absolutely, positively does not. Come on. Kipp and Arrod are probably wondering where we've wandered off to. I'd hate for them to come looking for us just when I've got my muzzle up your skirts."

"Pfft. I'm not wearing skirts."

"Good, because I was lying. I *wouldn't* hate for them to find me be-tween your thighs." He gives me a lascivious stare. "I think they should."

Gods. "Put that rock back in its place and let's get home. I want to touch you all over. I want to bite you in all the places the ratlings didn't."

The smile he gives me is pure wickedness.

After replacing the stone in the wall, we race back to the dorm, breathless with excitement. I'm getting more and more aroused with every moment that passes, and I can't wait to touch him. Can't wait to truly let go and just enjoy everything. I want his knot. I want his tongue. I want his gentle hands, his large callused fingers, his sweetly filthy words as he touches me. He pushes the door to the nest open, turning to look at me. "I want you naked. Right now."

A shiver of delight moves up my spine. "Same goes for you."

The moment we step inside, though, we run into Kipp and Arrod. They're sitting in the main study by the fire, and both look up the mo-ment we come in. Arrod's expression is delighted and full of relief as he surges forward. "There you are! We've been worried sick! You've both been gone for days!"

Raptor clears his throat and shifts on his feet. "We were at the hospi-tal first, and then we had to see Head Guild Master Rooster. Every-thing's fine."

"I'm glad to hear that," Arrod says, and he truly does look thrilled. He gestures that we should sit by the fire with him and Kipp. "Come and tell us everything!"

Oh, mucking hells.

Next to me, Raptor hesitates. He knows just as well as I do that if we sit with Arrod and Kipp to fill them in, we're going to be here all night. There's so much to cover. "Ah . . . it's best if Master Jay is here before we retell everything."

I nod, hoping I don't seem too anxious to get away. "Yes. Exactly."

Arrod's expression falls a bit. "Oh. He's not here."

"That is too bad," I say quickly. "Perhaps in the morning, then."

"Morning," Raptor agrees.

"Or perhaps just sum it up for us," Arrod says. "He might be gone awhile."

I hesitate. I guess we could do that, except I can't think of anything now other than how tired I am and how very much I'd like for my pussy to be licked by my minotaur lover right about now. "Um . . ."

"Yeah. . . ." Raptor rubs the back of his neck.

Kipp eyes me. He hops to his feet, shrugging on his battered shell with the ease of countless repetitions. Then he gestures at Arrod, indicating that the two of them should leave.

Oh good, Kipp gets it. I want to kiss his little lizardy face in this moment.

Arrod does not get it. He frowns. "Why would we leave? They just got back!"

The slitherskin makes a gesture that looks vaguely obscene. He licks his eyeball, points at us, then shakes his head.

"Ah." Arrod flushes, glancing over at us. "Right. Of course. We'll, ah, be back later."

Kipp trots past him, making a tiny fist.

"And we'll knock. Loud." Arrod trails after Kipp, as if he's reluctant to leave even though Kipp has made it obvious what our intentions are.

I should probably be embarrassed, but strangely, I'm not. This thing between me and Raptor has felt right from the beginning. He's always made me feel good. Cherished. Beautiful. Even with bandages covering random parts of my body and my plump arse hanging out of borrowed trousers.

Raptor turns to me, that sinful grin on his face. "You think they're gone?"

"If they're not, they're going to get an eyeful."

He huffs with amusement, heading down the hall to our dorm room. Once we're both inside, he shuts the doors and grabs the nearest sword, shoving it through the handles to prevent anyone from coming in. Then he turns a heated, almost predatory look in my direction. "Take your clothes off."

As if I need to be told twice. I undo my pants and shimmy them down my legs, but they get stuck at my boots. I switch to my tunic, but it's tricky to remove with just one good arm. I wriggle about for a bit and then, panting, give up. "I can't manage."

"Let me help." He moves to my side and rips my tunic open. A moment later, he's ripping my pants off my lower legs as I stare at him, open-mouthed.

"Seriously? Raptor, I'm running out of uniforms!"

"I don't give a fuck. You can wear mine." He crouches down by my feet and taps one boot, indicating I should lift it so he can help me finish getting naked.

Wear his clothing. He's insane. Raptor's enormous, bigger than some of the other Taurians, and very broad across the chest. I'm broad in the hips and chest myself, but I'm also a short, stout thing. I imagine just how his tunic would fit—tight in the tits and with long, floppy arms—and I start snort-giggling to myself.

"I mean it," he says, helping me out of my boots. "You can have anything of mine. Wear whatever you like or nothing at all. It'll make me happy either way."

Once my boots are off, I'm wearing nothing but the bandages around my bad arm. I'm glad we bathed in the hospital, because I don't want to take this moment to go and clean up. We've been waiting too long already. "You're still dressed."

He pulls off his tunic with one fluid motion and then drops his pants. It's the quickest undressing I've ever seen, and the look he's giving me tells me he's tired of wasting time. My gaze slides to his cock, fully erect, his knot hard and flushed at the base of his shaft. He strokes a hand down his length, and as I watch, a bead of pre-cum dribbles down the head. "You ready?"

Oh gods, am I ever. I'm breathless as I watch him. "You want me on hands and knees . . . or . . . ?"

"I want you on my face."

Hannai have mercy. That sounds like an excellent idea to me. I nod, wordless, and watch as he gets on the bed.

He lies back, his cock jutting into the air, and indicates I should come over. I approach him, considering the best way to tackle this. He's got horns curving to the front, so I'll have to be careful to avoid them. I touch the sharp tip of one horn. "I don't mean to be a naysayer, but how does this work, exactly?"

"You're overthinking. Come straddle me here." He pats his collarbone. "You can face my cock, and if you're good, I'll let you suck on it."

Those words shouldn't have the effect on me that they do. I make a needy little sound and hop up on the bed. I'm not graceful as I climb over him, not in the slightest, but he makes sounds of pure appreciation as I awkwardly clamber onto his chest. Once I'm sprawled over him, I press my good hand on his stomach and prop up a bit.

Immediately, he jerks me backward, and then his muzzle is between my thighs. Raptor licks me with one long, lascivious stroke, and I cry out, my thighs clenching reflexively. He gives my flank a tap, then grips my thick backside in his huge hands. "Perfect," he mutters between licks, his tongue making me crazed with one long, tantalizing lick after another. "You comfortable?"

I'm straddling his face backward, staring at the cock I can't quite reach and getting my insides tongued into oblivion. "Never . . . better. . . ." I wheeze.

"Good, because I'm going to be here awhile."

And he is. The wonderful, wonderful male takes his time with me, tonguing me all over before thrusting into me with a finger and commenting on all the "pretty" noises my now-wet pussy makes with every touch. When I'm close to the edge, that long, fascinating Taurian tongue slides against my clit, teasing it until I come, rocking against his face.

Panting, I collapse over him.

He nuzzles my inner thighs and my pussy, as if he can't quite help himself. It sends little aftershocks through my body, and I slide off him when this gets to be too much. I eye him with a dazed expression, but he just grins at me, very satisfied with himself.

"That was . . . incredible."

"It was, aye." He puts his hands behind his head, and the stretch of his big arms reminds me of just how many bandages he's covered in.

"How are your wounds?"

"Forgotten. Want to let me lick you again? I bet I can wring another orgasm or three out of you."

That sounds delicious, but I want to touch him first. I lean over his big thighs, staring at the cock I'm now very close to. It's heavy with arousal, his knot a vivid hue. The head of his cock is wet and sloppy with pre-cum, and I'm dying to lick it clean. "You haven't been bitten here by ratlings."

"Nah. Saved that for you."

"Thoughtful."

"I'm the most thoughtful of bulls."

"With the most impressive tongue." I lean close and tease a fingernail over his knot, watching as his entire body clenches and a fresh bead of pre-cum appears. With only one hand, I'm going to have to get creative with my mouth and the fingers I have available. I shift my weight, reaching for him while protecting my hand.

"Want to knot you," he rasps, and runs a hand down my flank. "May I?"

I bite my lip, because I don't know what's sexier—that he wants to knot me, or that he's asking permission. "Aye, but you're going to have to do most of the work—"

The words have barely left my lips before he's out from under me, and then he's lifting my hips into the air. I'm on my belly, my arse to the sky, and he runs a finger through the wet seam of my cunt, making sure that I'm slick enough to take him.

I moan, pressing my face against the bedding as he fingers me, my body making sloppy, wet noises. He grunts with approval and then toys with my clit. "You can take me, little bantam."

"I can." It's a breathless sigh of pure delight. "Give me your knot."

He pushes into me slowly, thoroughly, until my toes are curling. He's just as large as I remember, and he rocks into me with small, sharp thrusts, all the while telling me how good I'm taking him and how much he wants to bury himself inside me. How I'm his perfect, precious mate. When I'm stuffed full of his cock, I let out a whimper. I know there's more to come, and I'm full of anticipation. There's nothing to fear in a mate with a constant knot.

It's a blessing from the gods for sure.

And when he pushes deeper, cramming that thick band of his knot into my body and locking us together, I'm pretty sure I see the heavens themselves.

EPILOGUE

GWENNA
Months Later

Dere Ma,
    Today's the day. I wish you were here. Tell me you're coming to visit soon. Heck, you can come live with me, provided me and Raptor find a place to stay with an extra room. I love you and miss you. I hope you're proud of me.
        Love, Gwenna (for the last time)

THE GRADUATION CEREMONY goes by in a daze. I should be paying attention to each word spoken, each bit of praise that Head Guild Master Rooster lavishes upon the small group of students who stand in two neat rows at the front of the Great Hall. I should remember each word so I can write it to my mother, since she wasn't able to make it for the ceremony.

But I'm just so giddy that I don't pay attention to a single word of it. Instead, I keep stroking my new vivid blue sash that is as yet unadorned with pins. The fabric is soft and the blank sash is so full of potential, just like the battered but lightweight morning star attached to my belt. I stroke my sash and I smile at my husband in the audience, and I feel like a real artificer.

Raptor opted not to take part in the ceremony, even though his rank has been officially reinstated. He's gone through one once before, he said, and this ceremony should be about us. I stand with Lark and Arrod and Kipp at my side, while my gorgeous Taurian husband watches from the audience. He sits with Hawk and Sparrow, and while everyone in the audience looks happy for us, no one has that expression of robust pride quite like Raptor does.

There's a smattering of applause as Rooster finishes his speech, and then the crowd scatters. All the graduates stand there, a little dazed. This isn't the end of the ceremony, of course. After this, we'll go to the guild book that we signed when we initially began training. We'll cross out our old name and write the new one beside it, and then our official bird name will be added to the roster of working artificers. Last night, we met with the guild's official name chronicler to go over our name choices, so we wouldn't take one that's already in use. Each name has its own wax seal for sending official missives. Mine is already at home, waiting to be used for the first letter I send back to Ma.

At my side, Lark sniffs and swipes a hand over her face.

"Are you crying?" Arrod asks, disgusted. "This is a good day."

Lark elbows him. "Piss off, I'm not crying. You're crying."

"I'm not crying." He sounds affronted at the suggestion. "I'm muck-ing ecstatic. No more drills! Now we just get to do the fun stuff."

I loop an arm around Lark's shoulders and hug her. "Ignore him. You're allowed to cry." I know just how much this means to her. To all of us. But for Lark, the last six months have been extra emotional. She was given the opportunity to join as our fifth to take Hemmen's spot. Normally the guild would disqualify an entire Five if one member was considered unfit, but Hemmen's murder was seen as unfair to the rest of us (and rightly so). Lark's leg was still healing up, and she and Mereden had recently adopted their two children. She spent every weekend at home with them, just as Master Jay did with his widow, which meant that she had to work doubly hard every week to keep up.

So aye, I totally understand her tears. She thought she was going to be repeating for quite some time. To be in the guild now, able to take a name, able to earn a wage . . . it's the best. I hug her close and smile at Mereden and the children in the audience.

Sparrow races toward us, beaming. She hugs me and then Lark, and even Arrod. She drops to her knees by Kipp and flings her arms out. "Can I hug you? Just this once?"

He shrugs and allows her to hug him, his little body stiff. I know it's not because of the ceremony. He's thrilled to be graduating. His lady friend is in the audience, and I caught him blowing subtle kisses at her earlier. He just doesn't like touching humans. But everyone tolerates hugs today. I pat Kipp on his shell house in quiet approval. "Kipp deserves all the credit. If it wasn't for him acting as our sword, we wouldn't have gotten as far as we did."

Kipp preens at my praise, gesturing out at Raptor, who's coming toward us now that the ceremony is over.

"Oh, him?" I tease, loud enough for my husband to hear. "He's all right. Don't tell him that, though, or he'll get a swelled head."

In truth, Kipp and Raptor work as an excellent sword and shield for our team. Their opposite sizes serve them well, with Kipp able to race up and down the tunnel walls to do whatever it takes to move ahead or defeat the enemy, and Raptor sweeping through after him, bashing heads and clearing the way for the three humans. Arrod didn't like being "pushed to the back with the women" at first, but once he saw how effective our team was, he took pride in becoming our gearmaster. He natters on and on in our ears about how much oil our lamp is using or what supplies we're low on, and takes inventory constantly to ensure that nothing is missed. That leaves Lark as our medic, which she doesn't mind. Says she picks up tips from Mereden and jokes that she likes to inflict pain as she cleans our wounds.

It means I'm the navigator of our small group. At first I wasn't too sure how I felt about that, as the navigator is one of the most important positions in a Five. But with the dead whispering in my ears, it's impossible for me to get lost, and it seems a natural transition for my skills. I haven't had a chance to use my morning star in combat yet, but it goes everywhere with me, and Master Jay has shown me a few tips and tricks so I can be as effective a fighter as any.

The dead that speak to me are still too noisy. If anything, they're noisier than ever. But I'm better at directing them with what I want. Oftentimes, they simply want to be heard, and it's a matter of telling them that I'll listen to all if they speak one at a time. One at a time, I can deal with.

And if I get a ghost that won't listen? I have a big Taurian mate who doesn't mind taking me aside and kissing the five hells out of me until my focus is entirely on him. And if that doesn't work, well . . . I also have a ring piercing between my thighs, right on the hood of my clit. It's a Taurian wedding thing, and just having it there makes everything ultra-sensitive. If I have trouble concentrating, I can always squeeze my thighs super tight . . . which causes a different kind of distraction. But it all works.

Arrod flings his arms around Lark and me, hugging us. "We should go out somewhere to celebrate our new names and our status as official guild artificers!"

Lark politely peels his arm off and strides over to Mereden, kissing her and then picking up her son and carrying him on her hip. "Can we go somewhere kid-friendly?"

"Gods, why?" Arrod sounds horrified.

"Because I want to celebrate this moment with my family at my side, you hollow-brained pumpkin of a man."

Mereden chuckles, shaking her head. "We can leave if it's a problem. It's your celebration."

"It is," I agree. "And it is absolutely no bother. You're part of this crew, too." I slide out from Arrod's grasp and pull Sparrow in. "Just like Sparrow and Hawk, and Kipp."

Everyone looks around for the diminutive slitherskin, but he seems to have disappeared. He reappears a moment later, leading his orange-pink lady friend, Vik. The little messenger gives us a shy wave of greeting, the gleaming thick shell of her house dwarfing her form.

"Vik is invited, too, of course," I add. "But we need to sign the Book of Names first. I want to get mine recorded and done with."

"What name did you request?" Arrod asks.

Sparrow claps her hands. "Oh, is it 'Wren'? You seem like such a Wren to me."

"It's not 'Wren,' and it's definitely not 'Chickadee,'" I say, naming the two suggestions Sparrow gave me when we'd first arrived in the city. "And I don't want to put it out in the open until it's written down and it's mine. Bad luck and all."

"If it helps, I'll tackle anyone who tries to write it down first," Raptor tells me, leaning in and murmuring against my ear. I just tug on his nose ring. Silly, wonderful male.

Lark snorts. "You make your own luck. 'Sides, I already know what mine is."

I didn't realize she was going to switch names. "Um, is it 'Lark'?"

"'Mudlark,'" she says triumphantly.

Mereden just shakes her head, as if this is an argument she's lost one too many times already.

"What's wrong with 'Mudlark'?" Lark asks. "They're muddy because they get shit done. I want to have a fancy name change, too."

Mereden switches her daughter from one arm to the other. The little girl is sleeping against her mother's shoulder, drooling on Mereden's white medic robe. "And what are you going to do if someone comes along and wants to be 'Lark'?"

"Then I fight them and tell them not to. And if I lose, I get to be the dirty Lark. It's a winning situation all around."

Mereden pretends to frown, but her lips are curving in a smile. "Why do I even bother asking?"

"I have no idea," Lark agrees, and leans in to give her wife another kiss.

"All this kissing is giving me ideas," Raptor murmurs, nuzzling against my neck.

"Everything gives you ideas," I tell him, but I love his ideas. I love that he's constantly obsessed with touching me. It makes me feel so pretty, so needed. I love that his libido matches mine in every way. I caress his face, running a finger along his nose ring again and thinking about how there's a matching ring encircling the base of his cock. . . .

"Ugh," Arrod says loudly, interrupting my sexy fantasies. "Does everyone have a mate here but me?"

"Yes," I say.

"Yes," Sparrow and Hawk say.

Mereden just nods, rocking her daughter in her arms, and gives Lark another quick kiss.

Kipp looks at Vik. Vik licks her eyeball, whatever that means. It makes Kipp happy, though. He moves and presses his belly to hers, slithering up and down against her smaller form, and for a moment, the only sign of the two slitherskins is the two shell houses bouncing against each other.

"Should we cover the children's eyes?" Mereden whispers.

"It's only a greeting," Lark says. "But . . . maybe. And anyway, you're just jealous, Arrod."

Arrod's face is screwed up like he's a toddler who just found a bug in his soup. "Why would I be jealous? I can kiss as many women—or men!—as I want now. It's going to be so easy to get laid now that I'm an official artificer." He smooths a hand down his sash. "Artificer Cardinal, at your service."

Raptor leans in. "Cardinals are vain and dumb little shits. It fits."

"Hush." I giggle. Arrod is all right. I mean, he *is* vain, and a bit unintellectual, but he's got a good heart. We can't all be sharp. Gods know I still struggle with reading, though my lettering is getting better. As for Old Prellian? Forget it. I'm lucky that Raptor recognizes most of the basic symbols, because the glyph language still eludes me.

Master Jay comes over to our celebrating group, his arms spread wide. "My students! My Five! I couldn't be prouder."

"Because you get a percentage," Raptor says, giving our teacher a feral grin.

"Because this year has been hard on all of us," Jay continues, ignoring Raptor's teasing. "There are some classes you know will breeze through training, and others you know are doomed to fail."

Kipp flicks a hand on his shoulder, as if tossing something aside. Then he shakes his head.

"And you thought we were doomed to fail?" Arrod jokes.

"No. I thought I'd never met a messier Five, but I've also never met a more stubborn one. I figured that would carry you all through, and I'm glad to see I was right."

I'm glad there's no "even the women" comment. I know both Lark and I weren't expected to pass. The guild is incredibly sexist, and while they might look down on Kipp for being a slitherskin, he's still more palatable to them because he's male, whereas Lark and I are considered freaks for daring to step foot where men do. We had to train twice as hard for our solo tests, because we'd be graded more harshly. For the last few months, Lark and I have lived on that obstacle course after hours, practicing everything we could (luckily the kids looked at the obstacle course as a playground, so we were able to run it repeatedly). We studied twice as hard as Arrod. We worked with Sparrow on recognizing Prellian architecture and paint styles and maps of the old city. Even then, it was still too close for my taste. I'd had a judge on my solo test that made me do a second round because he "wasn't satisfied" with my performance. Luckily for me, my second round was locating an artifact hidden in the training tunnels, and I passed that with flying colors and quelled any arguments the old bird might have had. I could have had the dead just point me to a Greater Artifact and cheated my way through, but it wouldn't have felt right. I wanted to prove myself worthy.

It's always going to be an uphill battle to get respect, but I'm lucky that I have a big, protective, growly Taurian at my side who demands that everyone treat me equally.

"It sounds to me like dinner is on Master Jay's coin," Raptor declares, pulling me from my musing.

"Absolutely," Jay says, beaming at us. "My treat. I know just the place."

Arrod groans. "I bet it involves onions."

"It does," Jay replies. "Let's get you lot in the Book of Names so we can properly celebrate."

My stomach quivers with excitement. There's a crowd by the guild chronicler and the Book of Names, and a priestess of Asteria, who's blessing each artificer as they record their new moniker. Rooster stands nearby, puffed up with importance and in his finest clothing, but it doesn't bother me today. It seems appropriate, in a strange way, that he should bluster and shake hands as if he's a king passing out knighthoods. It feels like we've earned it.

Raptor notices my nervousness and nuzzles my neck again, and then gives me a not-so-subtle nudge toward the line of people. I step in behind Arrod, waiting for my turn, my nerves fluttering. By the time the feather pen is handed to me, I'm so nervous I want to vomit, and my forehead is beading with sweat.

The guild chronicler gives me that gentle smile, the same one he did last night when I'd first lobbed my name out there. "Will you sign the book, Artificer?"

Artificer. Me.

Satisfaction surges through me, chasing away my nerves. I lift my chin, nod, and take the feather quill from him. Painstakingly, I cross out my old name and write my new one in the Book of Names. It's symbolic, of course, of the end of our old lives and the beginning of our new ones. I'm in a daze as I set the quill down. The priestess blesses me. Rooster shakes my hand. Someone else does, too, but I don't know who they are. Then I turn and my mate is there. My big, pale Taurian with a look of such intense pride on his face as he gazes down at me.

Gods, I love him so much.

"Artificer," he greets me formally as I move back toward him. "It's done now."

"I can't believe it. Two years, and now I really am an artificer." I press my hand to my belly, as if clutching the corset under my clothing will somehow shore up my suddenly weak knees. "What . . . what happens now?"

"Well, now we go and have dinner and drinks with Jay," Raptor tells me, putting his familiar, heavy arm over my shoulders. He tucks me in against his side, and it's like I've always belonged there. "Tomorrow we put in for housing. We meet with our Five and decide if we want to stay together as a Five or hire out as artificers-on-standby until we can get a permanent Five."

Right. I know that. "We'll stick together. We all work well as a team."

"Aye, I don't think anyone's in a hurry to peel off. Not when you've got such a skill with *dowsing*." He says the word in a low voice, his dry tone full of amusement. We've been covering up my mancing as me being "skilled" with dowsing if anyone asks.

"So that's it?" I ask.

"That's it," my Taurian agrees, gazing down at me as if he could devour me whole. "Now we get to work, my pretty little Starling."

I like my name quite a bit when he says it like that.

ACKNOWLEDGMENTS

ACKNOWLEDGMENTS MIGHT BE the most difficult part of the publishing process.

(Just kidding, it's totally copyedits.)

Even so, acknowledgments are tricky, because how can you possibly round up everyone who's touched the book in your hands and somehow remember to thank them? But I'm going to attempt it!

(Cue me cracking my knuckles.)

First of all, I want to thank my Penguin Random House and Ace team. Anyone who has said that a publisher just prints the book and doesn't do anything else hasn't glimpsed all the work behind the scenes. I am continually in awe of everything that's done to make my books the best they can be, and am so grateful that you always work with me when I panic about something.

(I'm an author. We *always* panic about something.)

A huge thank-you to Cindy Hwang, my editor, who absolutely sees the vision for these books and knows just the spots to put her finger on to make the story better. I promise to be at least 50 percent less anxious about this one.

(Okay, 20 percent. Make that 20 percent less anxious.)

To Elizabeth Vinson, who hopefully doesn't cringe too much when I email all the time. Another big thank-you to Christine Masters (copyeditor), Yahaira Lawrence (production manager), Katy Riegel (interior designer), and Michelle Kasper (production editor), who saw the guts of this thing and helped me make it pretty. Please know that your jobs terrify me and leave me in awe at the same time.

To the art team, another thank-you! Rita Frangie Batour, I love how your mind works and how you always manage to package my book in a way that makes me go "Yes! Exactly!" It's like you have access to my candy-colored dreams. To Kelly Wagner, who did the fantastic cover art and didn't cry (much, hopefully) when she heard Ruby Dixon was writing more weird stuff and needed a cover. To lilithsaur, who did the interior art spread—your work is sublime, and it was so difficult to pick between what you sent! I adore you.

To Jessica Mangicaro (marketing), Stephanie Felty (publicity), and Kristin Cipolla (publicity), who tirelessly pushed *Bull Moon Rising* and are taking up the reins again (ha) for *By the Horns*. Just know that your enthusiasm for monster romance makes me cry with happiness.

To the audio team that made the audiobook so amazing—thank you to Felicity Munroe and Hiro Diaz for totally bringing it to life! Thank you to Iris McElroy and Gabra Zackman for the behind-the-scenes wrangling and pulling it all together.

I also need to give a shout-out to Alex Conkins, aka Conky. Conky does all the promotional art for me—if you've received a sticker or a bookmark inside one of my many books, Conky illustrated it. Thank you for always making room in your schedule for me, even when I email and am all "How fast can you draw a minotaur?" for varying reasons. I adore you as much as I adore your art!

To my agency team! Holly Root, Alyssa Maltese, and Heather Baror-Shapiro—thank you for your minotaur love! You let me be as weird as I want to be and somehow make it profitable.

To the booksellers who have supported me and held my hand at signings when I came in sweaty and panicked, and the ones who have emailed and asked for bookplates for stock in their stores because I'm a terrible potato and don't travel. I love all of you.

To my daily writing crew—Ella, Kati, and Lea—thanks for letting me "win" all our sprints.

To my parents, who are endlessly supportive. To my cats, who somehow manage to walk across the keyboard during all the steamy scenes.

To my husband, who still makes me laugh even though I know all his jokes. You're the first one to put a book on the brag shelf because you're proud of me. You tirelessly box special editions of my books for conventions because you want events to go smoothly for me. You help me troubleshoot my plots, and even if I don't take all your suggestions (I'm not sure the world is ready for a "horse with just a human face" as a hero), I love that we can work through things together. You're my biggest supporter and number one fan, and I love you so much. You make me feel lucky every day.

XOXO,
Ruby